NIGHTS
OF
VILLJAMUR

BALLANTINE BOOKS NEW YORK

NIGHTS
OF
VILLJAMUR

Legends of the Red Sun

BOOK ONE

Mark Charan Newton

Nights of Villjamur is a work of fiction. Names, characters, places, and incidents are the products of the author's imagination or are used fictitiously. Any resemblance to actual events, locales, or persons, living or dead, is entirely coincidental.

Copyright © 2009 by Mark Charan Newton

Published in the United States by Spectra, an imprint of The Random House Publishing Group, a division of Random House, Inc., New York.

SPECTRA and the portrayal of a boxed "s" are trademarks of Random House, Inc.

Originally published in the United Kingdom by Tor, an imprint of Pan Macmillan Ltd, in 2009.

ISBN 978-0-345-52084-5

Library of Congress Cataloging-in-Publication Data
Newton, Mark Charan.
Nights of Villjamur / Mark Charan Newton.
p. cm.—(Legends of the red sun ; bk. 1)
ISBN 978-0-345-52084-5 (alk. paper)
1. Murder—Investigation—Fiction.   I. Title.
PR6114.E975N54 2010
823'.92—dc22   2010009845

Printed in the United States of America on acid-free paper

www.ballantinebooks.com

2 4 6 8 9 7 5 3 1

First U.S. Edition

Book design and title page photo by Karin Batten

For Mick,
a father when you never had to be

Acknowledgments

*

My sincere love and gratitude to my parents, Kamal and Mick, for their continuing support.

Immense thanks to my agent, John Jarrold, who has been both consul and oracle; without his deeply valuable guidance and belief, this book would never have reached publication.

Peter Lavery, possibly the smartest man alive, and with a pencil in his hand, certainly the most ruthless. My deep gratitude to him, and also to Julie Crisp for helping to shape this book into something better.

Thanks to: Graeme Harris, for the late night conversations; Robert Thompson for the crucial advice; James Long for the wide-ranging discussions. And a special thanks to George Mann, good friend and sounding board.

And many writers continue to inspire and influence me, and I'm doubtlessly in debt to them all though they are too numerous to list. Nevertheless, keen-eyed readers will see open tips-of-my-hat to those who have shaped this genre, including Gene Wolfe, Jack Vance, M. John Harrison, and even Arthur C. Clarke.

"The power of the dead is that we think they see us all the time. The dead have a presence. Is there a level of energy composed solely of the dead? They are also in the ground, of course, asleep and crumbling. Perhaps we are what they dream."

—Don DeLillo, *White Noise*

NIGHTS
OF
VILLJAMUR

PROLOGUE

✳

This much was obvious:

They'd sent him to kill her. And here she was, weeks away from comfort, weeks across the Archipelago and halfway across the night. Still, at least it was a good time to be on the run.

The lanes of Ule were cold and body-thick. Flames illuminated everything, fire from within pits, or from torches. In the shadows you could see young men and women sitting up late, smoking, talking philosophy, all elaborate hand gestures, loud voices, a little laughter here and there. Children slumped bleary-eyed or asleep by their knees. Older people drifted past the stores behind, scrutinizing faded signs, something about their manner suggesting they might be hoping to find the moment where their lives had slipped away.

They just get in the way, Papus thought, *such is the nature of an Empire island. You can't stand still.*

The island of Folke:

An outpost on the fringe of the Empire, with Jamur soldiers waiting to launch a raid to push back a tribal uprising at dusk, also crowds of locals, passing travelers, morbid tourists. Paranoid, she would frequently see something strange, an erratic gesture between two silhouetted figures, a moment where they'd stare back at her, then she'd wonder at the meaning behind it. On nights like this, it was as if everything happened out of context.

She needed to return to Villjamur.

This far east it was said that war inevitably brought out the curious. They'd come in droves, as if they had forgotten about all the possible ways in which you could die. Despite all the cover these people offered her, despite all the places to hide—he'd be waiting for her, maybe within the trading crowds of the iren, maybe somewhere between the packed fishing stalls where old men chanted their prices in hybrid dialects.

"A charm, lord . . ." A grubby woman speaking in broken Jamur. Dressed in rags, reeking of manure. In her muddied hands she displayed several blackened bones. Her face was wrinkled, smeared with smoke-stained sweat, a worrying distance in her eyes that indicated she was too far detached from reality for simple reason. "Bone charms from slaves—holy items blessed by a Jorsalir priest, these. Please. I need coin—"

"I haven't got anything," Papus said.

The woman leaned forward so close that you could smell the death.

"Get out my way."

The crone muttered something, spit dribbling from her mouth. "Put your spirit in a *good* place. We sin too much . . ."

Papus drew a *sterkr* from her cloak, wafted it before the woman's eyes.

A subtle, contained crack of purple light, and the woman was forced into stillness.

Damn, that would've drawn him to me. Papus left the old woman in her statue-still pose, placed the relic back in her pocket, and continued to walk with purpose through the town. All the time acting as if everything was fine, nothing to worry about here, while wishing she could evanesce into the community.

Street corners became hubs of activity. Young lads in particular gathered, armed with dreams of battlefield fame. Women were here to offer their bodies to soldiers and those few travelers with money. Beautiful enough to make a living, but not enough to marry wealth, their place in the economy was unknown, and they each stood alone with expressionless gazes that said too much. Nearby, wine bladders exchanged hands for a little coin. Even the children were drinking to keep warm, but this was a festival night, and so the people of Folke didn't mind.

Papus scanned the town cautiously.

Every detail mattered to her. It could be the difference between dying and getting home to Villjamur.

Despite the eddies of locals that crowded her with a dirty intensity, she felt utterly lonely, a sensation that only heightened her fear of being murdered. Nights like this made her question her path in life, question who she was and where she'd come from, and if her life would amount to anything more than power and secrecy, power *in* secrecy.

—A man through the darkness.

Was that him?

Perhaps her route across Folke was too obvious. It was meant to be hectic here, provide her with some sort of cover. Should she rip through empty space, he'd find her quickly, if he was as good as she thought. He'd sense where she'd left, all right, sense where she'd gone, and he'd be waiting for her, waiting to beat her unconscious. Besides, you couldn't travel that far in one go, not if you weren't familiar with the surroundings. For all she knew, she could reappear over the sea and then drown in icy water.

Relics couldn't get you out of every situation, because life just wasn't that considerate.

A clamor of armor meant the Jamur soldiers were leaving the town to prepare for their coastal raid. She weaved through thinning tides of locals in their weather-faded clothing, wanting to be lost in their simple throng. As long as people were around her she'd be safe.

She had a relic to get to Villjamur, to show to the rest of the order. *He won't have it,* she told herself, a mantra by now, a repetition on the tip of her tongue to convince herself this was more than just a possibility.

Down a thin alleyway between two wooden buildings, then under a clothesline, out behind the town toward the coast, and all the time glancing behind to see if he was tracking her shadow.

In the background could be heard the thunder of the sea.

✳

Captain Brynd Lathraea of the Jamur Second Dragoons squinted through the dark toward the wall of water as it crashed onto the shores of Blortath, way off in the distance. Terns fled the wave, screaming as they scattered uniformly, like seeds thrown from a hand.

This was no *natural* phenomenon.

A hooded man was crouching in the shallow water, a few feet below, a device in his hands which he dipped rhythmically in and out of the sea. Occasionally he closed his eyes, tilted his head toward the night sky as if to perceive the world on some entirely new level. He was a cultist, from the Order of Natura—a minor sect—and he specialized in using apparatus that could change aspects of nature. Brynd ran a hand through his white hair. With a piece of equipment and a method that the captain could never comprehend, the cultist was throwing freak tides at Blortath so as to weaken their defenses before the Second and Third Dragoons launched their coastal raid before sun-up.

The mission briefing was simple:

Land.

Assist the forces approaching from the north.

Slaughter wherever possible.

In all the major towns and cities, any Froutan and Deltu prisoners were to be executed. As a lesson to prevent other tribes from uniting against the Jamur forces, the Emperor Johynn requested that no tribesmen should remain alive. This was an Empire island, had been for years. A simple statement, the Council would say, no point in rebelling.

Don't fuck with Imperial strategy.

The island of Folke was a different environment to Jokull. Murky sandbanks and sand dunes expanded along the rest of the shoreline. Brynd was standing on top of the foremost dune, long reeds clawing at his knees. Lichens smothered a few stray boulders. Everything here was a fraction wilder—not like the civility of Villjamur. In the distance, dark smoke from the warning beacons drifted around Blortath, only a short journey away by longship. Unseen, two garudas circled the island, and Brynd was becoming impatient for their reports.

The cultist began to load the tide. Groundswells commenced, tips of the surf rolled and then leaned, the water groaning under pressure, waiting to collapse but instead moving further upward in some unlikely physics. And an alien noise as waves banked up sharply in a thin wall between the islands, waited unnaturally in the air—then launched themselves toward Blortath.

Brynd wrapped his cloak around him, glad for the extra shirt beneath his uniform, although the additional layers made his new leather vest feel restricting.

"Hardly a bloody battle, this, is it?"

Brynd looked back to see who had spoken. A line of the Second Dragoons stood motionless in their black and green uniforms, leaning on their long shields, viewing the wave that rolled into the distance. The men and women weren't yet wearing armor, only the traditional brown cloaks, each with the Jamur star stitched in gold on the left breast. With them he had long stopped being self-conscious for being an albino human as well as their captain.

Among other things.

"And who said that, then?" Brynd asked.

"Me," said a distinctively higher-pitched voice this time.

Muffled laughter.

Kapp Brimir, a boy native to Folke, started squirming his way forward between the soldiers. More of the other islanders were visible in the distance gathered around their fires. The first voice certainly couldn't have been his, for Kapp was perhaps only ten years old. To avoid local uprisings, soldiers were told to be friendly with the local people before campaigns, but it was a difficult task with some of them. This boy seemed especially keen on annoying everyone. Kapp insisted on asking questions of any senior officers encountered around Ule: details about sword play, about how people dressed in Villjamur, about what they did for fun and did they dance.

"Yes?" Brynd said. "Your voice's pretty deep for such a young age, and you can swear in Jamur, too? That surprises me for a native. If this isn't much of a battle, just count yourself lucky. Were you looking for a full-scale war?"

"No." Kapp stepped forward, stood right next to Brynd, looking up at the soldier. "Doesn't seem very fair, though, using one of them." He indicated the cultist on the shore below.

Brynd said, "You'd rather we all died, instead?"

Kapp shrugged, stared out to sea, played with a lock of his hair as if he'd already forgotten their conversation.

Brynd said, "You want to be a soldier?"

"No way."

"Might be useful to learn how to fight one day."

"I can fight already." Kapp turned to face the unlikely tide again.

"Captain Lathraea!" someone shouted. It was the cultist, now wading up the sand without his relic. He was gray-haired, with birdlike features, a thin medallion strung around his neck, the symbol unclear in this light. "Captain, they've a cultist, too. They've got a bloody cultist!"

"Shit, how's that possible?"

"I don't know, but look." He indicated the wall of water coming back toward them, the lip of the wave breaking over itself.

Brynd turned in time to see Kapp pushing back through the troops.

"I think I can stop it, or at least weaken it," the cultist continued. "I'd get everyone inland, anyway."

"Thought *I* gave the commands." Brynd placed a hand on the sheathed blade by his side.

"This isn't the time for ceremony, captain."

"I suspect you're right."

"Have you seen the rest of my order?"

"Not for some time." Brynd shook his head. "Can't you lot keep a track of yourselves by using one of your own damn contraptions?"

"You'd do well to keep it friendly, brother," the cultist snapped, then ran down the shore, skidding on the sand, and placed his device in the water again.

Brynd commanded the Dragoons to move back, and the soldiers retreated up to the plains.

To the north of the island, tribesmen were clambering up the shore on to the grass ridge, axes in hand, and how they had arrived unnoticed, Brynd had no idea, because the garudas should have spotted them, wherever the hell they were.

If that boy really wanted a battle, Brynd thought, drawing his saber, *it's bloody well on its way.*

✳

Kapp ran so fast it seemed as if he couldn't stop if he wanted. The path was bounded on either side with broken buildings, and his feet thundered into the ground as he sped down Flayer's Hill toward his home.

He stopped as he heard the first wave surge against the landscape, rocking it. Then he turned back to watch seawater frothing as it spilled over the crest of the hill, sparkling in the moonlight. The water wasn't enough to fully breach the bank, but you could see that the next wave would. And he next heard shouting, then there they were, hundreds of the Emperor's Dragoons changing direction, marching now to the north of the island.

That albino soldier was leading them, his weapon raised.

The troops began to line up on either side of him. They locked their shields together, began to beat on the massed metal. As Kapp ran into the distance and downhill, the last image he had of them was that they were a *dominating* force.

He no longer wanted anything whatsoever to do with them.

The tribesmen clambered over the shore in an endless stream, the whites of their bone-charms visible, their axes held high, their flesh barely covered by primitive clothing.

Nothing made sense. Only moments earlier, the Dragoons on his native island were about to take another neighboring island under the Emperor's wing, but now it was *his* island that was suffering a coastal raid. Like burning insects, fires were scattering in Ule as people fled from the main town and out into wilder land.

Kapp had to warn his mother.

Arms aflail, he sprinted toward his home, a large wooden construct surrounded by a herd of half-asleep goats that swarmed away from him as he approached. He stopped when he heard a strange crackling. Frowning, he spun in a full circle to see where it came from, yet somehow it seemed to embrace every direction, fluxing through the air. He caught a glimpse of a spectral glow and headed toward it.

There were two figures beside a betula tree, both of them in black clothing, barely noticeable in this dim light.

One lay on the ground, a net of violet light surrounding him. The other stood above, a small metal box clasped in his hands, and it was from this the strange energy emanated. The one on the ground was screaming in pain, blood on his face. Kapp wanted to do something. It hurt him to witness someone in so much agony.

Scanning the ground for a fist-sized stone, Kapp picked up two knuckles of granite, then scampered in an arc to approach from behind. He threw the first stone, which hit the tree.

The standing-man turned.

Kapp threw the second stone that struck him square on the back of the head, and the man collapsed against the tree with a grunt of pain, dropping his box.

The net-light evaporated.

The injured figure suddenly rose, slashed a blade across the other's chest, then drew it again across his neck. His victim collapsed to his knees, shuddering, his mouth agape in either confusion or surprise, then slumped sideways.

The killer hunched over the corpse, panting, then concealed the box beneath his cloak.

Kapp was stunned by the incident. Apart from the wind sliding across the tundra, all sounds were improbably absent. Kapp felt an immense guilt, wanted to run. Had he actually contributed to murder?

As the remaining figure approached, Kapp experienced a sudden sense of calm. This was a cultist, or some official—you could tell by the medallion he wore around his neck. The rest of the outfit was elaborate, with the subtle red stitching of a small crest on one breast. The survivor was chubby, blond hair disheveled. Kapp watched in silence as the cultist knelt down before him, bloody scars webbing across his face in symmetrical perfection.

"Thank you, boy. Seems I owe you my life," the figure declared in elegant Jamur. He took Kapp's hand and shook it. Kapp was uncertain of the gesture.

"That's all right," Kapp replied in Jamur, dazzled by the man's intense blue eyes. They seemed unnaturally feminine . . . and there was no stubble.

He reached into his pocket and placed an object firmly in Kapp's palm. A coin, silver and heavy and stamped with strange symbols: a single eye, shafts of sunlight radiating from within.

It would probably be worth enough to buy his family home.

"I always pay my debts," the cultist continued. "Should you ever need a favor, you can find me in Villjamur. Show them this. Ask for me and I'll be found. Otherwise it'll not buy you much. Some may not even accept it."

"What's your name?" Kapp said.

"Papus."

"Why was that man hurting you?" Kapp nodded toward the bloodied body in the mud.

The stranger stood up, smiled in a way that suggested the whole story was too complicated to explain. "Because—among many things—I wouldn't let him have sex with me."

"I don't get it." Kapp frowned. "You're a man. Why would he—?"

"A one in two chance, boy, and you still got it wrong. Still, I don't get offended easily. The offer stands, should you ever need a favor. But first, I suggest you avoid this conflict. Go, take shelter in Ule." Then with a harmless laugh, she jogged into the distance as cries of war began to spill across the tundra.

Snow and ice are isolating creatures.
But there is nothing as successful in this world,
no ruler, no king,
that creates the illusion that
the land is bound together,
as one.

*Translation from Dawnir runes found
on Southfjords, circa 458 BDC*

CHAPTER 1

✳

GARUDAS SWOOPED BY, ENGAGED IN CITY PATROLS, WHILE CATS LOOKED up from walls in response to their fast-moving shadows.

One of these bird-sentries landed on the top of the inner wall of the city, and faced the dawn. The weather made the ambience, *was* the ambience, because the city forever changed its mood according to the skies. These days, there was little but gray.

The sentry was attached to Villjamur. He admired the citizens who were its fabric, from the slang-talking gangs to the young lovers who kissed under abandoned archways. All around were the signals of the underworld, discreet and urgent conversations in the dark. It was the only place he knew of where he might feel a nostalgia for the present.

His precise vision detected another execution taking place on the outer wall. Didn't remember any being scheduled today.

"Anything you wish to say before we release the arrows?" a voice echoed between the stone ramparts.

The garuda looked on with dull satisfaction from his higher battlement. He ruffled his feathers, shivered as the wind built up momentum over the fortifications, a chill quietly penetrating the furthest reaches of the city, a token of invading winter.

The prisoner, some distance away, wore nothing more than a rippling brown gown. He looked from left to right at the archers positioned either side of him on the outermost wall, their bows still lowered to one side. Down at the city-side base of the wall in its shadow, people marched circles in the freezing mud, staring upward.

A thin, pale man in green and brown uniform, the officer giving the orders, stood further along the crest of the wall, as the prisoner opened his mouth cautiously to answer him.

He merely said, "Is there any use?"

A girl screamed from the crowds gathered below, but no one bothered to look down at her except the officer, who said, "A crime of the heart, this one, eh?"

"Aren't they all?" the prisoner replied. "That is, of the heart and not the mind?"

A harsh rain, the occasional gust of something colder, and the mood turned bellicose.

"You tell me," the soldier growled, apparently irritated with this immediate change in weather.

Some sharp, rapid commands.

As the girl continued her wails and pleas from the base of the wall, the two archers nocked their arrows, brought their bows to docking point, then fired.

The prisoner's skull cracked under the impact, blood spat onto the throng underneath, and he buckled forward, tumbling over the city wall, two arrows in his head. Two lengths of rope caught him halfway down.

A primitive display, a warning to everyone: *Don't mess with the Empire. State rule is absolute.*

It was followed by a scream that seemed to shatter the blanket of rain.

The banshee had now announced the death.

With the execution over, the garuda extended his wings, reaching several armspans to either side, cracked his spine to stretch himself, crouched. With an immense thrust, he pushed himself high into the air, flicking rain off his quills.

He banked skyward.

Villjamur was a granite fortress. Its main access was through three consecutive gates, and there the garuda retained the advantage over any invading armies. In the center of the city, high up and pressed against the rockface, beyond a latticework of bridges and spires, was Balmacara, the vast Imperial residence, a cathedrallike construct of dark basalt and slick-glistening mica. In this weather the city seemed unreal.

The refugee encampments pitched off the Sanctuary Road were largely quiet, a few dogs roaming between makeshift tents. The Sanctuary Road was a dark scar finishing at Villjamur itself. Further out to one side, the terrain changed to vague grassland, but well-trodden verges along the road suggested how the refugees never stopped hassling passing travelers as they sought to break away from their penurious existence. Heather died back in places, extending in a dark pastel smear to the other, before fading into the distance. There was beauty there if you knew where to look.

The garuda noticed few people about at this time. No traders yet, and only one traveler, wrapped in fur, on the road leading into the city.

Back across the city.

Lanterns were being lit by citizens who perhaps had expected a brighter day. Glows of orange crept through the dreary morning, defining the shapes of elaborate windows, wide octagons, narrow arches. It had been a winter of bistros with steamed-up windows, of tundra flowers trailing down from hanging baskets, of constant plumes of smoke from chimneys, one where concealed gardens were dying, starved of sunlight, and where the statues adorning once-flamboyant balconies were now suffocating under lichen.

The guard-bird finally settled on a high wall by a disused courtyard. The ambient sound of the water on stone forced an abstract disconnection from the place that made him wonder if he had flown back in time. He turned his attention to the man hunched in furs, the one he had noticed moments earlier. A stranger, trudging through the second gate leading into the city.

The garuda watched him, unmoving, his eyes perfectly still.

✳

There were three things that Randur Estevu hoped would mark him as someone different here in Villjamur. He didn't *always* necessarily get drunk when alcohol was at hand, not like those back home. Also he listened with great concentration, or gave the illusion at least, whenever a woman spoke to him. And finally he was one of the best—if not *the* best—dancers he knew of, and that meant something coming from the island of Folke. There everyone learned to dance as soon as they could walk—some before that, being expected to crawl with *rhythm* even as babies.

Provincial charm would only add to this allure of the stranger, a little accent perhaps, enough for the girls to take an interest in what he had to say. A tall man, he'd remained slender, to the eternal envy of fat gossiping women back home. Altogether, he rated his chances well, as he advanced upon the last of the three gates under the dawn rain, armed with only his few necessary belongings, a pocketful of forged family histories, and a thousand witty retorts.

Randur already knew his folklore and history, had learned further during his journey. You had to be prepared for an important city like this, because Villjamur was the residence of the Emperor Jamur Johynn, and this island called Jokull was the Empire's homeland. Once known as Vilhallan, it had been a collection of small farming settlements scattered around the original cave systems, now hidden behind the current architecture. Most of the city's current population were in fact direct descendants of those early dwellers. Eleven thousand years ago. Before even the clan wars began. The community thrived on myth. With such a history, a wealth of cultures and creatures, the city was said to possess an emergent property.

Randur had been traveling for weeks. Somewhere on the way, on a superficial level, he'd become someone else. His mother was back in Ule, on the island of Folke. A stern yet strangely faithful woman, she'd raised him on her own in spite of the collapse of their wealth, which had happened when he was too young to know about it. He remembered hearing her coughing upstairs, in a musty room, the stench of death all too premature. Every time he entered it, he never knew what to expect.

She'd found him a "job" in Villjamur. It came through the influence of one of his shady uncles who was well connected on Y'iren and Folke as a trading dignitary, though he'd never shared his wealth with them. The man had always commented on Kapp's good looks as if this was a hindrance in life. Then that same uncle informed Kapp's mother that a man the same age and appearance as the lad had disappeared only the previous week. His name was Randur Estevu, and it was known that he was headed for employment in the Emperor's house. He had even been a rival of Kapp's at dance tournaments and in *Vitassi* bladework during the island's festivals. The young man had made enemies all right, boasting all too often that he had sanctuary guaranteed in Villjamur before the Freeze came.

"You lot'll turn to ice, fuckers," the lad had said at the time, "while I got me safe digs at the warmest place in the Empire. Can't say more, though, because I wouldn't want you lot getting in on my connections."

They'd found his body, or what was left of it, stuffed inside a crate on a decaying boat that hadn't left the harbor at Geu Docks for as long as anyone could remember. No one was even shocked the boy was dead. They were more interested in the old boat itself, as it seemed to fulfill some maritime prophecy someone had mentioned the week before.

Kapp then became Randur Estevu. Fled south with fake identification to the Sanctuary City.

He was told by his mother to seek his fortune there, where the family line might have a chance to survive the arrival of the ice. He had no idea what the real Randur Estevu was to be doing in Villjamur, as the stolen papers didn't explain. Besides, Randur, as he would now be known, had his own schemes.

He fingered the coin in his pocket, the one the cultist had handed him all those years ago, in the darkness, on that night of blood.

Garudas loomed above on the battlements beside the final gate leading into the city. They stood with folded arms. Half vulture, half man: wings, beaks, talons on a human form. Cloaks and minimal armor. White faces that seemed to glow in this gray light. During his few days in a Folke station of the Regiment—which he joined on a poetic whim, and primarily to impress this girl who was all longing glances and unlikely promises—the men talked much about the skills of the garuda. It seemed only a talented archer stood a chance of deleting one from the skies.

Soldiers had checked his papers at the first and second gates. At the third they searched his bags, confiscated his weapons, and questioned him with an alarming intensity.

"Sele of Jamur," Randur said. "So, then, what news here in the Sanctuary City?"

One of the guards replied, "Well, the mood ain't good, to be honest. People ain't happy. See a lot of miserable faces, both outside and in. Can understand it out there, like," he indicated the closed gates behind which huddled the refugees. "But in there they've got faces like slapped asses, the lot of 'em. They're the ones who're safe, too, miserable sods."

"Perhaps no one likes being trapped, even if it is for their own good," Randur speculated.

"Hey, they're free to fuck off any time," the guard grumbled. "Nah, it'll bring more than just ice, this weather."

After this final search, Randur continued through, and at last he found himself standing inside the Sanctuary City.

Whoever built Villjamur, or at least whoever designed its intricate shapes and eerily precise structures, could surely not have been a human. Garish buildings were coated with painted pebbles, while other oddities possessed colored glass in the stonework so they glistened like fractured gems. Randur stared around in awe, not quite sure which way to go first. Possibilities grew exponentially. The chilling rain transformed into drizzle then began to stop. Fish was cooking in some far alleyway. Nearby, two signs said "firewood." From the windows of one of the terraced houses, a couple of women started hanging out sheets. Two young men talked in some local hand-language, their sentences needing a gesture and a glance for completion. Ahead of him, roads branched on two sides, each leading uphill in a gradual arc, while pterodettes raced up the cliff faces looming in the distance. Kids were sliding on patches of ice in horizontal freefall. A couple walked by, the blond woman much younger than the man, and he judged them "respectable" by the quality of their clothing. Randur was tempted to make eye contact with the woman, and perhaps tease a reaction out of her. It seemed to matter, stealing a smile from that man's life. Not just yet, though. He had only just arrived. He had a cultist to find.

✳

In a top-floor bedroom, in one of the expensive balconied houses gracing the higher levels of Villjamur, a woman with a scarred face relaxed on top of a man who was still panting from his sexual exertions.

They kissed. Tongues slid across each other—only briefly, as it didn't quite feel right, and she wasn't sure which of them was causing that reaction. She pulled away, then clutched his chest, began playing with the gray hairs. His face was small, his features delicate, and his hands were rough, but at least they were touching her. Neither of them had ruined the sexual act with words, something she at least was grateful for. Meanwhile he continued to run his hands along her sides, rubbing her hip bones gently with his thumb, as if he had a fetish for the firm ridges of her body.

She pushed herself forward till her long red hair fell across his face. She then waited for him to brush it aside, and slowly, she could see the inevitable disappointment appear in his eyes, just as she had learned to notice it regularly over the last few years. At first his eyes remained fixed on hers. Then she saw his pupils clearly register the terrible blemish on the side of her exposed face. *This one's reaction isn't so bad,* she reflected. He had been a little drunk when they met, and his vision easily blurred. She had remained disappointed, though, in his overall ability to maintain his erection.

It always seemed to end up the same when she sought her own pleasure—something very different from when she was merely doing it for the money. Her job made it hard for her to meet normal men, certainly stopped her having a decent relationship. Her visible disfigurement didn't help either, that blistering down the right side of her face.

But this was her night off, and she had wanted a fling to make her feel better. She so much wanted to feel close to someone, had wanted that for so long.

In her younger days, she had known the world was cruel, how people judged you by first appearances. How that childlike prejudice against the unnatural could continue into adulthood as people merely found a way of better hiding their revulsions.

She pushed herself off him slowly, and then reached for her dressing gown. Walking over to the window, she looked out across the spires and bridges of Villjamur as if she was now trying to put the greatest possible distance between the two of them. In the opposite corner of the room, covered canvases of various sizes were stacked against the wall. She could still smell the chemicals from the painting she had begun yesterday evening.

"Wow," he said at last. "By Bohr, you're amazing."

She now gazed at the bruised skies hanging over the city, the last of the rain driving lightly across its architecture. Lifting the window sash, she could hear a cart being drawn across the cobbles, could smell the scent of larix trees from the forest to the north. She looked up and down Cartanu Gata and the Gata Sentimental, alongside the art gallery—a place where she doubted her own paintings would ever hang. People merged with shadows, as if they became one. Directly under her window, a man stumbled in and out of her vision, his sword scraping against the wall. For some reason she couldn't understand, each of these qualities of the city merely heightened her sense of loneliness.

"Your *body* . . . I mean, you move so well," he was saying, still praising her performance like they often did when it was clear they had little in common.

She eventually spoke. "Tundra."

"Sorry?"

"In the tavern, last night—the lines you used to get me back here. I suppose politicians are good with words. You said my body is like the tundra. You said I had perfect, smooth white skin, like drifts of snow. You even said that my breasts are as dramatic as the crests of snowbanks. You admired my breasts and my smooth skin. You said I was like ice incarnate. Yes, you fed me lines as awful as that. But what about my face?"

She immediately ran her hand along her terrible scar.

"I said you're a very attractive woman."

"Horses can be attractive, councilor." She glanced back at him. "But what's my face like?"

"Your face is lovely, Tuya."

"Lovely?"

"Yes."

He lifted his head up to take a better look at her as she dropped her gown to the floor. She knew what his reactions would be as the dreary light seemed to gather momentum on her bare skin. She reached over to a tabletop, picked up a roll-up of arum weed, but she waited until certain he was no longer looking at her before she lit it. The intense smell of its smoke wafted across the room, drifted out the window.

Still in vague shadow to his visions, she walked over to the bed, offered him the weed. He involuntarily grabbed her wrist, rubbed it gently between his fingers and thumb. His gaze was weak-willed and pathetic.

"You're beautiful," he said. "Delicious."

"Prove it, Councilor Ghuda," she said, climbing on his smile, watching him submit.

The roll-up fell to the floor, exploding ashes across the tiles.

❋

Later, when he had fallen asleep again, she thought about their conversation just before he drifted off.

He talked a lot, which was unusual for a man after sex. She reflected deeply on what he had said, about the *details* that he had gone into.

He had shocked her.

A man in his important position should surely refrain from talking so much, but he was probably still rather drunk. They had been drinking vodka for much of the dawn. He didn't leave her until the sun was higher in the vermilion sky, the city fully awake, and her breath sour from alcohol. When he did, there was no fond good-bye, no intimate gesture. He had simply slipped on his Council robes and walked out the door.

But it wasn't his casual exit that caused her upset, it was the words he had spoken before he slept, those simple statements he had maybe or maybe not meant seriously.

Already his words were haunting her.

❋

Afterward, as he did frequently, Councilor Ghuda imagined his own cuckolding.

Four years ago it had started, four years since he realized, that he couldn't invest all his emotions in one person, in his wife. He had caught her, Beula, in bed with her lips at work on a soldier from the Dragoons, and the image pursued him—his personal poltergeist—constantly undermining him. His sense of value in the world hung in the air like an unanswered question, and as a man he was unmade.

Sleeping with prostitutes helped his state of mind.

It was a fantasy, at first, an escape—then something more, a need for tenderness and cheap thrills with another woman. When he lost himself in the bad lines and the awkward over-stylized gestures, he managed to scramble something of an identity together. After the act, the women he paid for would watch him absentmindedly while wiping themselves down with a towel to remove any traces of him from their body. These women would not love him, and the words they spoke were not their own, but Tuya, the woman from last night, seemed almost genuinely affectionate, as if in Villjamur, a city of introverts, two introverts could find a sense of belonging—if only for a night.

Ghuda looked up as the skies cleared, red sunlight now skidding off the wet cobbles, and the streets appeared to rust. He stepped from the shelter of the doorway into the relative brightness of the morning. He needed to get to the Council Spire to start the day's work.

Whether it was a symptom of his guilt, he didn't know, but he felt certain he was being watched. He never requested a guard to escort him anywhere, in fact usually slipped away before one might appear.

There was much to deal with for the day ahead. Primarily he had to deal with the increasing refugee problems: the laborers from elsewhere that were flocking to Villjamur to survive the coming ice age.

People were heading to the various irens to trade and shop, overseen by soldiers from the Regiment of Foot, who patrolled along the streets in pairs. It was a trenchant policy of safety he'd personally initiated to ease the citizens' concern in these anxious times. You didn't want general panic to set in, even though the public fear of crime was more intense than its current levels actually warranted.

Up the winding roads and passageways, he continued.

On the way he encountered an elderly man sitting on a stool with a sign beside him that said "Scribe—Discretion Guaranteed." With one palm resting flat on the small table to one side, he sipped a steaming drink with a contented look on his face. There were quite a few of these men around the city, writing love letters or death threats on behalf of those who couldn't write themselves, including those whose fingers had been broken by the Inquisition. Ghuda speculated on what he might write to Tuya, the redhead he had just spent the night with. What would he say to her? That he would like to fuck her some more because she was so good at it? That was hardly the basis of an ongoing relationship.

The incline had become a strain on Ghuda's legs, so for a while he rested on a pile of logs heaped outside one of the terraced houses. Again, he had the uneasy sensation that someone was watching him. He looked around at the quiet streets, then up at the bridges. Perhaps someone was looking down at him.

He rose to go and heard footsteps behind him, running into the distance.

A shortcut led through to an iren, a trading area located in a courtyard of stone. As he stepped through a high and narrow alleyway, seemingly endless, his heart began to beat a little faster.

He quickened his pace.

He burst out onto the busy iren . . .

Then he felt as if his chest had exploded and its contents were spilling onto the cobbles. Except it hadn't, he was still in one piece, he was still alive, but he gaped down at the wound as it expanded, at his shredded robes exposing his flesh to the cold, damp air.

A truculent pain shot through him, and he screamed, trying to look behind him, but through welling eyes saw only a silhouette heading back, bizarrely upward, into the darkness. He stumbled forward, his hands clutching for wet stones, then began to spit blood on the ground. People were now crowding around him, watching wide-eyed, pointing. Sensing his life fluid filling the cracks between cobbles, the blood beetles came and began to smother him, till his screams could be heard amplified between the high walls of the courtyard. One even scurried into his mouth, scraping eagerly at his gums and tongue. He bit down so he wouldn't choke, split its shell in two, and spat it out, but he could still taste its ichors.

Councilor Ghuda was violently febrile.

✳

Standing outside a bistro with a rumbling stomach and a small pie raised in one hand, Randur watched the unsteady figure shamble toward him. People scrambled in fear, men holding their women protectively, as glossy beetles began to pullulate around the victim's gaping wound.

Randur stepped aside into an alley by a gallery, too stunned now to take a first bite of the pie. A small child screamed and turned to run, while the dying man—eyes wide and aghast, and coughing blood—stumbled on into the same small passageway. He stared straight at Randur, hunching to his knees just paces away from him. He continued to howl as the insects ripped at his flesh, tossing it into the air in a fine pink mist. He fell forward, and was silent.

Within moments, a banshee appeared into the passageway, as if she had been following the incident all this time. Cocooned in a shawl, her face was gaunt and striking against the untidy strands of jet-black hair. With a distant look in her eyes, she sucked in a deep breath, then began her keen, her mouth opening impossibly wide.

The sated blood beetles having scurried out of the passageway, a gathering crowd soon cast a shadow over the body. Randur having lost his appetite, handed the pie to an urchin in filthy rags.

"Welcome to Villjamur," Randur muttered.

CHAPTER 2

❄

Iᴛ ᴡᴀѕ ᴛʜᴇ ᴇxᴘʟᴏѕɪᴏɴ ᴛʜᴀᴛ ᴡᴏᴋᴇ ʜɪᴍ, ᴀ ʙᴀѕѕ ѕʜᴜᴅᴅᴇʀ ᴛʜᴀᴛ ѕᴇᴇᴍᴇᴅ ᴛᴏ shift the ground beneath him. Commander Brynd Lathraea opened his eyes, panting in the cold air, and looked up to realize that he was lying on the floor of a betula forest with dead twigs stabbing into his back. By his fingertips were wet knuckles of roots. He used them to help pull himself up, but his grip failed. He fell back, nauseous.

He tried to make sense of things.

Through the gaps in the trees, he watched a corkscrewing cloud of smoke, as branches swayed in the chilling wind. His ears were ringing. Strands of white hair blew across his face.

How had he got here?

The deck of a ship.

Then a blast.

He pushed himself upright, realizing how much his entire body hurt.

Next to him lay the remains of a wooden door, which he recognized as a hatch on his longship. His saber and short-axe were nowhere to be seen. Had his knife remained in his boot? Yes—*good*.

Through his daze, thoughts gradually returned.

As a commander of the Night Guard he had sailed to the shore recently, following the Emperor's useless orders. He had set out from Villiren, that sprawling mess of a trade city, their mission ensuring that Villjamur had a good supply of firegrain before the icy weather became too severe. He considered it a pointless task.

At the next attempt he managed to stand. Brynd then stumbled through the aphotic fagus forest, peering between its mottled bark for any sign of movement. His eyes caught subtleties, as he gripped branches, slipped on moss-laden rocks. At some distance on, he passed the disaggregated body of one of his Night Guard—and could tell it was Voren by the elaborate bow cast to one side. Doglike black gheels lingered around the corpse, their triple tongues and double sets of eyes shifting in rhythmic twitches around the open wounds, in a ritual as old as the land itself. Bones crunched.

Shapes shifted in the far umbrage either side and he questioned their meaning.

He recognized the boundaries of the Kull fjord, hills towering on either side of it, then fading into the distance. This was Dalúk Point, a natural port, but one rarely heard of outside military circles. Its rocky shores led down several feet to where the deep saline waters began.

The horizon was gradually filled with black terns flying in arcs toward the north. A strange serenity, as ominous skies loomed over the snow-tipped tundra in the distance. Brynd noticed an arrangement of stones on one dark hillside, signifying an upsul. It meant the Aes tribe had already moved further west across the island, perhaps to reach their winter camps. They'd be staying there a long time.

Above the constant sound of water on stone, the screams came echoing back, along the shoreline.

He limped around a nook of the forest that leaned over the water. "Fuck."

Two of his three longships had been totally destroyed. The smell of burning fuel was pungent. Tiny pyres floated on the water's surface, shattered wood and cargo were strewn around the shoreline, once-proud sails had become burning rags, propped up by masts that were sinking even as he watched. Three Night Guardsmen floated face-down, their cloaks ballooning with trapped air. Several soldiers were still fighting on the shore. At that moment one of them fell under the incoming arrows. They were fighting in close combat, with dozens of clansmen already dead or dying at their feet.

More tribesmen kept streaming toward them from beneath the trees, axes in hand. One shambled across his line of vision, his half-severed left arm gripped in his right hand. Blood stained the man's furs, war paint mixed with the sweat streaking down his face. Then an arrow exploded into the back of his head, shattering his skull.

Attempting to assess the situation, Brynd glanced across to the forest clearing nearest to the ships, where a few horses were still tethered to the trees.

As he shifted closer to the engagement, an arrow whipped across his face, and it skimmed across the stones to pierce the water. Following its origin, more figures were moving among the trees further up the shore, their axes glinting dully within the gloom.

He heaved an axe from a dead man's head, and shambled through the shadows until he came alongside a tight cluster of four of his men fighting under the remnants of the third and surviving ship. They looked to him when they could, then followed his directions.

He didn't recognize the attacking tribe's origins, but they fought inefficiently. He cleaved one in the head, then snatched the man's sword from his slackening grip. He pulled the axe free and threw it at another assailant. It wedged into his shoulder, and while the enemy was pinned in agony, Brynd rammed his sword through the front of his ribs. Warm blood poured onto his hands as Brynd tugged to free both weapons.

By now the remaining tribesmen were looking at him with wary fear—not for his fighting skills, but because of his color.

Perhaps they assumed him a ghost.

Another approached him. Brynd managed to knock away the savage's blade. He made a quick strike which his attacker tried to avoid, the blow splitting his left cheek. The clansman collapsed with a high-pitched scream.

One of Brynd's soldiers, meanwhile, had his head smashed in with a mace. Another received an arrow through his eye. In his peripheral vision, Brynd could see the gheels had arrived to maul the dead, flensing, then hauling out innards, trails of intestines vividly colorful against the gray stones.

Everyone suddenly looked up and the scene became inactive.

A flaming orb ripped through the sky from deep within the forest.

Crashed into the remaining ship.

Throwing up great hunks of wood.

"Fuck!" Brynd yelled. "Get away from here!"

The Night Guard retreated quickly up the shore.

"Head up into the forest!"

The fire spread rapidly, then another orb landed in the water. Brynd counted the time until the flames reached the cargo.

A white flash, and he pulled his cloak up to shelter his eyes, falling to the ground as the third ship exploded.

Noise saturated the air. Debris clattered on the stones around him, raked across the water, rattled the trees.

Men screamed as they were hit by burning shrapnel.

"Commander!"

Brynd stood and pulled back his cloak as he looked up to see who called his name. He shambled up the bank, glancing around wildly, while his men fought on.

"Commander," the voice beckoned, nearer now—from the darkness of the trees.

Fyir was lying on the ground, and as Brynd approached he noted he was clutching what was left of his leg. The stump had bloodied rags tied crudely around the end.

"Sir . . ." Fyir pleaded again, before screaming, tears covering his blackened face.

Brynd squatted beside him. "Lie still."

He peeled back the rags: Fyir's lower leg must have been destroyed in the explosion. The blond man's ear was also missing, a fragment of skull glistening in its place. "Don't think about this," Brynd said. "Think of something. Anything . . . Do you know who's attacking us?" He then slid a strip of bark between Fyir's teeth.

Fyir shook his head, wincing as Brynd tied some of his own torn-up cloak around the wound, and he screamed again, spat out the bark, moaning, "Ambushed . . ."

"Sabotaged," Brynd muttered. "No one was supposed to know we were here. There, that should hold it. You'll live, so that'll at least stop the gheels getting you. How badly does your head hurt?"

Fyir closed his eyes, squeezed out more tears, whispered, "Cultists?"

Brynd shook his head. "I doubt it was cultists. Since when do they use something as simple as arrows and axes? Have you seen anyone else?"

"What about . . . orbs?"

"Yes? What indeed?" Brynd reached into his top pocket, pulled out a small silver box. Inside it there were several colored powders in tiny compartments. He pinched a bit of the blue, and placed it under Fyir's nose. Within seconds the man's eyes rolled back and he passed out. Brynd stood up, placing the box back in his pocket. He was vaguely surprised at the severity of these wounds. The Night Guard were artificially enhanced, albeit slightly, and they were meant to re- cover quickly, suffer wounds hardly at all.

As he moved away, he gathered up a sword lying on the ground, a sharp Jamur saber. Pieces of butchered flesh littered the shore like after a cull of seals, and the skies around the fjord were black with smoke.

Another arrow skimmed past, and Brynd dived to grab a ragged piece of ship's timber on the rocks nearby. Using it as a shield, he ad- vanced toward the archers firing from the darkness of the trees. Shafts drove into the wood or clipped the stones around his feet, as he ran into the relative safety of the forest. Casting the timber aside, he headed further along the shore to hunt down the archers and what- ever it was that had launched the fire upon his ships.

On reflection, it might be foolish to attempt to eliminate person- ally an enemy that had obviously planned this attack in such detail.

But who? Why? All he was doing here was handling the collection of fuel. The Emperor had insisted on sending men he could trust, men for whom his paranoia was at a minimum. The Night Guard.

One of the enemy could be seen crouching at the forest's edge, peering out across the fjord. Like a hunter, Brynd stalked wide so as to keep outside of his target's range of vision, drew the dagger from in- side his boot. The crackle of the burning ships was enough to enable some stealth in his approach, and when Brynd was just twenty yards from his target, he flung the blade through the air.

It lodged in the archer's face and he fell silently to the ground. A second tribesman ran to his side. Brynd was on him, immediately scraping his saber across the man's throat.

This tribe wasn't from Jokull, or any other of the Empire's islands. The clothing wasn't local for a start, and there was no adornment save the bone charm hung around the remains of the man's neck. Brynd withdrew his dagger from the first victim, cleaned it off, placed it back in his boot.

Gheels crouched in the half-light, awaiting their moment. He decided to go back and wait near Fyir, killing only those who approached him. Revenge could wait until later.

✳

Nighttime, and in these moments Brynd's mind became ultrarational. Things became lists, strategies, probabilities. He knelt next to Fyir, a man in a resting state, now calm and peaceful. While he'd been away, blood beetles had begun feasting on Fyir's damaged leg, shredding the cloth Brynd had used to staunch the bleeding, and reducing his truncated leg by at least a hand span. In the process, the fist-sized insects had secreted a resin that stopped the bleeding and induced healing, so maybe they weren't completely a bad thing. Brynd had to scrape the creatures off with a saber, then split them down the center of their shells to kill them.

The skies cleared, and the world became unbearably cold. He couldn't yet light a fire because it would inevitably draw attention. Three horses were hidden deeper within the forest so they wouldn't be stolen. What strategy now? If only he'd brought Nelum along, a man who could generate plots in his head with simplicity, but Nelum was back in Villjamur, because Brynd hadn't thought he'd need him.

There had been several more explosions, sparks that shattered the darkness as barrels of firegrain were touched by the spreading flames, but Brynd was confident that the night ahead would be calm. Thirteen of the Night Guard were dead. That left five more unaccounted for, so he assumed them dead too.

Shadows had moved in front of flames for a while, a few hours back.

A featureless ship had rowed away.

Eerie stillness now lingered.

He could barely remember a time when the Night Guard were made to look so easy to defeat. The Empire's forces usually dominated battles, clearing rebel islands with brutal efficiency. All those years of early confidence since he'd begun his service for the current Emperor in the Regiment of Foot, then transferred to the Dragoons, and finally to the Night Guard. For his loyalty and renowned fighting skills, he had climbed to the rank of commander. Was he really so loyal? Or, because of the color of his skin, did he feel he always had something to prove?

He needed to show he was *normal*, steadfastly loyal to the Empire. That made his life easier. Being one of only a few albinos known in the Jamur Empire, he was used to being considered as a permanent outsider. True, people found him curious more than anything else. Their gaze usually settled on his red-tinted eyes, hesitating there a moment because of either fear or amazement, he'd never know— because people liked to stare, didn't they? As a result of his abnormality, he had worked on improving his fitness and knowledge with remarkable dedication.

He stared out from the cover of the trees at the fires that still burned where the firegrain had spread among the debris. Most of the grain would be underwater, soaked and useless. Some of it had caught on the wreckage floating along the fjord, and small fires lit its passage to the sea as if there was a festival for the water god, Sul. He wondered vaguely if priests from the Aes would come down to the shore to look for shells as a result of these fires to supply their divinations.

And what would they tell me tonight? That my luck's out? No shit.

He picked up an arrow he'd rescued from a dead soldier, held it close to see if he could work out its origins. Most likely it came from the island of Varltung, though there were no runes inscribed to indicate a maker. Varltung had a long history of resistance to the Emperor's forces. Being naturally fortified by its high cliffs, it was difficult for a sea landing. But, because of the Freeze, the Council was reluctant to acquire new territories.

How could a foreign force even arrive on Jokull, the Jamur Empire's main island, without anyone noticing? His mission here had been ordered from the highest levels in the Empire, with only the Council, its governing body, being privy to that information.

A man lurched out of the darkness.

"Ha! Some bloody Night Guardsman *you* are," the figure said. "Could've slit your throat in a heartbeat."

"I noticed you over an hour ago, captain, a hundred paces up the shore. With the noise you made, I'm surprised you're not on the rocks right now wearing several arrows." He looked up. "How long did it take you to realize I'm not the enemy?"

Captain Apium Hol ignored the jibe, instead paced around Fyir's sleeping body. He was stocky, pale skinned with red hair. On his breast, Apium wore the distinctive silver brooch of the Night Guard, a seven-pointed star representing all of the Empire's occupied nations, and it was only then that Brynd noticed that he'd lost his own.

"Looks like old Fyir here bit off more than he could chew," Apium remarked.

"Not even funny, captain. You should've seen him when he was still awake. Never seen a man in such agony."

"Beetles?" Apium inquired.

"Yes, some of it. He'd already lost up to his knee from the blast. I stopped the bleeding, left him here for a bit, and . . . well."

"At least it wasn't gheels. So, how many of us are left, sir?" Apium sat down on the ground beside Brynd with a groan.

"You're looking at us."

"By the balls of the dragon gods of Varltung." The captain shook his head.

"I wouldn't mention that nation's name right now."

"You suspect it's them?"

"Ah, who knows."

"So, what happened to you, commander?"

"Think I was thrown right from the ship into the forest," Brynd explained. "But the trees must've broken my fall. How about you?"

"I was on the shore when your ship . . . went up. Saw the archers heading into the forest, so I followed them. Got one of them, saw two others dead as I came back. I looked around for a catapult—because something must've propelled that fire—but there was nothing to see. Just an empty clearing. There were at least four of us on the shore— like, Gyn, Boldar, Awul—but they weren't there when I got back."

Silence.

To see your comrades die was something to be expected in the army. It was tough, of course. You formed a close bond. Men became an extended family. You saw more of the world together than most lovers ever would. There would be mourning, that was certain, as there always was. Brynd couldn't let it get to him right now, though, so he placed the issue into a region of his mind that he would later revisit.

"Any idea who did this?" Apium asked. "Not the clansmen, I mean, but who actually planned it?"

After a pause Brynd muttered, "It's a set-up. Someone in Villjamur wanted this to happen."

"But why?"

"So we're not properly prepared for the Freeze, I guess. Otherwise, no idea, really."

"Leaves us well screwed," Apium continued. "Do you think we should've brought a cultist along with us?"

"It's all well and good saying that now, but everyone wanted to keep this low-key. That was the whole point, wasn't it? Cultists would've only drawn more attention. And they would've *known* too, which defeats the objective. Although why all this secrecy just for a bit of fuel? I realize Johynn wants us relying on them less. You know, he even told me before we came away that he suspected the cultists would bugger off to do their own thing during the ice age. It's not exactly classified information that he wants to be able to manage things without them, get used to them not being around. He might be a little weird at times, but there's *some* wisdom there, I'll say that much."

"Hmm." Apium wore an expression of uncertainty. "Still, would've helped though."

"I'm going to be asking some awkward questions when we get back home."

"So you think we're going to be in trouble?" Apium suggested.

"It's not by any means an emergency. There's enough wood in the forests across the Empire to keep the home fires burning, for sure. This was more Johynn's doing. He was convinced the firegrain was needed—and you know what his mind's been like of late."

Apium stifled a laugh, then he pointed through the trees.

Two moons could be seen between the tall hills rising either side of the fjord, one moon significantly larger than the other, and both an ethereal white, hanging low in the sky. Astrid, the smaller, appeared sometimes to be unnatural, as if it was made of some pale ore, out of place even—something Brynd felt an affinity for.

The men stared for several moments. There was a sense of stillness. Stars gradually defined the hillside.

"Looking nice tonight, aren't they?" Apium said. "Strange to think they'll do it."

"What?"

"The ice age. Strange to think just the moons are causing it."

"When you think about it logically—"

"You see, that's your problem. I just said it's weird that it comes to that. You never just think plainly about stuff."

"It's not a plain world, captain."

"You need to get laid more often," Apium grumbled, lying back flat on the ground, his arms behind his head.

Brynd stood up suddenly. He could perceive movement nearby.

"What's wrong with you?" Apium said. "Touched a nerve have I?"

Brynd gestured for him to silence.

The red-haired man pushed himself upright to follow Brynd's gaze. "Can't see anything."

Brynd stepped to the right, his eyes wide, alert. Within seconds he knew Apium had lost him, could see the man's gormless face lit up by the moon, even at a distance. How Apium had managed to stay alive in the Night Guard was beyond Brynd. Perhaps he worshipped some outlawed god who knew something no one else did. The injections this elite group received on their induction should have worn off over the years due to Apium's excessive drinking.

Brynd took several slow steps over to where he had seen the foliage move. He reached carefully for his saber. Behind a sapling, he saw him. A man, naked, covered in mud. Brynd frowned, then reached for a stone from the ground. He threw it, the stone connected, but the man didn't move, didn't even flinch. Brynd repeated the action. Still no movement. He whistled back to Apium.

After a few seconds, his companion shambled through the forest to his side. "What's up?"

"There's a man over there." Brynd indicated the figure. "He's naked."

"Naked?"

"I said naked."

"You're right," Apium said. "What's he doing way out here with nothing on? Bit of outdoors action, eh?"

"How the hell should I know?" Brynd said. Little harm could come from investigating this, surely? There was no sign of anyone else around, and he was sure they were alone. "Let's get closer." Brynd led the way toward the naked man, who had remained still for some time. If he was aware of their approach, he didn't show it.

"The Sele of Jamur to you, sir," Brynd said, thinking the traditional Jamur greeting would prompt some response. Nothing. He looked the man up and down. "You, er . . . you must be cold."

Apium snorted a laugh.

The man still didn't move, just stared vacantly ahead. They stepped cautiously to within an armspan of him, noticing his face lacked blood as if totally drained of it. His eyes were slightly slanted, and they gazed directly past Brynd. There were strange wounds around his neck, then Brynd noticed that his head was shaven unevenly, so that tufts of black hair blossomed on it in patches.

"Looks dead, doesn't he?" Apium remarked.

Brynd reached out, prodded the man in the chest. Still no reaction. The commander took a bold step forward and reached out to feel his wrist. "Well, I'll swear by Bohr, he is."

"What?" Apium gasped. "Dead?"

"Yes. There's no sign of pulse." He let go of his wrist, and the man's arm slumped back to his side.

"This is cultist work, Brynd," Apium warned, reaching for Brynd's shoulder with fear in his eyes. "Nothing natural here. I don't like it. I've no idea what they've done to him, but we should send this fellow on his way and stay with Fyir. In fact, I think we ought to move off a little."

Although stunned, Brynd didn't know what to make of it. A hardened soldier, he was used to seeing the worst of life, but this individual out here spoke of technologies he was unaware of. What options did he have? If they killed this man, there might be more in waiting. Should he provoke it? In their depleted state, Brynd considered it best to leave things be and report it back in Villjamur. "I think you're right. This can wait. I'll maybe put it in a report."

They carried Fyir gently to the ruins of an Azimuth temple.

Little was known about that civilization, and hardly anything was left there aside from hidden and subtle masonry. One of the towers had fallen so that it rested flat against a hillside, just beyond Dalúk

Point, the lower side now wedged firmly into the slope. Lichen and mosses suffocated much of it, but there were still discernible patterns, squares within squares, that were known to be traditional religious symbols. It was thought that the Azimuth had worshipped numerology and mathematical precision, a sentiment he liked: looking for beauty in the most abstract of places. Brynd pondered this reverence as Apium fell asleep alongside Fyir.

The commander sat at the foot of the tower, his knees pulled up, back resting against the stone. His saber remained unsheathed at his side. Stars now defined the hills surrounding the fjord, and he concentrated on sounds, the way you always did on these shifts, hoping and yet not hoping to hear footsteps, maybe snapping branches, someone coming their way. But there was little activity apart from that of nocturnal birds and mammals, every one of their eerie calls reminding him how they were quite alone.

In fact, he began to feel he was barely there himself.

CHAPTER 3

✳

THE HARDEST CYNIC, INVESTIGATOR RUMEX JERYD THOUGHT, *IS OFTEN fundamentally the most romantic person, because he so often feels let down by the world.* He couldn't detect much romance in himself today, but all the cynicism he could wish for.

He could hear the rain driving against the old stone walls. He liked the sound: it reminded him of the outside world. Lately, he'd spent far too many days in this gloom, had begun to feel a little too disconnected from Villjamur. Everything the city stood for these days was something he found a struggle to perceive.

The rumel looked down at the returned theater tickets in his right hand, then his gaze switched to the note in his left hand.

It read: *Thanks, but it's just all a bit too late, don't you think? Marysa x*

Jeryd sighed, his tail twitched. It was from his ex-wife. They were a rumel couple, and had been together for over a hundred years. There were benefits in not being human. Not only was rumel skin tougher, but because of their longevity they could take time with things, have some patience. As a rumel you never ended up running around frantically after matters. You let them come to you. However, it made his being away from Marysa all the more painful, because it was as if he'd lost half his life along with her.

He folded up the paper, placed it and the tickets in the drawer of his desk. He would have to find someone else to take to the production. Or not go at all, just forget about it.

The Freeze was going to be cold enough without spending it alone. He sighed.

She'd hinted she was going to leave him, before that final day, but that was during one of the months of fighting between groups of the newly arriving refugees and Villjamur's far-right protesters, so a period where nothing really registered in his mind. The Inquisition had hauled in and executed several men—all disillusioned ex-soldiers of the Regiment of Foot—just to set an example, and it was known secretly that the soldiers were sympathizers with these extremists.

But it all meant Jeryd had been ignoring Marysa.

She liked antiques. In a city as old as this there was a plentiful supply. Sometimes, she told him, she hoped she would find a grand relic, one that the cultists had overlooked, maybe make a fortune with it. But Jeryd had his head in the real world, or so he said. It was only his job, after all. He brought home the trauma of these ancient streets, carried it as his own burden. Keeping order in a city of over four hundred thousand individuals was partly his responsibility, and when he came home there she was: parading some new item around the house, telling him eagerly about what its history might have been, researching it in those pointless books she purchased. A luxury! The Jamur society was the latest in an endless line of civilizations, and each had left their own funk and detritus. Of course, the cultists would have long claimed anything useful from the Dawnir remains. All that was left now was a hint that things were once greater—that life in Villjamur today was more primitive and less civilized than life under those ancient societies, the Qintans, the Azimuths, despite the city's constant attempts to hide that under the veneer of Imperialism.

It was only natural the couple would drift apart. One night she looked right at him, through him, continued that fixed stare, as if she was weighing up there and then whether to leave him. There was no argument, no discussion, and he didn't even want to ask in case he found out some harsh truth.

When the truth did arrive, it wasn't such a bitter exit, and that somehow made things even worse. Sometimes when he closed his eyes he could hear her footsteps as she departed, the sight of her tail trailing out before the door finally closed. The stillness of the room afterward. He didn't think there was another rumel man involved. He supposed there had never been *any* real man in her life, which was why she went. She had left only a forwarding address, and an instruction for him not to follow her there.

Jeryd was becoming increasingly dissatisfied with his life.

Not only that, but those kids from further along his street had been throwing stones at his windows again. Every winter they'd regularly arc snowballs into the door, and he'd end up answering it to encounter nothing as they vanished with urban skill down lanes and backstreets. They knew he was a member of the Inquisition all right, and that prestigious honor only made him more of a target. He had become a badge of honor, a snowball medal, the ultimate highlight of their day.

Bastards.

He looked up from his desk in mid-yawn as his aide, Tryst, entered his office. "Work keeping you up late, Jeryd?"

"Like always," Jeryd replied. "But I try my best."

He studied the young human form of Investigator-Aide Tryst, though didn't linger on his athletic physique, bright blue eyes or his thick dark hair. He wasn't even envious, strictly speaking, but the young man was a reminder of times long past—a hundred years ago, or thereabouts, when Jeryd had kept himself trim. Still, Jeryd retained a sharp mind, and he had his experiences.

Something wasn't right, however. "What's wrong this time?" Jeryd asked. "Is it about the promotions? You know I think you're one of the best aides there is. You're nearly family to me by now, but you're a human—and rules are rules."

Jeryd felt bad for not actually nominating Tryst to be promoted, considering the young aide had shown great promise, had done well to even achieve his current position. They'd worked on hundreds of cases together. Jeryd genuinely wanted to nominate him, but knew how the powers-that-be would frown upon it. Humans were simply not allowed to achieve senior positions in the Inquisition. They didn't live long enough, and it was as simple as that. A rumel averaged around two hundred years, which meant truly great wisdom could only be achieved by that species. It was an ancient ruling, decreed by the first Emperor, to help smooth over the uneasy coexistence of the two hominid races. You couldn't break tradition, so Tryst would go no further.

"It's not that," Tryst said, with a glance to the floor. "That's fine. I understand." Clearly, it was still a sore point, whatever he might say. "No, you'd better come and see for yourself. Warkur is out of the city, so they need you to take a look at the scene."

"I hope it's not the refugees again," Jeryd said. "We could do without another scene there."

"No, not that. It's a murder."

"Murder?" Jeryd said, standing up, his tail perfectly still.

"Yes. Very high profile." Tryst said. "We've only recently heard the banshee's keening. It's a councilor, this time."

✳

Randur studied the rumel investigator and his aide. They both wore official-looking robes in dark red, although the rumel wore brown breeches underneath, as if he never really liked his uniform. They were taking notes at the scene of the death, where Randur had been told to remain as a witness. He hadn't encountered many rumel on Folke and now wondered if it was their evolving alongside humans that resulted in both species becoming so alike in their thinking. Was it nature or nurture? It was probably a result of both.

The rumel was black-skinned, and you could see the coarse creases of age even from a distance, so Randur guessed he'd seen more than just a few winters. There were the usual rumel broad features with sunken cheeks, black, glossy eyes. He meandered around the alleyway as if with no real purpose, his tail waving back and forth with each step. Every now and then he'd turn his head to the sky, as if to check it for snow.

The iren behind was busy with traders and customers. A food stand was starting to cook thick hunks of seal meat, the smoke rising between the bridges and balconies higher up. Furs were available straight off the hide—bear, deer, lynx—so that you could craft them yourself in any number of ways. There were shoddy tribal ornaments and spurious island craftsmanship on display. They were manufactured on the cheap, but the people of Villjamur couldn't tell or, if they did, they certainly didn't show it.

Randur paid special attention to clothing, noting all the latest styles—tiny collars with little ruffs, pale earthy tones on the women that did nothing for them, two brooches worn where possible right next to each other. The swords people carried tended to be short messer blades, and he thought that they must be more efficient to kill with in the narrow corridors and pathways of Villjamur.

The Inquisition had eventually sealed off the area around the dead body, and they were now beginning to erect wooden panels to hide the death scene.

The rumel approached him, a cool and graceful individual.

"Sele of Jamur to you, sir. I'm Investigator Rumex Jeryd. Could you tell me your name please?"

"Randur Estevu, from Folke. Just arrived this morning."

"You're from out of town? I thought I could detect an accent. You speak Jamur well, though. I'm surprised the guards let you in."

Randur shrugged, a lock of hair falling across his forehead.

"Do you mind if I ask what you're here for? People from outside aren't generally admitted because of the Freeze, you see. We get all sorts of trouble here."

"Not at all. I've got employment at the Emperor's halls, and I've shown my identification at each of the three gates. It's all official."

"Right, well, we can't ever be too careful. We've got a bit of a refugee problem, as you've no doubt seen on your way in."

"Yeah, poor guys." Randur pulled up the collars on his cloak. "Are you, y'know, letting them all in before the ice comes?"

"It's not up to me, but the Council assure the people of the city that the matter's in hand though. So, can you now tell me everything you saw? Please, leave nothing out."

"Well, not much to say really. He came running and screaming from up there somewhere." He indicated an alley at the opposite end of the iren. "Beetles were already swarming all over his wound, then he just collapsed on the ground, right where he is now."

The rumel scribbled some notes in a small book. "Nothing else that seemed odd or out of place?"

"Everything seems a little odd to me today."

The rumel grinned. "Welcome to Villjamur, lad."

✳

Jeryd crouched by the body, taking in the details of the wound, how the blood trickled across the cobbles. A while later he glanced up at

Aide Tryst, who was stepping carefully around the confines of the alley. At the far end lay several broken frames and pots of paint from the adjacent gallery.

Around Cartanu Gata, especially where it intersected with the Gata Sentimental, nothing had changed for thirty or forty years, ever since it had been arrogated by the evening bohemians.

All along its lower walls were scribbles etched deep by knife blades over the centuries. Odes to lovers. Threats to all and anyone. Who watches the Night Guard? So-and-so sucks dicks. That sort of thing. Some of the cobbles were splashed with paint, too, and you could smell stale food despite the dampness. At night, lanterns cast long, feral shadows down here, and if there was no breeze the darkness was suffocating in such narrow confines. And there were always rumors of cultist-bred animal hybrids walking along here with awkward gaits before sunrise.

Weighing up all these possibilities, Jeryd was trying to build a picture.

Delamonde Rubus Ghuda. The victim—a human male, in his forties—was a senior member of the Villjamur Council. His ribcage had been open and exposed in a most bizarre way. The robes had just melted away around the wound, and some of his flesh appeared as if it had been scooped out. There were no traces of anything else around the corpse. Jeryd had never seen such an injury before.

This made a difference from the usual crimes he investigated. An old rumel like Jeryd could easily become bored with his job: people only ever committed the same few misdemeanors. You had murders, usually affairs of the heart; people stole things because they couldn't afford them; then you had the excesses of drug addicts. Generally it was about people either snatching more from life, or people trying to escape it completely.

But this crime had indications of something else . . .

Tryst paused alongside him.

"Not a pretty sight," Jeryd observed.

"Indeed not."

"What's this?" Jeryd shuffled over to one side, dabbed his finger to a cobble. A blue substance stuck to it.

"Must be paint," Tryst suggested, "from the gallery. Load of paint pots stored back there."

Jeryd stood up, wiped the finger on his robe. "No witnesses yet from there?"

"I'll get someone to ask questions. Knock on a few doors, maybe. I'm not hopeful, though."

"Get one of the others onto it immediately. I need to know if there was anything remotely strange going on here. Anyone unusual walking by. Any scuffles or swordfights, anything. And we need find out what he was up to last night and earlier this morning."

"Okay." Tryst turned to go.

"Meanwhile don't tell anyone about this," Jeryd continued. "I'll contact the Council myself, let them know. We can't do with this getting out just for the moment. The people who witnessed him die didn't necessarily realize his position, and I don't want Emperor Johynn finding out via rumors. Bohr knows it'd just become part of a conspiracy in his head."

Jeryd walked slowly to the far end of the alley, glancing up through the morning drizzle at three spires visible in the distance, and at the bridges that arced between them.

Tryst interrupted his thoughts. "Investigator, should we take him back to headquarters now?"

Jeryd slipped his hands in the pockets beneath his robe. He was studying the dead-end behind, where a heap of garbage lined the side wall of the gallery. Considering himself a man of the Arts, he had always wanted to visit all the galleries, but had never quite found the time for this one. Marysa had often mentioned it, painting a wonderful picture he never quite got to see. Then, again, she always did exaggerate. He'd seen far too much crime here over the years for him to look at this part of the city with naïveté. Especially nearby Caveside, where the buildings themselves breathed decay.

"Yes, get him back now," Jeryd said. "We could do with wrapping this up as soon as possible."

CHAPTER 4

❄

THEY RODE PAST HUNDREDS OF REFUGEES CAMPED ALONGSIDE THE SANC-
tuary Road. The numbers grew daily, conditions worsened. Filthy
children ran between tents on either side of the road, where grassy
banks had become mud baths. Livestock had been brought, too, and
makeshift pens had been constructed. The previous evening's fires
had been reduced to ashes overnight. This morning faces were glum,
and they looked at him with a sense of embarrassed pleading—these
were people, unused to poverty, who had never dreamed that this
might be where they'd end up.

Another city was growing outside the city.

People had come here in hope. Hope that they wouldn't be left to
freeze in the wild when the ice came. Hope that the Empire's main
city would be able to house them in its labyrinth. Hope that there
would be enough food and warmth. They'd come from Kullrún,
Southfjords, Folke, Y'iren, Tineag'l, Blortath—heard in their accents.
They had gathered whatever belongings they had and set off for the
Sanctuary City. But the city could only accommodate a limited number during the estimated fifty years of ice to come—that was the official line. The very government that ruled over them did not want to
offer them shelter. Had they been landowners, there might be an
open door, such was the way of things here.

Brynd felt pangs of sympathy as he moved past, a desire to help.
Behind him, on the cart, Apium was still half asleep.

"Captain," Brynd said sharply, and the man jolted awake.

"Eh? What? We're here, then, commander?"

The horses approached the main gate, a towering granite structure
framing huge iron doors.

"Sele of Jamur," Brynd addressed a city guard dressed in a blood-
colored tunic, who straightened his fur hat, and saluted.

"Commander Lathraea, the Sele of Jamur to you. Everything
well?"

"Been better," Brynd said sourly.

"Commander, we're obliged to ask you about the contents of the
cart."

Brynd nodded, knowing the security procedures. The guard
walked over to the cart, greeted Apium, pulled back the blanket covering their wounded passenger.

"Spot of bother at Dalúk Point," Apium said. "And he was one of
the lucky ones."

"What happened to him?" the guard asked, covering Fyir up again.

"We'd like to know that, too," Brynd confessed.

The guard gave him that knowing smile between soldiers. "Right,
in you go."

He signaled for the gates to open. As they groaned apart, twenty
more city soldiers advanced toward and around them, to prevent any
of the refugees from attempting to get into the city. Not that they
could, because there were two more gates to get past. And both were
firmly closed to them.

So the Night Guard soldiers entered Villjamur.

Today was Priests' Day in the city. Twice a year, otherwise forbid-
den religions were allowed such an airing. The streets were filled with
priests from the outlying tribes, allowed in on a one-day permit, but
watched closely by soldiers from the Regiment of Foot. Sulists gathered around their shell-reading priests. Noonists were standing semi-
naked in a circle, smeared in fish oils, holding hands and singing a
melisma while a bunch of city cats tried to lick the oil off their legs.
Ovinists were holding up pigs' hearts, as was their custom, allowing
the blood to drip from them slowly into their mouths. Apparently

this brought them closer to nature, but Brynd could think of less disgusting ways.

Aside from the devotees of the official two gods—Bohr and Astrid, worshipped under the umbrella of Mániism—no priests were normally allowed to practice in the streets. Tradition allowed only these two days of the year for citizens to be exposed to other religions. Brynd thought it all rather pointless, since even if you did decide to follow some other creed, you would be forced to leave the city to follow your new persuasion.

Brynd led the surviving Night Guardsmen along the main thoroughfares that would take them up on the next level where the streets and passageways became quieter.

Brynd leaped off his horse as a flicker of purple light caught his attention.

"What?" Apium demanded, puzzled.

"Back in a moment." Brynd headed off down the narrow passage, till he spotted a cultist slumped against a wall. The man was clutching a slim cylinder to his chest, from which purple sparks flew onto his bare skin. The device itself was somehow fixed to his hand, a web of skin keeping it in place. The man's face was contorted into a mixture of bliss and pain. Brynd turned away in disgust.

"What was it?" Apium inquired, as he returned.

"Magic junkie," Brynd muttered, mounting his horse again.

✳

"What?" Jamur Johynn demanded, looking up from his dining table.

The Emperor was chewing on a fish platter, now and then examining his food for stray bones. His distant gaze suggested he might as well have been eating a plate of lemons. At times, Johynn refused to eat at all and sometimes he would assure servants that he'd eaten everything, only for them to find remains of his plate on the rocks directly below the window, or maybe stuffed into one of the ornamental jugs. Whether it was because he suffered from anorexia, or was paranoid about being poisoned was anybody's guess. No explanations were offered, and no one dared to ask.

The dining chamber was a narrow room, but the numerous mirrors everywhere made the palace seem larger than it was. Early Jamur murals depicting gridlike astrological phenomena were painted between a myriad of identical arches. No one knew what they really meant. A row of plinths held the smoke-stained busts of previous Emperors, all Johynn's ancestors, like silent guests, while a handful of servants looked on, as always, from behind the pillars, neither wanting nor required to be seen. There was always a hint of fear in them as Brynd walked past, an inhalation of breath, a straightening of the back. Maybe they just feared this military intrusion because Brynd himself usually felt relaxed and informal in the Emperor's presence. They had developed over the years a relationship of intimacy, till Johynn could trust few people apart from the albino. Maybe that was because as Johynn had once hinted, it looked as if Brynd had some secrets to conceal himself.

"Killed to the last man, my Emperor. All apart from those of us you're now looking at."

"So this means . . . ?" Johynn made a steeple of his hands.

"No firegrain, Majesty, so the only resource there will be now is wood." Brynd stood to attention alongside Apium, but Fyir had been allowed a chair, a rare concession in the Emperor's presence.

"So, commander . . . ?"

"Our heat sources are therefore questionable," Brynd continued. "But let's not overlook the fact that half your personal guard has been slaughtered."

"No heat, no heat . . ." Johynn moaned, as if reciting some destructive mantra.

Brynd glanced across at Apium. The captain merely shrugged.

Jamur Johynn walked over to the window. "And how, how am I now going to keep the people of my city—of my Empire—warm?"

Brynd thought, *As if you give a shit about anyone who's not Empire-issued nobility or a landowner.*

"How can I look after them now the moons are in place? Everyone depends on me, Commander Lathraea. Everyone needs me."

"Perhaps we'll manage okay without—"

"Don't be ridiculous," Johynn snapped. "This failure makes it even worse for everyone. They're going to rebel and have me killed now, aren't they?"

"Who?" Brynd said.

Johynn turned to face him again. *"Them."* He tilted his head toward the window, and the city beyond. "My people."

"But it's not your fault an ice age is starting. There've been hundreds of years of accurate predictions, you were merely the Emperor to face the challenge. There's always stocks of wood—"

"But I have to look after them. It means four hundred thousand responsibilities. You wouldn't have a clue what that's like."

"They know you try to look after them," Brynd insisted. "Your Imperial lineage has always been popular."

"The ones already living here, perhaps. But any other idiot arriving from whatever benighted corner of this Empire they inhabit will be surprised when we can't let them enter. Then they'll hardly love me, will they?"

Johynn's voice started to falter. His fingers were drumming the sill as he stared out of the window again. Every movement suggested an increasing sense of panic.

Johynn said. "But I'm their savior, oh yes. It is my right, before the Dawnir, before the movements of Bohr and Astrid. *I'm their savior.*"

"My Emperor, perhaps this isn't the best time to ask, but do you know who else was aware of our mission?"

"What mission?"

"The one from which we've only just returned," Brynd said patiently, looking to Apium, who raised his eyebrows, shook his head, and mouthed the word "nuts."

"Only a few of our Council members—Ghuda, Boll, and Mewún. Chancellor Urtica, too. Only those four, no one else. No one else. No, absolutely nobody."

"Is it possible that any of them could've informed an enemy? Is it possible one of them didn't want us to succeed?"

Johynn spun around, approached Brynd. "Are you saying we've a traitor within our own halls now? For the love of Bohr, what next? Are you quite sure, Commander Lathraea, that such accusations have good foundation?"

"Our force was almost wiped out. You say no one outside the Council knew of our mission, yet we were ambushed. Sire, I'm only trying to find out who might threaten the Empire."

"You're a good man, Commander Lathraea. A good man. You

were all good men, you Night Guards." He leaned closely to Brynd, then whispered, "I can *trust* you, can't I?"

Brynd straightened up, bowing fractionally. "Beyond my life, your Majesty."

Johynn came closer still, the smell of alcohol on his breath now as intense as a bad perfume. "It's over."

"I'm not sure I follow," Brynd said.

"I've had increasing suspicions that someone in here is after me. They all are, maybe. They want to take my life, my existence. They want this." Johynn indicated the halls, the furnishings. "They want it all before the ice comes. I've heard them whispering in their chambers, making decisions for me. Doing my job for me."

"My Lord," Brynd said, "they're your Council. That's what they're supposed to do. No one is out to get you."

Brynd considered his own words, because perhaps that wasn't altogether the case. There was usually something devious going. This was government, after all.

Jamur Johynn took a step away from Brynd and looked him up and down as if judging his character in one simple gesture. A childlike gesture. Brynd began to feel self-conscious again. Johynn opened his mouth, but the door opened just then.

A welcome break as the Emperor's daughter walked into the room.

When he had first joined the Night Guard, he remembered seeing her, in her younger days, when she seemed confined in this building like a butterfly in a net. Hers seemed a delicate energy waiting to be restrained. Serious meetings would be interrupted by her childish conversations with her older sister, Rika, the heir to the Imperial seat, and their joyful shrieks filled the corridors with warmth. But those days were soon gone, departed at about the same time their mother was killed. Johynn had tried to replace parental love with treats and indulgences, something the little girl never seemed to desire, but altering her in some remote way.

Eir possessed a certain natural grace, a distinctive quality of manner. With short-cropped black hair, and tall for her age, her attitude to dress was cavalier, wearing items from any number of eras without caring how they matched. Her eyes were intense, her eyebrows two thin lines, and her face lacked the symmetry necessary to appeal to Villjamur convention. She liked to dress a little bit different. Despite her nontraditional looks, a queue of eligible suitors waited to claim her hand, and maybe decisions had already been made for her by her father over who she would be betrothed to. Maybe that was why she was rude to almost every boy she ever spoke to. For all her privileges, Brynd guessed it was no real existence for a woman in Villjamur.

"I apologize for disturbing you, Father, but the Dawnir wishes to speak to the commander."

The Emperor stared at her as if he did not recognize who she was.

Brynd intervened. "We were just discussing what our Dawnir could want—"

"Some more plots against me, no doubt," Johynn muttered.

"Should we see him now, my Emperor, if you've finished with our business?" Brynd asked.

"Yes, yes. Why not." He waved Brynd away, walked to the window. This time he opened it, allowing the icy air to enter the room, stepped aside, his fists clenched, then suddenly burst past them, out of the room, leaving the three men and his daughter behind with the echo of a slammed door.

"Hello, commander," she said.

There was always a slight informality between her and the Night Guard soldiers, engendered by their close proximity over the years. "Lady Eir, I fear your father's been drinking."

"And you think that's my fault?" Anger dissolved into disappointment on her face. He knew she had been trying her best to stop her father from drinking excessively, taking away half-empty bottles once he'd fallen asleep, had stared at him reproachfully with those big green eyes every time he refilled a glass. Now she just gazed at the wall as if some comfort could be found there, but there were too many mirrors to encourage her to look for long.

"Yes, I didn't mean to be harsh, but your father has islands and cities to help run. There's enough bad judgment being made in this city without our ruler drinking as well."

"I know, I know," Eir said. Her tone was confident, though her posture suggested it wasn't natural, that she had something to prove to herself. "Anyway, what happened to you all?"

"Ambush, and massacre. We're the remaining survivors from . . . from where we were sent last."

Eir said, "The firegrain trip? Who were you fighting?"

Brynd couldn't believe it. "Even *you* know about it. Is nothing sacred in these halls?"

"I'm sorry," Eir said. "Fyir, will you be all right?" She lay a hand on him kindly, a gesture that other men might envy.

"Suffice to say," Fyir squirmed in his chair, "that my soldiering days are over, Jamur Eir."

"Girls' talk," Apium snorted. Then, to Eir, he murmured, "No offense."

"None taken."

"He'll be up and about in no time," Apium continued. "We'll strap a decent bit of wood on that leg and he'll be back on horseback ready for training—"

Brynd gestured Apium to be silent.

There was a disturbance outside.

He hurried over to the window. *Shit!*

A scene was developing down below in the drizzle.

Emperor Jamur Johynn could be seen retreating to the outer edge of the balcony below, almost as if he was being backed into a corner. In his own mind he had probably reached such a position long ago.

Several guardsmen edged tentatively toward him, uncertain of how to act. A move forward suggested a threat to him. A move back might mean they would be too late.

Brynd fled the room to go and help.

✳

"Stand back," he shouted, pushing his way through the growing crowd. From this stone platform you could view the whole front section of the city, the spires, the bridges, the sweeping dark hills in the distance, even the sea in the other direction. Only a knee-high granite wall separated you from a vertiginous drop. Servants and administrative staff were here to witness the drama unfolding, and even some councilors had come to watch, too. The Emperor was still positioned as before, but he now faced the sky as if experiencing a purely religious moment. And maybe he was—in these moments you could never tell what was really going on. Brynd knew he had to stop him doing something stupid, had to bring the Emperor back safely into the hall. With the ice age setting in, Johynn would be needed as a national figurehead. People needed his guidance, his support, because in times of crisis you needed someone to reassure you it would be okay, even when it wouldn't be.

They needed someone to lie to them clearly and loudly.

"My Emperor, what're you doing?" Brynd called out, icy sleet gusting against his cheeks.

"It's easier this way," Johynn said. "As I said before, it's over."

His motions were awkward, like those of someone who had been drinking heavily. He regained his footing, shuffled further along the low parapets.

"I have no great words, commander," Johynn said. "Nothing profound to say, at the end."

"Please, I think you should step back a bit," Brynd argued. "Think about what you're doing."

"*Think* is all I damn well do, Commander Lathraea. All I do is think about things. All the time thinking."

"But the people of Villjamur need you," Brynd said desperately. "That's what you said earlier. That they *need* you!"

"Father!" Eir appeared, running onto the scene.

Whether it was because he lost his footing, or he genuinely intended to step off the edge, Brynd would never know, but just then the Emperor collapsed ungracefully off the wall, a flurry of his robes the last thing to be seen.

Everyone gasped . . .

Surged forward in disbelief.

Eir had to be held back, launching muffled screams into Brynd's chest.

A moment later they were greeted by the keening of the banshee.

CHAPTER 5

❋

"I'd like a room—just for the night, please," Randur said.

"A room?"

"Yes, a room. For the night." He fluttered his long eyelashes at the landlady, pushed a lock of glossy hair back in order to gaze at her more intensely, but she kept on peering down at the register.

"One night." She was old enough to be his mother—old enough, but not *actually,* so it was all right by him. You could tell she had once been a beautiful girl—her eyes showed you that, not so much a spark within them, but definitely something to provoke wild rumination. Short brown hair, good skin, a decent figure: not too much, not too little. Not that he really cared—he could enjoy any shape of woman. Most ages, too. Her white blouse, unbuttoned to reveal cleavage like a bad cliché, she made the most of what she had. Randur made the most of it too. Made sure she saw him looking. He gave her a smile, all teeth and soft eyes, trying to suggest there were things she needed to know about herself.

"Well, we're pretty busy at the moment . . . but I'll see what I can do." She turned with something he took and hoped to be a grin, walked away from the bar.

It was a crowded but clean bistro-tavern located on the second level of Villjamur. The furnishing was wooden throughout, tables were shiny from polishing, and it was crammed with equine decor: horseshoes, parers, rasps, farrier tools, riding boots on the higher shelves. Randur guessed the landlady was an admirer of horses, or a fan of horse riders. He noticed the whips.

Now there's a thought.

As Randur sipped his apple juice, he glanced about. He wanted to listen in on conversations, to discover what people talked about in Villjamur, to maybe capture the mood of the city. If you wanted to charm your way up the social ladders, you had to know what the main concerns of the local people were. You could perhaps learn something that way, because whatever image a city presented in the history books, it was the ordinary people who delineated the depth and character of a place, ended up molding the outsider's judgment and experiences.

". . . It's possible we won't see our Ged ever again," a middle-aged woman confided to her friend. "And Dendu's going to have to quit his work just to stay in the city. I'm not sure what we'll do . . ."

". . . Well, we're very lucky. I haven't seen my own child for ten years. But, I'm nearest family, so she can come to the city to stay with me, you see. And her partner, too . . ."

A smartly dressed man at a nearby table glanced up as a lady of around the same age approached him and asked, "Is anyone using this chair?" He shook his head, stood up as she sat down at the same table, then commented something about the weather as he lowered himself again slowly. Randur wondered how many people of his own age he'd ever seen make that polite gesture. Too few in this city, at least: maybe younger people felt threatened in some way. Or, perhaps, when people reached "a certain age," they felt themselves to be a dying breed, and considered it best if they stuck together. Either way, it was sweet to still see such courtesy enacted.

There was ubiquitous conversation about the Freeze, how the temperature was falling further. Always talk of the weather, but he also heard gossip regarding some of the outer islands of the Empire. And chatter about cultists acting strangely . . .

He focused immediately on the latter conversation.

". . . You shouldn't hang 'round there, you know. Cultists is bad news."

"But there were purple flames sparking from whatever he was holding, I'm telling ya," a swarthy lad explained to someone Randur took to be his father. There was something vaguely birdlike about their appearance, something similar about the nose.

"Anyway, this wasn't near any of those temples of theirs."

"Just steer clear," the older man said. "I've never trusted them, or their damn relics. All stupid magic if you ask me."

The landlady returned. "You're in luck. We've got a room. It's right next to mine, so try not to keep me awake."

Randur leaned closer and whispered, "If you promise not to keep *me* awake."

"You outer island boys," she said, waving her hand dismissively, repressing a grin. "You're all the same. Come on then, bring your bags, and I'll show you the way. What's your name?"

"Randur Estevu." He scrambled after her. "So, I take it you like *riding*?"

✳

A simple room—just a bed and a table and a chair. Some shoddy re-productions of island art on the walls. The window looked out at the rear of the building, which he actually preferred, as he didn't like the idea of being woken early by morning traders heading for irens.

He didn't bother unpacking much, as he derived an almost masochistic pleasure from having the entire contents of his life con-tained in a few small bags. It offered him a freedom he'd never before known. The idea that you could get up and go anywhere, at any time. What was more, he was living someone else's life. And he was living that one near the edge.

After a lunch of fish and root vegetables, he wandered aimlessly for a while, just absorbing the flavor of Villjamur. He felt a sense of melancholy about the people of the busy city. That wasn't surprising considering they were going to be confined more or less as prisoners here in order to have the best chance of staying alive through the ice. Families were being either torn apart or reunited, jobs were being lost, and people talked about a "Caveside" where most of the inhabitants would end up living. But few people ever seemed to speak of cultists.

He would have to ask someone.

"Excuse me, madam," he addressed an elderly woman with a basket of fish, "I'm trying to find a cultist."

Her eyes turning ferocious, she spat at him as she walked away. After another couple of such incidents, he realized that cultists were generally not much liked, but, finally, a little girl was prepared to answer his question.

"You'll find them on the level just before you reach Balmacara. Best to ask more directions up there."

Randur smiled at the somewhat grubby child, and gave her a couple of Drakar, thinking she might spend them more wisely than himself.

He walked on.

A black-feathered garuda with clipped wings was slumped in a doorway, rags across his legs, nervously smoking a roll-up of arum weed, and in front of his feet was a hat and a sign asking for donations for an ex-soldier. As he passed, Randur flipped him a couple of coins, and the birdman was grateful, creating shapes in a hand-language that Randur couldn't comprehend.

"Really, it's okay," Randur mumbled, wondering what happened to those who offered service to the Empire?

Around the next corner, two men stepped out from an alleyway. They wore brown tunics, heavy boots, no cloaks, and had a dirty look to them, as if they slept on the streets. He guessed them both to be around their thirties, but you couldn't be sure.

"Fuck you staring at me for?" one of them snarled.

"Sorry," Randur mumbled.

"Hey, gay boy. Nice shirt. Expensive, yeah?"

Randur felt suddenly conscious of his clothing: well-sewn black breeches, white shirt with all those traditional Folke cuts. A fine cloak on top. Did people in this city really object to men being stylishly dressed?

"Can tell by your accent you're not from around here," one of the men said, approaching. "So no one will notice if you disappear—isn't that so?"

"That's right. Disappear," the other man echoed. "Happens a lot round here."

Randur noticed the edge of a blade protruding from under a sleeve. "What's this about?" He stepped back.

"Money," one of them said.

"Ah, well, I can't help you there."

The street was now empty save for the three of them, the rattle of sleet having become more prominent over the last few minutes. The ambience seemed like a fight premonition.

"An expensive dresser like you, I'm sure you've got something on you," the other said. "A Lordil or a Sota would do us fine."

"Ah, and I thought he didn't speak, this one," Randur said.

"I'm warning you," the man snarled, wiping drizzle from his face. Short blades were produced, glinting weakly in the poor light.

"I really haven't got anything on me." Randur took off his cloak, scrunched it under one arm.

The first man lunged forward, swiping his weapon across Randur's midriff. Just as quickly Randur leaned away, took steps to one side, lightly. Then two to the other side. A dance maneuver modified for dueling.

"Come here, you bastard," the man said, enraged now, swiping repeatedly. He was grunting with frustration each time Randur slipped out of his reach.

Taunting them physically was fun. Made them lose a little control, become angrier. They stepped away from each other, coming at him from separate sides. Randur allowed himself to drop to the floor as they attacked simultaneously, then he kicked one behind the knees, watching him fall as Randur spun away.

"Look," Randur said as he wiped his wet hands on his breeches. "Let's just leave it here, and you can keep some dignity."

"Cunt," one of the men yelled, and lashed again. His blade flashed across Randur's knuckles on one hand, instantly drawing blood. Randur stepped back, kicked the knife from his opponent's hand, then kicked the man in the groin. The attacker collapsed in agony to the ground. As the other now made to attack, Randur ducked expertly, grabbed the arm holding the knife, spun him around and brought the arm down over his knee with a crack of bone. The man screamed in pain.

Randur retrieved the knife.

Sleet meanwhile became drizzle became rain sparkling off the cobbles. Randur was now drenched, his black hair limp, shirt clinging to his lean body, his cloak heavy with moisture. He glanced down at it dubiously, reached down again to rip a section off one of the men's cloaks, wrapped it around his stinging knuckles.

His attackers lay unresisting on the ground.

He walked away, flipping up the collar on his cloak.

*

Each of the lower levels of Villjamur looked much the same, but on the higher levels the buildings became taller, narrower, somehow more elegant. They were also built of a lighter colored stone— limestone rather than granite. Wealthier people lived here, or at least they were certainly better dressed.

A smartly turned-out man in a red cloak walked by.

"Excuse me," Randur said, "You don't know where I could find a cultist, do you?"

The man gave him a cold stare, but answered politely. "There's a bistro, just up there, near one of their temples. You'll likely find a couple of them drinking there."

Randur approached the bistro: a narrow, white-painted building that appeared to tilt to the right. He pressed his face against the roughly made window, but the glass was too steamed up.

He entered to find the place packed mostly with men. Several of the chairs had cloaks draped over the backs, a counter at the rear was serving pastries, and there was the faint smell of perfume from the only woman, sitting at a table by the door. He walked up to the counter. The girl behind it was short, blond, pretty—a suitable target if he didn't have other things on his mind. He ordered a drink made from juniper berries, like they used to make on Folke.

As the girl handed it to him he said, "Thanks. I love your hair."

"Really?" she said, eyes round and wide.

"Stunning." Sure that he had her attention, he persevered. He leaned forward over the counter to gaze at her absorbedly. "Look, miss, I don't suppose you know of any cultists around here, do you? I'm new to the city, and it's quite important."

"There's two, over there in the corner. Another just here. One there." She pointed them out in turn. "But if you ask me, you should stay away from them."

"Thanks." He handed her a Lordil for the drink. "Don't worry about the change."

He studied the various figures she had pointed out. The one seated nearest to the counter was of slender build, with a pointed black beard that enhanced his well-carved features. Randur stepped up to his table. "This seat taken?"

The man stared at his food. "If no one's sitting there, then I'm guessing not."

Randur sat down with his drink, took a sip. Beneath his black shirt, a small medallion glistened. On it was a strange symbol, two letter Cs, one reversed so that the curve touched what was a diamond between them.

"Girl at the counter mentioned you're a cultist," Randur said.

The man looked up. "What's that to you?"

Randur reached into his pocket and brought out the same coin he had been given all those years ago on Folke. He placed it alongside the man's plate. The man instantly stopped eating. Randur continued sipping his drink.

The cultist regarded him acutely. "And where would an island boy get hold of a coin like that?"

"It was given to me once by one of your lot," Randur explained. "Said her name was Papus."

"She's not," the man replied firmly, "one of *my* lot, as you put it." Something about the way he said it suggested that these cultists weren't so much the close bunch everyone made out.

"You're not a cultist, then?" Randur inquired.

"Oh, yes, but *she* isn't a part of my sect." He took another bite.

"Right." Randur stretched his hand forward to take back the coin.

The cultist stared at his recent wound. "Been in a fight?"

"Wasn't my choice," Randur muttered, bringing his arm off the table.

"Country boy ought to watch himself in this city," the cultist said.

"I can look after myself."

"Everyone says that. But, no one really can. What's your name, kid?"

"Randur Estevu."

"Well, Randur Estevu, I'll tell you something for free." The cultist rose from his seat. "There's a temple at the end of this road with a double door made of quercus wood. Knock hard on that, show them your little coin, and you may find you're in luck."

Randur stood up, offered his hand to shake. "Thanks, um . . . Sorry, I didn't get your name."

"That's because I didn't tell you." The cultist slung on his cloak and stepped out of the bistro.

❋

With a free hour ahead, her last appointment having not shown up, Tuya sat down to paint. Inspired by the current mood of the city, she was starting afresh. She wanted to paint something *fantastical* that spoke about the people of the city feeling trapped in their homes. Perhaps she would paint a caged bird of sorts.

She was wearing no clothes because, that way, there would be nothing to spill paint on except her unprotected skin. Similarly, she pinned her thick red hair up. Sitting herself on a stool, she tilted the easel so that she could look out of her window, across the architecture of the city, and she carefully noted the spires, the bridges, the pterodettes arcing across the sky. Water fizzed off the rooftops and suddenly the bell tower rang. She felt serene—all these pieces of the city coming together in a comforting collusion.

She applied blue paste to the small canvas using a knife and a wide brush. The paint was her own concoction. Using local pigments, she blended this paste with an ingredient that only she knew of—in Villjamur, at least. A cultist had given the secret to her before he died, having been a client of hers, when he fancied someone *normal*. The substance was grainy, opaque, and he had instructed her carefully on its qualities as rare as any other ancient relic the cultists used, perhaps originally ground by the Dawnir themselves. Or so the myth went. And myths went rather further than they should have in Villjamur.

From time to time she closed her eyes, let the cold breeze tickle against her body until it aroused her again. She concentrated hard, took her mind away from what she was drawing in order to perceive it in a different way. Life was all about perception, and art was important to her. Maybe it wasn't to the people who walked past her window or used her sexually, but for her the least chance to express herself became simply wondrous.

The creature she envisaged began to take form.

It was something like a pterodette—same scales and batlike wings—but it possessed a noticeably mammalian body. It was blue simply because that was the pigment she had chosen today. Though it stood no higher than a child, she'd built a strong musculature into its physique, so much so that it could probably break down a door.

It wasn't until the bell had struck again that she felt satisfied that she had finished for the moment. It wasn't meant to be precise yet, but would eventually take true form.

She stood up from her stool, stepped closer to the window. Sunlight was reflecting wildly off the astronomer's glass tower.

Turning, with the breeze at her back, she regarded her painting again. It was definitely coming to life. The blue creature was almost pulsing, as if drawing real air into its specious body. She now began to paint in earnest the background, the life-source of the creature, summoning abstract ideas that would feed its soul. Powerful urges thronged in her mind, a desire to fly off into the distance, to explore the Boreal Archipelago, this land of the red sun. Maybe to know freedom, of a sort.

Suddenly the creature began to peel itself off the canvas in fast, vacillating movements. It bubbled upward, shook itself . . .

And fell to the floor.

Tuya laughed and cooed as she picked her creation up and placed it on the windowsill. It crawled along, then stood up properly on four legs. Its wings spread. Tuya gave a cry of delight. She didn't know how she made it happen each time and, if she was honest, she didn't really care, because her art didn't just reflect life—it created it.

The creature flapped its newfound wings, then threw itself out the window. A gust transferred it to a new current, and it drifted across the spires and away from Villjamur, leaving her once again with that same sense of loneliness.

✳

Randur found the door eventually, an inconspicuous entrance on an inconspicuous street. Certainly nothing to suggest it concealed a haven for cultists. He might have expected some kind of inscriptions in the pale stonework surrounding the door, some elaborate decoration, something to indicate an elite building associated with the Order of the Dawnir, the oldest and largest sect of all. A nice plaque even. There was merely bare stone and a single hanging basket with thrift sagging over the sides. A city guard on horseback was riding by, and there was something in his brief glance that made Randur feel guilty.

He knocked on the door.

The hatch opened, exposing a man's face to the daylight. "Yes?"

Randur held up the coin. "I'm looking for someone called Papus."

The man's gaze was fixed on the coin. "Hang on."

The door opened with the doorman gesturing for him to come in. The doorman wore a black cloak, underneath which Randur could see a dark, tight-fitting uniform, almost military in its design.

"Wait here," the man instructed, and walked away.

The room was dark, but Randur could make out elaborate wood paneling, a few framed sketches on the wall. Incense burning gave a strangely comforting feeling about the room. It wasn't unlike the church of Bohr that had been built on Folke in the name of the Empire.

The man shortly returned with a chubby blond woman dressed similarly. The pair of them searched Randur for weapons, then sat him down on a wooden stool.

They asked his business in Villjamur. And questioned his request to see Papus.

He held up the coin again, explaining how she had given it to him. The pair looked at each other.

"She's busy right now, but if you want to wait here, we'll inquire if she can see you sometime," the woman said.

They left him slumped on the chair in that cold dark room. As his eyes became accustomed to the light, he had started to see the framed sketches in more detail. Diagrams of devices that he supposed to be relics, strange lettering surrounding each. He couldn't read Jamur as well as he could speak it, but this must be some older form of the language.

He waited there for the best part of an hour before he was finally summoned.

✳

He was led into a large stone chamber that obviously served as an office judging by the books and papers that littered the shelves and floor as if it hadn't been tidied in years. Tiptoeing around the clutter, he was told to sit on a chair by the large pointed-arch window. It seemed these were the chambers of Papus. The two leading him used the bizarre term in reference to her: the Gydja of the Order of the Dawnir. *A bit much, really* . . .

As he was left alone, staring through the window, a strange blue creature caught his eye. It flew down from one of the balconies on some higher level, arced awkwardly out of sight, then back into view briefly before banking up to one side.

The ancient chamber had a musky smell, with broken bits of masonry here and there. He knew the city was old, but had never imagined buildings like this would still be standing. Everywhere, there were books littering the shelves and even the floor. Moldy with their broken spines, pages stuck together, sprouting sheets of paper exposing diagrams and equations to the air. There were pieces of equipment, too, strange unrecognizable masses of metal, mechanical-looking insects, precise and advanced shapes.

Seeing all of this accumulated wisdom generated a feeling of inadequacy about his own education. He knew he was intelligent, but here was a more structured knowledge: ancient languages, history, the names of rare flora and fauna, whereas he mostly knew about swords and dancing and women. He had his wits, though, and you couldn't find every answer in a book—some were out in the real world.

The door opened, and a woman stepped in, garbed in the same outfit as the other two cultists. Her hair was darker than he remembered, and she was leaner.

"Who wants to speak to me?" Her voice was deep, her blue eyes dazzling.

Randur walked over to her, drew out the coin.

She took it and studied it. "Yes, I remember. Folke, 1757. You're the little boy that saved me." She handed it back, and gave him something like a smile. The severe lines on her face suggested that this was a rare gesture. "You've grown, I see."

"It happens," Randur murmured, placing the coin back in his pocket. "You said, at the time, if I ever needed a favor to come and find you."

"You have had a successful journey then, so far." Papus walked over to the table, and began to shuffle some papers. "Well, what is the favor?"

"I need to find a cultist who can stop someone from dying, or else bring them back from the dead."

Regarding him seriously, she put down the papers she was holding and took a step closer.

"I *did* save your life," Randur said lamely. He thought at this point it might be an appropriate reminder.

"Yes, so you did—but you're making an incredibly serious request, you realize? I mean, why would you want to live forever?"

"It's not for me. It's my mother."

"Oh, I see." Papus perched on one end of the table. "Could you just wait here for a moment?"

"I'm used to that by now."

Papus reached under her cloak with her right hand—

—and vanished in a flash of purple light.

Randur jumped up, as if scalded, and stepped toward the table. He scanned the heaps of books and papers as if they'd offer any clues. "Now how the hell did she do that?"

✳

Randur was back in the seat by the window, trying to fathom one of the books that he clearly didn't understand. He decided that he liked the diagrams aesthetically, however.

The door opened. Papus re-entered.

"I see you're using the door now?"

"Look," Papus said, "I do owe you a major favor, and I've talked it over with a few of my colleagues here, but I fear I must tell you that what you've asked for isn't really where our expertise lies."

Maybe he was naive, but this was getting frustrating. "You're magicians, aren't you?"

"No," she said, briefly.

"No?"

"No, we're much more than that. It isn't simple magic. There's a whole craft involved. We devote years to studying the subtleties of our technology."

It sounded like a speech recited many times before.

"You made a promise. So what d'you suggest?"

"Well, I'm referring you now to another sect. You've got to understand that we normally have nothing whatsoever to do with them. I'm not placing you in any direct danger, but you must be particularly careful. I'm only doing this, remember, because of your service to me all those years ago. I would not be doing it for any other reason."

"They sound pretty unsavory," Randur said. "I'm not sure I like where this is going."

"Let's just say that this is a tough time for the orders. Relationships are strained."

"So I gather your lot and this other group don't like each other."

"That is putting it *mildly*." Papus laughed. "But I'm now handing you over to them, and that is my favor to you in exchange. I don't think you'll ever understand just how big a favor it is." She paused, then explained. "We have radically different ways of thinking."

"How so?" Randur inquired, noticing the anxiety in her expression.

"They—the Order of the Equinox, they're called—like to . . . take the world apart. We prefer to put it back together. That's as easy as I can make it for you."

"Make it harder," Randur said. "I'm curious."

"They want to take the world to pieces, to find out all its secrets. To know how everything works, and they won't let anything like ethics get in the way. They're ruthless, cruel, and destructive. Whereas I like to unify, to keep order, observe a high level of morals. We give our help to the Council of Villjamur, and the Emperor, whenever they need us. But, nevertheless, it is to the Order of the Equinox that I must take you, if you're ever to find that which you seek."

"There are two sides to every coin." Randur had the token in his hand again. "How do I know that you're not just finding an easy way of getting rid of me?" He flipped the coin in the air so that it shimmered in the light.

She grabbed it even as it spun, and handed the coin back to him. "Come," she said. "I'll take you to meet them."

"Who exactly?" Randur said, his head tilted slightly.

"Dartun Súr," Papus replied, turning to leave the room. "He's the Godhi of the Order of the Equinox."

"Means bugger all to me," Randur muttered.

She said sharply, "It will, soon enough."

"One question," Randur said. "What was that thing you took from the man who was trying to kill you, all those years ago?"

"That's not important now. It was a weapon, it was meant to hurt people, but nothing fancy, nothing world-changing. Nothing prophetic. We just didn't want it in his hands. As I said before, Randur, we're the ones with morals and ethics. We're just trying to keep order, to safeguard things for the benefit of the Empire."

✳

Through the streets of Villjamur once again.

Down a route he wouldn't have noticed existed. Through constricted alleyways, along hidden bridges. Much about the city had faded, died—disused chambers and archways, remnants from another time with no place here anymore. As they passed under passageways he could hear carts being hauled above, and if he looked up through drain holes he could see people walking. Down here there were different styles of brickwork, crumbling stone where moss and lichen had colonized profusely near constantly dripping water.

"You know," Randur said, "the people who run this city could always ship those refugees from outside and set them up right here. It might be squatting, but still, if it means they don't die . . ."

She looked at him dismissively and Randur knew when to shut up. Papus gave the air that she knew a great deal, and would put down with great skill anyone who got a bit too clever with her.

They finally arrived at an underground chamber accessed by a door that you could barely see. Papus knocked, then turned to face him. "These are the only cultists who can help you in what you're looking for."

The door opened. A bald man in a gray cloak stood there to greet them.

"This is him," Papus explained to the doorman, an anxious look on her face. She then walked away quickly, and Randur found himself visiting his second cultist sect of the day.

✳

"So you see what I was promised." Randur was sitting across a stone table from the man called Dartun Súr, who was sprawled in the chair opposite. "And that's why I was told you could help."

The chamber exuded a wonderful smell that reminded Randur of some herbal wash worn by a girl he once knew. Otherwise the room was rather plain, with none of the carefully arranged relics, containers of strange liquids, preserved specimens, or crazy men with mad hair he might have expected.

Dartun leaned forward in his plush chair. He had an assessing gaze, and there was an unsettling, ageless look to those eyes. They shone too bright for the dim light. "An intriguing task, I'll give you that. But quite doable."

As an awkward silence stretched before them Randur examined the man. Dartun was annoyingly handsome, with his square jaw, gently muscled physique. He had somehow even found some sunlight in this city to give his skin a healthy glow. Despite the graying hair, his looks remained youthful, and Randur placed him at around forty years, even though he gave the impression of being a more experienced man.

"That's a smart cloak you've got there," Randur said to break the silence—and thinking he'd look good in it himself, with a little customization. "Very dark. What color's that?"

"Fuligin," Dartun replied. "That's a color darker even than black."

Another period of reflection, and Randur said, "So, d'you think you can help me?"

"Of course," Dartun replied, looking amused at the naive question. "That's well within our talents. It's one of my own areas of *expertise,* shall we say. No, my reflection on the matter is what can *you* do for us in return."

Randur knew that the favor Papus had given him was to introduce him to Dartun. He would now have to come to some agreement of his own with this cultist leader. "Well, if it's any help, I'm on my way to take employment in the household of the Emperor himself?"

"Old Johynn's place?" Dartun said. "Now that's certainly an interesting point. And what'll you be doing there exactly?"

"This and that," Randur replied coolly. This encounter was beginning to give him a sense of angst. He waited a moment before he asked the inevitable. "Would you want paying?"

"A-ha! Now that, Randur Estevu, sounds more like it."

"I would've thought that, being cultists, you could get your hands on all the wealth you needed. And what would you need money for anyway?"

"I love the way everyone assumes we can do anything, as and

when we please. Our technology is rather specific, you see. And, precious though they are, relics don't buy food or sustenance. I have an order to pay regularly: that's what keeps people happy. No, money is useful indeed. I think to cover our time and costs for this task . . . say, four hundred Jamúns should do it?"

"Four hundred!" Randur stood up with shock. Stunned someone could assign a monetary value to such a request. Was that how they did things deep in the Empire? Where was the fairness in that? He locked eyes with Dartun, but could see that the cultist leader wasn't a man to be argued with.

"Well, what price would *you* put on a life, Mr. Estevu?" Dartun said.

Randur sat down again, feeling miserable. Four hundred Jamúns? An impossible sum. Calculating that a Jamún was worth ten Sota, each of which was worth fifty Lordils, he realized you could buy up most of the farms on Folke with that kind of money. It seemed utterly alien to price up a person's life.

"Don't look too miserable," Dartun continued. "Just think about it, you'll be ensconced in Balmacara, where there're many wealthy people hanging about. I'm sure you can use your imagination in finding a way to ensure that some of that money comes your way. You're a handsome lad, and you'll find that being pleasing to the eye gives you a head start in these affairs."

Randur ignored the man's bluntness. He stared at the stone table nearby, at the small engravings around it, the runes. He wasn't aware of how long he remained lost in thought, but when he looked up, Dartun was still grinning at him.

Randur said, "Is there a time limit on this sort of thing? I mean, say my mother passed away today, how long would it be before it gets too late to . . . you know, do whatever it is you can do?"

"A fine question. Well, we experiment all the time, because progress is what I'm after. It's what this entire order is after: to distill the essence of life, to discover just whatever it is that makes us all *us*. So far we've successfully reanimated a man who had died up to two years before we worked on him, although his mind wasn't quite what it used to be. This is the result of generations of our research, Randur. We're not just some iren trader trying to offload a stack of cheap tat."

That was a relief to Randur. It provided some time for him to get hold of the four hundred Jamúns.

"A deal?" Dartun said.

"Yeah, a deal."

They shook hands.

"Could I just ask one thing?" Dartun folded his arms. "Why the hell d'you want to do this for your mother?"

A wave of nausea surged through Randur's body, as his mind raced back to *that* night, to the one thing he would forever regret. He needed to repair the damage that his lack of thought and consideration had led to. He needed to prove himself as his mother's son. After all, mothers brought you into the world. They then fed you, clothed you, showed you immeasurable kindness. They gave you everything they had. True his mother was a bitter woman sometimes, but that wasn't important. All that mattered to Randur, in retrospect, was that the one night she needed him, he had not been there.

He had failed her.

"So," Randur said, ignoring the last question, "what . . . I mean, how will you manage this?"

"Just leave that to the specialists, young man. Believe me, this isn't the first time I've been approached to play about with the laws of the cosmos. I've been in Villjamur for . . . a lifetime. Women come asking to be made prettier, or slimmer, or younger. Men come asking me to increase their virility. I've had prostitutes ask me to stop the pain they suffer in their jobs, have their internal muscles numbed or senses stopped so doing their work does not hurt them. I've even had drug addicts crying out for help. I've been around a long time, and I've seen it all, and I say to them all—let me see your coin, and I'll investigate if the technology exists."

✳

In a glass orb stationed in the corner of his primary workroom, Dartun watched the young man leave. The orb was linked to another on an external wall, surrounded by marbles as a decorative feature, and it displayed an exaggerated caricature slipping away along the backstreets of a black and white Villjamur.

So, this Randur wanted his mother to live a long time. *Fine, that's possibly simple enough—a few months or a year at the most.* He might even make her outlive her son if he was lucky. Randur had some charm, some vague charisma that appealed to Dartun. He would help the lad, but knew that the treatments would not last, knew that it wasn't a process good enough for himself. Dartun once possessed eternal life, thanks to the Ancients' technology. Once a year he had injected himself with a serum generated by relic-energy, a relatively simple procedure considering what else he had achieved—but now he was dying.

He discovered that the Dawnir relic technology was beginning to fail him the day he cut himself with a razor. Some time ago now: there it was, a red line through his skin. Standing up against the mirror. Candle brought close to his face. A line of cut skin that filled quickly with blood. Red liquid leaked into the sink, little drops of his own death.

He was suddenly aware of so many things that could kill a person:

A back-hoofing horse.

Disenchanted young swordsmen with something to prove.

Mishandling a relic.

Poisoned food.

There were banshees waiting at every corner.

He gathered as many of the relevant relics as he could find, spent sleepless nights in distant places until he could figure out what was going on and so prevent his aging, utterly convinced that he could find some solution.

Some cure for his forthcoming death.

And he hadn't yet. At the time he wrote down his thoughts in a journal, wondering about the words lingering after he had gone:

So how is it that I can still communicate from beyond the grave? How can I talk to you now? Words on the page, no less. Is this how we live on, in these little gestures? These trails left throughout our own existence—a note here, a pissed-off lover there? Something poignant we said to someone. Advice we gave. A joke we told.

Little pieces of ourselves donated to the world.

Is this what makes me live eternally?

Spurred on by these thoughts, and by the visit of Randur, Dartun went deeper into his labs to look at the Shelley tanks.

❋

A darkened room in the deepest corner of his order's headquarters. To one side seven corpses were laid out, claimed from the streets of Villjamur by good old Tarr, but he had hopes for the ones in the Shelley tanks: they were not dead to begin with. The tanks were arranged in two rows, the bathtub-like metal basins filled with regeneration fluids. Bodies lay submerged beneath, their lips touching underneath the surface of the water.

They were disturbed people, the mental patients, the radically disfigured, the severely disabled—people that Villjamur and the Jamur Empire did not wish to acknowledge, let alone look after. They had no opportunity to contribute to the Imperial system, and up until recently, they constantly stalked the backstreets with haunted looks on their faces.

He could imagine nothing worse than being forgotten about, than being shunned by every face that he ever looked at. One of the batch told him that when people would not speak to them, would not even look them in the eye, they may as well have been dead already. *Do we rely on being noticed by other people to confirm that we are alive?*

Dartun wanted to experiment on them: if he was successful, it would offer them a way out—if they could not die, would they be alive in the first place? He wanted to see if they could have their lives extended with his newly developed techniques. Then he could try them on himself.

Chemicals smeared the air.

Blindly, he lit a blue-glass lantern in one corner. Modified relics were submerged in each of one row's tanks, a faint purple glow shimmered above them: it meant they were ready. Riddled with pangs of anxiety, he walked over to the first, raised up on a waist-high platform, and the light on his face made him quite aware of his reflection in the thick fluids. Bombarded with test formulas, these bodies faced toxic chemical structures that no ordinary person could survive a minute of, let alone several hours.

Turning off the relics within, one by one, the fluids began to drain through thick pipes, polluting somewhere deep within the city. As the liquid levels descended, a male body was revealed, glossy and slick, naked and scarred with traces of minor operations and major rewirings—Dartun's attempt at preserving it. He plunged a syringe into its chest and within seconds it lurched and began to shudder violently. Its eyes opened and the figure clutched the air above its head, then gave a perversely bass baby's cry.

Dartun was ecstatic, drunk on optimism—had this attempt been successful?

It suddenly collapsed back into the tank, shaking silently. Then ceased to move at all, as lifeless as a pre-op undead.

Another failure.

He sighed, and repeated the procedure with the five other Shelley tanks on this side of the room, each one eventually falling uselessly into death. They should have been preserved, their internals had been rewired to prevent decay. He could see nothing but the futility of life in his experiments, and again he became depressed and sad. These people had no other choice and surrendered their lives to him, and he had let them down.

He could not even tell if it was good enough to convert to one of the undead.

Dartun was enraged. With only the dead for company, he kicked things about the room, and when someone from his order came in to see what was going on, Dartun indignantly shoved him back out again. He knew he was being immature and unstable, but that's what failure did to him. He hated it, hated that his own life was failing him.

Did anyone even think of their own death, or did they also assume the day would never come?

The days now seemed merely a heartbeat long.

All these failures had removed most of his options down to just the one. One decision, then, in honor of his recently acquired mortality: to push the limits of Dawnir technology to its fullest. If he was going to die, he wanted to do so as a legend—a name to be remembered—as a pioneer. There is so much in the world that he had spent his life detailing, and now he was going to put it into practice.

And not only that, but he needed to find some supreme relics, some intense piece of technology. Because any sufficiently advanced technology was indistinguishable from magic—and he had run out of technology.

At least in this world.

CHAPTER 6

❋

Investigator Rumex Jeryd sat at his desk, feeling like a victim. Already he had suffered from the first snowballs from the Gamall Gata kids. The street, central in the Kaiho district, seemed to breed the little buggers, but he couldn't move home, no, because they'd only follow him. The weather over the past day or so had been mainly sleet, so where they'd found such a supply of firm snow, he had no idea. Either way, the kids had woken Jeryd up much too early. As he left his house that morning, he could see their little heads cresting stone walls, attitude glaring from their eyes, communicating with whistles and urgent street-slang he didn't understand, calls of "Hey, *Jerrryd,* watch your back, yeah?" derisive calls of "Hey *Jerrryd,* where's your missus gone? You need us to keep you company? We *lurve* you, *Jerrryd.*"

You couldn't do much about kids like that. You could maybe arrest their parents, if they had any around, but the kids themselves would vanish fast through any number of broken stone alleys to avoid being caught.

Jeryd was old. He couldn't keep up with them. Couldn't keep up with a lot of things around Villjamur.

As he picked up a weekly news pamphlet on the way to work, he was shocked to discover that the death of the councilor was headline news. The case would now mean having to work with the Council, something he really wasn't looking forward to.

To his right lay a file, left for him by one of the night duty investigators. It detailed yet more violence near the city gates and the immigrant camp. Two refugees had been seriously injured with sword wounds to the head. People were even alleging rape. Accusations were flying everywhere. Meanwhile, the hygiene standards in the refugee camps were plummeting. There had been demonstrations by Villjamur's extreme right wing activists. They didn't want these types stealing what was "rightfully theirs" in the face of the Freeze. They didn't want disease brought into their city. Things were now happening at a level of hysteria no one was familiar with.

People were getting angrier, and more desperate.

✳

He spent an hour writing up notes from yesterday, while finishing a cold cup of tea the administrative girl, Ghale, had brought him earlier. She was dark-haired, attractive, but she didn't have a tail and her human skin was too soft for his tastes.

Jeryd peered again at his observations so far. Delamonde Ghuda was forty-three years old. Married, with no known children. Once elected, Ghuda had spent fifteen years on the Council, regularly endorsed by popular vote. Whatever the masses wanted, he was with them, and their vote was with him. He helped push through various educational and tax reforms, spent one year as Treasurer of Villjamur, before being promoted to overseeing all of the Jamur Empire's resources on behalf of the chancellor. That was a position he had held for four years.

So, who specifically would want to kill him?

At that moment, Aide Tryst entered the room without knocking. "Investigator, we've got a lead."

Jeryd looked up, stifled a yawn. "Great. Out with it, then."

"Witness statement has the deceased sighted the evening before in a tavern, drinking with a woman in her forties."

"Nothing unusual there, lad."

"They were seen leaving together, and rumor has it that she's a prostitute. Has a noticeable wound on her face. Another witness has the same two spotted entering a residential tower next to the gallery."

"Great, we now have a city councilor using whores. Like to explain that to his partner and the other councilors? I can bet you we'll have orders to keep that little fact quiet. And considering the Council's supposed to be a symbol of truth and probity . . ."

❋

Tuya wiped him off with a towel, which she then threw into a basket in the corner. The guy had only wanted a handjob in the end, which suited her fine. Said he didn't want to cheat on his partner, a last-minute change of mind. He lay on his back, panting for a while—men looked so pathetic after they'd come.

As she walked out of the room she said, "I'll leave you to get dressed. Just leave the money on the side and let me know before you go."

In fact he left her enough money to last her a week—four Sota and ten Lordils—and she watched him leave, dressed again in his smart robes on his way back to his office in the Treasury. It no longer amazed her just how ordinary her customers could be. They went back to their families, their wives, to their jobs, to their commonplace negotiations, and all the time nursing this guilty secret. Ah well, was what she did for a living wrong if no one got hurt? She wasn't one of those poor street girls who suffered sleepless nights under the guilt and shame, men coming and going like ghosts in their lives.

How had her existence got to this point?

Was the reason that she had become *capital*—goods and services?—was that why she would remain trapped in Villjamur? She suspected that her position was shared, in some ways, by many other ladies in the city. Mothers and housewives, and women like her who might actually earn money. For as long as women could be viewed in such transactional manners, their emancipation would remain incomplete. When had it become too late to change everything? Did she even choose this lifestyle or did it force itself upon her?

Sighing, she went back to her bed, lay down, drew the sheets over her. Watched the light through the window. Listened to the busy sounds of the city.

And closed her eyes.

❋

Jeryd knocked, and a woman eventually opened the door. She wore just a flimsy gown that wasn't going to keep out the chill. Red hair, a fuller figure, the sort that came with a little expensive dining now and then. Down one side of her face was a livid scar and Jeryd tried desperately not to focus on it.

"Investigator Rumex Jeryd, Villjamur Inquisition." He held up his Inquisition medallion. "And this is Aide Tryst. We're investigating the murder of Delamonde Ghuda, and we're hoping you can help us with our inquiries."

"Delamonde Ghuda?" she said. "Oh, my . . . Come in, please. Can I offer you something to drink?"

"No, thanks," Jeryd said.

Tryst took out a pencil and notebook.

She found two ornate wooden chairs, and placed them for the men to sit on near the window.

"Many thanks," Tryst said, seating himself.

"These are impressive." Jeryd indicated the chairs, but remained standing. He decided that he didn't want to get too comfortable. "Antiques?"

"Yes. Do you yourself collect, investigator?"

"Nah," Jeryd replied, glancing over at Tryst who merely stared around the room. "My wife was once a collector of sorts. Sometimes I tagged along with her to various markets. Never got into it myself, but I can recognize something half decent." For a moment he appreciated the fact that Marysa had taught him enough to pick out a decent antique. Then appreciation transformed into pain, again.

"*Was once* a collector. You're no longer married then?" Tuya said, sitting down on the bed, her crossed legs revealed in the gap in her gown.

Jeryd sighed, "We're here to investigate a murder, Miss . . . ?"

"Daluud. Tuya Daluud."

Tryst began taking notes as Jeryd began his routine, "You were seen with the victim on the evening of the murder."

"Yes," she agreed. "Yes, that's right."

"What exactly is it you do for a living, may I ask?"

She said, "You two are men of the world, I take it?"

Jeryd glanced at Tryst, then back to Tuya. "Where's this leading?"

"Follow me." She gestured them over to the elaborate door leading to her bedroom, paused them briefly with her outstretched arm. "Just a quick glimpse, okay?" Then she opened the door.

It was clearly a whore's boudoir. Luxurious bed, oils, candles, the large mirrors, the smell of sex. Jeryd stepped back out of the room, nodding to Tryst, who blinked rapidly. Tuya closed the door and turned back to them.

Only then did Jeryd realize just how tall she was. "None of this is of any concern to us, Miss Daluud."

"I know."

Jeryd placed his hands in his pockets, walked slowly around her living room, noting further the fine ornaments, paintings, furnishings. "Still, it obviously pays well."

"Yes, and there's no one else for me to spend the money on. But at least I get time to myself, and to pursue my other pleasures."

Jeryd paused, looking over at Tryst who was sitting by the window again.

Jeryd noticed the covered canvases in the corner. "You dabble in the arts, Miss Daluud? We allowed to take a look?"

"I'd rather you didn't," she said. "I'm rather shy of some things."

"Miss Daluud, would you be so good as to explain your dealings with Councilor Ghuda on the night in question?"

Tuya looked quickly between the two officers, before her gaze settled on Jeryd. "I was drinking by myself in that place next to the street iren."

"The Amateurs Tavern?" Jeryd inquired.

"Yes, that's the one."

"And you go there regularly?"

"Quite a bit. I like its character, and the view from its windows. When the first of the winter rain comes in from the sea, it makes the cobbles and the roofs all around it shiny black."

"Huh." Jeryd liked her engaging description. This woman obviously loved the city, but he needed questions answered. "What time was this exactly?"

"About seven, maybe even eight. I always take a book in there with me, and the time passes."

"So, you were in the tavern sometime after seven."

"Yes, and I was sitting alone to begin with, but after a while someone asked if he could join me."

"This was Delamonde Ghuda?" Jeryd prompted.

Tuya sighed, "Despite my scarring, he seemed to find me attractive. What can I say? Men seem to think I'm something special."

"And are you?"

He could see then that something shifted in her mind. Whether or not she now had respect for Jeryd, he couldn't be sure. "I'm sorry. And then what happened?"

"He sat down opposite, and I thought he was handsome. We discussed literature for a while, and he kept ordering drinks for both of us. He was altogether quite a charmer. I was lonely. He was intelligent. You're a man of the world, so you know how these things happen."

"Indeed." *Well no, actually,* he reminded himself. *It's been far too damn long since I've done any of that.* Jeryd sat down on the other chair, confirmed that Tryst was noting every detail. "And you came here afterward?"

"Yes," she admitted.

"What time was that?" Tryst asked.

"About ten."

"He was obviously a quick operator," Jeryd observed.

Tuya's laugh was surprisingly hearty. "I was lonely and he seemed fun. We came straight back here."

"You didn't notice anyone or anything strange on the way?"

"No. Nothing at all. Not that I was paying a great deal of attention."

"Okay, then what?"

"We came back here and . . . you know."

"You had intercourse?"

"Yes, investigator, but I prefer to call it making love."

"A little quick for love, don't you think?" A mild feeling of pique overcame him.

Tuya played with the ends of her gown.

"What time did he leave you?" Jeryd said.

"He was here until early the next morning. I was pretty much asleep when he finally left."

"And you didn't hear or see anything you would consider out of place?"

"Nothing more than you'd hear on any ordinary night. Drunks quarreling down below. Horses' hooves on the cobbles."

There was something about the way she smiled—she didn't seem happy when she did it. Jeryd stood up, looked at Tryst. The young aide got up and pushed his chair back.

"I think that's a start, anyway," Jeryd said. "We've got a few more people to interview." He didn't actually have any immediate plans, but he wanted to make her sweat a little by creating the illusion there was a lot to follow up on.

"You're off already?" Tuya said. "Surely I must be your main suspect?"

"If we need to ask you some more questions, I assume we can normally find you here?" Jeryd glanced once again at the antiques filling the room.

"Yes, although you might be advised to knock and wait first." She winked at Tryst.

Jeryd stifled a laugh at the lad's embarrassment.

✳

"So what d'you reckon?" Tryst asked as they were walking down the spiral staircase. His voice echoed hollowly against the bare stone.

"Too early to tell. The Councilor had a lot of enemies."

"Maybe his wife found out about this fling?"

"In just one night? Doubtful. This was a one-off thing, surely. Lonely woman, rich crafty man. I've seen it all too many times."

"Well, maybe my date with Ghale will have a happier ending."

Jeryd looked to his aide. "You mean Ghale, our administration assistant?"

"Yes indeed, the very same."

"Ah, too soft-skinned," Jeryd muttered, pushing open the exit door. "You need to get yourself something tougher. Something more like a rumel girl. They're built to last, you see."

"And when are you going to get another one, now you're a free man?"

Jeryd squinted up into a sharp beam of sunlight, as he stepped outside, and Tryst closed the door behind them. He couldn't think past Marysa: it was too soon since she had gone. There was too much for him to learn again. "Too old for those sorts of games."

"You're never too old," Tryst said.

"Well, I was never much good at all that stuff, anyway." He remembered immediately all the things Marysa had done for him, and how unfinished he was without her.

He headed off along the street, his thoughts returning to the prostitute and the dead politician.

CHAPTER 7

＊

Brynd waited patiently alongside Eir in the corridor outside the Council Atrium, the chamber where all the plans and schemes for Villjamur and the Empire were debated. They had sat there for hours. Brynd understood then that, as a servant to the Empire, his life was spent either arriving, departing, or waiting.

The two of them sat in a miserable silence, and he pitied Eir for having to witness her father's death when she was still so young. He tried to convince her that it was not her fault, that it was an accident. She hadn't wept openly, but when Brynd had gone to fetch her earlier that day, he could hear her sobbing behind the closed doors of her chamber.

However she stepped out to greet him as elegantly composed as could be expected.

After her sibling Rika had left, all those years ago, the younger girl had become more quiet, rather withdrawn. She shouldn't have had to cope with Johynn in his deteriorating state, not at her youthful age. Brynd wondered if she'd eventually come to see her father's departure as a release from his powerful emotional grasp over her.

Eventually, the large quercus doors of the Atrium were opened and they were both summoned inside.

The Atrium itself was a high-domed white chamber about fifty paces wide. The twenty-five councilors, each representing a sector of the city as stated by the old maps, sat in a circle of benches, ranged above them.

The Council had already been locked away for most of a day, anxiously deliberating the consequences of Jamur Johynn's death. They had ordered that the Emperor's mortal remains be cleaned up rapidly. As yet no one in the general population of Villjamur realized that their Emperor had killed himself. Palace servants had been threatened with torture and execution if any rumors were traced back to Balmacara.

Brynd and Eir took their seats silently in a wooden podium at one end of the chamber for esteemed guests, although Brynd felt more like a prisoner. On it was carved the emblem of the Jamur Empire: a seven-pointed star.

A low-level muttering rippled through the Council.

Eir was dressed soberly in a dark red shawl covering a black gown of mourning. Brynd took the opportunity to rid himself of the scars and dirt and memories of military ambush, and wore a freshly cleaned all-black uniform.

Though Brynd had earned the Emperor's trust over the years, he was never quite sure how this parliament reacted to his being albino. Brynd had his own suspicions about these councilors because of what had recently happened at Dalúk Point. If he scrutinized them carefully, perhaps one of them would betray guilt in his or her eyes.

Silence fell as Chancellor Urtica stood up.

Brynd glanced at him with secret disdain. You couldn't really trust a man who, it was rumored, had spent a year of his youth mixing poisons as an apprentice to a senior torturer for the Inquisition. Urtica was a swarthy, handsome man in his forties, his graying black hair cropped close to his ears. The Council uniform of green tunic and gray cloak fitted his slim body well.

"Jamur Eir. Commander Lathraea, welcome to the Atrium," he began in his smooth and deep voice. "As you will understand we've been debating our current predicament, and I'll get straight on to the details of what we've concluded. It may come as no surprise to you that we wish to bring the late Emperor's eldest daughter, Jamur Rika, back to the city. It is, of course, law and tradition that the closest senior relative should inherit the throne, ensuring there is an unbroken chain of command, as decreed by our divine father, Bohr himself.

Jamur Rika is to become Empress of Villjamur, being the most appropriate choice, we feel, in these uncertain times."

Brynd had anticipated such a move.

"Commander, we're now charging you to escort Lady Rika back from the Southfjords immediately. It should take you several days, and on your return there shall be a festival combining both mourning and celebration. It is essential that we look upon this as a positive move and not a crisis. As a senior member of this Council, I'll advise the new Empress at every stage. We will be happy to welcome her as the new ruler."

I bet you will, Brynd thought. *You'll use the poor girl's innocence and ignorance to drive through every selfish policy you've ever dreamed of.*

"Commander," Urtica continued, "we've set things in motion for your imminent departure, with a longship moored at the port of Gish ready for you to join it. Take as many of the Night Guard as you feel necessary."

"Yes, thank you," Brynd said. "Talking of the Night Guard, I take it you've heard what happened to us at Dalúk Point?"

"Yes, indeed. One of your men—a certain Captain Apium Hol, I believe—made it his business to inform all of the customers in several bars last night, as well as the entire main dining hall in Balmacara. I was myself told about it by a member of the kitchen staff. A most upsetting way to learn such news, for a man of my—"

"My point," Brynd interrupted, "was to discover how we came to be ambushed. Our mission was supposedly known only to high-level members of this Council." Brynd was staring directly at Chancellor Urtica. The man shifted slightly, but kept an expression of concern.

"This is indeed a tragedy, but such things do happen in military operations, commander. If there was a way—"

"I'm just trying to find out why my men died unnecessarily, chancellor."

"We will set up an investigation into this matter for you, but meanwhile your assignment is to escort back Jamur Rika."

"What if she doesn't want to return?" Brynd said. "It's no enigma she despised the Emperor for his treatment of her late mother."

"The Emperor is no longer with us, and it is your job to persuade her. We here need her. Villjamur needs her."

Brynd did not quite understand the urgency—it was the Council that dictated Imperial strategy, and Johynn had only really ever been required for his signature. "I'll leave tomorrow morning then," he agreed.

At that point, Councilor Boll interrupted, a slender, short man who would have looked like a child except for his withered skin and gray hair.

"Commander, there have also been a number of sightings recently," he began, "of phenomena we are not entirely certain of. We're getting reports of a series of murders on Tineag'l," Boll explained. "And people disappearing in large numbers. Admittedly these are only word of mouth from impressionable locals, and we've yet to hear anything from more reputable sources."

"You wish me to investigate? Report back on what I see?" This wasn't exactly the sort of mission Brynd was used to.

"More or less," Urtica concurred. "Nothing to concern yourself with particularly at this moment—at least not until you return. But you can understand our concern that something may be on the loose out there, picking at what's left of our Empire. Killing valuable subordinates."

"What's left of them if the ice doesn't get them first," Brynd said sharply.

"Indeed," Urtica said, then turned to Eir. "Jamur Eir, in this most unfortunate time for you, I ask that in the interim you take stewardship of the city on your sister's behalf."

"Of course, Chancellor Urtica," Eir replied flatly. "I shall do everything that is necessary."

"We will make a public announcement shortly," Urtica concluded. "Thank you both for your time."

A rather abrupt dismissal, but at least they were out of there. As he followed Eir from the Atrium, Brynd had to stifle a laugh. No sooner had he returned to Villjamur than he had to leave it again.

✳

Brynd was invited to take dinner with Eir, the temporary Stewardess of Villjamur. He had often eaten with the late Emperor, when their conversation would inevitably turn to his most recent mission, or battle tactic, but he had always felt uncomfortable when she was present, because he felt he should not be talking war at the dining table. Tonight, while she picked at the lobster, she was sitting bolt upright, still wearing that black gown which, in this light, made her pale skin glow as white as his own.

"How're you feeling?" he asked eventually.

A distance in her eyes, a disconnection. "I'm fine," she snapped. She looked down at her plate again.

The hides of various animals covered the walls and floors. As a fire spat loudly nearby, the poor lighting made the place look as if there were reanimated carcasses all around him.

"Are you looking forward to your sister's return?"

"Yes, very much so." Eir looked up, her eyes suddenly brighter. "It's been so long since she . . . since she left us."

"Do you think that she'll ever forgive him?"

"I hope so. It's possible. She's become a rather different woman since she embraced Mániism."

Brynd considered the point. "Perhaps the Empire will benefit from someone with such strong beliefs.

"Do you forgive him, if you don't mind my asking?"

"I hated him." Eir pushed her plate away, slumping back in her chair. "You don't have to stay here just on my behalf, commander."

Brynd replied, "I know that. But you're better company than most in this damn place."

She said, "I hardly think I'm good company for anyone at the moment." She was clearly struggling to control her emotions.

Brynd did nothing to fill the silence.

Eventually she spoke again. "Well, now that he's gone . . . This sounds awful of me to say . . ."

"No, go on, say it."

"It's like a burden has been lifted from my shoulders."

Brynd said, "Yes, I think I understand. Talk."

"I had to keep an eye on him all the time. That means I've not had much of a life here."

"Eir, you've had as good a childhood as you could expect in your position. Your mother would be proud if she could see you."

She continued, "But now he's gone, I don't have to do that anymore. I don't have to watch out when he starts drinking too much, or apologize to servants when he soils his bedsheets. I don't have to stand the other side of a locked door when he's ranting because of his paranoia. Yet every time I don't have to do something, these free moments, it reminds me he's dead."

"Which means you've got a life of your own back now."

"Really?" She smiled bitterly. "This isn't much of a way to go about things. Because of my blood I get treated a little better than most women in Villjamur, certainly. But there's a list of men waiting to marry me within the year, and I've never even met half of them. Think of how valuable their prize is now. I understand Imperial policies, commander. I understand my life will be little more to this government than supporting income flows."

"Sometimes, in this world, we don't have the option to find love," Brynd muttered, and realized he was addressing both of them. "Matters of the heart are not always for us to decide. Situations don't always allow it."

"Love." She almost sneered at the word.

Brynd motioned for the servant to take away their plates. As the boy left the room, he continued, "It's okay to be upset, Eir. It's natural to mourn."

"I'm not upset." Her tone had changed from before, and he could tell she was closing herself up, protecting her mind with walls.

Conversation had slowed, an awkward silence taking its place. Eir stared at nothing, occasionally closing her eyes completely as if to shut out the world.

After a moment he stood up.

"Are you going?" she asked, but she still wasn't looking at him.

"There's a good chance someone with my personality might make you even more miserable," he said, and a half-smile seemed to suggest she liked that comment. "The Dawnir wants to see me. Since I'm off soon, I'd better go and visit him now. Get some sleep if you can."

He left her alone in the room with the sound of his boots leaving and the spitting fire.

✳

Brynd set off along the winding stone passages until he finally reached the Dawnir's chamber, a secluded vault built some way into the cliff face, far away from the rich adornments of Balmacara. This was an ancient remnant of an older structure, the stonework of its walls worn smooth over hundreds of years.

Brynd banged his fist on the iron door of the Dawnir's vault. It looked rather like the entrance to a jail.

Slow footsteps sounded on the other side. The door opened. A shaft of lantern light fell upon his face. "Sele of Jamur, it's Commander Brynd of the House of Lathraea."

A gruff voice said, "Please, enter."

Immediately behind the door, the Dawnir stood, stooping slightly.

"Sele of Jamur," Brynd replied, and shuffled forward.

"I am very glad you could come and visit me, Commander Brynd Lathraea," the Dawnir said. "The times are interesting."

"As always," Brynd agreed, watching the Dawnir close the door behind him. Standing one armspan taller than Brynd, and covered in a bush of brown hair, his host wore a simple loincloth.

He always seemed to be hunching, probably because there was no one else of his height to talk to. His eyes were like large black balls set deep in a narrow, goat-shaped head, while his gums exposed a pair of tusks the length of a forearm.

"And how are you, Jurro?" Brynd asked. "I received word you wished to see me."

The Dawnir waved an impossibly large hand toward a chair. Three walls were lined with books from floor to ceiling, and more were piled up around the simple wooden furniture. There were beautiful bindings, and some had degraded significantly.

A sheep carcass was draped upon a table across the room, quietly stinking the place out.

"Could do with some incense in here," Brynd muttered.

After a moment of intense frowning, Jurro spoke. "Ah, a joke. Very good, Brynd Lathraea, very good. Irony, you call it, yes?"

Brynd reclined further in the chair, and picked up a book, but found it was in a language he didn't know. The fonts suggested it might be something from Boll or Tineag'l, or some other Empire outpost.

"That one is a history of dance on Folke," Jurro explained.

"Doesn't look like Folken," Brynd replied.

"Indeed not, Brynd Lathraea. It was written over a thousand years ago, and language changes."

Brynd pursed his lips, placed the book to one side.

"I was looking at it because of the Snow Ball that the highborn humans and the rumel have organized. I do hope I will be able to attend it."

"Don't see why not," Brynd said. "You're no prisoner."

"Indeed not, but I do feel like one at times. I don't get many true visitors either, just those hoping I can help solve their petty problems. Yet I am not an oracle. I know no magic. And, besides, as if I would know . . ." the Dawnir trailed off to replace the book on one of the shelves.

"So how does the study go?"

"Nothing new. No revelations. These histories of the Boreal Archipelago are fascinating though. There are many inconsistencies in the texts, which leads me to believe the history is deeper than is publicly known, and known less than is publicly history. And I have some . . . some considerable time on my hands. I'm in no hurry, therefore. The books I've read on the previous ice ages are indeed interesting. They seem to have been the bringer of death to many a good civilization, so I can see why our Council are anxious." Jurro pushed forward a large chair constructed from iron, with heavy padding. The Dawnir sighed thunderously as he reclined. He held up one large text, a leather-bound tome the size of a small tabletop. "This is called *The Book of the Wonders of Earth and Sky,* and it details eras so far ago that they are assumed legend. I read today our forests were once lost entirely. We now call trees by the names in which their seeds had been stored below the Earth. I read once again that the sun was once much more yellow than our own. If this is true, then our sun is losing strength, and it is dying slowly. There is, perhaps predictably, nothing within the pages to suggest my own origins. I remain full of pathos."

Brynd had heard many philosophical meanderings from Jurro. This creature had reportedly been within the city over a thousand years, nearly as long as this pile of stones had been called Villjamur. That's what Jurro himself claimed anyway. He had been originally discovered wandering the icy coastline of north Jokull, with no memory. Having survived this long, he was now assumed to be immortal, though Brynd wondered morosely what it would be like to live for so long without even knowing your roots. He himself shared something with the Dawnir in this respect. Brynd had been adopted as a child by wealthy parents, and therefore had no real concept of his own origins. Who would ever want to know where an albino came from anyway?

"So how about your health? Do you feel well?" Brynd said.

"No, I need more exercise. I envy you, endlessly on your little missions here and there."

Somehow, Jurro had just managed to belittle Brynd's entire career with a single sentence.

"You must take me along with you sometime, because I would like to see more of the Archipelago. It could jog my memory; I might recognize something of my own past. It might even be fun."

"Why not, if it helps at all? But, you obviously won't have heard about our latest mission."

Then Brynd gave the Dawnir the details of his last few days.

"Indeed, a complex situation," Jurro said. "I will put my ear, as you say, to the ground for you."

"Thanks," Brynd said. "You heard about our Emperor?"

"Yes. Again, curious. But his mind was never quite there, was it?"

"I'll be fetching his elder daughter to be our new Empress."

"Jamur Rika? Of course. Is she not a child still?"

"No, she's twenty now."

"How quickly you grow, you humans!" The Dawnir seemed utterly delighted at this observation.

They talked awhile longer about news from the city, the refugees camping outside the gates. And then Jurro began to ramble about the wildflowers of Dockull and Maour. Brynd could only listen to Jurro's expositions for so long, and gently interrupted him.

"Jurro, I don't suppose you know anything of the killings reported on Tineag'l, do you?"

"Killings?" Jurro made a contemplative steeple of his massive hands.

"I don't think it's tribal revenge. Perhaps a new creature, or something?"

"I know nothing about this—although, yes, I would like to know more. According to what I have read, there has not been any creature capable of large-scale killings for several dozen millennia. Fossils of such beasts exist, of course, on Y'iren. I will begin some research."

"Thanks," Brynd said. "I'd better be going now. I'll be back to see you when I return."

"Farewell, Brynd Lathraea," the Dawnir said, hardly paying attention.

✳

"You know what your problem is?" Apium said to Brynd. They were leaning over the bar counter in the Cross and Sickle. Close to midnight and the place was nearly empty. A veteran of the Ninth Dragoons slumped asleep in the corner still clutching his tankard, wearing the uniform he'd never need again. Two elderly rumel sat nearby in companionable silence. A fire crackled cozily nearby, and you could hear the *clink clink clink* of empty glasses that a serving girl was carrying into the kitchen. The tavern was one of those places that made an effort with its decor: engraved mirrors, imported dark woods, lanterns bright enough to make women feel comfortable drinking here.

"Go on then," Brynd said. This wasn't the first time Apium had explained to Brynd what his problems were. Certainly it wouldn't be the last.

Brynd took another sip of lager.

"You're a pushover," Apium continued. "That's what you are, a pushover. You'll take anything up the arse and not complain about it. You're just a bitch to these councilors."

"Really?" Brynd said. "Thanks for your support."

"Just stand up for yourself once in a while—that's what you should do. I would've given them hell!"

"You're not really one for diplomacy, are you?"

"Diplomacy's never won us soldiers a war."

Brynd pondered the inherent truth in Apium's statement.

"Perhaps you're right." As he spoke he realized that Apium's attention was drawn to the barmaid who was busy cleaning tables. "You with me?"

"I was with *her* in spirit," Apium stated. "I have been since we walked in here."

Brynd stared at him. "Stop leering. Haven't you got a sense of decency?"

"No, I'm not armed with a sense of decency," Apium said. "That way, my other senses are as sharp as they can possibly be."

Brynd laughed, shook his head, then glanced over the bar, silent in thought.

✳

Because they were carousing at the top level of the city, they didn't have far to walk to reach the military quarters of Balmacara. Brynd considered such privileged accommodation a wasted luxury, because they were so frequently away from the city on military service. This housing could so easily be used for refugee families. Instead, the chambers they occupied were set into the cliff face just to the north of the late Emperor's private quarters, and usually a minimum two members of the Night Guard remained in residence at all times, in case the Emperor should need to call on them in an emergency. Not that there had ever been one in Brynd's memory, but it was a sensible precaution.

As he was commander, Brynd's own chamber was by far the most extravagant, set slightly apart from the others. He liked the decor inside, a mixture of polished marble and slate, with purple drapes hanging on every wall. Hidden behind them were maps of the Empire's far-flung territories should he need to examine them quickly. It often helped during sleepless nights, to study these lands that he was charged to protect. It affirmed his sense of duty. Military medallions hung from the mirror on his dressing table.

Then he noticed the letter left for him on a side table. He lit a lantern before opening it to reveal precise details, provided by Chancellor Urtica, of where Jamur Rika was living near the settlement of Hayk, on the Southfjords. The letter also confirmed that Chancellor Urtica would like an interview with Brynd before he left, in order to discover further details of the disastrous ambush at Dalúk Point.

Brynd was disturbed by the thought of now finding time to come to terms with the deaths in his regiment, and discovering who was responsible for their ambush. Such quieter moments were difficult for soldiers, as the killings they witnessed worked over and over again in the mind. He would have to organize letters of sympathy to be sent to the families of the deceased soldiers—there was still so much to be done, and he must be ready to leave early the next morning. Brynd settled down at his desk for a couple of hours' paperwork.

✳

Brynd paused to look up at the clock. Not even an hour had passed, and he wasn't feeling particularly tired, but he decided the letters could wait. He needed some fresh air, he needed some relaxation. Perhaps Apium was right, and Brynd took life too seriously. The pressure was starting to get to him.

He changed out of his uniform into a featureless brown tunic, threw on a hooded cloak, then walked quickly out into the chill of the night.

✳

Brynd knocked on the door. The darkness felt suffocating, one of those nights when you felt like someone was watching your every move.

Brynd's secret would then be out.

And he would be executed on the city walls.

He was standing outside an inconspicuous doorway near Gulya Gata, not far from where painters from the gallery customarily loitered in the company of poets inside bistros by Cartanu Gata and the Gata Sentimental. Nearby, past the bad hotel in the exposed street, there was always the sound of activity: erratic laughter, retreating footsteps, the clink of glass or the scrape of metal. Depending on the mood of the city, it could also mean drunkenness, lovemaking, even a murder. Such sounds were interpreted according to your own degree of paranoia—Villjamur was constructed by a state of mind.

The door opened, and a slim young man stood there wearing only a flimsy robe. High cheekbones, thin lips, a wicked grin that Brynd could never stay away from too long. The young man brushed his sleek black hair back with his fingers. "Well, if it isn't my big war hero. Haven't seen you for a while."

"I've had a hell of a week," Brynd breathed, his gaze flickering from Kym's face to the ground. In a way it was a refusal to see himself reflected in Kym's eyes.

"You look like you have, too," Kym said. "You look bloody terrible. And you haven't even come in uniform. Well, you're a right scruff, but I can live with that."

"If someone catches us together while I'm in uniform we'll both be hanged. And think of how my unit would react if they discover the truth about me. My fellow soldiers are suspicious enough of me already." Having no wife might arouse suspicion normally, but at least being an albino gave him an excuse to hide behind.

Kym said, "You're just paranoid because of the color of your skin, honey. So stop being so self-conscious. People give less of a shit about you than you believe."

"I didn't come here to argue," Brynd said.

"Well, in that case, you may as well come in."

Still hesitant now. "Are you . . . alone? No one else here?"

"Of course I am, otherwise I'd say so."

Brynd followed him inside, looking around carefully before he closed the door. Kym was always so casual, and there was something deeply attractive about his carefree attitude. Or was it more carelessness? His lack of care was seen as a sign of strength by many. Women in particular were attracted to the deep confidence from which he drew his plenitude of sarcasm and humor and surreal wisdom. They felt the urge to be noticed by him, but he always came back to Brynd in the end.

"That a cut on your face?" Brynd had noted a thin line under Kym's eye, in this clearer light.

"Experienced some rough treatment, you know how it is. Well, you don't quite, I suppose, being all military and precise. This was just a little bit more than name-calling, though, a threat to inform the Inquisition. Just so happens the guy I was seeing at the time was tough, tall and muscled. Gave the guy who did this a broken jaw, poor bastard. Can't eat his meals without help now." Kym gave the gentlest of smiles.

"Indeed." Brynd was not sure whether to feel jealous or angry. He had no right to be either. "So how've you been? I see you've decorated the place again."

Brynd indicated the metal frame chairs, the elaborate new murals, the stylish new lanterns that cast shades of green and blue all around them. He found it impressive, Kym's ability over the years to always find something new to do with the place.

The first time they'd met was when Brynd was just a captain in the Second Dragoons. He didn't have such a high reputation to protect, so they were good days, relatively stress-free, when he could spend his evenings in lovemaking and easy companionship. The two of them would visit the galleries, even stroll on the bridges through the warmer evenings, just to get closer to the stars. But always in the darkness of the executioner's shadow because of a few lines in an ancient Jorsalir text. Back then, the Freeze was not something people even thought about, and he didn't have a crucial role to play in the Empire's development or safety, so he was less bothered about his reputation.

In those more directionless younger days, he went about the city screwing man after man. There were always places to find it, discreet clubs dark enough so married men could be hypocrites. He'd felt a discreet thrill at the fact that he could be killed simply for being what he was. It always made sucking a cock so much more *exciting*. Brynd had now settled on just one man—in personality a strange opposite that he needed more than chose, for reasons he never wanted to investigate. Perhaps it was the distinct lack of machismo in Kym, a quality that was so evidently postured during his time in the army.

"I sold a painting and got decent money for it . . ." Kym paused as he followed Brynd's gaze around the room. "It wasn't even very good, but taste is a matter of *taste*." He laughed at his own joke— something Brynd also found endearing. "So, I thought I'd give the place a new look. *You* could do with one, too."

Kym walked toward Brynd and the two men held each other for a moment while their expressions relaxed into something more raw. Brynd inhaled and exhaled deeply, waiting for the moment, waiting for the sign in Kym's eyes, and then they thrust their faces together, lips touching with a soft aggression, time falling apart.

Eventually Brynd withdrew with a sigh.

"I hate you, just invading my evening like this." Kym ran his hands along Brynd's arm, testing the ridges in his triceps. "I hate you, and love you. How long can you stay?"

"Only for the night, and I've got to be up early. Then it's not long until I leave the city again."

"I don't want to know." Kym placed a finger to Brynd's lips, and for a moment Brynd closed his eyes and tasted it.

Brynd parted Kym's robe, reached out, without really thinking, to feel the warmth of his body, more of a familiar reaction than an intention. He moved his palms very slowly down his lover's torso.

Kym shuddered. "Astrid, your hands are freezing."

Brynd smiled. "Sorry." He continued until Kym became hard, then kissed his stomach. "I've got something a little warmer."

Brynd fell to his knees, then took Kym in his mouth.

❋

Heading upstairs was something Brynd always enjoyed, as it prolonged the moment and the anticipation. Brynd taking solace in one of these rare moments when he could unbuckle the stresses of his complex, dangerous existence. It would be another one of those special nights in which he engaged solely with Kym.

A soldier, a battle hero, and this was the most dangerous thing Brynd ever did.

CHAPTER 8

✳

Brynd was up with the sun, or what could be seen of it in this dank weather. Sometime after the bell tower had struck five, he spent awhile poring over the maps of the Boreal Archipelago, Kym now a distant memory.

Then, leaving his chamber, he joined Chancellor Urtica for a simple breakfast in one of Balmacara's dining halls. They were the only two there, but a fire had already been lit to warm the great chamber. Aged Imperial standards hung in strips in various states of decay. Some of them were over a thousand years old: faded icons of faded glory.

"Please, commander," the chancellor began after a few mouthfuls, "tell me some more about what happened at Dalúk."

At least the chancellor seemed more interested this time. Brynd carefully explained all that had happened, produced the arrow. He insisted it wasn't so much who had attacked him that mattered, more the point of how they managed to find out about his expedition.

"You suspect that we've a spy among us, commander?" Urtica suggested.

"I would say, chancellor, that it might be likely. The loyalties of certain people within Balmacara are complex. Councilors possess external connections that Emperor Johynn wouldn't have been informed of. People with friends in distant places. If you call that the activities of a spy, then, yes, but it didn't come from my mouth."

"You could make a politician yet, my dear fellow."

Brynd didn't respond, just ate another mouthful.

Urtica picked up the arrow again. "Varltung, you think?"

"It's certainly possible, judging from the rune marks, while the metal work is definitely something I'd associate with non-Empire craftsmanship. I think it'd be worth you showing it to some of the experts in the arsenal workshops."

"I'll do that." Urtica looked from the arrow to Brynd, then back again. "Of course, if this was an attack mounted from Varltung, with the Freeze taking a firm grip, we may well need to brace ourselves for something more serious."

"You think?"

"We must fear that the Varltungs are getting ready to seize Jamur territories," Urtica said.

"You mean the islands nearby?"

"We must be ready to defend them, yes. The most northern and easterly islands are always heavily manned considering we see little war from there. But I suspect we must also be ready to now counterattack. They have killed some of our best men, commander. We can't allow this to go unpunished."

"Surely a campaign against the Varltungs is unnecessary—and likely to be unsuccessful, too? We've tried that before, several years ago. Decades, in fact. And what about the Freeze? You want to deploy all these men at a time when so many refugees are clamoring to get into our city?"

"Exactly so," Urtica said. "We must strike them fast and hard, and in a sufficiently damaging way that makes sure they can't counterattack for the foreseeable future."

"I would think the ice age means all this is pointless?"

"Not at all. Because of the Freeze, because of all these years of being locked away, we'll need those islands kept safe for our future generations."

Brynd said, "And you're so confident that any of us will survive at all?"

"Times will be very difficult, commander, and of course many may not survive. We don't even know the potential extent of the ice-cap. But it is possible that people will indeed survive, and safeguarding those islands would guarantee them the best possible chance of survival after the ice retreats."

✳

Chancellor Urtica had donated a few luxuries and a considerable sum of money for the brief journey—all of ten Jamúns' worth of the latter, broken into smaller coin: Sota, Lordil, Drakar. Brynd couldn't help feeling a bit suspicious, but accepted these supplies courteously. *Perhaps he is just trying to make me feel better after losing so many of my troops.*

They set off out into the cold gray morning.

Two pterodettes arced in the sky, their shrill cries penetrating the quiet of the city. Behind them they left the ringing of the hours for morning worship, the smell of breakfasts from assorted dining halls.

Waiting at the front entrance to Balmacara were the four men he had chosen. Stood by their immaculately prepared horses, patiently waiting to leave. Staring up at the sky, Apium was sitting on a black gelding alongside a vast, gleaming carriage which the new empress would travel in. The other three Night Guard soldiers, none of whom had been at Dalúk Point, were talking together quietly: fit, young, ideal for such a casual expedition. The two blond men were Sen and Lupus, twenty-six and twenty-two years old respectively. They could have been brothers, both lean, both tall. Both with those cutting blue eyes. Something almost wolflike about their appearance. They had risen dramatically through the army because of their talent, and they respected Brynd above all others. Brynd valued Sen particularly since the lad was easily the best swordsman he had ever trained. He constantly worked on developing his skills, so Brynd would lay money on him being the finest swordsman in the Empire within a year or two.

Nelum Valore, a heavily built black-haired man, was a little older. Should have become one of the Imperial academics, but he preferred life outside of musky chambers. Said what you could learn from books could be learned from the real world too. Brynd admired that quality, and made him one of the youngest lieutenants ever serving in the Night Guard. The man rarely discussed his Jorsalir beliefs, either, and the commander didn't know what to make of his dedication to gods he couldn't see.

These four were the best of the remaining regiment. In full uniform, black on black, the seven-pointed star glistening on their chests, they stood to attention, each with his left hand resting across his stomach.

"Sele of Jamur," Brynd greeted them. "We all set to go?"

"Yes, sir," Sen replied for them. "All weaponry's been fixed to the carriage and we've got our rations inside. Lupus arranged for the vehicle to be thoroughly cleaned overnight, so it'll be good enough for whoever it is intended." This last statement hung in the air, hoping for an answer.

Brynd peered underneath the carriage to confirm four crossbows and four spears were fixed to the base between the axles. Short-handle axes were there too, and none of those extra weapons could easily be seen, being a useful addition to the sword and bow each man would carry. Having the benefit of young eyesight, Lupus was a highly skilled archer, while Apium and Nelum used their mature strength for axe work, but knew their way around a sword as well.

"Good. I've requested for a garuda to track us in the skies—to scout around also, so that we don't get surprised again. So you know in advance, while we're away, the Council will make an announcement revealing that Emperor Johynn has died, and that his elder daughter, the Lady Rika, will become ruler of the Jamur territories. Villjamur will be officially in a state of mourning until our return."

"With the new Empress, I take it?" Nelum tapped the side of the carriage with his palm.

Brynd nodded, "Yes, we're collecting her from Southfjords. She knows we're coming to meet her, but not that her father's dead."

"Whose job is it to deliver the news?" Sen said.

"That honor appears to be mine," Brynd said grimly.

"I've heard she never liked him that much anyway," Nelum muttered.

"Meanwhile . . ." Brynd faced each of them in turn, "no flirting, no smiling—in fact, no talking to her, unless I say so. Just remember, she's your new ruler. You serve her loyally. We're her guard."

They nodded in confirmation.

"Just us five going?" Nelum inquired.

"No point drawing too much attention to our departure. It'd alert too many people that something was up. We won't get any trouble going to Southfjords, so no need to waste extra men. There aren't enough of us Night Guardsmen left, anyway. I'll have to recruit more after we return."

Silence passed as they reflected on dead comrades.

"Right," Brynd continued, "we've a longship waiting for us at Gish, and that's where we ride first. It'll take the best part of two days, so let's get going."

They all mounted their horses.

"You're very quiet today," Brynd remarked to Apium. The redhead was clutching at his stomach.

"Aye. Seems that I can no longer handle a bit of lager like I used to."

✳

In the center of the Atrium, Chancellor Urtica stood before the assembled Council. He flicked back his gray cloak dramatically, looking around with a falsely solemn expression. If he wanted to initiate a combat situation, he would have to be at his most persuasive, most charming. The reactions of the other members were uniformly glum.

"Fellow councilors," he began. "I've only this morning had a private meeting with Commander Brynd Lathraea of the Night Guard. He has informed me that he strongly suspects the Varltung islanders as being responsible for the surprise slaughter of his men."

Urtica produced the arrow that Brynd had given him earlier, passing it to the nearest councilor to hand around the chamber for inspection.

"Somehow these wretched people have found out about our secret mission to secure more firegrain, and are now planning to make sure we crumble before the Freeze properly settles in."

There was a murmur throughout the chamber, and someone spoke up, "Are you quite certain this is from Varltung?"

"Indeed, the armory will take a look to make sure, but we're confident it's from Varltung. They clearly knew of our plans and conse-quently destroyed some of our best regiment."

"But they're merely *barbarians,*" Councilor Mewún protested. "How could they do this?"

Urtica's voice became bolder, a well-rehearsed ploy on his part. He felt it important to inject some drama into these meetings. "I strongly recommend that we act on this outrage promptly. We should send a naval assault to seize the entire island and disable it, and take their re-sources. Who knows what they will be capable of later, whilst our city gates are closed?"

"Should the new Empress not decide this?" Urtica couldn't see who spoke.

Silence, for several heartbeats. "She'll have many other concerns once she arrives, and I don't think she is capable of conducting a mil-itary operation yet."

"I'm not certain we should consider going to war on such little ev-idence. How can you launch an attack without more definite proof?" It was Councilor Yiak, a chubby woman that Urtica had never liked much.

"We *do* have evidence," Urtica said. "But I can tell you need fur-ther encouragement on the issue. This is about defense of our Empire, about protecting it against crimes such as that perpetrated at Dalúk Point. I suggest we should have another debate this very evening, fol-lowing the evening prayer bell."

Urtica was delighted as the motion was carried overwhelmingly.

Councilor Boll then stood up, his skinny frame barely noticeable. His manner was nervous, his voice uncertain. "Um, I'd like to an-nounce briefly that we've had an approach from the Inquisition con-cerning the recent murder of our fellow councilor, Delamonde Rubus Ghuda. They would like to come into the Atrium itself to discuss the case."

"Indeed," Urtica replied. "But I'd recommend they come when we're not in session, and instead interview us one by one in our pri-vate quarters."

They all voiced their agreement, because Ghuda was a popular man, would be missed by all, and the sooner they reached the solving of his murder, the better. No one felt this more than Urtica. They shared the ideal that the city should be rid of the scum of refugees, that they presented the danger of disease and discontent. Urtica would endorse everything it took to find who had disposed of his ally.

✳

A few hours outside of Villjamur, on the road to Gish, Brynd caught a glimpse of a curiously caparisoned horse being ridden through a clearing in the betula woodland ahead. They had come off the main road some time ago, preferring instead to follow one of the smaller gravel tracks that ran along the coast. They had avoided the villages and hamlets of Eelú, Fúe and Goúle. He thought it best that as few people as possible were aware of their movements.

He could tell that the horse was from one of the famous gangs, but he wondered which one. He always found the gatherings of these horse gangs to be a wonderful sight, and he halted his men with a gesture, interested to see if they were racing today.

"What's up?" Apium said, following his gaze to the trees.

"Only a gang rider," Brynd replied. "Might take a look to make sure. Let's pause here for a quarter of an hour."

The gap through the larix led him onto an open expanse of tundra, where two horse gangs were currently assembled. There were mainly men as the lead riders, but some girls rode alongside, all dressing their horses similarly to whichever group they favored. Many wore leather, even daggers, since this was about raw masculine pride: young people dressed up with nowhere to go. Such gangs would gather on exposed areas of tundra to race one another, or just to hang out, drinking alcohol away from the eyes of parents or city guards, and at night they would lie with each other indiscriminately. During races money would change hands as the onlookers gambled on the winners, and rags of different colors were attached to the horses' legs or tails in a code Brynd didn't understand. Tribal tokens were fixed to the reins, personalizing the horse as far as possible, in mimicry of the military cadres of the Empire.

Behind the rival groups lay a flat dark plain, under a drizzle-filled sky, with the smell of forests and of salt wafting from the sea to the south. For a short while they would be happy enough here, all the cares and impending changes now forgotten. Two young men presently lined up their horses, paused, then belted across the horizon, the others cheering on in feral calls.

The sight of such carefree enthusiasm made Brynd feel he was getting old. He had youthful dreams once, which seemed to be traveling further and further out of his reach. Perhaps he should stay out of Villjamur when the gates would be shut for all those years . . .

The garuda suddenly landed next to him. Brynd didn't even flinch. He had spotted the creature hovering overhead only moments before.

With a chalk-white face offset by golden plumage, and large wings now tucked neatly behind his back, the garuda stood nearly six feet tall. He was wearing black breeches, with nothing covering his upper torso, revealing ferocious muscles beneath the downy feathers of his chest. Tied to the garuda's waist was a belt with two long sheathed daggers. The creatures were always an amazing sight. They now primarily inhabited several towering cliff faces at the Fugúl Colonies on the island of Kullrún, which was sealed off as a military training ground. There, over a thousand of them lived in caves. They had been an essential part of the Imperial armies for thousands of years. Although communicating with each other through shrill bird calls, they used sign language to interact with humans or rumel. How and when it had come about was anyone's guess, but such communication was essential to their joint campaigns.

"Sele of Jamur, wing commander," Brynd said.

The bird-man, Wing Commander Vish, then raised his arms to sign, *Why have you stopped?*

"We're only stopping to rest the horses. Did you spot anything on the way here?"

Just more refugees approaching the Sanctuary Road. There are probably at least a thousand camped outside the city now.

"As many as that." Brynd shook his head. "What'll you yourself do—during this Freeze?"

The wing commander eyed him expressionlessly, then signed, *What do you mean?*

"I mean, when the ice comes so densely that people are sealed in. That's not so far off now. You're intending to stay in Villjamur, right, for all those years? What're you going to do there?"

Just because the gates are closed, doesn't mean I can't fly. I can still serve the military, serve the Empire. You appear rather philosophical today, commander.

"I guess the Emperor's death will bring about changes for the city. Maybe I should be thinking of a change myself."

Maybe you have never quite felt a part of things in Villjamur. I always thought you were too self-conscious about the color of your skin.

Brynd looked away as if to cut him off. "Well if that's the case I've picked the wrong career." He wasn't aware garudas could be so perceptive. "I'm just getting old." Brynd laughed. "Perhaps I've started thinking about myself too much."

Then you'd be the same as the rest of your race.

"Come on. Let's get something to eat."

✳

Chancellor Urtica strode through the armory as if he owned the place, yet was almost knocked back by the change in temperature. Rows of men drenched in sweat were working at benches. They looked up to inspect the intruder, their white eyes startling against dust-smeared skin. In the background, a huge furnace burned violently, producing a heady smell. Everywhere, the *clunk clunk clunk* of metal being beaten and contorted into shape.

"Can I help you, chancellor?" A short, stout man, blond hair, wearing a short-sleeved black tunic and black breeches. His arms, shimmering with sweat, were totally smooth because continual exposure to the flames had burned away all the hairs. This was the Chief of Defense for Villjamur—in reality, a retired soldier who still directed the smiths according to battle orders.

"Indeed you can, Fentuk, my dear fellow," Urtica replied, smiling around at the other workers, who glared back skeptically. "Walk out with me, if you please, so that we're not heard."

"Sounds important," Fentuk muttered.

Urtica led Fentuk out of the building and over a darkened bridge nearby, where you could look directly across the roofs of Villjamur.

It was approaching dusk, a carnelian sky. House lanterns scattered throughout the city seemed to mirror the stars. The twin moons Bohr and Astrid hung on opposite sides of the sky, giving a brilliant light that seemed to catch all the spires and bridges in an ethereal glow. Some distance below them, a horse was being led along a dully lit street, its hooves clopping loudly on the stone. There was a flash of magic. A door opened and closed, chattering of women heard in between, and there was a lute playing sevenths in some tavern nearby, a dreary tune accompanied by an off-key singer.

One of those perfect Villjamur nights.

"So, Chancellor Urtica, what've you brought me here for?"

"Insurance." Urtica leaned against the parapet of the bridge. The wind ruffled his cloak and he shivered. "One can never be too certain who's listening in, these days."

"Listening in?"

"Listening in." Urtica reached under his cloak, produced the arrow. "I urgently need to know where this came from."

Fentuk took it, examined it closely. "Hard to tell in this light." He rolled it between his fingers, lifted it this way and that. "Well, it ain't Jamur," he continued. "Not from any of the islands to the west or south. My guess would be Varltung, but I can't be certain. Made very poorly, you see. Could also be Maour, Dockull or even Hulrr." The man pursed his lips thinly. "Why? Where d'you get it?"

Urtica clicked his tongue against his teeth. "It was found in the corpse of a Night Guard soldier. The commander suspects it was a Varltung ambush. I was hoping to get your confirmation, to support the case for a campaign against that nation, before the Freeze sets in."

"Oh, well, I . . . I couldn't say for sure it's from Varltung, no."

"Are you *certain* you can't be sure? We need to strike back against the Varltungs before it's too late." The chancellor waved his hands in the air to stress the point.

"No," Fentuk said. "I really can't be sure, not if it could mean war. Not on my word. Is this all the evidence you have?"

"We've more," Urtica said. A lie, of course, and he didn't think twice about saying it.

"I can't help you in this case, chancellor. I'm sorry." He handed the arrow back to Urtica, who concealed it beneath his cloak again.

"Was that everything?" Fentuk said, running his hand through his hair. "I have to be getting back now."

"No, there was something else—something much more important." Urtica looked around the parapet. He stepped in closer to Fentuk. "I must whisper this.

"I can offer you a substantial sum of money to make sure that you never have to step foot in that rancid armory again—we're talking safe accounts and country estates. All you have to do is confirm for me that this arrow came from a Varltung bow, and back me up officially if I wanted to initiate an order of war. You could do that for me, couldn't you, Fentuk?"

The chief of defense was solemn as he clasped the parapet. "I . . . I really don't know."

Urtica placed an arm around him. "I wouldn't like to say what might happen otherwise. I mean, there are some prominent promilitary Council members with significant investments in armory and ores—and in times of war their incomes and influence are known to rise hugely. Should they be denied this opportunity—and your name will be thrown about the Atrium—well, I have heard tell of punishment beatings for this sort of thing in the past. Such stories . . ." He shook his head and sighed for effect.

A moment later, as if ordered, a banshee began keening in the distance, somewhere possibly Caveside. As time passed, Fentuk was visibly shaken by this potential premonition. "How much money are we talking about exactly?" he muttered eventually.

Urtica smiled. "That's the spirit, Fentuk. You won't regret this. You should maybe join me for drinks sometime, socially."

✳

Brynd had ordered his men to set up camp for the night on the edge of a copse of trees seven hours' ride further on from the hamlet of Goúle, and just past the Bria Haugr, a conical hill that was reputed to be an ancient Azimuth burial mound. The surrounding fagus would provide them with some concealment.

They were now halfway to the military port of Gish. Brynd didn't want to travel via E'toawor, a significant port town and favored entry point to Jokull. He couldn't afford to go further north either, to the towns of Vilhokteu and, on the estuary of the River Hok, Vilhokr. He certainly did not need the eyes of common tradesmen, dockers, and farm laborers to be the first of her subjects to set eyes upon the new Empress.

As the sun set Brynd and Sen sparred with sabers a little to fend off the boredom. But as the sky became a bold shade of purple, it was clear that Sen was getting the better of him. The others, including the garuda, sat around the fire, backs against the wheels of the carriage, watching.

"He'll have you, Brynd," Apium said. "I can see your defenses falling apart. Sen doesn't even need a sword."

Brynd ignored the taunts.

"Go on, lad," Apium continued. "Aim low. Go for his cock—he's not got any use for it these days."

Finally they sheathed their sabers and Brynd turned to the others. "Time for a close-range scout. Sen'll stay here with the wing commander. The rest of you want to take a look around with me?"

Everyone groaned but they stood up.

Apium brushed himself down. "Which way we heading, commander?"

"I think we'll follow a circle going east, nothing too far out, just a few hundred paces. I need to make sure there'll be no surprises tonight." Brynd wasn't sure exactly how wary to be. This was Jokull, after all, and there hadn't been any serious fighting on the island for years—before Dalúk Point. Before that incident, the idea of any threat on the home island was something not even considered.

The others followed him in a huddled group, taking a three-hundred-pace radius around their camp. The terrain was largely flat, and away from the forest, an open view for leagues. Underfoot was a mossy grass that concealed rocks and dips. Apium managed to fall over just twice.

The sky blackened further. The glow of the campfire stood out as an intense beacon, revealing the silhouette of the carriage. Somewhere in the distance a wolf howled. Only one of the moons was showing—the larger one, Bohr—but it was now cresting the horizon just before leaving the landscape in utter darkness.

After a while, Brynd heard something strange in the distance. He had spent enough time in the wild to know that it was nothing natural.

He regarded the carriage.

Apium asked, "What's up?"

Brynd gestured for him to be silent while he scanned the scene with the enhanced vision which the Night Guard benefited from, but it wasn't enough for a clear identification.

Shadows moved across the landscape.

Nelum and Lupus moved alongside, staring back to the campfire. Lupus said, "I see something."

"Strap your weapons and armor tight," Brynd said. "Let's get back quietly."

The four soldiers jogged in stealth across the tundra, back to the carriage. Brynd began to slow, waved for the others to follow suit, then signaled for them to unsheathe their weapons. Lupus swiftly nocked an arrow, Apium and Nelum drew short axes, Brynd pulled out his saber. As they approached the campfire they spread out.

Sen and the garuda were nowhere to be seen, the only noise coming from the crackle of the fire.

And something was wrong, an uncertainty hovering in the air, and once again the environment became to Brynd a matter of statistics, of distances, chances, arrows spent. He turned back to study the copse of trees. He concentrated, heightening his level of perception.

To the other side of the carriage: a strange lump on the ground. It was difficult to make out in the darkness despite his superior vision.

He went over and knelt down next to it.

Lurched back in disgust.

It was Sen's head, severed cleanly, blood draining away from it in a small trickle between Brynd's boots.

Brynd hailed the others in an urgent whisper, and they ran to his side. The sense of shock among them was palpable.

Brynd looked up. "Stay calm. Stick together." He analyzed the scene as if the trees would produce instant answers. *What the fuck is happening on this island of ours?*

He noticed the trail of blood leading under the cover of the fagus trees. The rest of Sen's body must be there somewhere. The treetops fizzed under the night sky.

"Wait, commander," Apium whispered. "I don't think we should follow. Whatever did this to Sen is obviously skilled at picking people off quietly. Best we don't separate for the moment."

"You might be right there, captain," Brynd murmured, though uncertainly.

"What, we're just going to let Sen's death go without investigation?" Lupus said indignantly.

Brynd gestured for him to lower his voice. "One of the most promising young soldiers in the Empire is dead. One of our garudas has gone missing. So you think we should pursue this right now, at night, in the dark in the woods? There're just four of us now. Already two down." *Maybe I should've brought more men along, but no one but me could've known we were taking this route.*

"So we simply wait here," Lupus protested, "and get picked off one by one?"

A rustling from the trees.

Everyone looked toward the copse.

Three figures lurched forward and Lupus brought an arrow to anchor point, aimed it.

"Not till I say." Brynd held up a hand, but was reaching for his axe with the other.

The dark figures started running toward them.

Brynd signaled. Lupus released an arrow.

It whipped through the air, struck one of the intruders powerfully in the face. By then he was nocking another arrow, and soon another figure was falling to the ground. The final one stepped forward with sword raised.

Brynd hurled his axe through the intervening space.

It cleaved the attacker's face and he too slumped to the ground.

Then suddenly the unlikely happened: all three fallen bodies began struggling to push themselves upright, trying to pull out the arrows, with jerky, improbable movements.

Lupus fired repeatedly, pinning the bodies to the ground, twitching. And again they tried to stand with a jagged motion.

"Aim for their legs," Brynd yelled, running to reach under the carriage for a crossbow. Then, returning to Lupus's side again, he began shooting at the heads and torsos.

They fired until finally the bodies lay still.

"Cover!" Brynd swept in toward the dead, seized one of the corpses back into the light of the campfire. Soon the others had done the same with the rest.

Brynd began tearing open the ragged clothing on each of the corpses. "By Bohr, these men we've killed were already dead."

"Are you sure?" Nelum questioned, and was rewarded with a glare of annoyance from his commander. *Yes I'm sure. These things are fucking dead, many times over.*

"Look at this one. His skin is ice cold—blue, even in this light. He isn't even bleeding, just the remains of some black gunk. He's been dead for several days at least."

The soldiers remained silent.

"Draugr," Nelum said eventually.

"Y'what?" Apium demanded.

"Draugr. *Undead.* A purportedly mythical creature. Well, that's what it looks like anyway. Give it awhile longer and I suspect they'll be back to life, in some sort of manner. So we might want to make sure they're finished off properly, commander."

Even as soon as he spoke, one of the bodies began twitching, the fingers moving gently and impossibly. With a sigh, Brynd stepped quickly to the carriage and pulled out one of the larger axes. Over the next few moments he hacked away at the reviving corpses with relentless brutality, grunting as he hauled the metal blade down on them again and again, releasing his frustration in the process, and Apium soon joined in the frenzy with another axe till the camp was carpeted with bone and smashed heads. They then gathered the individual fragments together away from camp, and Brynd fervently hoped there was no way that they could resurrect themselves from that destruction.

"Now," Brynd demanded, with disgust on realizing he was covered in small chunks of flesh, "could you tell me about these draugr, lieutenant. Please."

Nelum had this scholarly way about him when he was explaining, always had done for the years Brynd had known him, and the act in itself was a comfort now, the return to business-as-usual. He began casually, pacing around in slow strides. "A few volumes of collected folklore report sightings of undead, mainly on islands like Maour and Varltung. Ascribed to distant mythology, mainly. So you certainly wouldn't expect to encounter them in this day and age, or for many centuries past. From the accounts I've read in bestiaries of the Archipelago, they're last reported about as far back as the Máthema civilization. That means myths of sixty thousand years."

"Yes, but *what* exactly are they?" Brynd interrupted impatiently.

"Exactly what I said: the undead. Corpses that in some way be-come animated again. Normally, their bodies have to be disposed of in certain ways, so I'm guessing and hoping your little dissection would have covered the requirements rather effectively."

"So what are they doing here on Jokull?" Apium broke in. "How did they ever get on the Empire's home island? With something as sinister as that coming ashore, you'd think some of the coastal guards would have noticed, eh."

"Your guess is as good as mine, captain," Nelum admitted. "I wouldn't say that they'd feel constrained by water though. Perhaps they didn't arrive, and were here to begin with."

"It can only be cultist work," Brynd said firmly. "You remember that figure we saw at Dalúk, captain?"

"Bohr's balls," Apium gasped.

"Eloquently put, captain," Nelum said. "But I don't see how— and I don't see why?"

"How? They've found some relic that'll do the job. But why? I can't answer that." Apium sighed. "Well, so much for a quiet night."

Nelum frowned. "I can't understand what they're doing out here, and why they're attacking us. It's as if they attacked on some primitive instinct."

"They're even frightening off gheels," Brynd observed. "And that's saying something. All this blood and not one gheel in sight."

"Commander," Lupus hissed.

Brynd stepped alongside him, peering out into the darkness. "What is it, Lupus?"

"Over there, about fifty paces. Looks like Wing Commander Vish." The private was pointing to the north, beyond the fringe of the copse, at a silhouette with wings protruding over its back.

"Keep me covered, private," Brynd whispered, then stepped for-ward to meet the garuda. As Vish came closer, Brynd could see that he was dragging his left leg along with both hands. One of his wings hung out raggedly to the side.

Flesh had been removed in chunks from his torso as if devoured, and his feathers were slick and heavy with blood. Brynd kept the saber in his hand as he supported the garuda along until they were back in the glow of the campfire. There, they eased him to the ground and wrapped him in strips of cloth torn from a cloak to serve as bandages. Finally, Brynd used some of his medical powders to knock the garuda unconscious so he wouldn't feel so much pain, and Nelum helped him stitch the wounds together.

I should've been more prepared. What the hell is happening here?

❋

The wing commander bled to death during the night, his story untold.

Brynd took solace in the fact that he passed away without pain. No one else had slept at all through the night, and they burned his body the instant the sun rose. As they rode off across the sparsely forested sections of tundra they looked back to see a thin stream of smoke carrying the garuda's soul away. The cold air was sharp against the dried sweat on Brynd's brow. It was, at least, enough to remind him that he himself was still alive.

CHAPTER 9

✳

Investigator Jeryd stepped into his chambers, bleary-eyed. The sun had been up for a short while, not that you could see it yet. His head was mostly clear—an impressive feat considering the amount of whiskey he'd imbibed. He never let it get too far and always knew when to stop. He'd seen too much of what happened to the lives of alcoholics to allow the same to happen to him. No, if you drank all the time, that meant you wanted to use it to control your life, as if that was the only solution, and Jeryd was not looking for control, merely one night of escape. Two hundred years of it had taught him that you could never control the world around you.

He slumped into his fine wooden chair with a grunt, and for a brief moment contemplated giving up his career. How had things come to this? His tail felt stiff, his body ached. As he rested his head in his hands he was staring directly at an envelope on his desk until it came into focus.

Marysa's handwriting.

Fumbling with eagerness, he tore open the letter.

He read it anxiously.

She wanted to meet him for dinner at the end of the week at one of their favorite bistros.

He tossed the letter on the desk, reclined back in his chair. So she wanted to meet him? That was a start. The Bistro Júula was where he had first taken her for dinner immediately after they had been married in a Jorsalir church. A dimly lit place, with wooden floors, patient staff, and crammed with large potted ferns that gave each table a degree of privacy.

He heard the bell tower strike thirteen: midday already, and he was meant to be meeting Tryst to look more closely at the body of Councilor Ghuda.

✳

Jeryd swore at the horse that splashed an icy puddle onto his breeches. Tryst, a good armspan away, stared at Jeryd in faint amusement as the offending carriage proceeded into the distance.

The iren across the road was packed. Cold in the shade of a nest of architectural monstrosities, dozens of stalls lined the cobbled streets edging this trading center of the city, not far from the Council Atrium. The investigator's hands were clasped behind his back as he glanced casually at the arrays of food imported in from the surrounding agricultural communities where cultists had been treating crops to help yields survive the bad weather.

Noticing a display of several pots, vases, ornaments, he made a mental note to investigate some of the antiques shops further away in the city's expensive iren district during his lunch hour. Maybe he could find an interesting object for Marysa, something to impress her when they met for dinner. Moving on, he guided Tryst up a spiral passageway leading to the next level of the city.

Along some of these higher roads they encountered some huge flies that must have just swarmed in, their wings a handspan wide. They were feeding near the stables of the chancellor's horses. They made a rather pleasant drone, and in a mildly disgusted way, he admired them. Usually they were harmless enough, occurring in twos or threes, the pterodettes keeping their numbers in check. It was not known if these giant insects had some collective consciousness, but he remembered investigating an odd incident last year, where a two-bit stage cultist used some of these creatures in his routine, to aid with his levitation. One night the insects picked him up, led him to a window, then promptly dropped him to his death. No one in the audience seemed to care that much at the time.

The investigator and his assistant reached a low wooden door set in an unimpressive stretch of limestone. Whereas much of the upper city was decorated and ornamental, this thoroughfare was plain to the point of functional. A remnant from earlier days, perhaps, in a city that had changed its perspectives innumerable times.

Jeryd knocked, turned to Tryst and explained, "This should bring some leads, I hope."

Tryst was silent.

"It was the Big Date last night, wasn't it?" Jeryd leaned against the wall, folded his arms.

"Yes, it was nice," Tryst murmured. "But we didn't kiss at the end."

"Bloody hell, it doesn't always have to end with a kiss. You should be happy it didn't end with a slap." He banged on the door again.

This time it opened, and a man with a haggard face beckoned the two of them inside, his white gown stained an alarming red down the front. "I'm sorry to have kept you gentlemen waiting, but I was in the middle of cleaning a corpse. My name's Doctor Tarr, and I'm pleased to meet you." He offered a wrinkled hand.

Jeryd eyed it uncertainly, and introduced himself and Tryst. So this was Tarr, then, a man who dealt daily with the dead. Jeryd wondered if he would be as jolly or remote compared to the other doctors he had worked with in the past. They were certainly an odd bunch, these people who chose to spend their day away from the living.

"It's interesting to finally meet you, after reading so many of your forensic reports these last couple of years," Jeryd said. "And interesting that we should meet over Councilor Ghuda, certainly my biggest case."

"Yes, yes, Delamonde Ghuda is a most interesting case." Doctor Tarr gestured for them to follow him.

There were no windows in the room they entered, which was lit poorly by lanterns. Due to a proliferation of dried flowers and herbs, the odor wasn't as bad as Jeryd thought it would be. There was a faint melody coming from another room. "You employ a musician here?" he asked in surprise.

Doctor Tarr stopped. "Why, yes, of course." He glanced at the investigator with mild disbelief. "The patients wouldn't like it if I dismissed our lute player."

"Patients?" Jeryd looked incredulous. "I was under the impression that this place was a morgue?"

"That's correct, investigator. However, I prefer a soothing ambience, even for the dead. He's not the best musician, but people need to earn a coin, given the harsh times ahead."

"Indeed," Jeryd replied. He thought he could hear a faint noise behind the sound of the lute. A buzz maybe, perhaps some cultist device to aid the process? Jeryd studied Doctor Tarr in the light of the lantern. He was a man perhaps in his fifties, with a slight stoop, weathered face, thinning blond hair, elegant fingers.

He led them into a smaller well-lit stone chamber with a stone slab in the center. The naked body of Delamonde Ghuda was displayed upon it, a white sheet keeping him decent.

Jeryd and Tryst stood either side of the corpse as Doctor Tarr pulled back the sheet.

"Now, as I stated in my report, investigator, these wounds look most mysterious. I've not seen anything like them before."

"Talk me through your findings, doctor, if you will."

"Well there were no *intrusions* to the body, meaning nothing had penetrated it, but, as you can see, there is a significant amount of flesh missing from the torso. Tissue appears to have been removed from this region." Tarr indicated an area from the base of the neck to halfway down the chest.

"When you say 'removed,' what d'you mean precisely, Doctor Tarr?"

"Exactly what I said. It's gone, *removed,* without any intrusion by a sharp instrument. I can't give you any obvious conclusion as to what did this, because I've simply never seen anything similar before, nothing like an ordinary knife wound, which is, of course, simple to recognize. That's why I wanted you to drop by, so you could see for yourself what an interesting case this is. You see, it's as if the flesh has been removed by some unknown substance that had either consumed the flesh or exploded it outward. The area of wounding is roughly circular, but you couldn't class this as a crime unless you established whatever the instrument was that caused this unusual wounding."

As Doctor Tarr went on to speculate on various possible causes, Jeryd began to realize he was wasting his time being here. He would have to go to the Council Atrium itself to find out if the popular Delamonde Ghuda actually had any secret enemies. While he was weighing up the options, Tarr was delving further into medical analysis. Jeryd wanted to leave, as the doctor unnerved him. The lute player merely added to this sinister atmosphere.

"Would you like me to show you some other victims," Tarr said, "to see how their wounds differ?"

"No thanks," Jeryd said.

"I'll just show you one more."

He showed them four.

They entered a chamber lined with recent corpses. Many of the bodies were male, and over thirty. Their faces were peaceful, their wounds dreadful—two inflicted by swords, one from a mace. One of them had clearly died only moments before Jeryd arrived.

Tarr was almost motherly in his pride. "This one took poison," he explained, standing next to a body resting on a raised platform. "It wasn't the poison that actually killed him, because he choked on his own bile. Note the dried blood on his fingertips. He spent his final heartbeats clawing at the stone floor on which he had collapsed." Tarr shook his head solicitously. It looked as if he wanted to stroke the body to comfort it.

Jeryd shuddered.

They came upon the lute player finally, a young man perched on a crate in the corner of one of the various rooms. The whole place was a network of small chambers. Its complexity reminded Jeryd of the interior of a lung. *What is the real point of this musician—to drown out their dying screams?*

"We really must be going shortly," Jeryd decided.

Tarr eyed the investigator fixedly. "I hope you can visit again. Not many people seem as comfortable around the dead as you do."

"My assistant and I, we're pretty used to being around corpses. It comes with Inquisition business."

"There's far too many that like to avoid being reminded that life tends to be a little shorter than we'd like."

"Some think it's too long," Jeryd said. "Suicide is less rare than you'd think, especially with the ice age on the horizon and families being split because of the lack of accommodation in the city."

Tarr walked over to inspect a young woman. "This one was raped, slaughtered, left on her doorstep." Her face was pale, calm-looking, as if her death came as a relief to the terrible moments leading up to it. "What a waste every time this happens. Very few people have a true appreciation of life. If we realized death might come upon us at any moment, do you think we'd waste time arguing or fighting or being idle?"

"You can't force people to appreciate such things," Jeryd said. "They've got to come to terms with it for themselves. And I suspect that it's rumel nature too, as well as human, not to want to think about it. It's all too sobering for most of us to cope with. Now, we really must be on our way. Do contact me if you need anything from us. Good day, Doctor Tarr."

✳

Tarr watched the two investigators leave, closed the door, then headed back into the chambers. He found the lute player. "You can stop now. They've gone."

Tarr heard that hum again, louder than before. The lute player disappeared into the darkness, leaving Tarr alone, where he waited until the humming ceased.

Dartun Súr entered the chamber.

The cultist leader had been working somewhere else in the building, the doctor did not know where. Maybe it was that damn strange cloak that allowed him to hide so effectively in the shadows. Tarr felt the tall man bearing down on him.

"Dear doctor, that was a wonderful tour you gave our investigator." Dartun gripped the other man's shoulder.

"Thank you, sir."

"So, what else've you got for me today? I've just finished working on that last fellow." Dartun clasped his hands, and looked eagerly around the room as if he were in an iren.

"Another one?" Tarr said.

"Yes, we must keep busy, you know," Dartun said. "That's what I was doing in the other room—just a bit of practice on an older corpse. And that was a nice touch of yours, covering it up with the lute player."

"Well I couldn't have the investigator poking around and getting suspicious. You should have warned me you were coming. The lute player was the best I could do. I bet our friend Jeryd now thinks I'm totally insane."

Dartun clasped his hands together. "Can't have the Inquisition prying around too much. I heard you saying you had some fresh ones? The fresher they are, the easier they are for me to work with."

"But those ones all have families," Tarr protested. "We've not had any unclaimed bodies arrive today."

"That's a bit of an inconvenience, really." Dartun frowned, rubbing his chin. He ambled around the room, his boots loud on the stone. "Listen, d'you think I could reserve the next unclaimed one that comes in? I'm having to . . . begin some other schemes of mine very shortly, and I might need to leave the city very soon. And I could do with a few more corpses, no questions asked."

He hated Dartun for this secretiveness, but he had been embroiled in it for far too long now. And it was no longer out of choice, since every time Dartun made a suggestion, it seemed to come across more as a threat.

"Right," Tarr said, "look, I'll try and keep one for you, but you know this really is most abnormal."

"So are most things, doctor." Dartun turned, something flashed in his hands, and even before he walked into the wall he had vanished.

"Why can't he just use the door like everybody else?" Tarr muttered.

CHAPTER 10

✻

Randur made his way through the increasingly bad weather up toward the Imperial residence of Balmacara, his traveling bags slung across his shoulder, his shirt soaked and clinging to his skin. Sleet to rain to snow to sleet, Villjamur was now only differing shades of gray, and he prayed to Bohr that the waxed leather on his bags was holding the water at bay or the rest of his clothes would be ruined otherwise. His long hair trailed lankly in front of his eyes. He was thoroughly miserable.

Shitting weather, he thought. *Just a day of sunshine, that's all I ask for.*

Balmacara was an intimidating sight, and its dark stone was imbedded in symmetrical lines, slabs of some shimmering-black material. It seemed impossibly high, almost reaching into the low cloud base. Bold pillars and arches, crenulations in the surface and crenellations crowning towers, all with a design nothing like he'd ever seen, and it didn't even seem to match anything in the city. The building loomed. It imposed itself upon Villjamur.

Having shown his papers to the guards at the gate to the outer compound of Balmacara, he was mortified to see yet more steps rising between two octagonal pillars marking the main entrance.

He wondered what he'd be doing if he was back on Folke. When he had left, people were starting to panic because of the Freeze. People in his hometown had begun building and excavating new homes underground. His mother, fortunately, was going to be looked after by a brother residing in one of the harbor towns, so he knew exactly where she'd be when he returned to find her with the cultist's cure.

As he dragged his sorry, soaking body up the steps to the door of Balmacara two men barred his way, ordinary city guards by the looks of them, red uniform, basic armor, fur-lined hats. After they checked his papers again, he was instructed to wait in the entrance hall.

Though impressive on the outside, Randur wasn't expecting quite this level of grandeur or skillful decoration inside Balmacara. In fact, the level of detail and wealth everywhere on display was simply arrogant. There were carvings of naturalistic foliage adorning every wall, every doorway. Gold and silver leaf glittered on the coving and picture frames. Floors and fireplaces were made from slabs of black marble, and elaborate lanterns shone along the main corridor, people's footsteps echoing some way in the distance.

Now this, Randur thought, *is definitely somewhere I could call home. A fine luxurious lifestyle to match my fine tastes.*

Another pair of guards escorted him to an antechamber. Within a heartbeat several more guards had entered, stared at him closely. Randur felt uneasy, began to reach again for his fake identification papers. Then suddenly he saw a young girl approaching defiantly through the corridor of guards. She marched up to him—all long strides and flowing hips, black-haired and definitely cute, but a little innocent for his tastes.

She stood there, and glared at him.

"Morning, lass." Randur offered her his papers.

She glanced briefly at them without saying a word. He knew enough about girls like that to know to put his documents back in his pocket.

"Randur Estevu." He risked offering her his hand to shake. "Can you show me where I need to go?"

"I am Jamur Eir," she announced, not even glancing at his offered hand. "I am Stewardess of Villjamur."

"Ah."

"I believe, Randur Estevu, that you are the man from Folke?"

"I am, yes."

"I am yes, *my lady*," she snapped. "Do they not teach manners on your island, or do they breed you all to be as backward as yourself?"

Well, so much for her prettiness lasting, with a scowl like that on her. He looked her up and down, still considering whether or not to keep on flirting. "I humbly apologize. *My* lady." He was never much one for formalities, unless there was a chance things might lead toward a little bedroom action.

"I was expecting someone a little older."

What was he supposed to say to that? A little older for what? "So was I," he returned, his face expressionless.

"Do you have a sword? I can't see one on you."

"No, they said I wouldn't be allowed to bring one in with me."

"Well, that's not very useful now, is it? How is a teacher meant to instruct without a sword?"

A teacher? What in Bohr's arse am I supposed to teach?

"At least you don't need one to dance, I suppose," Eir said.

"Dance?"

"Yes, dance. You did realize you were to teach sword *and* dancing, didn't you?"

"Indeed, lady." *Ha! So all I have to do is dance and fight!* "I apologize, but my thoughts were distracted momentarily, uhm, by the liquid depth and beauty of your eyes, my lady." There was a quiet groan from one of the guards, and he flashed her one of his better grins.

"I see there's nothing wrong with your island-boy oiliness." Eir was already turning away. "Balmacara is full of men. Don't think I don't know how the male mind works. Well come along then. We can't have you dripping water all over these floors."

✳

One of the servants showed Randur to his room, a small, well-decorated chamber with animal hides draped across the bed and floor. There was no glass in the window, but a thick tapestry kept the draft out, and a roaring log fire kept the heat coming. Several lanterns gave it a welcoming look. He considered it fit enough for entertaining ladies should the opportunity arise.

He dumped his belongings on the bed, then turned to the male servant. "Stewardess of Villjamur is a strange title," Randur probed. "What happened to the Emperor?"

"There isn't one, not at the moment." Little emotion came from the servant's answer. "The Emperor passed away a few days ago. The lady is in charge of matters until her elder sister, Jamur Rika, returns to the city."

Jamur Eir looked too young to be in charge, he reflected, but perhaps such a life of public duty had matured her. Her eyes had showed nothing for him to analyze.

Still, he was due to be paid a whole Jamún a month. Which was phenomenally high considering his food and accommodation were also provided.

Over the next hour, Randur discovered more about his new duties, about why they were hiring a dance master from so far away. "I mean, from Folke of all places," he had said with surprise. "I imagine there're numerous candidates to be found around Villjamur."

Why had the actual Randur Estevu been chosen? Was there some hidden agenda?

✳

When they met later, the Lady Eir herself provided the missing details. "We'll hold a dance competition, which is now a part of my sister's investiture celebration, called the Snow Ball," Eir explained. "The problem is that I can't dance particularly well, and it is known that Folke islanders are famous for their skills in that art."

What a ridiculous name for an event.

Randur remembered how very seriously they took dancing at home. It was more than just entertainment—it was a way of communicating, a kind of language, an art that had to be worked at, assiduously, that could tell stories, heal wounds, bring lovers together or drive them apart. Indeed, a physical expression of the soul. As a child he would often slip out of his mother's house at night to watch the local people expressing themselves in complex physical ways.

"And why sword skills? We know how seriously you Jokull folk take your fighting." He couldn't help a touch of bitterness as he said it, considering how the now-dependent populations of the Empire didn't exactly bask in the joy of Jokull's military dominance.

"My father's always warned that if I ever found myself in danger, it would be most likely from within the gates of Villjamur. I believe you on Folke have a special art of fighting at close-quarters."

"Yes," Randur said. "We call it *Vitassi.* It was originally part of *Vitassimo,* the dance which is one of our oldest traditions."

"Well, quite," Eir said, clearly losing interest. "The point being, my father urged me to learn some dueling style different enough to perhaps give me an advantage."

"This Snow Ball . . . Is it particularly important?"

"To some," Eir said. "It's to take everyone's mind off the Freeze. There is an award of around two hundred Jamúns for the winning participants."

Two hundred Jamúns. Randur tried not to show his eagerness. That was halfway to paying the cultist's fee. "I wouldn't have thought the money mattered to people like you—at the top of the social ladder, I mean?"

"Oh, it doesn't. We can buy anything we ever want."

Randur wondered why she had to say it with so much pride. "Well, with so much money, the people here must have all the happiness they could wish for."

"You might think that," she said, then left the room leaving him alone with the remnants of her melancholy.

✳

Randur couldn't put his finger on what exactly, but there was a strange mood in Balmacara. Everyone talked continuously about the gates of the city being closed. It made Randur wonder how he would ever get out of this city, should he gather up enough Jamúns to pay the Order of the Equinox. At all times, in Villjamur, it seemed there was someone, somewhere, talking about the impending ice. Many people prophesied doom—the end of civilization as they knew it. Randur himself generally lived for each day at a time, so tended not to think about the future. If it was something you could not see for yourself, why worry about it? He was more concerned with how quickly he could pull a girl.

And there were plenty of them in Balmacara. Randur was soon conscious of turning the heads of the female servants and courtiers.

He was used to such attention, so he smiled at the more attractive and winked at the least pretty ones. It helped that his personal guard was so ugly, too. There was a certain amount of tactical calculation in this, since a few of these women might have money he could extract with a kiss. Dartun's demands had forced such thoughts into Randur's head. Was he prostituting himself? This didn't really bother him. Sex was sex, and that was that—people made such a fuss about it.

He made sure always to be wearing good attire to mark himself out as a man of distinction, of rare breeding. He wore shirts as black as his own hair, the collar a fraction undone, britches worn tight, boots with pointed toes—as was fashionable in this city.

A declaration of intent. Here was someone to reckon with.

The next day he was taken to a small, rather poorly lit stone chamber in which the Lady Eir was waiting for him dressed in a baggy white outfit.

Randur studied her clothing, shook his head. "Well, for a start, you'll be better wearing something that fits to your body tightly."

"Really?" Eir said. "Why exactly would I need tight clothing? To enable the fetishes of your mind to flourish?"

"Lady, I'm afraid my mind gets its kicks from much wilder fetishes than that . . ." He shrugged. "No, I meant you'll get your sword caught in such loose material."

"I shall be wearing loose clothes most of my time. What's the use of training in things I won't be wearing when I'm attacked?"

"Whatever you wish. Now, first we'll need swords."

The door burst open.

What now?

Two city guard troops stepped in, then bowed to her. "My Lady Stewardess, Chancellor Urtica requires your urgent presence."

"What is it?" Eir said irritably.

"The chancellor's pressing for a motion of war, and this step requires your presence in the Atrium."

"War?" She frowned. "Who with?"

"The Varltung nation, my lady. There is now evidence that it was they who slaughtered our Night Guardsmen at Dalúk Point. Intelligence suggests they may well now provoke further attacks on the subsidiary nations of the Empire."

Randur listened carefully. Would the Varltungs really dare attack the Empire? If so his home island Folke would be first in line.

"Tell him I'll be there immediately." She turned her attention to Randur. "We'll continue this practice some other time. Meanwhile, the smiths are expecting you. You can choose any weapon you like."

"Cheers." He bowed and watched as she left the room.

✳ •

Out into the corridor, and he shambled around a corner into a gallery area where he spotted several richly dressed women about fifty paces away, their hair elegantly pinned up in the latest styles. His eyes lit up, a thousand opportunities flashing through his mind. For a moment he paused to watch them from behind the cover of what looked like the shell of a giant insect. At first he had taken it to be a suit of armor, but on closer inspection he realized the plating wasn't made of metal. It was the exoskeleton of some bizarre creature, pinned to the wall with a bolt, its mouth still open as if in a dying scream.

Randur shivered, regarded the women instead. He tried to listen to the snippets of conversation that echoed along the corridor.

"He's got a lot of Jamúns to his name, so I've heard . . ."

"Not quite sure he's marriage material . . ."

"Could you love him, though?"

"That's not the point, is it? He doesn't have to know what you might get up to on the side."

"Astrid knows I've seen better examples of a man . . . Not much physically, and he's also pretty old . . ."

"But still, there's a lot to be said for his house. I know I could be very happy living there. So I think you should go for him . . ."

Money-grabbing sows, Randur thought.

He took a deep breath, and proceeded toward them, arming himself with a few sweet lines to deprive them of their wealth.

CHAPTER 11

✳

THE HORSES RODE IN A RHYTHM MATCHING HIS HEARTBEAT, OR WAS IT the other way around? Brynd had done this for so many years it had become a dulled instinct, the sort of routine only noticed when he was not riding the length and breadth of the Empire. Brynd had been forcing his companions to ride until the horses were exhausted, only stopping at hamlets and villages, when the wilderness proved more violent than anticipated. Bitter winds, followed by harsh sleet. The few remaining Night Guards crested the hill that overlooked the port of Gish. It was a bleak landscape this side of the island. Low clouds skimmed the horizon, undermining massive skies.

Because of the recent deaths of his comrades, at nights when they rested he sometimes stared at his sword blade and at the white-skinned man reflected back, and tried to make more sense of himself. Perhaps he had grown used to the luxury of command, standing so far back from any direct combat. He had wanted this, an opportunity to prove himself a true man—because of his unusual skin tone as much as his sexuality. People always judged him in unspoken terms, so he had to respond with action only because that was expected of him. And look where that action had taken him—many good soldiers and friends, dead.

Maybe there was too much time to think on these journeys.

The estuary was crowded with sailing vessels of the Jamur Second

Dragoons. Brynd's own first regiment. Two dozen longships were blocking off one side of the harbor, allowing only a few fishing boats to pass out to sea. He could see the raised standards of at least two divisions—the Wolf and Eagle brigades—on the shore this side of the port town. Gish had only become a military port in recent years, following assessments of how the ice age might affect the navigational channels of the major island of Jokull.

Blink while reading the history of this region and you might miss that it had become a significant commercial center too, based upon supply and billeting of the army. It was now humming with armorers licensed directly from Villjamur, innkeepers, fishermen, wool merchants. And, below the gloss, the side of life that respectable people always looked away from: brothels, gambling dens involving big dog-fights or dice, slaves beaten senseless over a chore forgotten, and brawls between soldiers over a spilt tankard.

Brynd looked back toward the ships, deciding after his recent encounters that he wanted as many vessels as possible to escort them on the return voyage. If nothing else, it would provide a positive statement: Here she comes, the new Empress, and she's well protected.

✳

Two hours later, they boarded the *Black Frieter,* the largest of the long-ships docked at Gish. An old boat, once thought to house souls of the damned, it had been recovered from pirates decades ago, and now took its place in the Empire's fleet. Sea Captain Sang greeted them, if it could be called a greeting, then made sure the carriage would be well protected on the adjoining shore by several women of the Wolf Regiment. These quieter moments of travel always forced Apium to analyze the current status of the military.

Apium was always suspicious of the Dragoon Marines, despite them being a focal component of most military campaigns. They were a crucial force across the entire Archipelago, having developed effective techniques for short raids, and larger-scale invasions. A formidable reputation proceeded them, even though it hadn't been put to good use in recent years. An air of arrogance surrounded them; they assumed nothing could be done without their participation. Sang herself was the embodiment of this, a low-born, in cultural terms, who had achieved great things, and a woman only in physical terms. And even Apium was certain she was no lady, more vulgar in her manner than most male soldiers he'd known. She'd boasted to him once about all the islands she'd visited—travels around the entire Archipelago that no one else had managed. Said she'd even circumnavigated the Varltung islands, but he wasn't so sure, since there was no proof of such a voyage. She would customarily employ mainly women sailors, using the few men simply for raw physical chores. And he could make a good guess as to what services these might include.

Apium had joined Brynd, Lupus, and Nelum on deck; Brynd was commenting on the salt refinery recently built, and that as yet stood as nothing more than a precarious shack on the quayside. He was clearly unimpressed.

Gish was altogether a decrepit place. No major division of the army had been deployed from here for a good while, so many soldiers were rotting away here—their time taken up with gambling, brawls, casual sex. That, he reflected, was what you got from doing nothing more rigorous than training exercises.

Brynd was exceptional in taking the opportunity of using cultists to develop training strategies on Kullrún, an islet off the opposite coast of Jokull. Cultist technology was normally to scare men senseless, to drive back arrows, form illusions of troop movements, create phantoms that followed them long into their dreams at night. Any threatening scenario could thus be recreated, played out again and again, until the soldiers learned how to kill their enemy in the most efficient manner. A time-consuming business, but essential for producing the best soldiers. When it came down to it, when a soldier aimed an arrow at another man's face for the very first time, releasing it could prove difficult. And many of the soldiers currently in the Dragoons, Marines, or Regiment of Foot were fresh recruits who had signed up to avoid the hardships of the ice age since the military provided a guaranteed wage.

Boys and girls from the poorest parts of the Empire fighting for the richest.

Was that how all armies had been recruited throughout history?

✳

A few hours later, Brynd was the first to step down off the *Black Frieter* and onto the main island of Southfjords, under a massive sky filled with fast-moving cumulus, looming over a landscape littered with small wind-ravaged trees tilting at an angle. Terns arced over their heads, heading off toward their high cliff colonies further along the shore.

The four guards set off along a gravel track that cut up through a green hill, and Brynd suspected that those black-clad strangers, carrying swords and axes, would be an intimidating spectacle for a young woman who had been told nothing of why she was summoned home.

Even in decay the temple was an imposingly beautiful building, with its limestone arches and soaring spire flanked by two smaller ones. As Jorsalir structures went, this was certainly one of the more extravagant temples, more sizable than the churches Brynd had seen back in Villjamur. Maybe several hundred years old, so not remotely ancient by the Archipelago's standards, obviously it had been constructed in a period when the Jorsalir had commanded phenomenal power and wealth, unlike now, when the Council even levied tax upon them.

As they approached the building, three women stepped out, their green gowns whipping around their bodies in the wind like banners of war. The looks on their faces were just as grim, and Brynd asked his companions to remain still while he moved ahead alone.

Two of the women were aging slightly, graying hair framing their delicate features. The third was younger, but the graceful way she walked and her general demeanor made her appear ageless. He noticed a white dryas attached to her breast.

"Sele of Jamur," Brynd greeted them. "Commander Brynd Lathraea of the Night Guard."

There it was: that shocked look on their faces as they took in his skin, his eyes—always the same reaction.

"Ah, the albino? Sele of Jamur, commander," said the youngest of the three. "My name is Ardune, and I'm a priestess here. These two are my clerics."

"You received notification of our arrival?"

"Indeed," Ardune said. She blinked several times in the wind, as she looked back over his shoulder toward the other three men.

Brynd tactfully drew his cloak over his sword. "And does the Lady Rika know what has been happening?"

"She's been told very little, but has been waiting inside the temple for some time now."

"Right," Brynd said. "Well, I'm here to return her to Villjamur. We must leave as soon as possible."

"You're taking her away then," Ardune said. "Just like that?"

"She has a role to fulfill, priestess," Brynd explained. "We can't always choose what we want to do in life." *And I myself know all about that.*

"Indeed not, commander, but you cannot simply *take* her. She has a life here, you understand?"

"Yes, I do," Brynd continued, trying to be sensitive to the priestess's feelings. "However, she's been enjoying a quiet life here because of who she is. If she was a native, or simply a peasant, she'd never have been able to live in such a privileged position. Well, now the time's come for who she is to really matter. You understand, it's not just a few priestesses that this matters to—it's an entire Empire?"

Something faded in her eyes then, conceding defeat. "Quite. Well, please be sensitive. She's a person, not just a title."

"Of course I will. Remember, I'm the one who has to tell her about her father. I promise I'll not crush her."

Ardune appeared to have a genuine affection for Rika. Still, Brynd didn't know what to make of her, since he wasn't one to trust the mind of a Jorsalir. Not that they were untrustworthy in themselves, more that they had conditioned their minds to think on a different level, to question the world in a way no one else did. It gave them an air of superiority that he felt was unjustified.

Ardune led him inside the temple.

Rika's room contained minimal furniture, a few parchments on the wall, faded through exposure to sunlight, fabrics smelling of dried lavender, darkened limestone, a small burning fire in the corner. If there was indeed Bohr or Astrid up there, Brynd assumed they didn't much care for elaborate furnishings.

She was sitting on a chest, Rika, staring out of a narrow arched window, a book forgotten on her lap. This was clearly Eir's sister, although her face was more slender, making her cheekbones jut out unattractively. Her black hair was tied back plainly—no style in her appearance, no finesse.

"Jamur Rika, Sele of Jamur, I am Commander Brynd Lathraea and I have some . . . bad news for you, I fear." He hesitated. "Your father, Emperor Johynn—I'm afraid he passed away some few days ago."

"Oh," Rika replied. No emotion in her voice, nothing whatsoever. "Why, thank you for telling me this. It really is very kind of you to journey all this way."

Brynd held her gaze as if to work out what was happening in her mind. She appeared to be barely disturbed by the bad news. He may as well have just told her it was going to rain today. He knew she had problems with her father, which was why she had spent the last few years in exile here. Was that her anger forcing out any other emotions? Or was it her religious training, her perfectly controlled mind making her emotionally dead?

"The Council of Villjamur have nominated you as the one to inherit all that was your father's, since you're his eldest blood relative. You realize what this means?"

She met his gaze with silence, with a cold stare—no, a neutral stare, nothing in it. This girl seemed the embodiment of emptiness.

"Jamur Rika, you're to become Empress," Brynd said. "Ruler of the Jamur Empire, its nations, its people. I'm here, therefore, at the request of the Council, to escort you back to Villjamur immediately."

She stood, gazing out of the window again—at the sea, the clouds. Gulls screamed as they accelerated upward. More life in the natural environment than her reactions. "And what choice do I have in the matter?"

"Honestly?" Brynd said.

"Yes."

"Very little." He sighed. "You have a duty."

"I also have a life *here*, commander."

"Yes, that's not gone unnoticed," Brynd said, with a step toward her. He followed her gaze to a wild cat out on the grass below. It was ripping into a gull, blood covering the victim's white wings that were half-extended, broken. "Strong cats you have here, for it to bring down a gull."

"Indeed," she said. "Everything here is that little bit more . . . wild."

"Nature's creatures learn to cope in any conditions presented to them."

"It depends, of course, on what exactly those conditions are," Rika said.

Silence followed yet again, while Brynd stood next to her, hoping that this proximity might symbolize to her that he was at her side in more than just the physical sense. He watched the skies begin to bleed snow. Winds blew in stronger, the wall hangings rattled.

"I'll come with you," she sighed. "Just give me a moment to get ready."

✳

Apium hurled a pebble into the sea some distance away from the *Black Frieter.* It vanished from sight long before it pierced the water, lost in the eruptions caused by surf beating granite.

"Well, at least she's coming willingly," Nelum said, trying to light his pipe against the strong wind. He was failing miserably. "And, when she eventually strolls down here, we can embark and get her back home. And then we can put our feet up for a while."

Brynd glanced over at Apium.

"We can put our feet up for a bit, can't we?" Nelum said, examining their glances worriedly. He placed the unlit pipe back in his pocket.

"Not exactly, no," Brynd confessed. "Chancellor Urtica has informed me of some strange occurrences further north, and we've to protect the Empire by investigating. It's serious, according to eyewitness accounts. There have been reports of serious killings, and it's up to us to establish order, and to give the local populace reassurance."

"So why not send the Dragoons to investigate?" Lupus asked. "Why send the elite soldiers?"

"Lad's got a point there, Brynd," Apium said.

"Elite soldiers are required, and we've skills and training superior to the ordinary standards of the army. We in the Night Guard have access to some cultist-enhanced weaponry. After all, we're cultist-enhanced ourselves, let's not forget. And we possess better swords, bows that fire more accurately. And, anyway, I doubt that the sight of a massive army traipsing across the tundra would inspire any confidence that all is calm. It's easier to move in small groups, so I want one or two units with us, a couple of hundred soldiers at most."

"Maybe the armies are needed elsewhere," Nelum stated, his mind working ahead, processing all the possibilities.

"Not without my knowing," Brynd said. "You forget I've command of all the Empire's armies."

"So now we're to be galloping around after three-cocked unicorns," Apium grumbled.

"We don't know what these creatures are yet," Brynd said. "Unicorns or not, we shall go and investigate."

"Aye, maybe you're right." Apium chuckled. "Look, here's our Lady Rika."

CHAPTER 12

✳

As the sun rose lazily over Villjamur, Investigator Rumex Jeryd left his house in the Kaiho district. He walked past Gulya Gata, down alongside the irens near Gata du Quercus, Hotel Villjamur, and the inn called the Dryad's Saddle. There were a few eccentric shops down this way, high-end purveyors of drugs and erotica, where you could apparently find "love potions" conducive to controlled rape. Nothing like as described in romantic songs, and why the potions were allowed, he had no idea. That was Villjamur for you—as long as you had enough money you could get whatever you wanted, and to hell with ethics. You could wander these streets and become defined by your fetishes.

In the shadows of high walls, where the road curved down to the right, the kids of Gamall Gata were already waiting for him. From the top of the street you could clearly see the two main culprits, the two that were always there, each maybe ten years old, a blond and a redhead, layered up with warm clothing, thick gloves on, and with snowballs ready in their palms. Jeryd stared hard at the kids—he had to make them wonder for a moment if this was a mistake.

They did not.

The snowballs came arcing through the air, but exploded too short, smashed at his feet, and he smiled. "Not today, lads."

He turned, sniffed the chill air, began to walk away—

—A snowball slapped his head.

Bastards.

He could see the blond and the redhead running off, their arms windmilling with excitement, the others nowhere to be seen, then all that was left was the echo of laughter as snow dripped off Jeryd's head.

✳

Robes wrapped tight around him, snowballs nowhere to be seen, Jeryd proceeded along one of the lesser known paths of the city, his breath clouding in front of his face like a ghost that wouldn't leave him alone.

He ran what few details there were of Delamonde Ghuda's murder over and over in his mind. The case was particularly difficult because the number of people who might have a motive to murder the councilor were high. So, a high-profile death, and such a cruel way of dying.

The only likely cause could have been use of a relic, so that made a cultist the most likely suspect. But in general, cultists seemed to have no use for councilors, considered that they operated at a level above government. Above everyone else, in fact. And because of their valuable services in military campaigns, cultists tended to remain on good terms with those high up in Villjamur. So no, a cultist didn't seem likely after all, although he still had to consider them.

He would have to penetrate the Council Atrium to find out what projects Ghuda was working on before he was killed. It must have been something significant, if his murder was the best way to stall it.

And what about the woman, Tuya, who was the last person to see him alive? Nor was he looking forward to confronting Ghuda's wife to explain how he had spent his final night on earth.

On top of all of this, he was due to meet with his own wife, Marysa, this evening. And how was he going to persuade her to come back to him?

What a day.

Tryst had arranged to meet him later. The young human was currently "interrogating" a man suspected of burglary that had taken place in a street in Caveside. Jeryd let him get on with it on his own, because torture was something Tryst was good at—and it wouldn't necessarily be physical. Tryst had a gift for mental torture, would frequently have the suspect in fits of tears or else exploding with rage. Either way, he got what he wanted, which suited Jeryd fine so long as it was conducted within the legal guidelines. You had to do things by the book or those higher up would use it against you, some day when you happened to fall out of favor.

Jeryd loved this side of the city. He was now standing just beyond the Astronomer's Glass Tower, its bizarre octagonal structure towering above him, its expanses of glass capturing a rare moment of red sunlight that was trying to penetrate the cloud and mist. This side of Villjamur was certainly preferable to the neighborhood adjoining the caves. Unfortunately, most of his cases inevitably led to Caveside. Living conditions were terrible there, back where poverty was kept hidden out of sight. Inferior sanitation pervaded the area with a constant stench, though many might think it preferable to being locked outside the city.

Armed with questions, he approached a little house virtually hidden among its neighbors. Despite being so central within the city, people usually walked straight past the place as if they didn't want to see, without even knowing they were doing so. Its inconspicuous metal door was set in smooth pale stone. He knocked firmly and waited, and it was eventually opened by a raven-haired woman, her long, thin face pallid and gaunt.

She was a banshee.

"Morning. Investigator Rumex Jeryd. I have a few questions."

"Yes, of course." Her voice was soothingly deep as they always were—unless they were screaming. "Please, do come in."

Jeryd stepped inside her fragrant home, drawing his tail in behind him so that it didn't get caught in the heavy door. The house was intensely dark, the smell of lavender powerful. He'd been here several times before, and on each visit he wished they had put in a window to let in some daylight and fresh air. Colored lanterns burned, as did a small log fire. There were several women ranging from young to old, all wearing black, gray or white fabrics. They were sitting on chairs placed randomly throughout the house. All of them had similar gaunt faces, similar mannerisms. Some were reading or studying, others were weaving material. There was a claustrophobia here among these women, maybe sisters and mothers or something closer still, as if they were suffocating in unison, tightening their bonds on each other as they suffered. He never understood, nor commented on their situation.

"Please, be seated, investigator," the woman said. "I'll go and fetch Mayter Sidhe."

She left the room.

Jeryd sat himself down on a simple wooden chair. The furniture here was rustic—as if they couldn't afford anything else. It seemed out of place for a home so near the Astronomer's Tower and the richer irens, but maybe it had been here from generations ago. A few of the women hummed gently, rocking back and forth in their chairs as if mildly insane: not a comforting noise, more an eerie lament. Paranoia forced him to wonder vaguely if this meant he would die at any point soon, as if just being around them was putting him a step closer.

Mayter Sidhe suddenly arrived, the banshee who had been present at the scene of Ghuda's murder, and her wail had declared his death to the whole of Villjamur. Black-haired, white-gowned, young look-ing, too, but with that same haunted expression that the other ban-shees possessed. Blue eyes, with a strange distance within them that he could never understand. As with the others he had encountered her before, because whenever there was a death in the city, they were always the first on the scene.

He stood up as she appeared.

"Good morning, Investigator Jeryd."

"Morning, Mayter." He sat down again.

"So this is about Councilor Ghuda?" She pulled up a chair, sat next to him, and unnerved him a little, this close presence. This air of death.

"Yes," Jeryd said. "Just the normal procedure. But this has to be considered an extremely high-profile murder. The victim, as you know, was a very senior member of the Council."

"We're all the same, once we're dead, investigator. Our titles do not follow us."

"Right. But while the rest of us are still alive, there's work to be done that can make the whole . . . predeath concept a little easier to deal with."

"Point taken."

"So," Jeryd said, "I take it as usual, you knew he'd be killed."

"Yes, but not until he was."

Whatever the hell that means . . . "And it was too late by that point?"

"It always is. We're not lifesavers." She drummed her slender fingers on the table. For a moment Jeryd was distracted by the rings adorning them that caught the dull light of the room.

"No one suggested you were. So you were . . . in the area then? Or at least on the scene pretty quick."

"Yes, I was, as you say, in the area. I was merely buying some vegetables. Then came the vision—and you know what happens after that."

"Right," Jeryd said. "Up until that point, you saw nothing?"

"No more than any normal person would."

"What about after?"

"Again, no more than other people who came on the scene afterward. I got there in reasonable time, but I saw nothing strange."

Jeryd straightened. "Okay, so tell me about the vision you experienced, if you don't mind."

"It was like any other—the same glimpse through the eyes of the victim at his final heartbeat. Except . . . well, all I saw was a shadow, but it was like . . . like nothing I've seen before. A wild creature of some kind, I'd say. And then it seemed to disappear into the light— upward."

"Go on," Jeryd said. This was the first concrete statement he'd received so far. If you could trust a banshee.

"That's it, just a shadow. A creature I've never seen before. Then I knew where I'd find him. And I instantly felt as if I wanted to vomit, so I knew he was just about to die."

Jeryd said, "And you can tell me nothing more about the creature?"

"Nothing."

"What did it look like?"

"I can't tell." She began to seem impatient. "It was definitely not human or rumel. That's all."

"Okay. There were no flashes in your vision that might indicate who'd want him dead?"

"No, investigator. City politics makes little difference to our lives."

A chair scraped over to one side in the other room, and Jeryd glimpsed one of the other banshees rush outside. As she slammed the door behind her, one of the lanterns flickered.

He turned to regard Mayter Sidhe once again. "Anything strange happening that you know of?"

"Nothing that seems related. There're rumors of some of the Council members being Ovinists . . ."

Jeryd was aware those rumors had been circulating for years, the degrees of information depending on which tavern you drank in. Stories told of politicians gathered in darkened rooms drinking pig's blood. Divining secrets from these animals' hearts. Bathing in offal. Ritualistic slaughter. Even if it was true, it was all possibly harmless. How much damage could you do with a dead pig?

"Well," Jeryd said, "I've not seen any evidence of such practices. And it's very hard to bring the law down on those who think they're above it. Short of forcing them all into a Jorsalir church for cleansing, there's not a lot we can do."

Faintly, in the distance, there was a scream, and he realized that it must have come from the woman who had left a few minutes earlier.

Meanwhile, Mayter Sidhe regarded him with an unsettling gaze. Jeryd never knew what these banshees really thought about anything: they never opened up, never showed any emotion. Yet they seemed to get distraught and upset whenever a death was near, as if they felt the same pain, and were sharing it with the sufferer. Nor did they ever seem to age. Mayter Sidhe herself could be anywhere between forty and ninety years, yet she looked eternally young, didn't she, and even vaguely beautiful. If anyone knew much about the secrets of these witch women of Villjamur, they didn't share them. Amid all gossip purveyed in the taverns of the city, the banshees were least spoken of. Perhaps it was a healthy fear that they could announce anyone's death simply at their own volition. As there existed the possibility it could be your own death, he felt it was best not to anger them.

Jeryd realized he would get no further information here, so he said good-bye, then proceeded on to interview the person who he was least looking forward to talking to.

✳

Up here the houses were also tall and narrow, three-floor constructions, most elaborately decorated with ridiculous statuettes of angelic creatures. The place reminded him of the ghost plays he'd watched in the underground theaters when he was still a young rumel. Beula Ghuda, of course, already knew about her husband's death, something at least for Jeryd to feel relieved about. Dealing with dead bodies and criminals was much easier than talking to the relatives of someone who had died in suspicious circumstances. You had to look them directly in the eye while being prepared for any number of reactions, any number of extreme emotions.

How could this happen?

What do you mean, dead?

You bastard, don't lie to me.

In his more morbid moments, back when his wife loved him still, he would wonder how she might react to being informed of Jeryd's own death, and played out her possible reactions as if he was a fly on the wall. No matter how many years he had been in the Inquisition, these parts were often the most difficult, and as he knocked on the door the feeling was still as unpleasant as the very first time. A fragile-looking blonde answered it. She was about mid- to late-thirties, a green silk dress draped loosely over a tiny frame, with a face as gloomy as the banshees he had just been visiting—and you couldn't blame her for that, could you, at a time like this?

"Beula Ghuda? I'm Investigator Jeryd. Would it be all right for me to ask a few questions relating to . . . to your recent loss?"

"Yes, of course, investigator," she said. "Please, step inside."

Inside the house seemed as grand as the exterior, overloaded with what Jeryd considered were pointless ornaments and bad taste. To be rich in Villjamur seemed a waste of money: all they did with their wealth was buy unnecessary objects. The city having not been under threat for so long, the Empire having expressed its dominance far and wide, the result was that the wealthy citizens of Villjamur had become more attached to their material comforts, and the gap between the richest and poorest had only bloomed.

Beula Ghuda sat him down in an over-warm room full of jeweled lanterns, colored lights. Rich fabric, desirable brand-weave from Villiren, was draped from each corner of the ceiling to the center point. There was a large window of the highest quality glass, from which were views over the summit of the city walls to the snow-flicked tundra beyond. The room smelled of stale incense, and he guessed by the number of books lying casually around that Beula was something of a lady of leisure.

"How are you managing?" Jeryd began tentatively.

"Oh, so-so." She gave an ironic wince that he didn't find unattractive. "Truth is, investigator, we were not really that close—in the end."

He was surprised by her matter-of-fact response, but it made what he had to say a little easier. "I'm sorry."

She shrugged. "Yes, these things happen."

She perched herself on the edge of a cushioned armchair of a style so typical of the era of the previous two Emperors, Gulion and Haldun, with motifs glorifying combat carved into its thick wooden side-panels. She clasped her wrist with the other hand and stared to the floor for some time. He gave her some time to gather her thoughts.

Eventually, she glanced up. "So, how can I help you?"

"Were you aware of his final movements?" Jeryd said.

She looked right past him. "No."

"I'm afraid it's not what a wife would want to hear."

She shrugged.

"He was last seen leaving the apartment of another woman. She has confirmed that they spent the night together." He held her gaze for as long as she would allow.

"I understand, investigator," she said. Then added, "What was she like?"

"You mean the woman he was with?"

"Yes, the woman."

"She was a prostitute by profession, although I believe it wasn't something he paid for in this instance."

"That's a relief," she murmured bitterly.

Jeryd contemplated her words. It wasn't as if he actually under-stood the female mind these days. He gave her a moment before he spoke again.

"You know of anyone who might want him dead?"

"Other than me? Is that what you mean?"

"No, I mean because of his activities within the Council, mainly."

"Well, there were plenty who were jealous of his success, but he was a popular man other than that."

"Were you aware of any controversial new policies he was cam-paigning for?"

"No, regarding his work, he never really talked much to me. You know, for such a popular man, he wasn't all that popular here at home."

"If you don't mind me saying, you seem fairly comfortable with his death."

"I'm a strong believer in Astrid, investigator. I therefore believe in rebirth, and that he'll be reborn soon in a position reflecting his be-havior here in this past life. You know, investigator, I did love him in my own way."

Jeryd felt sympathy and some concern. He himself wasn't much of a religious type.

"Over the last year or so I was hurt that he stopped coming with me to church. He wouldn't pray in the Bohr section, and seemed to forget all about spirituality. I'd even almost say he'd discovered some-thing else."

"Something else?"

"Yes. As if something took his mind. I say this only as I'm a moral and spiritual woman, but it was like he stopped being the man I knew, and began operating with a different set of beliefs entirely." She stood, turned to the window. "Just look how much it's snowing now!"

Jeryd stepped alongside her, looked out across Villjamur.

The snow had begun to fall as hard as he had ever seen it, leaving the spire-crowded skies of Villjamur looking even more claustropho-bic. *By Bohr, this is enough to fuel those brats in Gamall Gata for several weeks now.*

Despite the thick drifts building up, it was hypnotic, gentle. Beula began to cry quietly as if the snow itself had altered her emotional state, bringing on some primitive madness. Jeryd walked away to the other side of the room, as he always felt uncomfortable with the intensity and depth of emotions that humans seemed so ready to express.

He watched her crying at the window, framed by the snow falling outside.

CHAPTER 13

✳

RANDUR STEPPED BACK WITH A FLAMBOYANT GESTURE, WATCHED EIR tumble to the cold floor, her sword slipping across the stone in a sideways fall. She cursed at him as she retrieved it.

"Pretty keen to inflict a wound, weren't we?" he remarked. "And I didn't realize you Imperial ladies had such a sweet way with words."

Eir pushed herself up, panting heavily, much more than anger in her face.

"With *Vitassi,* you shouldn't fight with the heart," Randur reminded her, sauntering back to his starting position. "Such sentiments are likely to make you appear brave in your obituary, admittedly. You weren't mindful enough. You weren't in the *moment.* You let anger cloud your skills. Remember, it's not all about the sword—that's simply an extension of you."

Eir eyed him with contempt, and he had left many bedrooms in the dawn light to be familiar with that look. She moved in to attack him again, but was then rapidly on the defensive as he forced her into a series of classic *Vitassi* postures. Metal clashed, boots scuffed on stone, noises so familiar to him, that at times like this he could often forget he was still even holding a sword.

"Good," Randur said. "That's much better." He sighed as he pushed past her, then slapped her buttocks lightly with the flat of his sword, deliberately fueling her anger, working her into a rage, forcing her to get more control of herself. He tripped her up, and she fell forward.

"I hate you." Eir's lip began to bleed.

He walked over to retrieve her sword. "I'm not here to be liked. I'm merely here to make sure you don't get yourself killed—an unlikely task, as it currently stands. And for the moment, you still need my help."

"And you expect me to actually *dance* with you after all this humiliation?"

"No, *you* expect me to dance with you."

She sat upright with her legs crossed, appearing to contemplate her bruises.

He offered his hand to help her up, but she ignored it and got herself on her feet once again. Randur handed her back the sword. "Well, anyway, your sword technique's improving and I can see you've got some good potential. You could be fighting with the Dragoons within the month."

She said nothing, began walking stiffly away, then she stopped, and he followed the line of her eyes to the window. A cold wind gusted into the chamber.

They stepped together to that opening in the thick stone walls which looked over one entire side of the city. The view was partially obscured by numerous bridges and spires. A thick fall of snow drifted down from the gray sky. In its smothering embrace, the horizon was no longer perceptible.

"So much of it," Eir murmured, lost in her thoughts.

"Yeah," Randur said, becoming lost in his own.

✳

Dartun watched the young boy snatch the relic from the group of cultists. The lad had guts, he'd give him that. Those men weren't from his order, and were simply holding the device out for all to see. Too cocky, too arrogant, not nearly careful enough. *The fuckers deserve to lose it.*

Dartun drew his fuligin cloak around him, absorbing shadow, then followed the boy who now ran in his direction, a scruffy little chap dressed in thick rags, obviously from Caveside. Darting down an arterial series of alleyways, the boy had soon lost everyone except Dartun.

Last night he had coughed so much he thought he would emit blood, and he had never felt like this before.

The cobbles were slick with snow in the sun since the last snowstorm. Some streets had already been washed down with salt water. The wind worked its way relentlessly through the cramped alleys. Dartun cornered the boy finally at a dead end where buildings towered up on every side, leaving the pair in shadows. A strange serenity prevailed this far away from the main streets of the city, suggesting that the further he walked down these passageways, the less easily he'd find his way back.

"Hand it over," Dartun demanded.

The boy eyed him with a mixture of curiosity and arrogance, obviously weighing up the cultist. His blue eyes were dazzling. "Fuck you, mister."

Dartun laughed. "Some spirit in you, I see."

"What's it to you, wanker?" The lad shuffled from one foot to the other, looking for a way past.

"Just give the relic to me." Dartun extended his hand. "You don't want any harm to befall you."

"No, it's meant to be mine, it's my destiny," the boy said. Then, he threatened, "I'll use it on you."

"You really don't want to try that."

"No?" The boy reached into his pocket then was holding up the silver device itself. It looked like a compass, a subtle navigational tool of some kind, perhaps used to divine directions.

"No," Dartun insisted.

The boy ignored him, flicked the relic open, began to press on it at random, looking to and from Dartun with eager eyes, and all Dartun did meanwhile was take several slow steps backward, guessing what might happen, wondering only what form it would take.

A ball of purple smoke erupted, extending in every direction.

Just enough time to see the skin of the boy peel back before he became a myriad of chunks of flesh and bone, which distorted then liquidized as if it was paint. Dartun had ducked in time before he heard the gentle explosion, bringing his fuligin cloak over his face. He felt the remains of the child hitting him first then slapping against the cobbles.

Dartun stood up to regard the mess. Blood was sprayed in a circle all around the relic, which remained intact on the ground, a glistening unstained piece of metal. Mere fragments of the boy remained: the odd bone, a tiny segment of skull. At least his fuligin cloak was so intensely dark that the stains were barely showing up on it.

Primed with an explosion detonator. Haven't seen one of those for a while.

"They'll never learn," he said out loud; he reached down, scooped up the relic, pocketed it, then walked away.

Two nights earlier, he had felt a stiffness in his legs that he'd never noticed before.

❈

Four days ago, he had grazed his hand on stone, drawing blood.

He'd looked at his injury for an hour, contemplating why this was happening, contemplating that narrowing line between life and death.

If you cannot die, it means you're not alive to begin with. And now the system of relics is gradually failing me.

Dartun repeated this mantra over and over again in his mind, forcing himself to believe it. Home, in a darkened chamber within the headquarters of the Order of the Equinox, he stared at the relic taken from the dead boy. Every relic was somehow protected against use by any lay person, the secrets of handling it known only to the numerous cultists who frequented these islands. Ignorant meddlers were poisoned for their trouble, or corrupted by holding something unknown, the lucky ones only losing a single limb. Other relics used bolts of energy to stop the heart, and some used a toxic gas. Their fate was never pleasant, but it ensured that cultist secrets remained exactly that. And so it had worked for tens of thousands of years.

He held the artifact up to a shaft of light penetrating a slat in the wooden shutter. This new relic was a type of *wend*, that would have assisted the Ancients in their travels. Even though it wouldn't help him regain his immortality, he was always delighted to find another relic, whatever its powers. This one was a particularly wonderful piece of equipment. The internal materials were not of this era, that was nearly always certain, although the casing was some form of current silver, so perhaps it had been modified. Round, fitting easily in the palm of his hand, it absorbed the thin beam of light from the daylight outside, and it held his attention endlessly.

Dartun considered himself the best cultist around. He could not only use relics, but modify them, developing his own devices from the ancient wonders. He could combine them, could manipulate the different technologies for his own research and, over his abnormally long lifetime, he had made countless notes, developed theories, tested them, tried to fill in the numerous gaps in knowledge. He had pushed the boundaries of what was known and, by doing so, blurred the boundaries between life and death. But there was something evading him that he wanted to achieve. And he wanted to attain it more than ever because of his sudden awareness of mortality.

This is the way my world ends, he reflected: *not with a whimper, but with a fucking big bang.*

Again, today he had contemplated the signs of his aging.

Deeper lines in his face.

Gray hairs.

Aches.

Cuts and grazes on his skin.

These were the legacy of mortals, things he hadn't been used to. Every time he identified one of these minor deteriorations, he would stand still and examine it for the best part of an hour, trying to accept the fact that he was dying. It took over nearly every part of mind-space. There seemed no room to think of anything else.

He finally placed the relic to one side, walked over to one of his numerous bookshelves, selected a notebook. From another shelf he drew a map from a large stack. Then he lit three lanterns, placed one on his desk, set to work.

Last month he had suffered a migraine for two days. His first such inconvenience in hundreds of years.

The main subject of concern for everyone in Villjamur, on Jokull island, and every other island of the Empire, was the Freeze—the ice age, long predicted by astronomers and historians. But it had to have its good points, and for Dartun, it meant that he could finally investigate one of the celebrated myths of the world.

The Realm Gates.

The mythical doors to other worlds. It was said that the Dawnir built them, the race that constructed the islands under the red sun, to link worlds with others. Some priests whispered that there would be direct access to the realms of the gods, some said that instead you could walk straight to the realms of hell. No one seemed to know for certain and, as a result, many assumed that they were simply stories spread by Jorsalir priests. Dartun himself had spent hundreds of years documenting all the historical accounts available. But he had access only to what the empires of the west had detailed, a skewed history. The nations of Varltung and further east passed on their history by word of mouth only, by the warmth of a fire no doubt. *Romantic*, Dartun thought, *but it only gives me one side of the picture.* He had, however, pieced together the rough location of where he thought the Realm Gates lay. That meant traversing endless water, over the seas to the north of the Empire's domains, way beyond Folke and far north of Tineag'l. But the Freeze had now caused the formation of thick and stable ice sheets. It meant he could now explore those regions more easily, without being knocked endless days off course by the hazards of rough seas.

The coming ice age meant he was finally able to travel to other worlds.

The fact that his immortality was fading only spurred him on to achieve this quickly, didn't it, because there was no more luxury of time. So he would soon be leaving Villjamur accompanied by members of the Order of the Equinox, some who had already left in advance. They'd find new worlds to the north. And there was always a vague, desperate hope in his mind that somewhere in these new worlds would lie the technology to help him prolong his life. He had little else to bank on.

There was a knock at the door, and he looked up in surprise. "What is it?"

"It's me, Verain," replied a female voice.

He registered her slender figure before her face; as he tended to do, even though her face was equally exquisite—slender and symmetrical features beneath rook-black hair. She always wore a snug-fitting dark uniform, too. Dartun had come upon her as an orphan girl using a relic to entertain customers for money in some questionable Caveside tavern. Firstly he wondered how she had got hold of it, then he wondered how she had learned to use it. It turned out she'd stolen it off a cultist who'd been trying to get her to give him a blow job, so she'd taken what was his after he'd shown her how to use it. She was only thirteen at the time, but quick-witted from the start. Dartun had immediately hunted down the cultist in question, one from some useless, minor sect. He had beaten him with Dawnir energy and left him with just enough life so that he could realize he didn't really have a life anymore.

It was soon obvious that even at such a young age, Verain connected with the Dawnir technology in a manner worthy of any cultist. So he decided to take her in rather than leave her on the streets of Villjamur. Ten years later, they had entered a relationship. He was flattered by the young woman's attentions, perhaps, but when he had been immortal he found it easier that way, to be attracted to someone for their looks only, rather than connect with someone who would inevitably die before he did.

Verain smiled at him with one side of her face, as she always did. His attraction to her was mainly sexual. Being immortal meant that he would frequently lose the partners he'd form emotional ties with. None of them had wanted to live forever, even on the rare occasions when he dared to offer that gift, so he had been hurt more times than he cared to remember. It was these lighthearted, purely sexual partnerships, that brought him most pleasure, and as little pain as possible. Even now he knew he was dying.

"Some of the others are setting off to reach Tineag'l by boat," she announced.

"Are the first lot there already?"

"Not quite, but any day now."

"Okay," he sighed with relief. Everything was now starting. Everything was about to be put into action. All his years of experience and study and knowledge would soon be tested; his theories, his hopes, his desires fulfilled.

"Are you feeling okay?" Verain said, noticing his exhalation.

"Do you think I wouldn't be?"

"No. It's just . . . well, things are going to change, aren't they?"

"Of course. That's the nature of the world."

"I'm just worried, Dartun. You've been so different these past few weeks. You once said if I ever got scared I was to come to you. But what if it's *you* I'm scared of?"

"Me?" Dartun laughed. "Why be scared of me, you of all people?" He walked over and took her hands in his. Then he kissed her forehead in a way that was more parental than lover.

She glanced up at him with that familiar distance in her eyes. There was a lack of understanding, he sensed—perhaps a lack of willingness in her to understand him. But maybe she couldn't.

It was possible no one could understand him.

"Go to the others," he said, "and tell them to prepare. Next stop, the north. Then we'll find somewhere warmer."

Somewhere I might recover my immortality once again.

CHAPTER 14

※

People showed signs of moving around the city out of context.
They arrived places late, routines were disrupted, because normal
routes were blocked in places. More time was needed to navigate the
usual paths, and it was as if everyone had now come out of their
homes simply in defiance of the longest winter they'd ever know. For
many humans this extended season would be the last they would ever
see. For rumel there was a greater chance of seeing the summer again,
to watch for that moment when the trees and plants would explode
with life.

Jeryd was annoyed that people kept stopping suddenly, right in
front of him. More than once he considered delivering a small ad-
monitory slap to someone's head. It was always here they tended to
pause, gazing around at the old Azimuth-inspired architecture, the
smaller domes and intricate sandstone squares that contradicted the
rest of the later additions to the city, which rose generally taller, and
were hacked out of local limestone. Still, he liked the feeling of the
snow under his boots, that crisp compaction.

Home to a lot of the oldest shops in the city, this street was a
haven for antiques dealers, traders in exotic products, spice dealers.
On one side stood three cheap hotels. But things changed significantly at night: the street in front became the hangout for dealers of

less respectable substances. Quick hand movements in the moonlight, and something illegal was exchanged at an extravagant price. It was where you might meet a cultist who needed quick money, and some said that you could buy weird animals, sleek-looking hybrids, but Jeryd had never seen any in all his years.

As Jeryd headed down a narrow side alley, memories came flooding back of regularly accompanying Marysa here when they were both much younger. He couldn't think of the last time she'd actually held his hand, but when they were still in love she'd drag him along to look at all those items that appealed to her. He was once so keen to learn about her interests, to discover more about her. It must have been over a hundred years ago when he first started coming down this way, waiting outside the shops in the sun, enjoying a moment to himself as she rustled around inside. He still wanted to hold on to the idea of his being with Marysa, even if things didn't work out this time. Perhaps, in his old age, he was becoming sentimental, like humans did. Perhaps there were fewer differences between the two hominid species than anyone cared to admit.

Stepping over a bolting rat, Jeryd entered one particular antiques store that looked familiar, and the door chime rang. His eyes adjusted to the murkiness, taking in piles of antiques stacked awkwardly wherever you looked, suggesting that one misjudged step on an uneven floorboard would bring about an expensive catastrophe. An old woman was standing behind the counter, while another stood with her back turned about ten armspans away. They looked identical, both in similar overdresses, the sorts with floral patterns like the ones you used to see about thirty years ago, but now faded from overwashing. Knickknacks and ornaments spilled on the floor amid random furniture. Strange instruments, pottery, art were propped up against any available wall space. Desperately, he hoped there were no spiders under all these objects waiting for him: because arachnids were this tough investigator's hidden shame.

Jeryd stepped carefully around the large room searching for something that might appeal to Marysa, some small token to impress her, to show her that he still loved her. Was there possibly one item that could do all that on its own? Probably not. He tried desperately to think about the things she used to like, cursing his inability to make a decision. He scratched his head as he leaned over tables, picking up items, replacing them immediately.

Ever so slowly he started to mumble in frustration.

"Talking to yourself, investigator? Maybe she'd like some of the brass instruments over there. They're enough to pique the interest of the most ardent collector."

Tuya was wearing a light-blue robe, a color rarely favored in current fashions, with a straw hat tilted down over the side of her face. He tried not to let his vision linger on her lissom figure, that could be noted despite her thick clothing. Pouting lips, all cheekbones and soft edges, there was an uncomfortable intensity about this woman.

"You said your wife collected antiques, so you're here to buy her something, aren't you?"

She fingered a wooden statuette by her side. "You should at least consider some of the items over there. There're some fine nautical gadgets."

Tuya led him away.

She explained the various items to him in a way that unsettled him, though he couldn't work out exactly why. Maybe because he remembered similar times with Marysa. He wondered if it was wrong to be talking so casually, and made the decision to be wary of her charms. Greater rumel in the Inquisition than himself had succumbed to feminine wiles.

A musky smell in these rooms, the stale aroma of time having passed, the remains of forgotten civilizations. He found it odd that people should want to collect many such items, even though they did not know their original purpose. He thought about what objects he owned himself, and if in a thousand years they would each become a mere ornament on a rich lady's dresser. Perhaps some of the shit scrapers he used to flush out of the gutters would become some gift to charm a pretty girl. He smiled at the thought.

Tuya continued to point out and describe things, but his mind began drifting to his own past again.

"Rumex, you're not listening, are you? How're you ever going to win a woman's favor if you don't pay attention while she's talking?"

"I always did when she was around," he said, a little annoyed. What business was it of Tuya's anyway? Did she get her kicks from sifting through other people's lives? "Well maybe I wasn't a very *good* partner."

"But you could be," she said.

"And you could tell me how?"

"So long as you don't mind talking about such intimate things with a murder suspect."

The pressures of his personal life were beginning to distract him from his job for the Inquisition. Yet above all he needed to sort out his private life. It felt uncomfortable to be here with her, but every minute he spent with her, he might be able to observe her closely, find out who this secretive woman was, and, more importantly, to probe her further about her involvement with Ghuda. "No, it's fine. Just don't take it personally if I'm obliged to arrest you later," he said, and raised a questioning eyebrow.

She seemed to like that. "Of course. Besides, because I spend a lot of time alone, I could do with the company. In my time, I've listened to a lot of men talk—and let me tell you, men do talk, if only to the right woman. You know my profession, so I get to peek into a lot of lives, see a lot of destruction—the amount of hidden secrets and lies that keep a partnership intact . . ." She looked intently at a small metal clock and picked it up. "And, besides, I'm just making my living doing something I enjoy. If they didn't come to me for their kicks, they'd only go elsewhere. I'm not the problem—just a symptom."

"No one suggested you *were* a problem," Jeryd observed bashfully.

She put the clock down, tucked a loose strand of red hair behind her ear. "Anyway, what I'm saying is I know quite a bit about relationships." She laughed to herself, some hidden irony perhaps. "Yet I myself have never held one together. But, I'd like to think I could help you. And your partner obviously had good tastes." She gazed at Jeryd intensely.

He looked away awkwardly.

"Relax, investigator," she said, laughing. "I meant she liked quality *antiques*."

"I know that," Jeryd said, defensively.

"You shouldn't take things so seriously. You're so full of melancholy. I think you work too hard. What would you do if you didn't work?"

Jeryd frowned. "I'm not sure really."

"It's scary for some people to think what they'd do if they didn't have to work constantly. I think that's why many do work so much: because they're frightened of stopping."

"What's all this got to do with helping me get Marysa back?"

"Because you've probably put your work ahead of her most of the time when she needed care and attention. You didn't listen to her enough. You didn't make her feel special. You therefore never earned the right to be loved. I dare say you worked so hard because you didn't feel comfortable loving her."

"Compliments corner, this," Jeryd muttered dryly.

"It's a reality check," she said. "I can tell by your face that I've hit a nerve."

"Maybe you have. Look, I'm meeting her tonight. What could I do to . . . *seduce* her?"

She proceeded to give him some advice at length.

It was as if the secrets of womankind were being revealed to him.

He even had to make notes.

"So," he said, after being numbed into silence by her advice, "what should I get Marysa as a present?"

"A good-quality antique, one that could also be thought of as a relic. It'll arouse her curiosity, will mystify her, play on her mind. You must be on her mind *always*."

"Of course." Jeryd folded his arms, leaned back, playing it cool. Yes, he could appear confident, he could persuade Marysa to come back to him. This seducing business was clearly a breeze. "You're pretty clued-up on all this stuff."

"I know." She seemed satisfied with the compliment.

Turning to what he was genuinely more confident about, Jeryd risked another attempt to dig for information, now that she was more at ease with him. "So how did you really get to know Delamonde Ghuda?"

"You don't ever ease up on the work front, do you?" she said.

"My lunch hour is over, I fear."

"I met him in a tavern, Rumex. That's all. He's just one more handsome man I went to bed with. A man I wanted to sleep with out of choice. Not a crime, is it?"

It should be, he thought, but then he didn't really understand his personal feelings in this. As a rumel who was out of touch with the way the modern world worked, he often understood himself even less than he did others.

✳

Dusk, and standing outside of the Bistro Júula. Jeryd stared up at the pterodette that had narrowly missed excreting on him. The little reptile flew up to perch on the roof, looking down at him.

"Not on these robes, you won't, my friend," Jeryd said confidently, empowered by the advice of another woman.

Antique present tucked under his arm, carefully wrapped. He wore fine silk robes, in black, over a white silk undershirt with matching handkerchief. The outfit had cost him nearly a Jamún. He had shaved with an expensive blade earlier on, too. Consequently the breeze felt chillingly fresh against his smooth cheek, despite his thick rumel skin. He had even—though he would never admit this to anyone else serving in the Inquisition—scented his white hair with fragrant oils.

I may stink like a tart's dressing table, but every little bit helps.

He tried to remember everything Tuya had told him. He had reread his notes a dozen times, and it put him in mind of those Inquisition entrance exams, back in his youth.

Jeryd cast an eye at the nearby clock tower. She was bound to keep him waiting—she always did. He felt nervous, as if this was their first date. The sky was darkening fast, the tall buildings becoming even blacker against it. Birds and pterodettes arced hypnotically above the countless spires. Lanterns were being lit along the street, their colored glow catching the limestone. Sandalwood incense wafted from one of the taverns further upwind. Maybe he was going soft, but he thought the scene rather romantic.

There she was, Marysa, walking slowly along the path to meet him, hips swinging slowly as she came up the hill, and his heart was beginning to race. She caught his eye as she came closer, then looked at the ground. For a moment neither of them said anything. Her elegant, black robe was slightly darker than her skin, with a colored scarf wrapped around her neck. Her white hair was tied up with something that sparkled, no doubt some current fashion he wasn't aware of, and the colored makeup around her eyes opened up her face in new ways. Her tail swayed back and forth sinuously.

"Hello," Jeryd gulped. "You look incredible."

"Thank you," she said. "And I like your new robe."

He hadn't heard it for so long, that soothing voice. "Oh, this is for you," he forced himself to say, handing over the present. "Just a little something you might be interested in." He tried not to contain his eagerness as he urged, "Go on, open it."

She unwrapped it quietly, and her face lit up. The gift was small, possibly some ancient navigational device, only a handspan wide, with an intricate mechanism.

"An antique," she said in awe. "Looks almost like a relic."

Jeryd stood back, arms folded, feeling pleased with himself. "Should keep you busy for a few days trying to work out what it is."

"It's really wonderful." She kissed him on the cheek, a gesture that could have meant anything, so he tried not to interpret it with wishful thinking.

"Now, shall we?" Jeryd indicated the nearby bistro.

✳

After a deep initial awkwardness, the night went better than he could have imagined. He *actually listened* to her for the first time in years. Her main focus these days turned out to be ancient architectures—particularly newly discovered remains of the Azimuth Empire, undergoing restoration work here and there. She told him at length of the ancient Azimuth civilization: the great causeways now strewn under a hillside, the skeletal palaces submerged under marshes. While she had been consorting with the archaeologists, bones of ancient creatures had been found, great mastodon ribcages unearthed near the coast, mammoth quidlo squids, human remains several armspans in length, even unknown beasts with three skulls. She gradually painted for Jeryd a vivid history of the Boreal Archipelago. Why had he never found her so fascinating before?

Gestures came and went, light touches to the wrist, a smile after meaningful words, catching each other's eyes through the flame of the candle, every nuance so much more powerful, so much more lingering than before, as if the very fact of being apart had made them realize just how much they filled a gap in each other's life.

Inevitably they got round to the breakdown of their marriage, whereupon Jeryd confessed to being a poor husband. She then gave him a list of demands, should they give it another go.

They were not unreasonable, he admitted, all to do with time, attention, details. Even he could manage that. He stopped short of pleading with her, was merely happy to be with her once again. And she responded positively to that, he hoped.

✳

Later that evening, he walked her home to her temporary residence— a room on Gata du Seggr, the other side of the Gata Sentimental, where you found a lot of old soldiers living in retirement. She whispered to him that it would not be right to spend the night together, so at the door he merely pressed his lips to her hand, then turned away into the darkness.

✳

On his way home he couldn't help but notice that he was being followed by someone with heavy footsteps, but there was no incident. Once inside the door, seeing with clarity how much of a mess his house was, Jeryd decided to have a quick tidy up. Afterward he sat naked on his bed by the burning woodstove, with his head in his hands, his tail motionless, his expensive new robe folded neatly on a chair in the corner. There was an ache in his chest as he reviewed the evening in his mind. Things seemed to have gone well, but he didn't want to get his hopes up. Becoming overoptimistic could lead to the very worst kind of disappointment.

It was interesting how Tuya had changed the way he looked at his marriage, at his entire life. She had been amazingly succinct in pointing out his errors, had been the only one ever to locate a direct channel to the things that were essential in his world. Without Marysa there would still be so much . . . emptiness. Emptiness which he had previously tried to fill with so much work, in some vague attempt to avoid thinking about how bad things had become.

He reclined back on the bed, began to drift off to sleep.

✳

He was woken by footsteps, heels clipping the cobbles beneath his window. His heart missed a beat as the front door opened then closed. He twisted round in his bed, rubbed his eyes, peering at the clock. He realized he had been asleep for only half a bell. Footsteps up the stairs, footsteps to his bedroom door. With one eye he watched it open, pretending he was still asleep.

A figure approached his bed, paused.

"Some inquisitor you are," Marysa chuckled. "What if I was a thief?"

Everything I have is yours anyway, he wanted to say, but didn't. She kicked off her shoes, slid her dress down, eased herself onto the bed. They kissed, and he was gentle with her, and as they made love she would bite his chest gently, and arc her back like a bow.

Tonight, and for as long as I'm alive, he promised himself, *it will be all about her.*

✳

Outside Jeryd's house, Aide Tryst was leaning against the wall watching the glint of the moon on the slick cobbles. He had sifted through the backstreets to get here, mannered and methodical in his stealth, sliding by the tenebrous traffic of Villjamur, past all the hustlers and the slick magic and weird hybrid beasts that filled the hour with a night-noir exoticness.

And now Marysa's gentle groans came down to him occasionally above the noise of the breeze.

In his hand he held up the heart of a pig. Blood dripped along his arm under his sleeve as he silently incanted an Ovinists' mantra, the words forming in a hushed murmur on his lips.

I curse that man, he thought. *Because he won't promote me to the position I deserve, yet instead of solving Brother Ghuda's death he's wasting his time with that wife of his.*

Yet all the time he pretends to be my friend.

In his semitrance, Tryst's thoughts drifted, took control of things again. How had he got to be here, outside this house, in the middle of the night, so full of rage and jealousy?

As he reflected, memories came back to him, the ones of his youth, back when the summers seemed endless. The cottage just south of the city where his parents lived. His father, that colossal bearded man, a priest of Bohr, and an alcoholic, who abused both

Tryst and his mother. His mother herself, small and fragile and beautiful, so undeserving of the hell his father brought home with him. Tryst loved her, wanted to protect her with every instinct of his being.

But to his father she meant nothing, because Bohr had become everything, a god Tryst could never see, and perhaps that was the reason why Tryst had become an Ovinist.

Because he excelled at his lessons, it was his mother who fought for him to stay at school as long as possible, even as his father's drinking habits and bouts of violence worsened. She invested in him a sense of motivation, of freedom to get on in life, not to be held back by conditions. Perhaps some of her own fears laced her words. When she died of some mysterious illness, it destroyed his optimism. Strangely, it broke his father too, and Tryst didn't expect that. So now that it turned out Tryst couldn't expect any more promotions in the Inquisition, he thought back to those days constantly, relived those moments of helplessness again and again.

His mother had told him he was so clever he could achieve anything, and now Jeryd was stopping Tryst from *achieving*.

Tryst slid an ornamental dagger from his sleeve. He cut a slice of the pig's heart, then took a bite to show his devotion to his new god—the one that had helped process his bad memories.

But he still could not do much about the problem of Jeryd.

Seething, he walked home, contemplating ways to hurt the investigator.

CHAPTER 15

✳

VERAIN PULLED UP THE HOOD OF HER FULIGIN CAPE TO ESCAPE THE COLD wind that channeled through the passageways of Villjamur as if it was chasing her, haunting her like a relentless ghost.

As she continued on her way, old men leered at her from hidden doorways, called out to her with degrading suggestions. Some were so drunk they were falling against the walls yet even then they were requesting sexual favors. She had half a mind to use a relic to castrate them—at least that ought to cut short their fantasies. She merely flashed a short sword by their faces as she passed, but their voices continued to pursue her long after she had gone. Otherwise there were only the cats infesting the alleyways, but she actually appreciated their company.

She felt so isolated now. She was going to betray her lover.

For that's how Dartun would see it, there was no hiding from the truth. He would scarcely care if she left him for another man. He scarcely ever had sex with her, certainly never bought her gifts. It wasn't as though she wanted much, just some vague show of affection—was that too much to ask? But that wasn't the reason she was about to betray him.

Over the past year, she had seen him become obsessed with his projects, even down to little things that kept him from interacting with others for days. Somehow he had retreated into his mind, and become totally self-obsessed with his plans to step across the threshold of the world. He was going to tamper with the very nature of reality by opening a gate to another realm and stepping through it.

Dartun frightened her with his ambitions.

These were things that ought not to be decided by one man alone. Others should be warned, and if she—his lover—suspected it was immoral to proceed in such a way, then she should at least find a way of opening it to debate, shouldn't she? It was after all a decision that could affect her home.

She passionately loved Villjamur, with its antiquated buildings that leaned on each other through neglect and decay. Amid architecture that often contrasted violently in places, centuries of history were jammed in together, tens of thousands of diverse inhabitants crisscrossed in a mosaic that made up the daily life of the city. Without a family to now call her own, the city represented that familiar link to her childhood, her anchor, something she could always turn to in comfort. No one in her order liked her due to her proximity to Dartun. All she had in her life was the city. She would often walk across the bridges alone, looking down at the hundreds of citizens surging past, lost in their own thoughts. Nothing should be allowed to threaten their world. Orphaned at a young age, she had been passed between people she did not know, never feeling settled, never appreciating the love or guidance of a mother or father, or those gestures that defined who you were. Villjamur alone gave her context. It was while growing up on the streets of the city that she became involved with the cultists. It was in Villjamur that she learned about right and wrong. The place had taught her who people really were, no matter what strata of life they inhabited. And Villjamur had taught her that most fundamental truth—that most people were the same, because of experiencing similar sufferings, pains, and pleasures of existence. In the end they were all of them equal.

She asked Dartun what if something came through the doors that he would open into new worlds? And he had told her, quite simply, that if something escaped into this world, if something contaminated the islands and then Villjamur, so be it. His life and the importance of furthering knowledge was more important.

So torn between her lover and her city, she had chosen Villjamur. That was not because she loved him less, but because she had to weigh up the happiness of more than one person. Here, she told herself, was a whole city to potentially protect.

Verain's destination was a featureless stone building, located somewhere off the usual avenues. She knocked on the door and a hatch slid open. To the questioning face behind it, she displayed her cultist medallion. She hoped that the mathematical equal symbol would be enough to declare the importance of the matter.

"What?" the face asked.

"I need to see Papus, Gydja of the Order of the Dawnir. It's urgent."

"Wait there a moment."

Minutes later the door opened, and three cloaked and hooded figures stepped out into the darkness of the street. "We'll need to search you before you can enter," one of them explained.

Verain nodded, handing over her blade. Three pairs of arms worked her over, prodding at her in vaguely abusive ways, but, eventually, when they were satisfied she carried no relics, she was led inside. She was made to sit on a simple stool in a bare, wood-paneled room, the only light coming through the open door from a lantern hanging on the wall. Since there was no fire, she watched her clouded breath catch this dim light.

Nearly half an hour passed before a silhouette appeared in the doorway. It paused, clearly examining her, then demanded, "Why are you here?"

"Who wants to know?" Verain stood up.

"I do," the figure replied sternly. "I'm Papus." She carried a candle into the room and began to light others until eventually Verain could see her face clearly.

What Dartun had told her about Papus had not been complimentary, but then he would say such things, because apparently she was a strict woman with so many ethics and morals that even her own sect feared her. There were stories though of her connections to those high up in the Empire, so she clearly was the right person to approach. And she was a powerful cultist: perhaps second only to Dartun. She would know how to process the coming information.

"My name's Verain Dulera, from the Order of the Equinox." She followed Papus as she placed the final candlestick on an empty shelf on the wall.

As the woman turned to face her, Verain was surprised by her masculine features.

"I know who you are," Papus said.

Verain pulled back her hood.

Papus said, "And I see Dartun likes pretty ones."

Verain was suddenly conscious of her own attractiveness. Not that Papus herself was ugly, but Verain had learned from other women that beauty was something everyone reacted to differently. "It's because of Dartun that I'm here, actually," Verain said, crossing her arms in front of her defensively. "I've got some news I must give you."

"And I'm expected to trust this news from a rival sect? Furthermore, news about the least trustworthy man who ever handled a relic?"

"Please listen to me," Verain said. "If he knew I was here then my life would be in danger."

Papus gestured her to silence. "I know plenty of things regarding Dartun Súr, many you wouldn't want to know. I doubt what news you have will change my opinions of him. But what information could you possibly have that would make me detest your lover even more than I do already?"

Verain explained to her Dartun's plans to open a door to another world.

Papus snorted laughter. "And you yourself believe that he will actually find these doors?"

"He's had a long time to find out about these things." Verain wilted internally, having hoped that this woman would appear more receptive and reassuring.

"Why are you telling me this?" Papus demanded, propping her chin on her hands with her elbows on her knees, producing a defeated kind of body language.

How could she relate that she was scared of someone she loved. "Because I care for him," Verain replied. She didn't think Papus would understand, so she went on to explain. "I care for him a great deal, despite the way he is to me, or rather isn't. Dartun may seem languid to these matters, but he's not cruel or anything. I'm starting to think a lot of other men are the same as he is—just too caught up in his own world."

"I think you'll find," Papus said, "that most people are rather caught up in their own world. Men and women, rumel and human, that way they can escape the real one."

"I just wanted someone else to know, who could do something about the situation if something came through into this world. And since yours is the biggest order, you're obviously the most influential."

"Apparently so." Papus sighed. "Thank you for reassuring me."

✳

Dartun hunched in one of his special chambers. There were several lock mechanisms to pass through, with complex codes. He needed sanctuary at times, a place in which he could retreat, a place that more importantly offered somewhere for him to work in peace. No one knew of this place, and they would not have been able to find it. It was where he kept his more important relics. This small, dark metal-lined room was it, deep underground in his order's headquarters. He lit a candle and set about his search.

He was looking for the *uphiminn-kyrr*. It was a relic pioneered initially by one of the legendary underground cultists, the ones who worked alone without a sect but were skillful and elusive. Feltok Dupre was sometimes thought to be more a rumor than a person, a cultist who was said to have taken to alcohol and operated now in Villiren for coin to get by. The *uphiminn-kyrr* was his development, and he had sold the designs to a handful of cultists. Dartun was one, and he had been able to construct the device himself from complex plans that he thought initially were impossible to work with, written in old text and with root words he could barely understand. It took several years before he realized he had not in fact been conned.

Where is it? For a moment he leaned against the wall, pressure suddenly escalating in his head. It hit him just how much he wanted to do this, to find a new world, and to find a cure for mortality again. Why did people have to die? Why did their own worlds have to end? He fought back an urge to cry, something he wasn't used to. What had become of him? The lump in his throat seemed unmovable. What would Verain think of him, like this? Well perhaps she would see that he was normal, after all, a quality it was often obvious she craved from him. He just couldn't be the man she wanted him to be. He wanted to discover things, didn't he, to push the boundaries of what was known, not to settle for something quiet. Yet she was the only girl who had affected him in recent memory. He knew that, often escaping into her company, her tender affections. Only last month they shared drinks in the corner of a bistro, just like a *normal* couple, shrouded in that anonymous darkness brought by their fuligin cloaks, and they talked of things that didn't matter, things that he never knew about her. That she never wanted to be a mother, even though she loved children—because of her own orphaned upbringing. That she disliked sweet foods—something he surely should have noticed. That she feared ever being imprisoned, and would suffer nightmares about it periodically.

It seemed there were worlds to discover in her, too.

She meant something to him, but his newfound situation of losing his immortality had changed the context in which he lived—and he could not let her know she was important to him, not if he was going to die. If only he had just a few more *guaranteed* years, some time to discover more about these islands that lay under the red sun, about what everything meant, about where their civilization had come from. Such a history had always been there to discover, *somewhere*. If only he had more time.

If only . . .

There it was, the *uphiminn-kyrr*, a hexagonal box constructed from some metal that he could not identify. It was certain there was no known current stock of this ore. It possessed a sheen similar to steel, but the properties and structure were different. Glass dials indicated the points of a compass, with marks indicating degrees of trajectory. He took the box to his chest and left the chamber.

✳

Later, early evening, up on one of the bridges, staring blankly into the wind like he was doing so much these days. If he had so little time left alive, why was he spending much of it experiencing such existential crises? A laugh snapped him out of it. No one was around on this bridge, leading between one derelict building and one disused theater. Occasionally a gust would draw his fuligin cloak across his face, forcing upon him a darkness so total he thought it death itself.

The *uphiminn-kyrr* was to clear the skies as best as possible. The clouds were potent these days, and they needed dispersal if he was going to travel north for long periods. He placed the device on the ground, set the dials for maximum trajectory, then set it to start. There was a timer that he salvaged from another relic, so he was never quite sure how efficient it was, so he remained focused on the device from a distance of twenty paces. It was like waiting for a firework. The sounds of the city drifted up from below, bottles clinking, a little laughter, reverb of horses' hooves navigating tight alleyways, every night so similar.

Eventually, a fizz—a light glow from the *uphiminn-kyrr,* and a small ball of white light launched with velocity into the skies.

He did not know how long it would take to know if it had worked, or even if the effects would be useful, but he had to do all he could.

CHAPTER 16

✻

J ERYD WATCHED THE NIGHT SKY VIBRATE WITH LIGHT AND COLOR. MARYSA held his arm tighter. She shivered a little, and he couldn't tell if it was from the cold or the eerie event above their heads, but it wasn't important, just that fact that she was holding him once again, just like old times. As the lights reflected off her glossy black eyes, he was so grateful to be with her again. It had taken her absence to make him realize just how much she meant to him, and he was shocked that, as a rumel, he was actually *suffering* from such emotions as humans normally did. He had always assumed that it was that rumel quality of level-headedness that put them a notch above their hominid cousins.

"Rumex," Marysa breathed, "isn't this wonderful? What's causing it?"

Jeryd had no answers, and his tail was perfectly still in contemplation. "Perhaps this is some prior indication of the ice age? Perhaps not. I'm even willing to put a few Drakar on it being some kind of cultist trickery."

They were both hypnotized by the display, these beams and flickering shafts of light changing form and color in front of the stars. All around them, other people were equally entranced, craning their necks to see more clearly between the tall buildings, stepping out on balconies, scrambling for the higher bridges, as if getting closer would enable them to understand the bizarre occurrence any better.

Jeryd had taken Marysa out for a few drinks that evening and to watch a golem dance display put on by cultists from the Order of Pugandr. He had been genuinely impressed with the dwarfish, claylike creatures that skipped about on stage.

But all through this magical evening, he couldn't quite shake the feeling of being the victim of observation, even when he found himself lost in contemplation of the extraordinary events in the sky. This was a city where at night you would easily see shadows stepping out of alleyways behind you, or hear the sound of ghostly feet scuffing on the cobbles. It was a city that bred paranoia.

But who cares if someone is tailing me, just as long as it isn't those Gamall Gata kids.

✳

Randur stared out of the window, his slender, naked body illuminated by the weirdly ignited sky. His sword, garments, and boots lay scattered on the floor somewhere behind him as he grasped the edge of the window frame to watch the varying colors shoot across the heavens. A diffuse glow of green and red undulated like an immense curtain drifting in a slow breeze. Impossibly high. Impossibly wide.

Lady Yvetta Fol stepped up behind him, placed her palms on his buttocks. "Impressive," she said, sliding them slowly up and down, then giving a gentle squeeze.

"Yeah," Randur said. "I've never seen the sky look like this before. I wonder what the hell is happening?"

"I wasn't talking about the sky." She slapped his rump. Her many gold rings stung his bare skin, and he shuddered at the cold metal. Her breath crept slowly up the back of his neck as she moved his long hair to one side. Her fingers skimmed the ridges of his shoulder blades and spine. She kissed one shoulder hungrily.

As he turned around, her palms continued to move across his lithe dancer's torso, which she had already compared favorably to that of her husband, old and fat and lazy, and she murmured something vaguely about waiting for him all her life. But he couldn't keep this up all night. Where the hell did she get her appetite from? It made him wonder if she had been storing up frustrated libido for years, releasing it all tonight, on him, and now he was the prey instead of the hunter.

His lips touched her rings, caressing the display of wealth. Earlier he had cautioned her about a thief, one of Randur's latest fictions, suggesting that a wave of crimes was washing through the upper levels of the city, with wealthy ladies being targeted for their vulnerability. And after seeing the concern on her face, he pressed her fingers to his lips and offered his loyal protection for the evening. "You simply don't need all these right now." Randur slipped the rings from her fingers, dropped them discreetly into one of his upright boots. "You're beautiful enough just as you are, my dear."

Eyes creasing, she gave one of those small exhalations of pleasure, like the ones he had been hearing all night. "You really think that?"

He placed a finger over her lips. "I imagine *every* man would."

"Well certainly not *him*."

Him would be her husband, the influential Lord Hanton Fol.

Her gray hair was now ruffled after making love three times already. For a lady of fifty years, she was still slim, only mildly wrinkled. He had enjoyed what they did tonight—she was certainly a skilled performer, despite the dents in her confidence from her husband's complaints, and the fact that he was always sleeping with much younger women, whenever he was actually in Villjamur. Lord Fol was a wealthy landowner, who supplied the army with crucial foodstuffs distributed to their garrisons across the Archipelago. Lady Yvetta was rich in her own right, owning a substantial estate on Jokull, and also several trading ships. Randur was aware of these facts from gossiping with the servants before he came here. He confirmed her value from the proliferation of jewelry and ornaments that were crammed into her balconied mansion.

Her hand cupped his groin, and he groaned, partly in pleasure, and partly in dismay. She began kissing his neck, holding her lips for a moment on his collarbone. He ran his hands along her spine, noting the suppleness in her aging skin. *You can mix gain and pleasure so long as you're doing things right.* He was now pushed against the window frame, the glass chilling his back. Her hand continued to work on him, perhaps a little too eagerly.

Oh please, not a fourth time . . .

To the bed again, sliding his hands along her legs, his tongue licking feverishly from her ankles to her thigh, until she couldn't stop groaning. The soft light from the window—the heavenly display—enhanced every curve of her body, smoothed every line of aging. At an agonizingly slow pace, Randur's mouth advanced across her body. She groaned ecstatically, her fingertips gripping the bedsheets.

A thumping at the door.

Randur stared into her startled eyes.

Bugger. He whispered, "Who is it?"

"How should I know?"

Thumping again. A voice shouted, "Lady Yvetta, this is Anton!"

Yvetta whispered, "My husband's brother."

Shit, Randur thought, immediately checking for an obvious escape route. The window, the exit of so many a lover in the night, seemed an appropriate choice.

"I know you're in there, Yvetta," the voice continued. "I was brought news that you entered your chamber in the company of some young man. I can't allow our family name to be disgraced in this way."

"Nonsense," she shrilled. "I'm utterly alone."

Randur leaped off the bed, threw on his shirt and breeches.

Yvetta hurried over to the door to intercede.

While she wasn't looking, he flipped a couple of bracelets from the dresser into his pocket.

"There's no one here, Anton. Really," she protested.

"Let me in to see for myself," the voice said.

"Give me a moment," she said. "I must make myself decent."

Randur, meanwhile, had alternative concerns: "*Where's my other fucking boot?* Oh." He grabbed it, fled to the window, opened it silently then stepped out on the balcony. Before he closed the window again, he blew her a final kiss, and whispered, "When you next read some sweet stanza, think of me, as I will of you, *my love.*" She returned his gaze with a look of anxious foreboding.

It was a freezing cold night. Colors still drifted across the sky, but there was no time to appreciate the view. With one of his boots still in his hand, he emptied its contents and pocketed the jewelry.

As the sound of raised voices came from within Lady Fol's room, Randur quickly shoved his boot on, leaped to the next balcony with his dancer's agility, then climbed up to the roof. There must, he reflected, be easier ways to acquire some money. Careful not to slip to his death on the icy stonework, he edged along until he came upon an emergency spiral staircase. He descended it quickly, then jumped out onto the street.

"Evening," he greeted a couple walking by, waving while he began to button his shirt. "Lovely night, isn't it?"

✳

Commander Brynd Lathraea stared up at a sky fragmented into color, vivid streaks of red and green drifting across the darkness like sheets of rain. They had been back on the island of Jokull for a day, and they had stationed further up the coast. Another hour or two for them to get to Villjamur, but after Dalúk Point he was painfully aware of how badly their plans might be kept secret. They had then camped for the next night a fair distance up the coast.

"Shit me," Apium said, clambering off his bedroll, and nearly stepping on the dying fire as he scrambled to Brynd's side. "Bollocks." He brushed sparks off his cloak.

Brynd stood with hands on his hips, craning his neck to see through the overhanging trees. The other two Night Guardsmen approached them, but said nothing, just stared entranced at the massive light show above.

"What in Bohr's name is that?" Apium muttered eventually. "D'you reckon it's something to do with the Freeze?"

"Cultist work that, captain, without a doubt."

Nelum agreed, "Indeed, this is nothing natural."

"I said earlier something strange was happening all across the Archipelago," Brynd muttered. "I don't like it at all."

"Always the cheery sort, aren't you?" Apium said.

Brynd glanced across to Rika's carriage. By now one hundred soldiers from the Dragoons were stationed protectively in a perimeter all around their camp, while pairings of troops patrolled further out. He was deliberately monitoring an hour's journey in every direction, so if there happened to be any more draugr, they would be taken out quickly. Brynd wasn't taking any further chances, either with his remaining men or his precious charge.

Two hours after the heavenly display had finally faded, a female private from the Dragoons guided her horse quietly through the forest toward them.

"Commander," she saluted him, then dismounted.

The other three Night Guardsmen leaped to attention, then gathered around their leader.

"Yes?" Brynd eyed the solid young woman.

"Commander, your presence is requested urgently."

"Apium, Nelum: stay here. Your life before the Empress's."

"Sir," the two men said in unison. They drew their swords and took up position by the carriage.

"Lupus," Brynd turned to the third, "come with me and bring your arrows."

"Of course, commander," Lupus replied.

The two jumped on their horses, followed the Dragoon into the darkness of the betula forest.

"Private, what's the issue?" Brynd inquired as he ducked to avoid branches, his saber in hand.

"Those draugr creatures you warned about earlier. We've spotted some."

"How many are there?"

"Approximately fifteen, it seems, commander—at the edge of the forest, on the Baering Moors."

Brynd was above all determined to not let these creatures harm the new Empress. And furthermore he wanted to find out where they came from, what their motives were or who had sent them. He'd never heard of such a thing in the Empire, so why now, why on Jokull?

Through the trees, hooves thudding against the forest floor, twigs snapping as they brushed past.

They finally came across a group of Third Dragoons, the Wolf Brigade of around forty men, their helmets glinting in the light of the moon. Their official standard—a white wolf rampant, against a green background—leaned against a tree in the forest clearing. Brynd was reassured at the number of soldiers assembled.

Their sergeant stepped forward, a blond woman wearing the familiar black and green uniform of the Dragoons. She sheathed her sword, placed her wolf's-head shield to one side. He saw her face was tracked with abrasions from the tribal campaigns she had led successfully awhile back.

"Commander Lathraea," she said. "I'm Sergeant Woodyr. Has Private Fendur explained the situation?"

"She has," Brynd confirmed.

Lupus jumped down, tethered both his own horse and Brynd's to a tree.

The three of them then proceeded over to the edge of the forest. Quietly, she pointed. "Look."

Brynd's eyes narrowed.

Across the moorland, about a hundred and fifty paces away, stood a group of draugr, the moonlight from the moon Astrid casting bold, eerie shadows across the earth around them. Wind blew constant ripples through the short grass, but the draugr didn't move, only their fluttering garments. It was an ethereal picture.

"They've been standing there, as if unwilling to move, for some time," Woodyr explained. "At least half an hour now since we first discovered them."

Brynd's eyes grew accustomed to the scene, seeing the figures were dressed in rags, merely strips of cloth hanging off their flesh, both men and women. "Have they done anything at all yet?"

"No, commander," the sergeant confirmed.

"Has anyone approached them?"

"Not after your earlier warnings. We waited for you to arrive to assess the situation."

"I'm glad to hear it." Brynd turned to Lupus, said abruptly, "Shoot one."

The private walked to the very edge of the forest. With a clear aim at most of them, he nocked an arrow, brought it to anchor point. "Any one in particular, commander?"

Brynd tilted his head, said, "Try that one." He pointed toward the nearest motionless figure. "Aim for the head. We know that a body shot isn't all that effective."

Lupus released the arrow. It whipped through the air and struck the draugr in the eye with a crack as the skull shattered. The creature fell to the ground under the force of the blow, twitched slowly, like a fish on dry land. None of the other draugr reacted. They merely remained stationary in the moonlight, staring ahead, or at nothing at all.

"Cover me," Brynd ordered. "And sergeant, line up all the archers you've got. Make sure they watch my back and keep the rest of those things away."

"Yes, commander," Woodyr replied, and returned to her unit.

To his left, the archers lined up against the fringes of the forest.

Brynd made his way across the moor, stepping tentatively over the soggy grass, crept up to the creature that Lupus had just shot. Its skull had been split by the force of the arrow, the shaft still buried deeply. Stitching around the creature's neck, a black line evident across its blue-tinted skin. Brynd unsheathed his sword and poked at it, but it didn't respond, maybe it couldn't sense the touch of the metal against its skin. A worrying sign.

Brynd glanced back at the forest, reassured at the metal glinting in the moonlight, the swords and arrowheads at the ready should anything happen to him. He walked on between the other draugr. Their heads were all tilted to one side, making them appear to be asleep—except he could see their eyes clearly reflecting the moonlight.

He approached one of the creatures that looked like a woman, the long blond hair stirring gently in the breeze. He scraped his sword down one arm, drawing black fluid from beneath the skin. The draugr didn't react, obviously couldn't feel any pain. Was this in any way a human after all? He realized that, whatever they were called, these creatures were not alive in any normal sense, but in all his years in Jamur service he had never seen anything like these.

Returning to the fallen draugr, Brynd untied his belt, hooked it around the creature's ankles, dragged it back to the edge of the forest, his feet slipping on the grass, and all the time looking back to check that none of the others were now following.

Sergeant Woodyr came forward to help him. "What do we do, commander?"

"I don't see these ones as a threat exactly, but I think we should shoot them all down. We'll need a barred caravan, then pile them in and bring them back to Villjamur. They can't be left standing out here. Make sure to cover them up so the public don't see them. There's enough panic in the city already."

"Sir," she saluted, then gave her men the order to fire.

Dozens of arrows were instantly let loose.

CHAPTER 17

✻

Randur entered the complete darkness of the caves of Villjamur. It was the first time he'd ventured here, mainly because everyone had warned him of the perils. Too many unsavory characters, they claimed. You'll get your head kicked in. Robbed. All the worst villains in Villjamur live there.

And that was precisely why he was heading this way.

It was the smell that got to him first, a rancid, surprisingly humid odor. The first street he came across was like those on the lower level of the main city, the same kinds of taverns emptying out drunken men and women who were clawing the walls to guide themselves home. Shops all closed, ghostly presences in the night. The few colored lanterns burned steadily, however, in the absence of any breeze. Stray dogs pursued their solitary paths through narrow alleys. People walked by with hoods raised, giving them all a needful anonymity.

Randur slid his hands into his pockets, could feel the jewelry, sharp and cool against his palm. He didn't know exactly how he should be feeling about his latest behavior, but he would sell the stuff and use the money to pay Dartun. Surely granting his mother the gift of life counted as a positive moral act. He could be doing nothing wrong if he was saving a life. Lady Yvetta would barely miss those trinkets, and he would continue doing the same with many other women in Balmacara. *I'm fine with this,* he decided. Lady Yvetta was hardly going to expose herself by branding him a thief.

An excellent plan had been initiated. Randur's fictional thief, the one that stole from rich lonely ladies, had been spotted. Or rather, Randur was spreading rumors to anyone who would listen about a short, fat, blond man that dressed in baggy breeches—crimes to fashion too!—who had been sighted on more than one occasion, slipping from windowsills into darkness. Randur even suggested that the culprit might have been loitering near Lady Yvetta's apartment the previous night. His tracks had to be covered. He had managed to blag himself this far through life—another set of lies would hardly hurt him. But from now on he would have to select his women and jewels with more caution.

The further he penetrated them, the caverns became bizarrely higher. Some of the spires from the main city could have easily fitted under here. There was the eerie high-pitched sound of bats echoing far off above, and there was a lot of thick smoke due to the lack of ventilation. How far back did this strange section of the city extend?

He came across a fenced-off open section, like an excavation. It was about fifty paces by a hundred, stretching back from his path to the rock of the cave itself. By the light of a lantern stood a hooded man working with a shovel in his hands.

"Hey," Randur hailed him.

The man stopped digging. "Fuck you want?"

"What's going on here? Archaeology dig?"

The man laughed. "Graveyard, mate. A new one."

"New one?" Randur echoed, resting both hands on the low wooden fence.

"Yep," the hooded man said. "They've filled all the deeper holes down in the caves. Our esteemed Council raised funds for a building here to be cleared, so we could fill the land it occupied with the dead."

"Thought they always burned the dead. It'd save room, too, wouldn't it?"

"Aye, you're right." The man began to chuckle. "Only thing is, this place here is for murderers they've executed." He leaned forward conspiratorially. "Burying them keeps their spirits trapped here. Can't

have their foul spirits passing on to the next realm, can we? Ha!
They'll be filling it up quick. Take it you've not been down this way
much? Where y'headed, mate?"

"I'm not sure exactly," Randur said. "I'm looking to sell something."

"Whatcha got?"

"A few bits of jewelry," Randur replied. "Not on me now though.
Any dealers down this way?"

"Depends. You won't get much cash down here unless you go,
well . . . even deeper underground, if you follow. See, shops here
in the caves ain't likely to hold much in the way of jewelry. Would
soon get stolen."

Randur said, "So, where do I go to find such a customer?"

"That depends. You can look after yourself okay?"

Randur peered into the hooded darkness concealing the man's
face. "I reckon as well as anyone in this city."

"That's the spirit, lad! Couple of taverns further in's what ya need.
Probably a half bell's walk if you carry right on down this road. Look
out for the Jinn or the Garuda's Head. You just tell the bar staff there
that you're trying to offload some goods. There'll probably be some
sort of brawl in there most likely."

"Thanks for that."

From under his soiled cloak, the man extended a bony hand that
appeared utterly bloodless, as if he should have been lying in one of
the graves himself.

"Right," Randur acknowledged, and reached into his pocket for a
coin.

"Much obliged," the man murmured, and headed back to tend to
his graves.

✳

Deeper in, the houses became much more cramped together. Randur
peered through lantern-lit windows in the crudely built shacks to see
large families huddled together inside—cheek by jowl, as his mother
would have said. Amazing that the sunlight would never penetrate
this far to brighten their lives. The walls were so flimsy that every
sound could be heard by the neighbors. What must it be like trying to

sleep with babies crying all around them in the night? Not even gardens in which children could play, and the damp washing was strung up in front of their doorways. Everywhere monotonous shades of brown, gray, black. Surely if those refugees outside the city knew what it was really like to live in Villjamur then they would prefer to take their chances with the ice.

The outline of a vague shape was stretching across the entire roof of the cavern. Something up there glittered faintly like starlight. But that would have been impossible.

And it suddenly struck him how completely anonymous he was in Caveside. Despite his new position at court, he was now in an alien city where no one had heard of him. That gave him a peculiar sensation when he paced the muddy cobbles.

Suddenly, from a building to his left, two men burst onto the street brawling. A cloud of alcohol followed as several men piled out of the tavern after them, cheering them on. Light from the open doorway spilled out on the grotesque scene. The brawlers cursed each other and rolled about on the ground. They punched each other's faces and grabbed each other's garments as if to frantically swap clothes.

I reckon this must be one of the places I'm looking for.

Someone from the crowd stepped forward and kicked one of the fighters on the head with a solid-looking boot. It snapped back, neck broken, its owner lying perfectly still. The other man got up, brushed himself down, patted the killer on the shoulder. Together with the gathered onlookers, who were muttering approvingly, they returned inside. Randur studied the inn's sign. He had indeed arrived at the Garuda's Head, a crudely whitewashed building, with a pair of external torches burning. As the corpse lay on the ground in a pool of blood, a banshee could be seen approaching in the murky light. Randur stepped quickly into the tavern.

Everyone turned to stare as the stranger walked toward the bar, the sound of conversation dipped. Even with a shelf of candles distributed around the room, the place was barely navigable. The walls were plain, with little decoration, just the odd dull and faded painting of battle and hunting scenes mainly, the odd seascape. Fishing nets hung from the ceiling, wood paneling glowing behind. He tried to gauge the tenor of conversations, but all he could hear was the hushed mumble of men talking into their drinks.

Randur leaned boldly against the wooden countertop at the far end of the tavern. Rough-looking types stared at him suspiciously through a cloud of pipe smoke. He could smell arum weed, lager, and fish being fried in some other room. The counter was littered with tankards and used plates that no one had bothered to clear up.

Randur produced a knife from out of his sleeve, and slammed it on the counter followed by a handful of coins, which eventually rattled to a rest. "Lager," he announced to the grubby man standing behind the counter.

"You'll need more money than that," the fat barman replied, wiping sweat from his cheek.

Randur laughed awkwardly, pretended to rummage in his various pockets. He placed another few Drakar on the table. "That's all I've got."

The barman counted the coins slowly before grunting what sounded close to an approval. He turned to one side to pull the drink. Having given that little display, surely no one would think Randur worth robbing.

A gray-haired man propped to his right, muttered, "Pretty flashy blade that." He indicated the onyx-handled knife that Randur had placed on the bar counter. "You wanna be careful you don't get it taken from you. You can never be too careful in Caveside, like."

"I wouldn't worry yourself," Randur replied defensively.

"Just sayin', like." The old man blew his nose into his hands, which he then wiped on his breeches.

Randur frowned at this display. The man who had addressed him was so thin and starved looking, he appeared half-dead. His cloak was in good condition though, and still a deep green. He wore several polished copper bangles and brooches, all bearing leaf motifs, and even his boots were particularly well-shined.

Randur decided his neighbor wouldn't be able to give much trouble. "Thanks for your concern." The barman placed the tankard of lager on the bar. Having remembered his identity wasn't real, he felt safe in continuing the conversation. "I'm Randur. Who the hell are you?"

"They call me many things round here, young Randur . . ." the old man began. There was an authority in his voice, the sort that made you suspect some kind of prophecy was imminent.

Randur waited for a moment as the man stared ahead aimlessly. "Well, you going to tell me one of them at least?"

"You can call me Denlin."

"Well, Denlin, what do you do exactly, apart from propping up this bar?"

"Ex-soldier. Jamur Eighth Dragoons—and for forty years, too. Forty years of the military."

Randur sipped his lager casually. "So, what did you fight with?"

"Longbow and crossbow, lad. I was an archer by trade, before my eyes started failing me, that is."

"And is that why you quit?" Randur said. "Your vision failed you?"

"Wasn't that really," Denlin said. "I'm no dribber—I can still bring down a garuda from the sky on a windy day." He looked down at the beer-stained floor. "Admittedly my vision's not what it used to be."

"Well anyway, Denlin the Archer," Randur raised his tankard, "here's to things not being quite what they used to be."

"You seem too young to be mouthing words like those," Denlin muttered. "Those're words only a man who's lived a bit should be saying."

Randur shrugged. "You don't have to be old to know that life will throw a good deal of shit your way."

They clinked tankards.

"So, lad, tell me," Denlin said, a new froth of beer on his lips, "what brings you Caveside?"

Randur checked the barman was out of earshot. "I'm looking for . . . certain people."

"Know a lot of people, me," Denlin pressed. "Who you looking for? Anyone specific?"

"Look," Randur decided suddenly that the old man could be a lead, "I need someone interested in buying some stuff from me."

"Buying and selling, yeah? Hmm. You wanna be careful with your valuables round these parts."

Randur said, "D'you know of anyone who might be into regular trading with me?"

"Well that depends, lad," Denlin said. "Depends what needs trading."

Randur leaned closer to the old man. "Look, I screwed a lady, and I took her jewels. I need to make myself some coin, and I need it quick."

Denlin burst into a hoarse laugh. "Ah, I used to do a bit of that myself, lad. Ha! You sort of remind me of me."

I truly, truly hope not, Randur reflected, leaning back to examine him. *That would not be a great reason to continue living.* "Anyway, can you help me out?"

"Maybe, maybe not," Denlin said. "What's in it for me?"

"One in every ten coin is yours," Randur said. "I've got a lot of jewels already, and I plan to have a lot more. You'll end up making a fair bit out of me."

Denlin nodded thoughtfully, then brought a pipe from out of his pocket already loaded with arum weed. "You in some kind of trouble, lad?" He lit the pipe. "Someone who wants coin this way has gotta be havin' some problems."

Randur shook his head.

"You in trouble?" Denlin pressed. "Got the Inquisition pounding at your door? A wife who's blackmailing you?"

Randur snorted a laugh. "I have my own reasons. But, all you need to know is that I owe a bit of money to someone."

"You need this cash quick then, like?" Denlin took a sip of lager. "Worry not, lad. I'll soon sort you out."

"No funny business, though." Randur picked up the knife, flicked it in the air, caught it by the handle, before concealing it within his sleeve again. He finished his lager, slammed the tankard on the counter. "So we've a deal, Denlin the Archer."

"That's a name I like the sound of, y'know—Denlin the Archer. Yeah, we got a deal, lad."

"Good," Randur said. "So, where can we find a buyer?"

"Look around you, lad. There's dozens of buggers in here who'd buy anything you can offer."

"Have they got enough cash though?"

"'Course they have. Why d'you think they can afford to spend all their time drinking?"

Randur shrugged. "I guess so." Maybe the barman had not been rooking him after all.

"Give me half an hour and sit over at that table in the corner." Denlin indicated a bench at the far end of the tavern in a dark corner. A small brass instrument glittered next to it in the half-light. "I'll be back with some punters, but you'll need to get another round in though."

Randur sighed, rolled his eyes, ordered them two more tankards.

"Thought you didn't have any more cash on you," Denlin crowed, concealing a smug grin behind his tankard as he took a first gulp.

Randur muttered, "Your ability to see through me is admirable. I guess your vision isn't all that troubling."

Denlin raised an eyebrow in acknowledgment. "Looks can be deceiving down these parts, lad. You just remember that, and you'll get on fine."

✳

After Denlin had made a quick inspection of the jewelry Randur had to offer, he disappeared without another word. Randur sat at the table on his own, staring out into the darkness and the smoke, listening to the furtive chatter, wondering how long the tavern would stay open.

He took a look around at the other customers. There was a blond woman crying into her hands while the man reclining next to her was smoking away, uninterested in her distress. An old man was now standing at the counter without any shoes. On stools alongside him sat two laborers, covered in dirt, the grime suggesting there were mines underneath the city. Detritus of every kind was scattered across the floor, including specks and spots of something he took to be blood.

It suddenly struck him just how many physically damaged people he had encountered in the city. Many had hands missing or savage wounds across their faces, black eyes and ripped ears. One man nearby had a leg severed beneath the knee. Knives were brandished openly, and swords rested against the tables, on open display.

Randur hadn't really thought about it before, but he guessed that was what you should expect in a world where the sword, axe, and arrow formed a common language. The inhabitants therefore wore the signs of constant violence. He ran his hand across his own pale face, reassuring himself in the absence of any wound. You made your own luck in this world, and you played the cards you were dealt. He had been lucky so far, but put it down to *Vitassi,* nothing more.

Denlin returned with a square-jawed swarthy man, dressed only in a black tunic in a gesture of defiance to the coming ice.

"This is the gentleman I spoke of," Denlin said to his stocky companion.

Randur stood up, offered his hand. "Randur Estevu. I'm pleased to meet you."

The swarthy man nodded. "Coni Inrún—trader."

"Well, please take a seat," Randur said, wondering if this man was capable of uttering words of more than two syllables. All three of them sat down at the table.

Coni leaned forward. "Denlin says you got jewels."

"That's right," Randur said. He reached into his pocket, drew out an emerald set in a silver ring. Resisting any temptation to flamboyance, he placed it on the table before Coni.

The man pulled out an eyeglass and began to examine it in detail. Randur glanced over at Denlin who merely raised his eyebrows.

"Very good," Coni said. "Good workmanship this. Where d'you get it?"

"An old lady gave it to me," Randur lied. "Decided she didn't want it anymore."

"Hmm," Coni said. "Give you five Sota. Not a bad price for this."

"I'd expect at least a Jamún for this," Randur said.

"Seven Sota," Coni said.

"Nine," Randur said.

"Eight."

"Nine, and that's it," Randur said.

"I'm sorry, Mr. Estevu," Coni said standing.

"Eight it is," Randur said.

"Okay." Coni sat down. He produced the coins, picked up the ring. "You got more such items?"

"A few, but not as good as that one."

The two younger men went on discussing the jewels that Randur had stolen for over half an hour. Denlin meanwhile had remained quiet, merely observing the transaction while keeping one eye open for trouble. With his first commission payment in his pocket, Denlin bought exotic drinks from the counter, including the legendary Black Heart rum. At first Randur refused, but the old man insisted they were not that strong. After Coni had departed with much less coin, but a good stash of jewelry, the men drank progressively. Candles burned low around them, men came and went from the tavern. Denlin related tales of his exploits in the military, himself and Randur talking the way an old man and a young one tended to do. Wisdom was shared: Randur happy to listen, Denlin happy to talk.

Randur drank and his eyes became heavy. He wasn't used to such quantities.

It wasn't long until he reached that point where he knew, in his heart, he was well . . .

. . . and truly . . .

. . . *gone* . . .

CHAPTER 18

✳

Jᴇʀʏᴅ ᴇɴᴛᴇʀᴇᴅ ᴛʜᴇ Cʜᴀᴍʙᴇʀ ᴏꜰ IɴQᴜɪSɪᴛɪᴏɴ, ᴀ ᴅᴜSᴛʏ, ᴄᴇʀᴇᴍᴏɴɪᴀʟ office in which the arch-inquisitor and his three aides of justice were already seated at a large marble table. They greeted him with the barest of glances.

Not a good sign.

It was a wood-paneled room with an expensive stained-glass window overlooking several of the lower levels of the fore-city of Villjamur. Shafts of colored light filtered through, and a fire crackled welcomingly at the far end. Various ancient decrees, written on cloth, hung from the walls, something to inspire the current office-holders, they said. Or in Jeryd's eyes, something to remind him of all the forms he had to fill in daily. Still, it was nothing compared with the level of state control that the Council could impose elsewhere.

The arch-inquisitor himself was a brown-skinned rumel who had served nearly two hundred and twenty years in the Inquisition, and he could tell you about his life all right, giving endless narratives that always ended in him wondering what had happened to so-and-so. Because his tough old skin was so wrinkled, Jeryd initially had trouble making out where the aged rumel's eyes were. All three were dressed formally in the uniform of the Inquisition: crimson robes, with a medallion representing a crucible.

"Investigator Jeryd, please be seated." The arch-inquisitor gestured to an empty chair.

Jeryd pulled his own formal robes aside and sat down. How he hated these meetings. He felt as if some people in the Inquisition lived only for moving paper from one file to another. They were not his kind at all, as he liked to get out and about. He placed his notebook on the table, met the drifting gaze of the senior inquisitor.

"My aides inform me that you intended visiting the Council Atrium. Is this the case?"

"Yes, arch-inquisitor," Jeryd replied. "And it's been approved, I believe, by these very same aides." He indicated the three rumel sitting next to him. "They've all given me the go-ahead, so we can maybe make this investigation quick."

The arch-inquisitor leaned inquiringly toward each of his aides in turn. They muttered their agreement in unison, like a hypnotic lament for Jeryd's boredom.

"Very good then. Now, Investigator Jeryd, I've asked you here very simply to impress on you the fact that whenever one of our investigators ventures up there, inevitably a commotion is caused. We've famously not got on all that well with councilors. They don't like us poking around in their matters."

"I understand, arch-inquisitor, but I'm investigating the death of Councilor Ghuda. In this case I think they'll be very cooperative, in case it should happen to any of them also."

"Indeed, Investigator Jeryd. But we can't be certain it wasn't one of them who had him removed."

"That's a possibility. But if they've nothing to hide, they'll let me go about my work."

The arch-inquisitor gave a hollow laugh, which evolved into a cough. His aides passed him a wooden cup, and the old rumel slurped gratefully. "Well, we've a frayed relationship with the Council, I fear, so please don't ruin it further."

Jeryd said nothing, thinking, *I don't give one iota as long as things get done and the streets are safe again.*

✳

The air was constantly filled with a bone-chilling sleet, enough to make you think that the sky was breaking up, that you would never again see the sun. People opened doors and windows to the same dismal sight every morning, hoping for a little sun, perhaps naively. It sent disappointment through the city like ripples on a pond of depression.

Jeryd showed his Inquisition medallion to the guards at the city level where Balmacara stood. The three grim-looking men eyed Jeryd and Tryst suspiciously, even more so after Jeryd reminded them of the rights of the Inquisition—including freedom of the city of Villjamur, free pass to all quarters of the Empire, which was the sort of privilege no guard wanted to hear. The pair of visitors left their horses to be led off to the stables to one side, and proceeded to climb the main steps leading to the Atrium.

Chancellor Urtica came to meet them with a well-rehearsed grin, a lightness in his step.

"Ah, the investigator," Urtica said cheerfully. "I'm delighted to welcome you to our humble chambers. May I ask you how you'd like to proceed?"

Jeryd shook his hand. "I'm Investigator Rumex Jeryd, and this is Aide Tryst."

"Aide Tryst," the chancellor acknowledged. "Sele of Jamur to you both."

Jeryd noticed a strange look in Urtica's face, a sort of flicker of facial muscles—the classic, knowing look that suggested he might have met Tryst before. And if that was the case, Jeryd wondered how it would have been possible.

"As you know we're here to follow up on the murder of Delamonde Ghuda," Jeryd confirmed.

"Good." The chancellor's face darkened. "He was . . . a close friend of mine. Any idea yet who might have committed such a foul crime, investigator?"

"Some leads," Jeryd said. "But there's a lot of questions that still need asking. I'd like to see Ghuda's chambers, and trust that everything has been left exactly as it was?"

"I can't guarantee that precisely, but much of it is how it was."

"Have you been in there yourself?" Jeryd inquired.

"Of course. Many of the documents were worked on by the two of us."

"You were close then, it seems. Did Ghuda have any enemies? Anyone who would've wanted him out of the way."

"We all would," Urtica smiled. "It's the nature of our position. We can't hope to please everyone, all the time."

"That's not really answering my question, is it?" Jeryd said, perhaps more sharply than he should have.

"I can't think of anyone who would specifically want him killed, let's put it that way." The chancellor glanced past Jeryd, down the corridor. Jeryd followed his stare. Some of the other Council members were heading through a large marble arch. "You'll have to excuse me, investigator, but I've a meeting to attend. Feel free to contact me again, once I'm finished."

Urtica brushed past him, proceeding down the corridor.

Tryst meanwhile was staring absentmindedly at a tapestry on the wall.

Jeryd turned to the guard escorting them. "Show me Ghuda's chamber."

✳

Smooth stone, dark wooden panels, the smell of decay—such were the chambers in which every Council member performed his or her administrative duties. The decoration and carvings were old yet rich, as if, Jeryd thought dryly, to remind each official of the wealth they enjoyed at the top. Something that said *Look how far you've come.* Plinths held small busts of the Emperors of the current dynasty: Haldun, his son Gulion, Goltang, and of course mad old Johynn himself. Parchments were heaped upon a large wooden desk situated beneath a window that was carved in the mock-Azimuth design: simple rectangles, elegant precision. The view wasn't spectacular: a dreary sea and the sheer cliff face. Pterodettes had nested in the crevices of the latter, and their faces stained it in bold gray streaks. Nonetheless it was certainly an improvement on Jeryd's office.

The investigator had sent Tryst to interview one of the guards about the councilor's daily movements, something to get an impression of his typical routine. Jeryd was beginning to suspect his human assistant. The way he made eye contact with Chancellor Urtica had been rather unsettling. For the moment, Jeryd thought it best to get him out of the way. In this job, you had to follow your hunches.

He sifted through some of the parchments and scrolls strewn on the desk. They detailed movements of monies between some of the outer-island estates and Villjamur—most of the land across the Empire was owned by private individuals through inheritance or conquest. That way, the most efficient farms could be rewarded, and advancement in techniques easily encouraged. But recently large movements of funds were being treated as suspicious, especially if they were possibly being used by the wealthy to smuggle extra servants and laborers into Villjamur before the Freeze.

None of this stuff was of any use to Jeryd, however.

He moved on to a decree of death imposed upon several thieves from Caveside, for attempting to smuggle in refugees. *One law for the rich,* he sighed. He perused a scroll for transportation of grain to the Dragoons now being sent to Folke. He read about a landowner who was selling up all his properties before he came to the city to escape the ice. He read documents authorizing the movement of slaves from Folke to the mines on Tineag'l.

All in all, it was uninspiring stuff, and none of it seemed quite right, as if they had been left deliberately on his desk to create a positive image of Ghuda. Nothing damaging would have been left for the Inquisition to discover. These were politicians, after all.

There must have been somewhere that Ghuda concealed his private documents. It was always the way with councilors—their deceit and self-preservation was legendary.

There must be a loose stone in the wall, or maybe an opening behind a wooden panel. He felt along the walls first—no loose bricks. He tapped along the wood, but it all seemed to be set firmly against stone anyway. He approached the busts, eyed them. He picked up the one of Goltang, the Emperor who had died over two thousand years ago. Jeryd wondered how the artist could ever have carved something true to life. Goltang was the man who had created the Empire leading to its domination of the Boreal Archipelago, the land of the red sun. A history of brutal campaigns, then raping island resources and forcing subsidiary tribes into labor in his name. The history books said that he was exporting progress. And he did all this without recourse to cultist technologies, something his successors couldn't cope without.

Jeryd set Goltang down, picked up an image of Johynn. The first thing he noticed was how light this statue was in comparison. He brought it to his ear then shook it. Something rattled inside. With a smile, he casually dropped it on the floor. It smashed into several large fragments, but with a piece of paper sticking out underneath.

Tryst entered the room without knocking. "Everything all right in here, sir?"

"Oh, yes," Jeryd said blandly. "I just got a bit careless and knocked one of these chaps off their plinths with my tail. How're your own inquiries going?"

"So, so," the human replied. "I'm gradually building up a picture of his routine. All pretty dull stuff if you ask me."

"It's all essential, though," Jeryd pointed out. "I don't suppose you could fetch me a mug of hot water, could you? This cold weather's playing havoc with my poor old chest." He coughed for a little effect. "After that, why don't you head back to the Inquisition chambers while I stay here and plow through all those documents. I'll see if there's anything worth taking away with us."

"You sure?" Tryst's voice betrayed suspicion. "I don't mind helping you."

"No, it's okay. I need the silence to concentrate." Jeryd began to cough violently again, resting one arm against the wall to enhance his performance.

"Certainly, investigator. I'll fetch your hot water." Tryst left the room, shut the door behind him.

Jeryd bent down to pick up the piece of paper. He unfolded it fully, regarded the strange lettering and symbols. It was clearly written in some sort of code. One symbol at the top, though, he did recognize: a rough sketch of a boar. Instinctively, he looked back to the floor, began rummaging through the broken pieces then paused to pick up a blue gemstone, a topaz. This was the first lead, since topaz was supposedly the secret emblem of one particular religious cult.

It seemed our friend Ghuda had been an Ovinist.

✳

Jeryd didn't understand the significance of Ghuda's connection to that underground religion, nor did he have any clue about what the lettering meant on the accompanying parchment taken from the statue. Back in his apartment, he contemplated these items at length.

After a while, he dropped another log on the fire, took a break to look out of the window. Nighttime again, and, despite the cold, Villjamur vibrated with activity. Off-duty soldiers had come thronging in search of company for the evening. They staggered between taverns and street corners, bellowing and whistling into the chilly air. Such intemperance was becoming more noticeable as the Freeze became a reality. Youths climbed on walls to throw snow at citizens. Running footsteps faded into the distance. In the neighboring buildings, squares of light emerged at the higher levels as lanterns were lit for the evening. As his eyes focused, Jeryd noticed figures appear at these windows, gazing out across the city, perhaps staring right back at him. Directly below his own window, he suddenly noticed Marysa approaching quickly, wrapped in a thick winter cape, returning from her day of study in the library. As he waited for her to come in, he sat down at the table.

A moment later, she pushed the study door open with some force. She was breathless from her rapid progress, and walked straight toward the fire.

Jeryd rose to greet her, squeezed her cold hands gently. "How was your day?"

"Rumex, I swear someone was following me." Her dark eyes were wide with panic, her tail twitching anxiously from side to side.

"Following you?" His tone became serious. "Please, sit down and I'll make some tea. Tell me, what did you see?"

"I'd prefer some whisky." Marysa sat down at the table.

As he handed her the glass, she continued, "I didn't get a good look at him. Every time I turned to look, he'd be gone. I know it sounds silly, but I swear that someone was there."

Jeryd placed a hand on her cold knee as he sat alongside her. "You're not being silly, because these are strange times. How did you first realize you were being followed?"

"Footsteps—always the same footsteps. I'm not going mad, I swear."

"It's all right," Jeryd soothed, giving her a look that confirmed he knew she wasn't making it up. He hugged her more tightly.

She sipped her whisky with urgency. "Who could it be?"

For a moment he wondered if it had something to do with his own work. Perhaps someone was frightening her to get at him? He kissed Marysa's hand reassuringly, and she curled into him, resting her head on his shoulder. The intimacy made him feel like they were a couple again, that he could look after her. There was something so reassuring about this, and it affected him deeply.

He had no plans to let her go for the best part of an hour.

CHAPTER 19

✳

Shrouded delicately in lantern light, Tuya rested her hands on the windowsill to gaze out through the night. The window was open slightly and, because she wore only a white silk evening robe, the stirred air rose the hairs on her arm. The moonlight from Astrid was now concealed only slightly. Pterodettes arced upward toward the nearby cliffs as a few pedestrians stalked the frozen streets hunched up in thick clothing. Not a time to be out. Why could she never connect to Villjamur? What was it that made her think she belonged outside the city?

She thought she could even hear refugees huddled outside the gates, in the icy conditions. Maybe it was her imagination, but the thought ceaselessly saddened her. Surely there was no need for them to remain outside?

She considered what Councilor Ghuda had revealed to her that night, which perhaps other than the councilors involved, only she knew. Surely she owed it to the city, owed it to herself to divulge it.

She needed to give something back to Villjamur.

She turned back to her painting, remembered who was next.

She began to apply herself to her only escape from her tenebrous world. She lifted up a brush and began to *create*.

Lines of paint spread thickly. Diagonals, verticals, curves. A body began to form.

Once she had finished, she stood back, her white robe splattered. This was certainly one of her most sinister pieces. There was no theme with such creations, no references, no premeditated allusions.

She walked to a mirror, noting her hair was a mess that would need fixing.

A gust of wind abruptly blew out the lantern beside her, bathing her in darkness. Already the pigments were beginning to glow, a subtle light pulsing with the regularity of a heartbeat.

She lay on the bed, her gown parting across her angled knee, gazing toward the window as the wind stirred her curtains. The glow in the room brightened, and she stared down her body.

Councilor Boll would die tonight.

✳

Councilor Boll stepped out of the chamber facilities, realizing how he always hated communal toilets. It never seemed right to be engaged in a conversation while taking a shit. Especially to Councilor Eduin, who might have only just crept out of someone else's arse, for all Boll knew. Why did anyone expect you to conduct a conversation in those private moments? You couldn't exactly walk away from the situation either.

Boll shuffled down the corridor toward his chamber in Balmacara. He had to prepare for an early morning meeting with Chancellor Urtica, who apparently, judging from a message he had received only an hour ago, had discovered a brilliant method to eliminate all the unwanted refugees from Villjamur, involving someone from the Ovinists drawing on their expertise with poisons. But the last thing they wanted was for thousands of people to die on the doorstep of the city. That simply wouldn't do. They should die somewhere else, Boll reckoned, with subtlety, far enough away so that the stench of death wouldn't drift over its gleaming spires and bridges. The citizens of Villjamur deserved better treatment than that.

Boll entered his own chamber, which was littered with a collection of gold antiques from previous ages. Like many people in this city, he had a fondness for a previous era but didn't know why. In his case he wanted to absorb as much as he could about the great Dawnir creations, of the legendary Pithicus race that was wiped out by the

Dawnir in the War of the Gods. His shelves were accordingly crammed with texts on the Máthema civilization, about the Azimuths who followed. He also possessed an expert knowledge of the history of the Jamur Empire. That was his main strength, his knowledge of previous civilizations. He prided himself on it. He would stop people to get them to ask him questions about it—*go on, anything from any era*—and then he would let his words wash over them, a one-way conversation to say *I know more than you do.*

The lantern light was caught in myriad places around the immense room. He stood at the window, scratched his groin, watching the lights in other houses being doused for the night, one by one. Then he lay down on his feather bed, picked up a history book entitled *Mythical Azimuth Battles.* He began to read, but the prose was so dry and lifeless, that not one sentence registered, and he drifted off to sleep.

✳

Boll woke in darkness. All the candles had gone out. The shrieking of pterodettes just outside made him strangely vulnerable.

"Must be the damn wind," he grunted to himself. He climbed out of bed to shut the window that had blown open. Then he shivered, uncontrollably, sensing that he was not alone in the room.

He leaped onto his bed, reached up to the shelf above it, then stepped back down with a short sword in one hand. Circling with bare feet on the cold tiles, he held the blade out in front of him. His heart was beating so violently in his ears it seemed to suffocate all other sounds.

In the corner something began to glow, and eventually took on the form of a decayed corpse with luminous bones. In one, clawlike hand it held a gleaming metal axe.

"What . . . what d'you want?" Boll stammered, drawing his night robe tighter with his free hand.

There was no response, and Boll noticed the creature possessed no reflection in the adjacent mirror. He quivered with fear as it came nearer, seeing directly through the gaps in the glowing bones. The thing barely owned a face, just crudely assembled features of two sockets for its eyes, a black circle for its mouth. "I have money . . ." Boll began pleading.

As the ethereal skeleton towered over him, Boll slashed the blade in some vague attempt at self-defense. It merely stood there regardless, the sharp metal passing through it as if slicing water.

The axe in its hand seemed real enough. As the blade descended Boll twisted to one side, but it still crunched into his shoulder generating an explosion of pain. He howled, sprawling flat on the floor, his right arm now functionless, blood pooling around him. The next blow gashed his groin, severing an artery before thudding into the floor tiles.

CHAPTER 20

❋

INVESTIGATOR JERYD WAS NOT AT ALL AMUSED.

He just stared thoughtfully at the wall, sipping a cup of tea, and for a long while no comment issued from his lips. Eventually, with a sigh, he said simply, "Another councilor?"

"Councilor Boll," Aide Tryst confirmed, standing close by Jeryd's desk.

"Councilor Boll." Then, contemplating the paperwork, Jeryd said, "Bugger."

"I understand the body is now in the possession of Doctor Tarr, but he's spent all morning in the House of Life."

"What the hell's he doing there?" Jeryd grumbled. "Bohr, he's a miserable git."

"Meditating, I believe," Tryst said.

"Well, let me guess," Jeryd pondered. "Bizarre wounds again, no useful evidence, a general waste of time and utter confusion for all involved? Just more stress and paperwork for you and me?" Jeryd pursed his lips. "How many people know about it?"

"Well, according to the servant who found him, not many. He contacted another member of the Council who lives nearby, who in turn contacted Doctor Tarr's people to remove the body immediately, then he sent word straight to us."

"Well, that's one thing to be grateful for, at least," Jeryd said. "So, we've got ourselves a murderer with a taste for butchering members of the Council?"

"So it seems," Tryst agreed.

"Let's drop in on Tarr again, then I think I'd better have another chat with Chancellor Urtica."

✳

The Hall of Life was one of the more depressing places in Villjamur. Though close to the astronomer's octagonal tower, it was located at a much lower level. The only access was via several stairways that spiraled deep down into the city. Reaching it required negotiating a complicated labyrinth of dark passageways, and rumor had it that if visitors strayed too far off the main route, they might never be seen again. It was like a route to one of the lower realms, a symbolic reminder of the final journey.

If Doctor Tarr even needed reminding of death, he had come to the right place. There, deep underground, in a high-ceilinged cavern, it was said that a candle was lit for every child born in the city. They burned there in the thousands, arranged in neat rows that extended on all sides.

It was an ideal place for meditation, as encouraged by the Jorsalir tradition—somewhere for contemplation. People entered and departed, some to sit quietly, some weeping, others staring blankly at the candles.

Time became lost in deep contemplation.

Doctor Tarr was seated on a wooden bench to one side, surrounded by shades of darkness, a metaphor for death.

The doctor glanced up briefly then resumed his contemplation of the burning candles. Symbols of the fragility of existence, the slightest draft could blow out these flames, at any moment.

"Right, let's go talk to the morose git."

Tarr sat up sharply as the words echoed across the vast chamber. He recognized Investigator Rumex Jeryd, emerging from one of the stairwells with his human assistant.

"Ah, Doctor Tarr." Jeryd approached him. "Sele of Jamur to you."

"And to you, investigator," Tarr replied, standing.

"What on earth are you doing down here?" Jeryd inquired. "Surely you're familiar with the trappings of death by now?"

The doctor gave a gentle smile that rather unnerved the investigator. "Familiar, yes, but prepared, no. I've seen too many mutilated corpses, and Councilor Boll's murder has to be one of the most horrific sights I've ever encountered."

Jeryd said nothing, merely glanced across the sea of candles before them. Finally he said, "I don't understand why you're here though. Surely you should be examining the body?"

"There's not too much left of it to examine, truth be told," Tarr said. "I've come to realize through the years, investigator, how life can be so easily, and so horrifically, taken from us. This Empire has led an easy existence over the last few decades. No major wars, no great plagues, no crop failures on a large scale. Every single one of us has been safe, as if we have never left our mother's knee. Look at the flames, both of you. Yet we are a besieged city, investigator. Disease attacks within our city walls, and every sunrise takes us yet another step toward our inevitable death. One wonders what happens afterward, on the other side."

"Will you tell us what you've found, doctor?" Tryst interrupted.

"Of course," Tarr said. "You're quite right to ask. Come to the mortuary later though. In all honesty, there's little to see, since his body was hacked into mincemeat."

He sighed gently. These days anything seemed possible in Villjamur.

✳

"I honestly knew nothing about it," Chancellor Urtica confessed, the shock on his face genuine enough for Jeryd. He ran his hands through his hair, now clearly lost for words.

They were standing inside the door of Boll's chambers, staring at the huge bloodstain covering the floor. They stared, for what seemed like an entire bell. It had spattered the walls, too, and even the glass on the window was smeared with gore.

Jeryd was quietly grateful that at least the body had been removed.

"First Ghuda . . . and now Boll." Urtica's gaze flicked about anxiously.

And next you? Jeryd wondered, recognizing the fear in the councilor's expression.

"Please excuse me." Urtica turned, and left the chamber.

"Bit of a mess, all this," Jeryd sighed.

Tryst approached the worst of the carnage with a narrow step. "Guess we should have this cleaned up before we examine the room thoroughly?"

"Soon enough," Jeryd agreed, "but let's just take a look around first."

For over an hour, Jeryd and Tryst examined every corner of the room. They rooted assiduously through all of Boll's books, documents, even ornaments. All the time Jeryd was careful to keep his tail well tucked in, away from the crimson mess. He finally did a search for hidden drawers, checked for concealed panels—but found nothing out of the ordinary.

He was about to give up when he noticed a stain on a mirror. As he brushed his finger against it, Tryst stepped next to him. "What've you got there?"

"Blue paint," Jeryd said in surprise, holding up his hand to inspect it.

"Was he an artist in his spare time?" Tryst suggested, staring at Jeryd's finger.

"I doubt it," Jeryd replied. "There're no sketchbooks. Not even any paintings on the walls—only tapestries. So how did he get blue paint on the mirror?"

"You reckon it's important?"

"Everything can have some importance, Tryst. The good investigator must always think that."

Tryst walked away stiffly, as if wounded by the minor reprimand.

But Jeryd continued, "You know, on the day of Ghuda's death, I saw some blue paint stains on the cobbles, right beside his body. At the time we assumed it was probably from a pot spilled on its way to the nearby gallery."

Tryst stood by the window, staring out across the snow-burdened skies. "So we have a link between the cases? It's not much to go on."

"It's something though," Jeryd said. "And it's more than we had before. Bohr, it seems we hardly even get a body to examine this time around."

He pulled a handkerchief from inside his robe, wiped the blue paint from the mirror, then from his finger. He wrapped it up deftly, concealed it beneath his clothing, and made his way back toward the door.

✳

"Doctor Tarr," Jeryd said later, "we're here, as agreed."

"Good afternoon, investigator," Tarr said, beckoning Jeryd into the mortuary. "The human has not come with you this time?"

"No, he apparently had some administrative tasks to see to," the rumel replied, stomping his boots to rid them of snow. "Maybe the sight of Boll's chambers was enough to put him off."

"But not you?" Tarr said, cheerfully.

"No, I guess not then," Jeryd laughed dryly. "Maybe I've developed a stomach for such things after all these years."

They proceeded into the depths of Tarr's workplace, where a single lantern struggled to provide light. Its oil flame flickered as he shut the door. Jeryd found himself still pondering Tarr's presence in the Hall of Life. Why would a man so used to working with death bother to go there in the first place? He had clearly been in a state of intense soul-searching when Jeryd had found him there, so perhaps there was more to Doctor Tarr than his surface demeanor implied.

The doctor led him to a table on which lay a large metal tray about two armspans wide, three long in length.

"What've we got here?" Jeryd inquired.

"This is it, investigator." Tarr gestured toward the contents of the tray. "This is Councilor Boll."

Even Jeryd was amazed. In all his decades in the service of the Inquisition, he had never seen a body *left* in this horrific state. He had seen the results of torture, of fierce battles, of poisons that ate a body slowly—but nothing like this.

At one end of the tray were assembled the bones of the late councilor, or what was left of those that had been fragmented into finger-length pieces. The other end contained the "flesh"—a grisly pink and red mound like you might see in the gutters of a slaughterhouse. The stench was powerful.

Jeryd said in awe, "How could this have been achieved?"

"With a large axe, and plenty of time," Tarr said. "I would reckon the murderer to have been kept busy for nearly two hours."

"At least he was dedicated to his task then," Jeryd muttered, scanning up and down the tray. "And yet no one seemed to notice?"

"This was relentless brutality, investigator. It was evil, pure and simple."

"You were right, doctor, I don't think there's anything for me to examine properly here. I'm going back to warn the Council Atrium immediately. If something like this could be done in such secrecy, any one of their members could be next. I'll see myself out." Jeryd turned away.

As he stepped outside, he took a deep breath of the sharp evening air. He stroked his chin in disbelief, for a moment not actually wishing to catch this killer. Did he really want to encounter the individual who could turn a living being into slush? And how exactly would that confrontation go? Excuse me, sir, but I think you . . . Then no more Jeryd.

What had Villjamur come to?

He pulled up his hood, slid his hands deep into his pockets, strode off to find where he had tethered his horse.

✳

"Chancellor Urtica," Jeryd insisted, "I'm not sure you understand. You'll need to consider maximum security. Double, triple your guard. I fear there may be someone intending to pick off councilors one by one."

Urtica stared at him in alarm.

"This is a serious matter," Jeryd continued, feeling he had got the man's attention. He was seated opposite a large table, in a pleasant wood-paneled chamber. The fire burning in the corner had nearly died to ashes. The rumel and human had already been chatting for half an hour.

"I see you don't collect many things," Jeryd said, looking around.

"It makes for a purer mind, investigator." Urtica sat back in his chair sipping tea. "It makes my work more efficient. Less to distract me that way."

"Maybe I should try that and clear the crap out of my chamber,"

Jeryd said. "Anyway, as I asked you earlier: what might have linked these two councilors? What common projects could they have been working on? Such a link might help me find a motive."

"And as I keep telling you, investigator," Urtica said, "I just can't think of *anything*."

There was something intransigent about his tone that Jeryd found frustrating. There was an air of superiority, a suggestion that he considered himself invincible. Perhaps it concealed something darker? Jeryd wanted to challenge him, *You know something and you're hiding it.* "Remember your own life might be at risk."

"We'll ensure all these corridors will be filled with guards by this evening."

"May I ask as to what are the most important concerns to the Council at the moment?"

"Is it really necessary for you to know such things?" Urtica sat back in his chair, staring into the fire.

"Perhaps," Jeryd shrugged. "Perhaps it may offer some clue to the reason for these killings. After all, any of you might be next."

Urtica merely nodded methodically, as if coming to terms with the threat. People reacted differently to such situations, didn't they, some not caring much at all, others getting into such a panic that they never left their homes.

"Our main current concern is the Freeze, of course," Urtica said. "It raises a number of crucial issues, the most important being the refugee crisis. There are already an estimated ten thousand of them camped outside the city gates, as you know."

"Go on."

"We're working on several solutions"—Jeryd noticed Urtica's expression alter slightly—"but ultimately, it will be up to the new Empress. She will make the final decision on what to do."

"How are other cities of the Empire coping?" Jeryd said. "Vilhokr, Villiren, E'toawor, Vilhokteu?"

"As well as can be expected. People have flooded in from rural areas. They're accumulating grain supplies and fuel, building icebreaker longships, imposing rationing. Like us, they see it as a challenge. Investigator, there will be many fatalities because of this ice age, and everyone is working hard to ensure that ordinary folk will survive."

"And you really care?" Jeryd said boldly.

"It's not about caring, necessarily, rather it's about making sure a city continues functioning. If you care too much, you get personal, and if you get personal, you inevitably fail. This is a business, investigator, pure and simple."

Jeryd observed the body language of this consummate politician. Urtica crossed and re-crossed his legs repeatedly throughout their conversation. Also, he rarely made eye contact, and was obviously uncomfortable being questioned about Council matters.

"Tell me, Chancellor Urtica, do you know if any of the councilors like painting as a hobby?"

Urtica looked up, raised an eyebrow. "I haven't a clue, investigator. Why do you ask?"

"I found small traces of fresh paint near both bodies."

Urtica merely shook his head. "I've told you all I can."

Jeryd stood up. "I think I've done all I can here."

Urtica said, "Could you put another log on the fire on your way out? It tends to get very cold in here."

Jeryd paused by the door. "Yes, I suspect it does."

On his way down the corridor, Jeryd thumped the wall in frustration. Two murders, linked by only one bizarre similarity: paint. Why was there a dab of blue paint next to each corpse? Were they trying to fight their way out with a paintbrush?

The chancellor was no help so far. Neither was Doctor Tarr.

Suddenly he remembered how the suspect Tuya painted in her spare time. It was an obvious connection, maybe too obvious, but it was the only thing he had to go on. But why would an alienated prostitute want to kill top-level politicians, and so savagely? It just didn't seem quite right. Perhaps she might have some suggestions to help his thoughts, and he decided he would visit her very soon.

But not tonight. Tonight he would be going home to Marysa.

Everyone deserved a life of their own—even an investigator.

CHAPTER 21

✳

CHANCELLOR URTICA MADE HIS WAY DOWN THE CRUMBLING STAIRWELL, glancing back every now and then, just in case, just to be sure.

He held a lantern high, drew his cloak around him. A gust of wind rattled down from above, transforming his shadow into increasingly esoteric shapes. Urtica was descending into a little-remembered quarter of Villjamur. Deep underground. Messages were etched across the stone, bearing the names of lovers and enemies from across the ages. Bats, rodents, lizards, all competed for dark corners, like a reverse image of life on the surface. The smell of their feces was intense, but this did not deter Urtica. He had dealt with more shit than this in his time.

For half an hour he descended, knowing the way well.

Faintly, he heard chanting. It meant he was nearly there. Voices were raised in an ancient variant of common Jamur, the language in which the Ovinists still sang. They were engaged in prayer—but not to Bohr or Astrid, or any approved deity—and that would change, wouldn't it, when his time came.

A battered wooden door heralded the end of his route. After knocking seven times, the hatch slid open, curious eyes appeared. A flicker of recognition, then the door was unbolted, opened, and Urtica stepped inside.

A hundred candles were reflected in wall mirrors to create an unlikely brightness. Incense filled the air, as smoke wafted across the far side of the immense room. Dozens of black-robed, black-hooded men and women sat on benches facing the far wall, which was hung with ornate tapestries. Below them was a plinth supporting a metal tray containing a selection of pigs' hearts rescued from the city slaughterhouses. The chanting continued as Urtica walked toward the front of the chamber, the hoods turning minutely as everyone's gaze tracked his progress.

When he arrived directly before them, a young blond girl stepped out from their ranks, leading a pig on a leash. She was dressed in white silk, which clung to her slender frame as she approached him, the pig shuffling behind her absentmindedly. No sooner had Urtica stepped before the congregation, than his audience drew out their rapiers simultaneously, brandishing the narrow blades in the air until silence fell. Urtica beckoned the girl to stand behind him, then raised both hands above his head. The swords were lowered and, once they were all seated again, Urtica began speaking.

"Neophytes, minors, majors," he intoned.

"Magus Urtica . . ." the congregation replied in a chorus reverberating against the ancient stone walls.

"My brothers and sisters, I have grave news on certain matters. Last night our esteemed Majorus Boll was brutally murdered in his sleep. This is the second member of our holy order to have been killed recently."

Murmurs all around. Beneath the hoods were familiar faces, their eyes glistening like those of beasts reflected in firelight. Among them there were several Council members, in shadow, all of them concerned for their own safety.

Urtica held up his hand for silence. "Jamur Rika will arrive in Villjamur shortly, and I feel this interim period is an excellent opportunity for us to profit. I intend to make myself Emperor of the entire Jamur territories, and once in position, I can assure you all greater powers, greater influence."

"How will you remove Jamur Rika?" someone inquired from the front row.

"All will be revealed in good time. But now, for our holy rituals!"

Applause filled the huge underground chamber, then solemn chanting in the ancient language. The little pig squealed in fright and the girl had to struggle hard to keep it under control. Urtica beckoned her over to stand in front of the sacrificial plinth. He loomed down over the tethered creature, tucked it under one arm, produced a knife from his sleeve. He held the blade high, smiling wildly, the room heady with smoke and adulation.

Quickly, he lunged across the young girl and slit her throat.

She crumpled to the floor, her white silk robe reddening like blossoming roses. The pig eagerly thrust its snout in her lifeblood.

"I promise that the sacred pig—our god reincarnate—shall feed well under my rule!" Urtica thundered. The swords were held high again, the cheers and chants rising to an eerie crescendo. Urtica stood with his arms raised, breathing heavily with excitement. Sweat glistening down his forehead, he indicated for several men standing in the front row to approach him. The first was Aide Tryst, his head covered slightly by the hood, the lanterns casting subtle shadows across his face. The handsome young investigator held out his hands as Urtica lovingly offered him a pig's heart.

"A word with you later," Urtica whispered.

"Of course, Magus." Tryst retreated with a deferential bow, and the next man stood ready to receive his dripping reward.

✳

After the proceedings, Urtica walked with Tryst back to the city proper.

As they traversed one of the bridges, Urtica paused to lean on one of the thick stone parapets, examining the city from this great height. A sea mist had come in, now filtering through the city. Occasional citizens appeared, walking it like ghosts with lanterns held out in front of them. There was the stench from crates of rotting vegetables discarded in corners behind bistros and taverns, disturbed occasionally by cats rooting through them for rodents. One of the tavern doors opened spilling light, and a group of men piled out into the cold evening air, singing wildly about a previous Emperor who had wrecked carnage all across Jokull.

Urtica glanced up to some of the narrow windows on the spire towers. Faint dabs of light, shadows moving inside the warmth. After a nod of confirmation from him, Tryst lit some prerolled arum weed, the embers glowing at the tip. Urtica didn't mind a few bad habits now and then.

"I love these bridges, Tryst," Urtica confessed. "They offer such a wonderful view, you can see nearly everything going on. And still, even after all these hundreds of years, the citizens below us always forget that other people can watch their movements at any time."

"Indeed, Magus," Tryst said, stepping up alongside the chancellor. "Anyone would think the whole place was designed with voyeurism in mind."

"Perhaps," Urtica sighed. "Yet I love this city. There is so much that it can do."

"A pity the ice age restricts it," Tryst said.

"Not a lot we can do about that," Urtica said. "However, it'll only last for a few decades. We inside can outlive that." He then eyed the refugee camps, and the smoke-striated sky.

"It'll mean we come back stronger, afterward." Urtica slapped the stone with his palm, turned to face Tryst directly. "Your commander. Investigator Rumex Jeryd. What do you honestly think about him?"

"Honestly?"

"Honestly."

He took another drag on the roll-up and breathed slowly into the night. "Well, Magus, it's complicated. I mean we used to be good friends, and admittedly, he has helped me a lot. But now I feel differently because he's thwarting my promotion."

"All about the age thing?" Urtica suggested.

"Indeed. Because I won't live as long as a rumel, he reckons I'll never become experienced enough. So, he won't do anything to help me. He won't even try."

"Of the fellow himself, then—is he a competent Inquisition officer?"

"Oh, yes, he's good at his job. But he'll never break with tradition. Won't even try." He scowled. "I think I deserve better."

"Well, I'm not sure I like the sound of him too much," Urtica said. "Now, I don't want him removed either. That would only draw attention. It might suggest corruption in the Council. No, if he's as good as some folk say then I hope he'll find the murderer. I find something unnerving, though." Urtica shivered as a damp wind stirred his robe. "I want him to find the killer, yet I don't want him delving so deeply into Council business that he might stumble into Ovinist territory. Not now, with all these plans I have for us. He strikes me as one who takes his work extremely seriously, and I can't risk him exposing us."

Tryst said, "You wish me to help in some way?"

"Yes, tell me if there's anything we can distract him with so he does not dig too deep."

Tryst related the renewed relationship of Jeryd and Marysa, that he messed up things with her before, couldn't afford to do so again.

"This might prove useful," Urtica said. "Perhaps you could distract our investigator by somehow disrupting their relationship. I don't know how, but don't kill her or anything. That would knock him off the case completely, and all I want is just a little distraction. Something that will keep his nose out of Council matters and concentrating only on surface issues. Anything to keep him on the streets hunting the killer."

"I'm sure it can be arranged." Tryst frowned. "I only need to find a way."

"You know, you've proved very useful to me, Tryst. I would like to see you standing a little closer to me in the future. We've got some important schemes to develop, particularly regarding the refugee situation." Urtica waved an arm vaguely toward the edge of the city. "Those vermin beyond the walls, spreading their filth and disease. I need someone to help me deal with them. When the time comes, it won't be a pretty job at all. So do you reckon you're up to it?"

"Magus Urtica," Tryst smiled. "It would be an honor."

"Good, then let me tell you more about my proposals on the matter, my dear boy . . ." Urtica turned his gaze once again to Villjamur.

CHAPTER 22

✳

I<small>T WAS</small>, R<small>ANDUR</small> <small>CONCLUDED, PUSHING HIMSELF OFF THE COBBLES OF AN</small> alley next to the tavern, an unwise decision to drink so much and so quickly.

He felt damp grit on his palms, and the muscles in his arms quivered as he levered himself upright. His head ached so much he wanted to cut it off. He looked up to see Denlin perched on top of a small wooden stool nearby.

Still drinking.

Still talking.

"Morning, lad," Denlin said cheerfully.

Randur collapsed to the ground with a groan, and the old man burst out laughing.

"Trouble with you youngsters is, you think you can keep up with us. But we've been at it for years, lad. I was drinking this horse piss before you could let go of your mother's teat . . ."

"Bollocks," Randur muttered, then groaned again. His hair was disheveled, mud plastered all over one side of his face. There was a faintly foul smell he hoped he had nothing to do with.

So, another night of drinking with Denlin. This ritual had been going on for days, the cycle repeating itself: seduction of a lady, take what pickings he could, then flee into the darkness of the caves where

Denlin would soon arrange a buyer. Celebrations would ensue, naturally, and it wasn't normal for him to drink this much, but last night he had a particularly good haul. A diamond bracelet snatched from a sixty-year-old widow. Her age hadn't limited her sexual appetite, but it had taken her an age to reach orgasm, and she lay so still afterward that he thought she was dead. As he left she kept murmuring thankyous.

Before he had stepped into the night, he managed to swipe his most expensive trophy yet.

A clock tower chimed, each strike ricocheting around Randur's head. He counted eight hours, and realized that within the next one he had a dance lesson with the Lady Eir. He cursed loudly.

"What's up, lad?"

Randur said, "I've got to go." He stood up at last, brushed himself down, his damp clothes stinking of smoke and alcohol.

"Well I'll be here when you need me," Denlin said.

"I'll be back as soon as I've got more stuff to sell." Randur turned and began to hurry away through Caveside.

He abruptly frowned, noticing the unusual light. It shouldn't be daylight down here, not still underground, though it occurred to him that he had only ever visited the caves at nighttime, and now it was morning.

Randur rubbed his eyes again, looked up. "Well, would you look at that . . ."

Light ran in strips down the underside of the immense cavern, as if he was standing under the glowing ribcage of some gargantuan beast. These ribs sparkled like glass. At the apex, in the very center of the cave, shone a bright hub of light that intruded from the outside, directly from the brightening sky above. There were similar smaller hubs located at intervals throughout the caves, each one projecting light to this neglected expanse of city. Perhaps this was the real Villjamur from time immemorial, not the other city that every traveler saw, or the one the wealthy and powerful now lived in.

But this was no time to dawdle, or speculate. He was late, and reeking of alcohol. He sprinted back to Balmacara.

✳

It was the same morning that Commander Brynd Lathraea was bringing the new Empress to Villjamur, and a large contingent of the Fourth and Fifth Dragoons was riding toward the city through the mist. The horses' hooves thumped on sodden tundra, leaving a muddy trail. It wouldn't be at all difficult for anyone to follow, but there were so many troops in attendance that you need not fear a surprise attack. Brynd rode directly alongside the carriage in which Rika sat with the windows veiled. Apium was astride his horse, one of those pulling the vehicle, while Nelum and Lupus were riding directly behind. All around them on either side, keeping pace precisely, were columns of Dragoons.

The Lady Rika herself was the center of all this.

Brynd eyed her frequently, but couldn't tell much from her expression. He suspected she understood exactly what was required of her in her new role, with its responsibilities. He also knew she had not seen Villjamur for several years. Its daunting walls and the three entrance gates had been there seemingly forever, but there were now differences, inside and out. The ice age was upon them, with thousands of refugees huddled outside. Families were being torn apart, there were suicides and murders daily.

And her father, the Emperor, was dead.

✳

"Your breath, Randur Estevu, smells as if a horse has just passed wind. I trust you've a decent reason for entering my presence in such a state?" Eir folded her arms as she examined Randur.

"And what would you know of a horse's bodily functions, a pretty little rich girl like you?" Randur slumped into a chair in the minor chamber he had commandeered for dancing lessons. The fire was spitting rather too loudly for his liking, even though tapestries covered the windows in an attempt to exclude drafts. Randur was at least grateful for the dim lighting, since his head pounded even when confronted with a candle. His pupil was today wearing one of her green silk numbers, something he had to admit she looked particularly attractive in.

If only she could shut her mouth for more than a second.

Placing his head in his hands, he began to massage his scalp. "Oh, Bohr."

"And may I ask how you managed to end up in this state?" Eir inquired.

"You may not," Randur groaned, glancing up at her. Her face displayed an expression of disgust he wasn't used to seeing from women. He was a man of style, after all, so maybe things weren't looking so great.

"Do you realize who you're talking to?" Her tone was indignant.

"Sure I do," Randur replied.

"Yet you obviously have no respect for me?"

"I'm sorry." Randur stood up, gave her as sarcastic a bow as he could manage, given the pain in his head. He wasn't in the mood for this formal nonsense.

Her expression suggested that she wasn't sure whether he was being serious. "I thought you requested for a drummer to help us with the timing?" she persisted. "Maybe he has got himself into Astrid-knows-what trouble, like yourself."

"I wasn't in any trouble," Randur protested, rubbing his eyes. "I can handle myself just fine on these streets."

"I'm sure you can," Eir said tartly. "Now I demand that you tell me where you were and what you were up to."

"Caveside, if you must know." He began to pace around the room in the hope of walking off his headache, occasionally stepping over to the window. Right now the cool air was the freshest he'd ever breathed.

"Caveside?" Eir said, frowning. "Whatever were you doing down there? While you're in residence here, you ought to conduct yourself with more decorum. It's a bit reckless, don't you think, fraternizing with all those thugs? I've heard stories about serving girls who ventured down the wrong street and—"

"D'you have any idea what actually goes on down there?" Randur snapped, glancing despairingly at her. He shook his head. *Bohr, how damn spoiled are people around here?*

"Well," Eir replied, "I have been told of all sorts of thieves and murderers. Soldiers gone bad."

"Yeah, well maybe there are some of those," Randur admitted. They were so silent for a while he could hear the wind racing through Balmacara. Upon understanding the words she spoke, he said,

"You've lived here all these years and never actually been down there?"

Eir gave an impatient shrug. "I don't really have much time for the business of such people. Why should I risk stepping foot in that darkness?"

Randur grunted to suppress a laugh. *How could this girl be even temporarily in charge if she doesn't have a clue about half the type of people in her own damn city? It makes me glad I never grew up in a place like this.*

Randur was feeling tired, knew he was getting grumpy as he always did when he hadn't had enough sleep. That, combined with his hangover, meant he was pretty pissed off. "What is it with this place, this *legendary* city of sanctuary? The jewel of the Jamur Empire, the largest city in the Archipelago, yet you've got thousands of refugees camped right outside the gates, while the city's rulers turn a blind eye on the millions of ordinary citizens who don't own huge acreages of land, or who haven't grown fat off tribal slave labor, or what's practically wage slavery. They're just not real to you, are they?"

"*Everyone's* real to me," Eir said.

"Reckon *you're* even real yourself?" Randur sneered. "What kind of life have you ever led to make you so real?"

"A dutiful one, thank you. I've had pressures and responsibilities."

"Responsibilities. Right. I bet you've always had every last thing done for you."

"And who exactly are *you* to tell me this? I should have you strung up from the city walls as an example."

"That's exactly my point, see?" Randur continued, unabashed. "You just deal with life the way a spoiled child would. You want to eliminate someone just because he tells it how it is. What kind of ruler does that make you, if you can't even deal with ordinary people?"

She walked to the tapestry covering the window, drew it back and gazed over the countless spires of Villjamur. "This is the only city I've really known. I've heard of the other places—Vilhokr, Vilhokteu, Gish. I've never visited them, never needed to, was always advised not to. Maybe I've been fortunate in my position and upbringing, but . . ." Anger now flared in those eyes, and frustration. ". . . Just because I haven't had to work for my living, doesn't mean my entire life has been worth less than anyone else's."

Randur suspected he'd hurt her, thought right now it was difficult to care. He had a throbbing head, a mouth as dry as a desert rock. He was angry at this rich girl. Her superior attitude added a whole new rancor to his thinking.

"For your information," Eir said, "there's perhaps a little more to me than you might think. I'm not a bad person. I've not wished ill on anyone. Every time we practice dance or combat you make a reference to my fortunate upbringing as if it was something you missed out on. Well, it isn't that lucky being imprisoned in a life you don't necessarily want. So maybe I'm a little short with people at times. To use a phrase of your own, maybe I do get *pissed off.* Some of us can't just go on pretending to be someone we're not."

If she knew anything of his past, of his own secrets, she didn't show it. This was all getting a little bit near the knuckle.

She continued, her voice significantly softer, "Perhaps you yourself should show me the other side of this city then, if you really think it would do me some good?"

"Like I'd be able to sneak you out of this place with no one noticing. I'll probably lose my head for that—but sure, why not? If you're genuinely up for it, we can find a way. But, look, we should be doing dance practice. Let's learn a few steps, shall we? I'll count time for us, in the absence of our drummer."

Eir approached him. They assumed position, fingers locked, a close embrace, and more than ever she seemed small and vulnerable in his arms. She was now in one of those moods where she didn't seem to want to look at him, wanted to pull as far away as possible in each dance step. Maybe he would try to patch things up between them by just shutting up.

The door opened to reveal one of the resident guards. "My Lady Stewardess, there is some urgent news."

Eir stepped away from Randur quickly, as if she had been caught in some lewd act.

"What news?" she demanded.

"Your sister Jamur Rika's entourage is getting near the city, my lady. Garudas have sighted her carriage just under two hours away."

CHAPTER 23

✳

THE RETURN OF THE ELDER SISTER, RIKA, BROUGHT THOUGHTS OF HIS own family to Chancellor Urtica. Families were an important issue to him.

After all, he'd killed his own.

They used to ridicule him, and he just couldn't cope with that, no, not the everyday references to sneering at his shortcomings. Gathered around the table at night, *every* night, they would start to berate him for his failings, especially his mother. Even when he qualified for the junior ranks of the Council his family would carp at him for not progressing up the ranks quickly enough. They would question his lack of friends, they complained that he didn't earn enough; it seemed everything he did or did not do became a target, a focal point for savage criticism. Fearing that this constant undermining would ultimately limit his career prospects, the young Urtica decided one night that enough was enough.

Dispatching them had been a joy, a creative wonder, the kind of ingenious ploy to smile about as he remembered it. He contrived a way of tricking them into dropping something lethal in each other's food. One night just after he had turned eighteen, a treat to rid himself of all the shame and humiliation, the sheer joy of watching them cough up blood, retch bile, yet still take time to berate each other shrilly as they realized what was happening. He had a watertight alibi—paying off several old friends for their word, with promise of power to come—and he'd faked an entry in his mother's diary. When the Inquisition came they declared it an open and shut case. Sympathy had come pouring in from neighbors, for the poor boy so tragically orphaned. When he finally got away from their condolences, he began to savor the thrill to be obtained from the godlike power to terminate life. While he was engaged in the business of removing his family, he had taken the liberty to forge new wills—with ancient Jamur runes and seals and all—leaving more distant family members ostracized. Charitably, he gave them a little, because he was nice like that, but the majority of the wealth and estates came to him. *Forgery,* he thought at the time, *is such a blissful art.*

And soon there were others to suffer at his hand, like his older cousin in a freak sailing accident off the coast of Jokull, whose drowning was followed by a few drinks at the quayside celebrating the sudden inheritance of family estates on the east coast near Vilhokr. *A glass to you, dearest cousin, for the comforts with which you've provided me. Cheers!*

With his new-won independence and income, he had turned to the Ovinists. The traditional gods reminded him too keenly of his pious family. After all, a new faith for a new man!

Vaguely the whore he used last night had looked like his mother, a slender waif of a girl with sharp features. It brought back some complex thoughts to his mind. *What does it mean, sleeping with a substitute for my mother? And in sleeping with whores, well, he was just becoming like his father, wasn't he? Bohr, families can fuck you up* . . . Urtica slid out of bed, walked over to the fire to throw another log on it, then on went his favorite green tunic.

A guard entered the room. "Sir, Commander Lathraea approaches the city with the new Empress."

So, she was back at last, and it was time to see exactly how easily he might manipulate her.

He walked over to a window, pulled back the tapestry to reveal the view over the fore-city. A gust of wind whistled in, but he didn't even feel it.

Such beauty, such potential . . . Until his gaze focused on the refugees camped outside the gates of the city, their numerous little fires already coughing smoke weakly into the air. Their makeshift homes stretched far into the distance, where disease was spreading rapidly. Decent people feared leaving the city. Resentment at this encroachment was growing, and with it a feeling of hatred.

Other concerns loomed now in his thoughts, first and foremost the final campaign against the Varltungs. He had to convince Commander Lathraea to be out of the way so that Urtica himself could assume full control of the military. The Empress, too, would need to be persuaded to put her trust in him, but that fitted in nicely with the troubles now erupting on the northern fringes of the Empire. In fact he needed Brynd's expertise in handling this crisis, so that wasn't just a lie.

✳

Rika leaned out of the carriage, looked up at the gray sky. The wind whipped her hair around her face as she pulled strands of it back. "Why have we stopped?" she asked.

Brynd rode over, the spires of Villjamur towering behind him on the hilltop, and the sight of the city sparked a thousand memories in her, and she was overcome by a strange sensation in her stomach. This was the home of her youth that she hadn't seen for years. A part of her that she had almost forgotten about. It was an uncomfortable feeling to realize she wasn't that same person anymore. A famous ancient scribe had once recommended never returning to a place with happy memories, because it could never be the same. What about bad memories—would they diminish too?

She had to confront the girl—now woman—she had once been, and remember the day she had walked out on her family. Well, her father, anyway, but he was gone now.

"I wanted to advise you of a problem, Jamur Rika, before you approach the gates of Villjamur." Brynd steered his horse till he faced her directly.

His sinister appearance: burning red eyes, black horse, black uniform, narrow white features belied his true nature. The brooch of the Empire glistened reassuringly on his chest. She had never seen anyone quite like him in her life. There was something about his demeanor that said she was safe in his hands, that he would protect her. It was those things that really mattered, not the color of skin or eyes.

"What is it you're saying, commander?" she demanded, hoping she sounded very much like an Empress.

"I must warn you there are thousands of refugees outside the city gates. They are hoping to find protection inside the city during the Freeze."

"And they can't come in?" Rika said.

Mild regret in his eyes, despite his military firmness.

"No," Brynd admitted. "It's been decided there's a limited capacity for Villjamur once the gates finally close. The city has to protect its own interests during the many years of ice to come."

"So please stop me if I'm incorrect in my assumptions that no one can come into the city? And these people will die here. In front of us. As we watch on?"

"Pretty much," Brynd said. "But they'll die anyway. Meanwhile military personnel will be allowed in and out—or people with the right documentation, of course. It's the only way the city could last for so long."

Rika pressed on, "And nothing can be done? Nothing in our hearts can be found for their plight?"

"Not my place to say, Empress," Brynd replied. "There are many other things I'm involved with at the moment. As soon as I'm equipped and rested, the Night Guard will be leaving to investigate some skirmishes in the north."

"How significant are they, these skirmishes?"

"Too early to tell, my lady."

So much for her to take in. She could have done with Brynd staying with her for a while longer, because although alarming on first sight, he radiated confidence, a quiet compassion—as much as any military man could. "Commander, can I trust you?" she said. "I feel . . . quite vulnerable here. As if people might take advantage of my naïveté."

"Empress. I was sworn in as one of your father's favored guard, to be sent on any mission in his name, to uphold his honor. As his chosen successor, you inherit my service also, and that of my soldiers. Of all the Jamur armies, in fact. And as soldiers we're not paid to think about our orders, and we serve only your word. Though I can fully appreciate how great that responsibility must seem right now."

She sat back further into the carriage. "Thank you, commander. Your skill with words and encouragement is a great help to one so new and unversed as myself."

She then heard the commander order the escort of Dragoons to move on, and the carriage was in motion.

Next stop: Villjamur.

✳

Lines of troops kept back the refugees by sword and bow, making sure none dared closely approach the roadway. They formed two distinct lines on either side of the route stretching all the way from the city gates, and she could hear the helpless moans, the cries of fear as metal was brandished in their direction, and the cursing of soldiers as they shouted for them to keep back, stay off the road. The stench of their encampment was awful, intense.

She was the Empress, or would very shortly be, so surely she must do something to stop this ill-treatment of her own people? Or perhaps this was the first lesson she would learn: her own powerlessness to achieve everything she might wish.

Brynd was riding to one side, and turned to nod at her briefly before again scanning the troubled scene. She saw the gaunt, muddied faces of *her* people staring at her carriage between the lines of Dragoons and horses. Shouts of commands. Then the gates of the city were opening, whereupon more soldiers streamed forward in a clatter of armor and weaponry. Garudas circled above her, ever watchful, as screams from the refugees reached a crescendo.

Her eyes widened at the alarming spectacle. All this fuss just for her—she refused to believe it. The carriage rocked its way onto the cobbled streets of the city, and within a few moments she was inside Villjamur, safe, the noise of the refugees muffled as the doors closed behind.

Then they stopped. Was this where she must get out? Again that uncertainty.

The commander leaned into the carriage. "We'll now progress through the main streets of the city. People may stare in at you. They don't really know you from sight. You may remind some of the older citizens of your mother, perhaps . . ." He stopped at that sensitive point, and changed tack. "Many of them probably don't know the current state of rulership despite the announcements that should have been made."

"Very kind of you to warn me, commander. But I'm sure I'm capable of looking after myself."

Brynd retreated, ordered the entourage to ride on.

Rika stared up at the city, *her* city, its landscape furnished with a sense of possession, so nothing would be the same as before.

Everything was as she remembered, and bittersweet memories lapped over her. The dreamlike spires that disappeared up into damp mist. The hanging baskets everywhere encaging the beautiful flowers of the tundra. The soaring bridges, the gray-red stone, the ever-busy people. And Balmacara in the center. Her own history came back in flashes: a childhood spent staring out of windows at these same sights, not being permitted to have much contact outside Balmacara. Days of boredom. The trauma of her father beating her mother, of beating Rika herself. And little Eir brightening random moments with her naïveté, a child's voice echoing down the corridors. It was amazing what mere clusters of assembled rock could do to the mind.

Forget about all that. It's the past. Think of the future.

✳

Her sister already stood waiting for her inside, her face erupting in emotions. After the initial formality, Eir and Rika embraced for what, to Brynd, seemed like a season. The fond memories were returning, the gradual remembrance of their idiosyncrasies, all reflected in the softness of their glances and the way they would touch each other's arms.

After a long interlude of whispering, they seemed to remember that other people were gathered around them, listening, waiting.

The young page showed them into a formal chamber where several members of the Council were seated, all immediately rising to their feet.

Brynd and the rest of his Night Guard followed silently.

There he was, Chancellor Urtica, walking over to the new Empress. He took her hand, pressed it to his lips, after he briefly went down on one knee. "Jamur Rika, a great honor. As your chancellor, may I welcome you to Villjamur, on behalf of the Council. Your presence here in this difficult time is most reassuring."

"Hey," Apium muttered to Brynd, "he's not wasting his time in greasing up to her, is he?"

Brynd grunted a quiet laugh. He looked across to Nelum and Lupus, who stood silently, watching the Empress's every move—as they had been trained to do for her father.

"Who's that swarthy looking stick of a fellow over there?" Apium whispered.

Brynd followed his gaze to a thin, handsome man standing in one corner of the chamber. With glossy black hair that cascaded down in curls, he wore smart clothes of the kind usually seen on the outer islands, but updated to make a splash in the city. He seemed a bit of a clichéd dandy—even to Brynd. The man stood tall, his chin raised, his head angled in calculated postures. Several ladies of the court were huddled close to him, and every now and then he'd flash them a rehearsed grin.

Brynd raised an eyebrow. "I've never seen him before. Why not ask one of the servants."

Apium stepped away and returned moments later.

"His name is Randur Estevu, and apparently he's Lady Eir's tutor for sword and dance. I think I remember Johynn talking about getting someone in. I don't know, holding a bloody dancing event because the Archipelago's about to be plunged into an ice age. Ridiculous, if you ask me, these bloody nobles."

"Aren't we ourselves technically nobles?" Brynd said.

"Aye, but, uh, at least we do something useful, not just prance about to music."

"Last time you danced you cleared the floor—and not in a good way."

"I had a bit to drink, I'll admit. Anyway, why should a soldier need rhythm?"

"Good sword skills," Brynd explained. "I'll bet that waif of a man can look after himself."

Brynd regarded the curious-looking newcomer, this Randur. He certainly had good dress sense. The man suddenly looked back at him. They stared at each other for a heartbeat, then Randur glanced away.

Brynd turned his attention to Urtica, who was still fawning upon the new Empress, with forced laughter, fake smiles, overstated gestures—it was enough to make Brynd feel sick.

✳

Later that afternoon, the sisters were allowed time in private, once it had been decided that Emperor Johynn's state funeral would take place in the morning. He was to be buried in the crypt under Balmacara, inside the caves, just like every ruler before him. For all other citizens, their bodies were burned on a pyre, much in line with the ancient tribal religions. It was thought that cremation sped their spirits toward one of the otherworlds, depending on how your life had been lived. Emperors alone were destined to stay in Villjamur forever, their bodies in the caves, decaying till they became part of the city, part of legend itself.

Their bones becoming Villjamur's bones.

Brynd discovered that after he'd gone, news of the Emperor's death had sent a slow shock wave through these corridors. Councilors had flapped around the place, murmuring portentous utterings, but all the time adding to a sense of unease. Brynd himself had noticed this malaise grow in the short time since his return. It manifested in a general lack of confidence, in an escalating mood of fear. But perhaps this mood was exacerbated by the coming of the ice age.

An initial ceremony would take place as the red sun rose. Then as the sun set, Rika would be proclaimed Empress, therefore finishing a day to change history—or at least the history books. Brynd had stationed two soldiers from the Night Guard outside Eir's and Rika's chambers, while he himself liaised with Chancellor Urtica, at that politician's request. The two men met in the War Chamber usually reserved for discussions on battle tactics, and perhaps this was the first indication to the commander that something was wrong.

Brynd opened the door to find Urtica standing at the far end of a massive stone table, his back to a spitting fire. No tapestries garlanded this room, only lanterns and examples of ancient weaponry on the walls. As he entered Brynd realized the conversation wouldn't be going his way.

"Commander, do step inside and close the door. Hell of a draft coming in."

Brynd shut the door and approached, his steps clicking in the awkward silence. "What's the problem, chancellor?"

"War, commander," Chancellor Urtica sighed. "I fear it's war."

"And why so? I've been away for less than a month, so what can have arisen? Surely we should be looking for peace at all costs in these distressing times?"

"Of course, but our experts have now analyzed the arrow that you retrieved from Dalúk Point. It was indeed a Varltung shaft."

"Really?" Brynd said, his eyes narrowing. "But I still don't see why the Varltungs would make a raid on us."

"Yes, well, these are strange days. Furthermore I've intelligence from our garudas suggesting that the Varltungs have planned more raids—now that our city is at its weakest. So I was forced to put some defensive plans in motion after you left. Troops are moving across the Empire as we speak."

"What intelligence exactly?" Brynd said. Were the city's forces already marching to war without his knowledge?

"Not only from garudas, but rumors from various outposts. So I have initiated troop movements for a coastal raid on the Varltung nation. I'll be using cultists from the Order of Dawnir to help, too, as I want to stop any chance of our outlying islands being assaulted after our city closes its doors. It is a purely defensive tactic, and we aim to minimize casualties, and work *with* them once they submit."

"And you're absolutely certain of this strategy? Surely, as commander of the armies, I should be allowed some say in this decision. Surely I should have some *role* in this?" It appeared that Urtica had already made up his mind even before Brynd had left to fetch Jamur Rika. Now it wouldn't surprise Brynd to learn that soldiers were already dying.

"That's certainly true, and I will need your agreement. The Council felt constrained to pass an urgent order of war in your absence. The Empress must be briefed immediately. More Dragoons and Regiments of Foot are currently being readied, but there's now another threat, for which I think your personal attention is more essential."

Brynd analyzed every word that Urtica uttered, scanning for the gaps in what he said to find the real story. Being chief commander of military operations appeared to mean little to these politicians, these articulate men who had no direct experience of combat. They just rolled the dice from a safe distance, not understanding the real costs in terms of resources and emotion.

Urtica said, "You were aware of your next task, I think, even before you returned here. Those killings on our islands further north—on Tineag'l to be precise."

"The mining island?"

"We've now had two reports of largescale massacres there. Towns have been wiped out, and so far hundreds have died—possibly thousands. I sent a garuda to investigate and he hasn't returned yet—that was some time ago now." Urtica reached across the table for a parchment, passed it to Brynd. "This however came through to us."

Brynd read the message.

> *To Emperor Johynn, and the Council of Villjamur*
>
> *I must alert you to a potential crisis as we've had reports of terrible events occurring on Tineag'l. Many have been fleeing atrocities of an unknown nature, that quite frankly leaves me to be astounded. There have been severe numbers of disappearances on Tineag'l, and interviews have been held with those who have fled. There is something killing whole communities, cleansing entire cities and towns. I estimate from listening to those escapees, and by studying old maps, that tens of thousands may no longer exist. It is rumored, that a host of many thousand refugees are fleeing from the north on foot, and it will take them some weeks to reach the south tip of Tineag'l. But when they reach it they will sail to Villiren. And good sirs, we can't cope with such quantities in our city. Already we've local people seeking shelter from the ice, so what is Lutto Fendor to do? I request you send aid, in whatever form possible, to this city and investigate the atrocious incidents on Tineag'l before this evil spreads here to the island of Y'iren. We are but a humble trading city, so we are not equipped to resist, or indeed help the refugees fleeing these killings. We need protection. Send it quick!*
>
> *Your servant, and in the name of Bohr and Astrid, and of the Jamur Empire and Council.*
>
> *Lutto Fendor, Portreeve of Villiren, on the island of Y'iren*

Brynd glanced twice over the parchment, noticing it possessed the mark of Jorsalir, a discreet symbol of the moons in each corner, behind the star of the Empire. That meant it was official all right, blessed by the priest, but Brynd tended to ignore those kinds of blessings. He grunted. *So Fat Lutto actually does his job, for once.* He handed it back to Urtica. "Yes, this is bad news all right. You wish me to assemble *what* exactly?"

"I think at least a few units of Dragoons, plus a cultist from the Order of the Dawnir should suffice. And the rest of your Night Guard, of course. But I'm not sure we can spare much more than that just yet if we're to organize a proper defense against the Varltung nation. Remember, they won their freedom six hundred years back, they've defeated the Empire's forces once. And they've enough population to furnish a few hundred thousand fighting men if they can unite all their tribes. I would like to make them . . . *submit* before the Freeze becomes too severe. So I'm leaving this matter in your capable hands." Urtica was silent for a moment as he contemplated some of the maps lying in front of him.

"You don't think this is a more important issue than the Varltung operation?"

"You know very well what Lutto's like. He can be . . . *inaccurate* in what he says. He's fat, he's lazy, he's a gambler, and a criminal."

"But he's in charge of an entire city and he's panicking," Brynd said.

"In charge because he rigs the voting. Anyway, I think that given the information so far, the greatest issue lies on the eastern fronts. Should you need more men, you can send for reinforcements. Oh, incidentally, that Dawnir friend of yours has been grumbling about wanting to go with you."

"Jurro?" Brynd said, puzzled. "Why does he need to come anyway?"

"Why not take him with you? The activity might finally jog his blasted memory, and then we can get some useful information out of him. I mean what's the use of an Ancient if he doesn't have memory? I don't want him just rotting away reading books for another several generations and only have the benefit of his misery to put up with. Take him with you, let him see a bit more of the world. Before the ice sets in."

Brynd considered just how exactly he could take one of the Ancient race on a scouting mission, traveling through towns where he'd undoubtedly be mobbed by villagers who would see him as some kind of oracle, some savior to them in the ice age. That was the exact reason he'd been hidden for so long.

"What of the firegrain?" Brynd said. "Have the remaining stocks of grain and oil been calculated?"

"Of course," Urtica said. "Anyway, there's wood remaining on Jokull, and plenty on the other islands. That's what the military will use for their warmth. That's what other cities are relying on. Emperor Johynn was just mad sending you out there in the first place. Now, shall we thrash out some details about the current crises facing the Empire? I believe our two fine minds should deliver some decent logistical analysis, what d'you say?"

"Yes." Times were awkward all right. He would prefer to be in control of the raids on Varltung, or else remain here to stand by the new Empress, but this threat, on one of the fringes of the Empire, appeared urgent, and what the hell could be causing it anyway?

"Why all this effort to subdue Varltung now? This Freeze could last thirty-odd years, and much of the Empire will be changed as we know it. Hell, there may be no Empire left when we come out of hibernation."

As Urtica met his gaze, it seemed a gust of wind came in from somewhere, flickering shadows adopting new postures across the old walls. "Commander Lathraea, I don't think you fully understand the purpose of the Jamur Empire?"

"I'm not sure I follow."

"I didn't think so. What does an empire do? We extend ourselves, we acquire new territories. We take control there. We grow. We make progress. We seize the world for our people, and we give them additional wealth as a reward. You're a military man, commander. I expect better of you than to doubt our purpose."

"Bohr, we've not had a skirmish in years—except for that incident on Dalúk Point, of course. And the lack of military action has been a *positive* thing. We've found more diplomatic ways to establish relationships with tribes locally. You think I've risen to the top of my career by rearing to fight everything I come across?"

"Did it never occur to you that you've risen so far so quickly because you were adopted by a wealthy family? That's how things work in Villjamur. I'd hoped for more from you, Commander Lathraea. There's a population of some millions out there that it's our responsibility to feed and nurture. We need to raise them from the squalor of their mud huts, and give them a better quality of existence. Your role isn't that of politician, but as a guardian of the Empire. That now means going to Tineag'l, to prevent a bigger threat than even the Varltungs may prove."

The chancellor had a valid point, even if Brynd didn't trust him, wondering how much of what slipped off his tongue was sincere. There were far too many bizarre happenings recently to trust the politicians, and perhaps the recent cycles of the moons were affecting more than just the weather. Maybe they were creating some kind of insanity across the Boreal Archipelago, generating a subtle tension you couldn't perceive exactly. And in the years to come, things would only get worse.

CHAPTER 24

※

JAMUR RIKA PERCHED ON THE WINDOWSILL STARING OUT ACROSS THE early morning snowflakes sifting through the air in thick flurries, collecting on the rooftops, on stationary carts, upturned barrels, walls. People were shuffling in and out of bleak streets and alleyways, avoiding the worst of it, miserable faces sheltering from the sky, only children looking up with glee, maybe not understanding what it meant.

She could breathe the tension even from up here.

All a necessary distraction, but she had to turn around and face her bed chamber eventually. It was so unfamiliarly full of luxuries that weren't her own—not that she'd possessed many before anyway. Leading a life studying Astrid had meant little need for such accoutrements. Purple furnishings, numerous gold and silver objects that she had no idea how to use, that perhaps had no real use anyway. Over there was the white silk gown she must wear for her father's burial in the crypts. Its layered silk was so much richer than the simple, black cotton she wore to sleep in.

And why should those refugees have to suffer when she enjoyed all this? She wanted to help them somehow, had already drawn up an idea to present to Chancellor Urtica at the earliest opportunity. To feed them, send aid, a food package from the city, from the new Empress. A positive move that would say she was trying her best. Even after only a brief moment back in Villjamur, it seemed as if the Council made all the decisions. But if she was going to insist on one thing it would be that.

Sleep hadn't come easy. Innumerable criers had stalked the evening until late, announcing her father's funeral to the echoing walls, their clear voices filtering through to her dreams, filling her slumber with visions of death and rebirth.

Rika felt trapped in a place that wasn't home, with such great responsibility. Jorsalir training had at least given her the luxury of accepting her fate. Now she felt such a longing, but for some time she didn't know what for. Perhaps she missed the remoteness of Southfjords, where there was little to occupy her mind except the daily texts, interrupted with a few thoughts of her sister. That those days could never be repeated made them all the more desirable. She must seek out a priestess in this alien city, so that she could have the benefit of Astrid's aspects to guide her through this difficult period.

✳

She couldn't let her past go. She had tried for so long to avoid it, had perhaps even fled the city to escape thinking about it. Always, when abroad, her life came back to her in images:

Shafts of sunlight bleaching stone floors. Eir crying after being covered in flour in the kitchens. Pock-faced tutors issuing grammar instructions while it rained. The first time she ever saw a garuda. The day the tapestries caught fire in the dining hall. Two servants kissing with intensity against the wall of one of the studies. On a balcony eating an apple in the fading autumn heat. A city cat licking the sole of her bare foot—its tongue strangely rough.

Rika and Eir had played frequently about Balmacara from a young age. There were so many corridors to explore, so many rooms that meant nothing but the challenge of exploration, tall windows offering vistas of Villjamur's great bridges and spires, and they were curious young minds with endless days ahead. Time was not a concept with which to be concerned.

Many of the city guard were charged with their protection, soldiers humbled by nursery duty. She often wondered what these towering, muscular men, swords at their waists, must have thought of these two tiny girls in ridiculously expensive dresses. Their training left them somehow inadequate for this new duty. She remembered the glances when two new guards were asked to watch them as they played. The men would look at each other, shrug, then merely stand there. By the end of the day they would inevitably be on their hands and knees, Eir and Rika riding their backs, brandishing wooden swords, and their mother would burst in the room laughing. The guards would retreat later, blushing.

Rika laughed. *I bet they enjoyed it really.*

They would try to lose them, Eir and Rika, try to vanish and cause panic. Once Eir managed to hide for an entire afternoon on top of a bookcase in one of the libraries while soldiers trotted along the corridors, checking every room, and their mother would vacillate between annoyance and worry. Knowing where she was, Rika would slip in every hour with some sweets for her.

"Are you coming down yet?"

"How long has it been?" Eir had said, brushing down a cloud of dust with the side of her arm.

"You should come down before they clip you round the ear. Eir. Ha! Ear Eir! You're named after an ear!"

"Shut up or I'm never coming down. Worse, I'll say that you scared me up here, and made me stay here and cry for ages."

"You wouldn't," Rika said.

"I would. So how long has it been?"

"Four hours."

"Give it at least two more. This book is good. The sweets are good. Anyway, I like the fuss being made. Makes a change."

Eir had always been the one less likely to follow instructions, the younger sibling, testing the rules that had been first set for Rika. And she had a point: they would often be ignored. They were children, so she should not be so harsh on them. Their father was busy being Emperor. A tough man, he shouted at them and their mother for no noticeable reason. Then there were the beatings, memories she tried to repress. One could see the neglect upon her mother's face, the withered features while in conversation with him, occasional bursts into tears as she sat staring out of the window. She had been beautiful. Sleek black hair, a pretty, oval face, tall and regal. Such dramatic clothing. Girls would help her select outfits, makeup, jewels, perfumes. Every bit the Emperor's wife. To Rika she was how ladies were supposed to be in the first instance, a role model for the glittering things that simply don't matter. Back then Rika would sit on her bed, dazzled, feeling lucky if her mother tried some of her items on her, smiling. She remembered her breath smelled of mint leaves—

A knock at the door.

For a moment she considered not answering. If she remained seated here by the window with her memories, it was possible that her day wouldn't even begin. As soon as she got up, events would inexorably be set in motion—events that would lead to her being declared sovereign of the Jamur Empire. Instead she could just sit here and stare out at the city, allowing the hypnotic flakes of snow to take her mind away.

Easy to understand why her father had eventually become insane.

"Rika, are you awake? It's Eir."

"Just a moment." Rika rose to let her sister enter, pleased it was not another stranger.

Eir marched to the center of the room, a heady waft of perfume following. She was wearing an outrageously fashionable red gown, high collar, black sleeves, her hair slick with oil, her face made up like nothing Rika had ever seen before. A fake red tundra rose nestled on her breast.

"You're not even dressed," Eir observed.

"No, I'm not," Rika sighed. "I was watching the snow and just thinking."

"You'll have plenty of time for that," Eir said. "We've got decades yet to go blind from the whiteness of it all, they say. The Night Guard and Council are assembling, as are all the major families."

"I've got a little while yet before I need to get there," Rika said. "I'm not sure how I'll cope here, with all the fuss they make. How does one get anything done with so many other people interfering?"

"I simply don't know," Eir confessed, now sprawling across the windowsill. "It's kind of fun to have such a bother made of us from time to time."

Rika smiled. "You've become such a spoiled little brat."

"Don't . . . you're sounding like Randur."

"Who's Randur?" Rika demanded.

"No one." Eir clenched her hands in a nervous manner.

"Indeed." Rika took a step closer. "He wouldn't be that young braggart strutting about these halls flirting wildly with every woman he meets, would he? I have certainly noticed him. Don't tell me you're predictably falling for his charms too?"

Eir laughed. "You've hardly been here so how could you even think that. No, I can barely stand having to dance with him."

"So you're close to him, are you? Is this a frequent occurrence?" Rika folded her arms.

"He's only my instructor."

"Is he at least any good?" Rika inquired.

"*He* seems to think so, at least."

"He's certainly a pretty man," Rika conceded, inviting her sister to open up to her obvious infatuation.

"Don't let him hear you say that. He'd not let you forget about it in a hurry. Anyway, I don't want to discuss him." Eir stood up. "Now how soon can we expect you to bless us with your presence?"

"Just give me a few minutes. I'll be down."

Eir kissed her sister on the cheek, went to leave.

"One moment," Rika said.

So many years had passed, and she now considered how her little sister had developed into an attractive young woman. Rika walked over to her, grasped her hands. It felt easy to be open with her. "Eir, I'm scared, at times, that I don't think I can ever be an Empress. I'm not strong enough to do this. I just don't have the experience—"

"Rika, you're the bravest most sensible woman I know. You left this city to spend your life on a fringe island with nothing more than a few peasant farms and Jorsalir structures for company—that in itself takes quite some strength of purpose. You have spent time studying religion, so you possess a moral code that frames your thoughts. And, besides, now that father's gone, it may be fun because everyone will want to impress you."

After a brief silence, Rika said, "Are you sad? I mean, that he's gone?"

Slowly, Eir put her arms around her shoulders, and Rika enjoyed the warm embrace. To be able to be close to her sister again moved her. They held each other for a minute. Eir whispered, "I only feel upset because of the relief he's gone, and because now I might have to start growing up and taking responsibility."

✳

To Rika's surprise, hundreds of people turned to face her as she stood at the top of the stairway leading down from the balcony, and the noise they made was alarming. It wasn't as though this would be quiet, the death of the only person in the city that had been known to everyone.

Those who weren't military wore vivacious dress, like her sister, that strange tradition in Villjamur to wear the brightest colors to see off the dead. There would be no morbid reflection here, guaranteeing a funeral day more colorful than any normal one.

At the foot of the stairs was a wheeled catafalque bearing a wooden casket.

Her father's body.

Although she knew she should, she didn't really feel all that much for him any more, but why was that? Had she spent so long alienating herself from the more basic human emotions that now she didn't know what to think, or was it a relief at the passing of this man who had been so cruel to her mother, a man who had loved no one but himself?

Standing in a row immediately behind the casket was the Night Guard, what was left of it, just eleven members currently. Commander Lathraea stood to attention at the front of them, a vision of darkness in his black uniform, his pale face shining like some ghostly beacon.

Councilors loitered behind him, and then various nobles, in bright robes, further back. Ordinary citizens from the city had been allowed access to this privileged level, so crammed themselves, shoulder to shoulder, into any adjoining street that provided a decent view. All around the city she could see people watching from balconies, standing on walls, leaning from the windows of countless towers. Many of them were waving to her, and there was an element of excitement about the entire city. There would be narrations tonight, as there always were—they would linger on Emperor Johynn's life until the red sun rose. There would be wine, beer, dancing. A few late-night walks where people would be saying how lovely she looked or what a sad time for her to follow in her father's footsteps.

Rika strode down the steps to join her sister by her father's casket. Some part of her wanted to lift the coffin lid, to see what his face looked like one more time, to wonder if her anger would be rekindled, or if she would open up her heart to him only to be met with a cold silence.

Commander Lathraea stepped forward with a nod and some whispered instructions.

The procession journeyed along the twisted streets of the city, Rika the only one on horseback, elevated so all could see their new ruler. Her mount towing the deceased was somehow vaguely symbolic. Despite the freezing weather, the crowds cheered. Old women threw tundra flowers across the passing carriage. For nearly two hours they progressed, a sad trail of sodden flowers marking their passage toward the underground crypt.

✳

Anyone who was anyone in the Jamur Empire made themselves present there in the darkness of crypt. Every Emperor of the Jamur lineage was buried here, four thousand years of blood kin. It had begun with Jamur Joll, who had first led his people into the ancient town of Vilhallan, as it was known then, after a legendary battle, there proclaiming himself Emperor and ordering the three encircling walls of Villjamur to be built. Johynn would be buried alongside his father, Emperor Gulion, the one who drowned twenty-six years previously with more than a little rumor surrounding the incident. Rika looked on with a strange realization that this is where she herself would be buried, among these hundred of candles, in an eternal stone prison.

✳

"War?" Rika gasped. She leaned back in her chair, stared into space. The word echoed in her mind, summoned up feelings of guilt, of shame. War meant death, and she would be complicit in causing it. It didn't even seem her decision to make—the Empire would do what it needed to without her say in the matter.

Two lanterns burned in the room, and a candle on the table and a fire. Animal-head trophies hung on the wooden-paneled walls, which bore the carving of ancient runes. The sense of history here was humbling.

"It's an essential, I assure you," Chancellor Urtica said. With one upturned hand, he gestured at the maps spread out before them, then moved the candle to cast a light over the Empire's islands of the western Boreal Archipelago. "Our armies have gathered here on Folke, near the garrison town of Ule. It's our largest fortified area in the east. I'll admit that initially my concerns about war were as yours clearly are. But we've reason to believe there will be a serious attack on our territories from these tribes." Urtica clutched the edge of the table. "I've taken every step I can to defend our lands, Empress. You need not worry on that count." He stepped back to warm himself by the fire.

Rika stood up to get a better perspective on the geography. Seven nations, dozens of islands and rocky outcrops that once meant nothing to her, and even now were abstract, a collection of lines and color on paper. "Chancellor, what does all this mean, precisely?"

"It means, my lady, we're sending thousands of troops over a period of time, the first of whom are marching or sailing east even as we speak. It is quite necessary to protect our people."

It seemed rather odd, defending people by launching an assault on another island. "Can we afford such an enterprise?"

"That should not be of concern. We councilors have made sure that coin has flowed into Villjamur regularly. It is mainly cultists who are expensive when deployed, but we've little choice but to use them from time to time. I have taken measures to ensure that our tax revenues increase by cutting Veteran Pay, and taxing the well-stocked pensions of those already in the military." He turned to present her with an earnest expression. "Essential, if this Empire is to protect itself."

"Well . . . if you're absolutely certain it is necessary. And the Night Guard?" Rika inquired, thinking of how useful Brynd had been. "Are they going too?"

"They are . . ." Urtica hesitated, "required to tackle separate incidents, Empress."

He told her of events on Tineag'l, a genocide, a potential refugee crisis on a scale never before seen.

She nodded, didn't want to admit any further lack of knowledge and, being a woman, felt that this was a particularly important position to maintain in a male-dominated arena. No matter how enlightened a civilization was, she felt that war always seemed to bring out some primitive urge in men, a need to demonstrate strength.

"My lady, I know there's a lot to take in." The chancellor smiled knowingly.

Perhaps he didn't mean to sound patronizing, but he did. And he was right: there was such a lot to take in. "Then I'll leave this matter under your control, chancellor. Although I would be very grateful to be informed of every military movement undertaken."

He gave a gentle nod. "As you wish, Empress."

"On another matter, I would very much like it if food could be sent out to the refugees."

"Sorry, my lady?" Urtica replied, his eyes showing something like surprise. Or humor.

"I would like those people to be fed as best as possible. Even if just this one time. Think of it as a welcoming gift from their new Empress. Just because they're outside our gates and homeless, does not mean they are not our responsibility."

Urtica's expression remained calm, yet contained a glint of something she couldn't read. "An *excellent* suggestion, Empress. I'll draft up orders to put to the Council, although it may take some time. I can see you have your mother's compassion."

"Do I?" Rika's reply was full of melancholy.

"You do indeed. It was a great shame that she died in such . . . suspicious circumstances."

"There was nothing suspicious about it." She said the words before she had a chance to consider them.

"You think," Urtica said, "that you know who the killer was?"

Again, the ghosts returned.

As a child, one day when her father was looking for her mother, Rika told him that she was with one of the guards in the private gardens. Such an innocent comment. She didn't think he might see something sinister in her contact with this other man.

"It was suggested by many that my mother was having an affair with a soldier from the Dragoons, and somehow my father found out. Very soon her body was found in one of the lower levels of the city, lying flat on the streets. She bled to death, my father told us, tragically while on official business—whatever that may have been."

Urtica gave a brief gasp. "Surely you don't think your father was responsible for it?"

Rika remained silent. Yes she did, but she wasn't going to let him know that.

Urtica pressed on. "A price was offered to find her murderer, wasn't it? Forgive me, but this was quite some time ago. I'm sure the matter was thoroughly investigated."

"The Inquisition found only more paperwork, chancellor."

"It must have been a difficult time for everyone."

"That was probably the year that father began to find it difficult to trust people, preferring his own company for great lengths of time. I remember that servants would take bottle after bottle of wine to him. As the months went by he was less fussy as to the quality, just that it was still coming. I suspect that was the start of his deterioration."

"Perhaps," Urtica agreed. "The mind does suffer greatly under the stresses experienced in office. But I hope you will trust people in Villjamur a little more than he did." A smile. "Things are very different these days."

✳

A quarter of an hour later the chancellor sent a request for a garuda soldier. While he waited, Urtica began writing down a list of orders. Eventually one of the city's bird-soldiers entered the chamber. Urtica examined the creature, its white visage startling, even in the dreary light of the room.

You requested to see one of us? the flight lieutenant signed.

Urtica tried to remember the appropriate words and the symbols, what the hand shapes meant, unused to having to read them himself. He was no mere soldier after all. "Yes, take this order to the military garrison at Ule, Folke." The chancellor handed the garuda a document. "Show it to every captain you see. Should my note be destroyed en route, memorize these words: 'At the command of

Empress Jamur Rika and the Council of Villjamur, you are commanded to organize a front line facing across the northern and easternmost shores immediately adjacent to Varltung. A total of two thousand troops must be placed in key positions ready to receive longships that will set sail from all the military bases on Jokull. Mission summary: ensure total submission of the Varltung race with as few prisoners as possible.' "

The garuda made a harsh squawking sound in his throat. *Sir, is this correct? You wish all of them to be killed?*

"Who are you to question my orders?" Urtica could see the frustration evident on the bird's face. "You've been bred specifically for military use, so don't let emotions get in the way. Anyway, we cannot afford to look after prisoners during such times as these."

So be it, the garuda signed, then gripped the scroll in his humanlike hands.

Urtica eyed the tiny feathers that grew on the creature's arms, then looked him straight in the eye. "Did you memorize those instructions?"

The garuda signed. *They are not easily forgettable, sir.*

"Good." Urtica sat down on the chair before the maps and regarded the garuda casually. "I'll send follow-up instructions, but the scroll you possess contains details of troop allocations and movements, and none of this is up for discussion. Every captain will understand and act accordingly. Now, go." He waved him away with the back of his hand. The flight lieutenant twisted sharply, generating an unnatural breeze somehow with his body shape, then left the room.

Moments later, Urtica stepped over to a tapestry on the wall, peeled it back. A view of the city was unveiled, and he watched the garuda flying off across the spires and bridges, gliding out toward the east.

Urtica brooded on the predicament. He could tell no one of his negligible manipulations, of course—people just did not like to see the bigger picture. Because of the evidence provided by hired tribal thugs at Dalúk Point, this Empire had now been offered an excuse to expand. The loss of a few Night Guard soldiers proved only that they weren't as wondrous as they liked to think they were, the posturing idiots. The Empire now had an opportunity to take more resources, more wood and food and ore, in defiance of the Freeze. They could claim another nation in the east, and this ancient Jamur Empire would become even more glorious.

That was the bigger picture.

CHAPTER 25

✳

STARLIGHT WAS ALL THAT WAS AVAILABLE TO GUIDE BRYND AROUND THIS labyrinth of streets. They turned and twisted at various angles, and Brynd recalled how when he had first explored them years ago, he had been puzzled how they backed around on themselves, always leading him in the opposite direction. A shortcut here, a hidden path there, and you found yourself arriving at unusual junctures, some new territory not only in locational terms but even within your own psychology.

But tonight was different. He knew exactly where he was headed.

There was a permanent ethereal sheen to the stone from which the city was built, and to travelers it would look like some ghost construction, nothing real. He might have been walking in a dream.

He eventually found the right door, knocked, waited. It was answered by Papus herself, the leader of the Order of the Dawnir, clothed totally in gray, with only her face visible beneath her hood, which she held down as she stepped out into the moonlight. Under her chin, her medallion was just visible, though its symbol of an upright palm held no meaning for him.

"I received your message," she whispered, her words turning to mist in the chilly air.

"Do you think you can help?" A sense of urgency had crept into his voice. Shifting weight from foot to foot in the cold, he rubbed his hands together impatiently.

"Possibly." She glanced into the darkness behind, closed the door and stepped out into the alleyway.

They continued through the night, stepping over mounds of litter left at the rear of clustered housing, and it took them an hour to make their way to Caveside.

The city docks were used daily by the fishermen who pushed out their kayaks or larger vessels in constant relays, day and night. Each hunted different species of fish from the contiguous seas, sometimes beyond. Their catch fed the city, and despite the closure of the gates, the docks would remain open, now the only free route in and out of the city. Soldiers were stationed everywhere to prevent the smuggling in of refugees on boats. City guards, recognizing their commander, greeted him accordingly. Through a tunnel of houses to his left he could see starlight glistening above the water.

Papus herself had been quiet, preferring silence to conversation, and Brynd was fine with this. He had a lot to be thinking about anyway. They'd worked together before, and Brynd had already told her of his next mission, of his requirements.

Most cultists desired little involvement with Empire business. They were a complete mystery at times, had their own agendas full of hidden intelligence, and the balance of power could shift between their orders overnight, leaving a whole new arrangement to be negotiated. He knew less about their relics, of course, since they used their own methods to keep them secret. They had done so for thousands of years, and some of these orders were as old as Villjamur itself.

He led Papus to one of the large granite buildings at the far end of the harbor, a featureless structure with no windows at the front. He knocked on the door, which was answered by a female soldier from the Second Dragoons. She saluted him.

"Are they here?"

"Aye, commander. Downstairs."

She stood to one side as the two of them stepped inside. This was one of the military jails, and they entered a room about fifty paces long lit by four lanterns. Metal bars lined one entire side, behind which waited the figures he had ordered to be brought in.

"Here they are," Brynd gestured. "Draugr."

"Draugr are just myths." Papus stepped closer.

The imprisoned figures were difficult to see in the dim light, all huddled together against the rear wall.

"We've found them here on Jokull, wandering around aimlessly, though another group attacked my unit earlier—and I noticed one at Dalúk Point, though I'd no idea what it was then." He came and stood next to her, resting one hand on a bar. On the floor was a puddle of black liquid, which he assumed to have seeped from one's wounds. "One of my men described them as draugr, and he's quite an expert on such things. Anyway, it seems these things were already dead when they attacked us on that occasion, but this lot seem fairly harmless."

Papus didn't react, merely eyed the group for some time before she said, "Bring one closer to me. I hardly believe such myths survive on Jokull."

Brynd called out, and three uniformed women unlocked the gate and, with caution, ushered one of the creatures out. The thing stood motionless as Papus examined it closely, trying to deduce answers. Brynd followed her gaze as she moved the lantern up, down, sideways, skimming light across different parts of the naked torso. This one would once have been a woman, her body now exceptionally anemic; her skin was stretched taut around bone, so the ribs extruded as if she were a famine victim. Yet beyond minor visual signs of putrefaction, she was *still alive*.

"Can you tell me anything?" Brynd said.

"Well this one certainly appears dead." Papus replaced the lantern on the wall. "Yes. Quite dead," she repeated.

The three soldiers returned the draugr to its cell, then returned upstairs out of earshot.

"I don't think it's actually a draugr," Papus said, "not in the true sense, at least."

"No?" Brynd folded his arms expectantly.

"No, I think these have been brought back to life by other means."

"But how?" Brynd asked. "And by whom?" He watched Papus, and could see the confusion registering on her face. It struck him then that she was clueless. For someone of such advanced knowledge, that was alarming.

"I don't know how exactly, but I've my suspicions about who is responsible."

"Who?"

"Dartun Súr, of the Order of the Equinox."

Brynd was surprised at the answer, a cultist so close to Villjamur. "He keeps a very low profile normally, doesn't he?"

"He does, yes, but this is very much like something he'd be capable of. I've heard rumors of him being able to preserve life; though that sort of thing isn't common knowledge, not even in *our* cultist circles."

Pretentious cow. You're only human, like the rest of us. Brynd said, "Well, your circles aren't our circles, Papus, so please enlighten me."

Papus appeared to ignore his sarcasm. She was probably too concerned with feeling as unknowledgeable on the subject as he was. "Well, this isn't right if these creatures are being used to . . . kill."

"And once they start killing, the bastards are difficult to stop," Brynd muttered. "The ones who attacked us had to be chopped in pieces, and burned, just to be sure. If it's really your *friend* Dartun, then he's breeding them to kill."

"You think we're all friends?" Papus asked. "You should know better, commander. Anyway, I suspect he's up to something serious at the moment."

"Something I should know about?"

"No, this is strictly a cultist issue, so it can be solved by us alone, commander."

Brynd's tone became more menacing. "I know you sects have had your fights and bickering in the past, but so far you've always kept it to yourselves—that's fine. Now, you're affecting the rest of us, and you're endangering the lives of Empire soldiers. And Bohr knows what you're doing to ordinary citizens out in the country."

"I'm not doing anything," Papus snapped. "There's some other trickery being misused, involving some ancient relic no doubt. But I now thank you for making me aware of it." She turned away.

"What, you're just going?" Brynd said, surprised at how annoyed she was getting.

"And what did you honestly expect me to do, commander?" she said, frowning. "I've told you, this is some ritual I have no experience of."

"Can't you help us at all?" Brynd said. "I've got to leave the city shortly, and I'll be out of Villjamur for some time. I'd prefer to know that something was being done meanwhile to investigate this matter, because I've no idea if we'll come across any more of these things. This lot may seem pretty docile, but they can transform into savage killers. They're not to be taken lightly." He grasped one of the bars as he gazed at the draugr again. "There are too many strange things happening these days. It's as if this ice brings with it a certain madness."

"I'll do what I can, Commander Lathraea, but not for your sake, or even the city's. This business has much larger implications, if Dartun really has gained access to the elements of life and death. There are things that could change the world as we know it. Think on it, commander. If people can be brought back to life in such quantities, think of the implications." Papus drew her cloak around her and walked silently up the stairs.

CHAPTER 26

✳

Given all the hysteria of a new Empress arriving in Villjamur, Eir had hoped for a better night of celebrations. It was now days after her father's funeral, but this final evening of celebrations had been talked about and anticipated so highly by everyone from councilors to servants. People in the city had been looking for anything to hang their good mood on given the assault of ice, and Rika's new position had certainly offered them that.

But as the evening's festivities died away, Eir found herself seated at a table being lectured on how the general behavior of ladies in Villjamur had diminished of late. Lord Dubek was a cousin's stepfather, a gruff old man dressed in the same dreary blue garments he always wore. Though nearing fifty, he was rumored to have a keen eye for younger women. As his vision drifted across her exposed shoulders, she pulled up her green velvet gown and glowered at him.

"Thing is," he said, swilling a cup of red wine, "we live in an age with little war. Your generation is ruined by that. You've all grown up without hardly ever seeing real fear in your parents' eyes . . ." He brushed down his mustache, and leaned in a little closer.

As she looked across the hall for more interesting company, her vision settled on Randur Estevu, her instructor. He had nestled himself in among a group of ladies of Balmacara, regaling them with some improbable anecdote, no doubt. Amid the ripples of female laughter, he stood, and it was easy to see how familiar he was with them, touching their arms, nodding in earnest at whatever they said to him. A lingering look, kisses on the hand, smiles as choreographed as his dance.

She wasn't quite sure what to make of him.

That man possessed more than an air of mystery, especially since he often went sloping off into the city late at night, Caveside of all places, and what could he possibly want there? Yet he was a good instructor of both swordsmanship and dancing, and Eir realized she had learned a lot from him, even though she would hate to admit it.

The gaggle of ladies dispersed, leaving Randur alone with one other, the Lady Iora, a woman twice his age. Eir frowned at this. Although Lady Iora was an attractive woman, there was no longer any spring in her step. A bad narrative raced just behind those sad eyes. It was well known that Lady Iora was a recent widow, her husband having been found dead beneath a naked if somewhat mortified servant girl back in Villiren. It was a matter of heart, they said, or rather its failure, and despite the irony, Lady Iora had then sold her husband's estate, having decided to settle in one of those fine old apartments on one of Villjamur's higher levels before the Freeze took a grip.

Eir watched with growing suspicion as Randur clasped the aging beauty's hands in his own.

He leaned toward her as if telling her rare and private things. She nodded and they both stood up to make for a discreet exit.

On a sudden instinct Eir decided to follow.

✳

Having grabbed a black cloak, Jamur Eir stood in the shadows outside Randur's room. Only moments ago she had witnessed Lady Iora, in disheveled clothing, walk off down the corridor.

Eir didn't know why she was still waiting here, as though expecting something else—and why was she not asleep, like everyone else in Balmacara? Why was she, a princess of the blood, hovering outside some island boy's chamber? She didn't even like him that much. Sure, he was good to look at, in some vaguely feminine way, but his arrogance diminished any real attraction: the way he'd strut—not walk, but strut—around the halls like he owned the place, like he deserved to live here.

Maybe she was interested in his life, because, after all, Eir had spent her entire childhood being protected, housed in this place with guards to ensure no one might hurt her. This was all well and good, but it was certainly tedious at times. She remembered when she and Rika used to occupy themselves playing games along these corridors, while their parents would argue. She had seen very little of the farflung regions her family governed. Dragged around, heavily protected by her teachers, to look at boring old buildings, there was little chance to meet men, and those she did encounter always seemed too petrified to talk to her.

But this Randur was someone who was finally *interesting*. The fact that she'd heard through servants' gossip that he went to the caves made him more so. What was it he got up to? For some unaccountable reason she wanted to find this out, but it looked like nothing was going to happen tonight.

No sooner had she thought that, when the door opened. Randur stepped out.

She pursued him down the corridor, her careful footsteps whispering over the tiles. Guards queried her route, but she lied to each of them, stating a Night Guard soldier was to meet her shortly. For a place that pretended to be so secure, it seemed remarkably easy to slip away.

❋

It took Randur half an hour to reach the Garuda's Head. The door was open, as it nearly always was, throwing a square of light on the street outside. There was little noise from within, but Denlin sat at a table with a fat man, several cards laid out before them under the glow of lanterns. Denlin noticed Randur's entrance, but remained focused on his game.

A crowd stood around them, whispering amid urgent laughter.

The fat man he played with, dressed in a scruffy brown tunic, held his head in his hands. There were beads of sweat across his forehead as he stared at the cards with his mouth slightly open, as if a knife had been shoved in his stomach.

"What's it to be?" Denlin said to the fat man.

His opponent poked one thick finger at a card in the middle. Denlin flipped it over to a gasp from the crowd. An image of a dragon on the upturned card meant Denlin was the victor.

The fat man simply gazed at the card for some time as those watching gave an almost embarrassed laugh that suggested they'd seen this guy lose a lot of money before, that this might even be his weekly routine before he disappeared penniless into the deep night. He clutched the table, shook his head.

Denlin held out his hands to collect his coins.

"A pleasure." He gathered up the cards, left the table.

"You're late this evening," Denlin said to Randur, as they walked to the bar.

"Yes. She fell asleep on me. Twice."

"Not during, I hope?"

"As if."

"Well, spare me the tales, lad. Been a long time since I dipped me wick, like. My drought's moved into its second year." Then, to the landlord, "Two lagers."

Randur glanced around, noticed a stranger standing at one end of the bar, a hood pulled over his face.

"So," Denlin said between sips, "what you got this time?"

Randur handed over two gold rings, each set with a precious stone. "Either of these any good?"

Denlin put the items under the light, tilted them this way and that. His face screwed up into wrinkles, highlighting his age. "Not bad at all, lad. Who's this lot from?"

"A Lady Iora," Randur replied. "Recently widowed, and damn wealthy as a result."

The hooded stranger gasped, then looked down at a tankard.

Denlin glanced quickly over to the figure, then at Randur. "You gonna tell me who your mate is?"

"I'm sorry?" Randur said.

"Your pal who came in here with you." Denlin indicated the hooded newcomer.

"I came alone," Randur said, then, to the stranger, "Mate, does our business interest you?"

The figure made to leave, then Denlin grabbed one arm. The stranger gave a high-pitched squeal.

"Den, stop that." With a shocked realization, Randur walked over, pulled aside the hood. "Lady Eir, for fuck's sake, what are you doing here? How the hell did you get out of Balmacara?"

Her eyes widened with uncertainty, then all she could do was stare at the floor. Her hair was disheveled. No makeup, no jewelry, nothing that might indicate her position, but down here they only knew her as a title, not a face.

Randur drew her hood back up, then took her outside, Denlin following.

"Eir," he hissed, "what're you doing here?"

She spun around in the dark street, and suddenly she was as passive-aggressive as usual.

"Actually, Randur Estevu, I think it's you who should be answering that question. I've just witnessed you admit to stealing, and from a lady of the court, what's more. You've stolen within Balmacara, so I should have you executed. You're nothing but a common thief. I should've known better."

"She's got a point there, lad," Denlin concurred from the doorway of the tavern.

Randur looked back at the old man. Fortunately there was no one else within earshot in the dirty backstreet. "Thank you for that, Denlin."

Randur looked to Eir, sighed. He took some time to think of a suitable answer, then shrugged. "You're right, I've stolen. Maybe I can explain. Though I reckon I should be getting you back to Balmacara before the sun rises. It's not safe here."

"I think a common thief is the last person who should be responsible for my safety, don't you think?" She folded her arms, glared at him.

Randur took a deep breath. *Be careful what you say, Rand. You've blagged your way into the city, and now your mouth might get you kicked right back out again.*

Denlin stepped forward, stood in between them. "This, uhm, who I think it is? Jamur Eir?"

Eir stared at Randur, unspoken questions in her gaze, waiting for reassurance.

"Go on," Randur prompted.

"Yes, yes it is," Eir said. "And who are you?"

"Friend of the lad, here, that's all."

"A thief too?" Eir said.

"Ha! No. Though some might call me that, especially in there."

Denlin gestured vaguely toward the tavern, then scratched his head, ruffling his already messy gray hair. "No, I'm an odd-job man, like. I do a bit of this, a bit of that. You need something, I'll find it—for a price of course. At your service, my lady." He took a bow.

Randur couldn't decide if he was being sarcastic or not. "Den, you think you could leave us alone for a bit?"

"Anything you have to say," Eir snapped, "you can say here, in the open."

Randur looked between them, sighed. "I don't know about you two, but I want a drink." He went back into the Garuda's Head.

Denlin scratched his crotch, followed, muttering, "At last, some sense."

"What, you're going to just leave me out here alone?" Eir protested.

Randur turned in the doorway. "You want answers, step into my office."

✳

"I'm a thief, yes," Randur admitted, then took a swig of his lager, staring at Eir across the table. She clasped a cup of watered wine from which she took occasional sips, making a face as if she'd sucked at a lump of salt. "But, I'm stealing with good reason."

"Doesn't every thief?" Eir said.

"She's got a point, lad," Denlin said, then belched.

"Thank you, Denlin." Randur glared at him. Back to Eir, he continued, "I'm stealing because I need the money to . . ." He paused for a moment. He might as well tell everything. "To save my mother from dying."

Eir's expression softened.

"From tunthux."

Denlin whistled. "Nasty."

"What's tunthux?" Eir inquired.

"The slow death, they call it," Denlin volunteered. "Can take a few years for someone to die from it. At the end they say you bleed from every orifice, blood pouring from your arsehole—"

"Thank you, Denlin!" Randur interrupted. "We don't need to hear all that." Then, to Eir, "My mother is dying and I came to Villjamur to find a cure, from a cultist. I need to raise money, you see, since a cultist won't do it for nothing. And that's why I'm taking things—jewelry, gemstones—from certain women I give . . . *satisfaction* to. As you yourself explained, Eir, I can't exactly take stuff from Balmacara, so . . ."

"So you seduce vulnerable ladies of the court for their wealth," Eir sneered. "How honorable of you."

"I gave them plenty in return. I give them excitement and attention, albeit for a short while. They certainly aren't getting it from anyone else, so is that so bad? That I satisfy them? And besides, who would say a thing if it was a young woman accepting the odd trinket from her older male lover."

"That's different," Eir protested, rather uncertainly.

"Is it really?" Randur said. He gripped his tankard, took a sip of lager. "Is it really so different for a man to expect payment?"

"Whoring," Denlin offered. "That's what that is. At least common whores is more honest about taking money, like. And I've known some lovely ones in my time . . ."

"Thank you, Denlin." Randur wondered if the old man would ever shut up. "All I'm doing is giving some emotional and physical attention to certain neglected ladies who need it, and taking an unofficial fee in the unspoken market. The jewelry I take is in order to save my mother's life. If you're going to get all moral over this, I still reckon I've got the higher ground—so there you have it. I'm working to get my mother's life back, but I'm still a little short in coin."

"How much do you need?" Eir said suddenly.

Randur tried to read her expression and said, "Four hundred Jamúns."

As he took a sip she said, "I can get that for you."

Randur nearly spat the drink on the table. "Really? You can?" He wanted to be a gentleman, to refuse her kindness, but despite his inherent politeness, despite his pride, he couldn't refuse something like that—because his mother's life depended upon it.

For a normally proud man, he wasn't feeling much pride right now.

"Yes," Eir said, "that is, if what you say really *is* true."

"You think I'd lie about a thing like that? If that's what you think, you can keep your fucking money." Randur stood to leave, shuffled along the table. A few customers turned to watch. "Fuck you looking at?"

Eir rose with him. "Randur, don't. I'm sorry, I didn't mean that."

He looked at her for a moment, then sat back down. He wasn't sure he'd really have walked out, but it was one of those gestures, a little drama in a situation that required it. And it was time for him to show a lack of trust—why was she willing to give him so much money, to help him so blatantly? It made him highly suspicious. For someone so solipsistic, he rarely *believed* in himself.

"I'm sorry. I don't understand though. Why do you blame yourself for her illness?"

"Because I was more busy having fun than being there for her—being there for my own mother. I was too young and selfish to notice."

"You mustn't blame yourself . . ." Eir began.

"Well, I do. I have to save her. That's why I'm here, in this miserable city."

Her brow furrowed. "So, does that mean you're actually not my genuine sword and dance instructor?"

"No, I'm not the *genuine* Randur Estevu." He then explained how he'd been able to enter the city.

"And your real name?" Eir said.

"Can't be much worse than the one you're using," Denlin suggested.

"I'd rather remain known as Randur Estevu, for the time being anyway."

"Fine. And you will at least continue teaching me dance until the Snow Ball is over?"

"If I'm not hanged for theft, meanwhile, sure," he said. "Although I'll need to leave soon afterward—once I get whatever the cultist gives me—and then get back to my mother."

Randur wasn't sure what to feel at this moment. Jamur Eir was sitting here, in a dingy tavern in the roughest area of the city. It was not only bizarre enough that she had followed him all this way, but also was now going to give him all the money he needed to pay Dartun Súr. He had assumed it would take much longer to get the funds, so what did he feel now—gratitude, relief?

"Why're you being so kind to me?" Randur demanded.

"I think what you're doing here is quite brave—especially since you're doing it all for your mother. I in particular can appreciate the importance of a mother in someone's life . . . And if it means you don't have to service every rich widow in the city, then I'd feel—then that's good."

Randur tried not to show his sudden confusion at her words. He would never understand the female mind. "I truly appreciate it, I really do."

"One condition," she said.

"What's that, then?"

"That I can come with you back to Folke. I want to see some of the Empire. I've been sheltered too long. My sword instructor would certainly seem an acceptable guardian in the eyes of those in Balmacara."

A smile on his face. "You have a deal. Now hadn't we better get back?"

Eir nodded a yes.

Denlin seemed to have fallen asleep. The old man's head had tipped back, his mouth slightly open.

"Den!" Randur banged the table.

"Whassa . . . Oh, must've drifted off." He slapped his own face to rouse himself. "What's happened then? You two all patched up and in love?"

"We're friends again," Randur said, standing up. "We're off now. Looks like the sun's nearly up."

"Aye. So, I guess you won't be coming down these parts again, if the lady's paying your debt."

Was he really sleeping all that time? "No, I guess not as much as before." Randur felt a little awkward. Despite Denlin being crude and obnoxious, they had a bond, had spent a good few nights drinking and laughing together. "Thanks for everything. We've had some good times down here."

"Aye, well, don't be a stranger, will you." Denlin offered his hand. "Always welcome at my place, too. Enjoyed those card games we had there, without the riff-raff."

The two men shook, but Randur noticed how the old man had discreetly returned the rings that belonged to Lady Iora into his hand.

Randur shook his head. "Cheers, Denlin. I'll be back down here sometime soon—only, just for drinks this time."

"Well you'll find me here, doing a bit of this, a bit of that." Denlin glanced to Eir. "Look after the lad."

"He'll need more help than I can offer." Eir stood up quickly, walked out of the tavern.

As Randur reached the door, he looked back and tossed one of the rings back to him. "Buy yourself something smarter to wear."

"And waste good lager? You've a lot to learn, Randur." Denlin peered down into the bottom of his tankard.

A smile was all Randur could offer. Anything else would've been too awkward.

Randur and Eir stepped out into a bright Caveside morning.

People newly woken were venturing out into the streets, where boys were drawing carts of dubious-looking vegetables to the market. The sign outside the blacksmiths said "No Jobs." Two officers of the watch were talking to a man sleeping in a doorway, demanding if he had nowhere else to live, and would he mind moving on.

It really is another world down here, Randur thought, turning to Eir. "Are people going to worry if you're not back in Balmacara soon?"

"Why do you ask?" She regarded him with those big eyes. He thought for a moment that they might trap a man who wasn't in control of himself. There was a vulnerability in her expression, he realized, something that made him want more from her. You have to be savvy to avoid situations like that. Trouble was, he didn't think he was much able to deal with it.

"I want you to see something. I really think you need to see it."

✳

"Well, this is home. Ain't a palace, mind, but I like to think there are those who'd kill for a spot like this." Denlin stood back proudly as Eir gazed around his home. He hastily cleared away a couple of cups, as if the gesture would improve the appearance of the place.

The room was tiny, probably just a quarter of the size of her own sleeping chambers. Two lanterns illuminated the room in a dreary shade of brown. Simple wooden furniture, one small table with several chairs and Jorsalir ornaments scattered here and there. Religious paintings on the wall, in frames that had seen better days. The walls were crumbling, and even the incense burning in an adjacent room could not disguise a smell of dampness in the air.

Outside in the streets a banshee began her keening, and everyone turned to face the window instinctively to confirm it wasn't themselves.

"There goes another one," Denlin complained, "and there'll be more as these temperatures plummet further—especially down this street, where a lot of oldies like me live." Denlin quickly moved aside some wooden plates. "Damn sister of mine, but I suppose she does have her hands full."

At that moment a bundle of noise came piling down the narrow stairway. "Uncle Denny!" three young girls shrilled in unison, as they pawed at his cloak. Dressed in identical white night dresses, they paused to stare at Eir with uncertainty, before turning their attention to Randur. "Randy!"

"Hello, you lot." Randur picked up the youngest, a blond angel with dark smudges all over her face. "So how're Denlin's little golems?"

"Oi, we're not golems," the child griped. "Denny, tell him we're not golems." She began to pull at locks of Randur's long black hair.

"Indeed you are all golems," Denlin said, his face creasing with delight. "But, girls, I want you to be on your best behavior now because we've a very special visitor." He tilted his head toward Eir.

"Oh no," Eir objected. "Don't be wary on my behalf. Pretend I'm not here."

The girls all stared at Eir with renewed awe.

"Lovely to meet you all," Eir said, self-consciously. "Have you all just woken up?"

"Well, yes," the tallest said. "Actually we've been up for ages, thanks to Opri's fidgeting. She even woke our mam up with her kickin'."

Eir looked to Denlin in disbelief. "They all sleep in the same bed?"

"Aye, lady," he replied. "It's a small house, like. Big compared to most down here, and there's only room for one bed. I'm out most of the night you see, while they sleep, earning some coin. Then when I come back in the morning, the bed's all nice and warm for me. And when they all wake me up again in the evening, the bed's all nice and warm for them."

Eir said nothing to that. Denlin allowed the girls to go out and play in the streets, but only as long as they fetched some water back from the well.

It was then that Eir turned to Randur, her face showing distress. Coming here, seeing how people actually lived in her city, might do her the world of good, he reckoned. The girl needed some enlightening.

"I'd offer you some tea," Denlin apologized, "but I ran out last week. And as for food, well . . . we haven't got too much in just now, you see. The lad here has been my main employer, so to speak, in recent weeks."

"Oh, no, I'm quite all right," Eir said. "Really. I never realized quite how . . . well, it's very tough for you, isn't it?" She took a seat at the table, resting her elbows on the grimy wood.

"Aye, miss." Denlin subsided onto the wooden chair opposite her. "Times is tough, and not many jobs down this side of the city. I mean, you got your traders and smiths. You got your leather workers, bakers, craftsmen, that sort of thing naturally. You got a lot of gambling going on—dogfights, mainly—and some stranger things happening in the really old caves. You get cultists there—just the rubbish, solitary ones. Ones that's addicted to their relics like it's a drug. They make a fair living by tricking people, like. People'll buy anything with their last coin if they think it might help them. But I ain't sure how long it'll all last when the Freeze sets in. Meanwhile, people find odd jobs, and wealth trickles about. There's usually something that needs doing, like, even if it's not really legal."

He gazed silently across the table for a moment, his fingers prodding at the wood delicately as if searching blindly for solutions.

Denlin then continued. "Some people get desperate, head right down through the caves to the old mining systems. Sometimes they disappear for days. Older men, mainly, remembering the old tunnels. They come back covered in blackness, but clutching a bit of precious metal, a gemstone found here and there." He grinned. "Bit of a metaphor, that. In times like these you find people quickly forget coin as a currency. They start bartering, trading things for favors. There's a lot of whores in that respect—women and men too. This anarchist group is gaining some big interest in trying to stop that sort of thing, aye, and they've got the support of a lot of women who want proper equality." He absentmindedly placed his hand on a copy of the pamphlet *Commonweal*. "People's starting to feel like slaves to those what gives us jobs, like. I shouldn't be saying this, lady, but if you want to know what the real world is like then . . . Well, it's all nice and fancy up there, but you can be blinded by all those sparkling trinkets no doubt." Again there was silence, and Randur was surprised by its intensity. Denlin continued. "Anyway, trade used to come in from the docks—so you'd get the odd exotic treasure from Randur's island, and from your Blortath, Tineag'l, Y'iren. Most things pass through Villiren, to be honest. There's still the odd religious trinket from Southfjords and Jorsalir priests come pushing some text. There's a lot that rely only on their faith in those two gods to get 'em through the night. Then there's the gangs, humans fighting against young rumels for no reason other than the right to trade something exclusively. Some nights the banshees don't stop keening. Other nights you hear nothing at all, and have to wonder if that's worse."

Eir was focusing intently on every word.

"But it's not *all* bad! Here am I painting you such a nasty picture of your fair city. No, you get the nice things, too. For instance, there's a much better spirit of community this side. You get a lot of communal dances on street corners. Drums beat, fires are lit, and then people make pretty shadows, laughing over a bit of drink and food. There's not much else to do, you see."

Randur glanced at him suddenly. "When does that happen next?"

"They pretty much occur when people make them happen. I'll let you know about the next one, soon as I hear word of it."

"Yeah, us two can come back and join in," Randur said. "They've got a fancy dance up in Balmacara soon, you see. We could do with getting some practice among others."

"Oh, it won't be as grand as your *fancy* ones up there," Denlin grinned. "No polished floors or big feasts. No fancy music."

"Never mind," Randur said, thinking this sounded better all the time. "I'm sure the Lady Eir would like to see how dance should be performed properly."

Glancing up to Randur, she smiled her reply. Then she faced Denlin once again. "Thank you for your insight."

"Pleasure, miss," he said.

She reached beneath her cloak, brought out a gold Sota, placed it on the table.

"My lady . . ." Denlin muttered.

Randur had never seen the old man so short of words.

". . . I can't accept such generosity. I . . ."

Eir said firmly, "For the girls."

CHAPTER 27

✳

ANOTHER ONE OF THOSE ICY MORNINGS ON WHICH NO ONE WISE REALLY wanted to venture outside. But Investigator Rumex Jeryd wasn't one of those intending to stay sensibly in the warm. For once he would have given a lot to go out, rather than be slumped here at his desk. It might have been warm, but paperwork was dull. And unfortunately the arch-inquisitor was visiting later in the afternoon to follow up the Council murders, and Jeryd hadn't progressed a great deal on the case. Not only that, but there was need for an investigation into a surge of organized crime against the refugees camped outside the city gates. Groups of men, and some women, stalked the evenings, launching weapons from the higher walls of the city to rain murder on those they feared would threaten their survival. Apparently some of those were beaten up by the supposed anarchist group from Caveside. All official attempts at dissuasion were ignored, because it was the nature of mankind that these antirefugee groups wouldn't be persuaded by logic alone.

Jeryd was expecting a visit this morning from Investigator Ful-crom, a relatively young, well-groomed, brown-skinned rumel who, Jeryd suspected over the years, was a homosexual. He could never admit it, but Jeryd thought he could hear it in the gaps of his sentences. Jeryd considered him a damn good member of the Inquisition. Fulcrom had solved the North Caveside Rapist case. He had discovered who organized a raid on the Treasury. He had stopped a vicious child molester as he was about to strike again.

Fulcrom and Jeryd had now been chosen to address the refugee crisis in more detail, but because of his existing workload Jeryd had passed on the bulk of the actual planning to Fulcrom.

Besides, Jeryd wanted to have more time to spend with Marysa. Things kept getting better between them, and he was maybe even starting to really enjoy life. He was not uxorious, but who would have thought that simply holding hands and kissing, as the snow fell about them in a garden of glass flowers, could be so enjoyable?

But she still had the occasional feeling that someone was following her through the icy streets after dark. He imagined that whenever she whirled round, her long coat flowing around her, all she would hear would be boots scuffing the cobbles as they departed in haste. Or maybe a sharp inhalation of breath from some dark corner. He had not told anyone else in the Inquisition about this yet; he felt embarrassed to do so.

Jeryd pulled a key from his pocket, slid open a panel on the wall, drew out a small chest, unlocked it. Inside was the Ovinist letter that he had discovered in the broken statue. He knew only that this was the banished cult somehow at work, but the actual contents he could only guess at. Maybe this was something for Fulcrom's acute mind to work on, and as the thought came to mind the young rumel entered Jeryd's chamber.

"Sele of Jamur, Investigator Fulcrom." Jeryd stood up to shake his colleague's hand. "Cold morning?"

"I'd say," Fulcrom replied. A cool confidence about his movements as he shook off his damp cloak, hung it on a hook on the wall.

Jeryd threw a couple more logs on the fire, stoked it to entice some more heat. A cloud of smoke wafted straight back into his face like a cultist trick, and he stumbled back to his desk, coughing.

Fulcrom was one of those rumels that looked almost human in his features: soft skin, prominent cheekbones, a friendly look in his eye that told you he was pleased to see you. He possessed a likable and trustworthy manner that made people open up to him. Jeryd considered the other rumel undoubtedly handsome, and Fulcrom always wore the smartest gray tunic under his crimson Inquisition cloak. Despite the slush outside, even his boots were much cleaner than Jeryd's.

"Please." Jeryd indicated a cushioned chair over by the window.

Fulcrom made himself comfortable, gazing out to see what he could observe of the street below.

"Anything interesting happening?" Jeryd asked.

"Just the usual problems—people being smuggled into the city, and a couple of brutal murders Caveside. As for the refugee situation, I've got a list of names that involves some pretty senior people."

"How senior?" Jeryd glanced back to the fire.

"If I said it went all the way to the top, would you be surprised?" Fulcrom shifted in his seat.

"The Council?" Jeryd said.

A nod.

"I wouldn't be surprised at all," Jeryd said, trusting his years of experience. "What exactly do you know?"

"I think there's someone at work in the Council who wants these refugees completely removed. Someone who thinks they're too much of a stain on Villjamur. Coin's moving between someone close inside to some of the gangs Caveside. Don't know who it is, but . . . Well, you get the idea."

Jeryd made a steeple of his hands as he considered his colleague's words.

"Any thoughts?" Fulcrom said.

Jeryd leaned in, and whispered, "I bet you that Urtica himself is behind all this somehow."

"It goes *that* high? What makes you say so?"

Jeryd went to retrieve the scroll he had found in the image of the dead Emperor. As the younger rumel scanned the document, Jeryd explained, "Found that inside a hollow bust of Johynn in the office of that murdered councilor, Ghuda. I know it's an Ovinist text, but I can't work out what the hell it means."

Fulcrom raised an eyebrow. "Looks like an old runic text, if you ask me. Ancient stuff—judging by the forms of the letters I'd say a thousand years old, at least."

"Can you interpret it, though?" Jeryd said. He walked around the desk to stand before the fire. "I've been trying on and off for days, but nothing comes to mind."

"No," Fulcrom admitted. "But I think I know someone who can."

"Who?"

"The Dawnir."

"What, the one living in Balmacara? Do they even allow access? I know his existence isn't common knowledge in the city."

"Well, you're a member of the Inquisition, so I'm sure they'll allow it."

Jeryd shrugged. "These days, who knows."

Fulcrom handed the scroll back to Jeryd, who placed it safely away once again.

"So," Fulcrom said. "You suspect Urtica's behind it? That's a bold claim to be making."

"I know," Jeryd said, "and I've not got any hard evidence. There were rumors a while back that he was involved with the cult. And he reacts evasively to questioning, though I wouldn't think he's behind the murders. He seemed genuinely shocked at the horrors located in Boll's chambers. You want my opinion, he doesn't have the stomach to be a killer, at least not at firsthand. He's more your manipulator, behind-the-scenes kind of guy. The only thing I can assume is that he might have been up to something with Boll and Ghuda. Well, after what happened to them, he must be shitting himself now."

"So, how exactly d'you think he's involved?"

"I've no real idea. The Council murders are the most bizarre I've ever come across. You know what the only clue is, if you can even call it that?"

Fulcrom shook his head.

"Paint."

"Paint?"

"Yeah. I found a smear of paint in Boll's chambers, amidst all that blood. Then I remembered I found paint by Ghuda's body, too."

Fulcrom appeared to be processing this fact carefully. "So, some sort of artist or craftsman involved? You sure it's not a cultist?"

"Seriously doubt it, because they live by their own rules. Plus why such spectacular, unsubtle deaths? That's not their style at all. They're more stealthy in their methods."

"Maybe the murderer decided to paint an image of his victims? As a keepsake perhaps . . . I don't know, I'm just throwing things your way."

"The paint could mean anything," Jeryd said gloomily. "All I can do now is check every jobbing artist in Villjamur."

Jeryd was suddenly struck by inspiration. "Damn!"

"What?" Fulcrom said. "I can tell you've thought of something."

"Damn," Jeryd repeated, and sat back in his chair. He laughed, his tail thrashing from side to side. "How stupid of me. All the time I've been telling myself it wasn't her."

"Who?" Fulcrom sat straighter.

"The prostitute that Ghuda spent his last night with, she had paintings all over her place. I think I should pay her another visit. Maybe I'll send Tryst along to keep an eye on her. I just thought it was *too* obvious, and therefore it didn't seem right. Only thing is, if she is involved, why?"

"Who knows why anyone does anything," Fulcrom said. "Many of our actions are a lot stranger than they need be. Especially humans, led so easily by their emotions."

Jeryd felt uncomfortable, recalling how susceptible to emotions he himself was.

✳

"This way, investigator," the guard gestured.

Jeryd followed his lead, all the time mulling over his thoughts, the red and gray military uniform at the periphery of his vision. Ten minutes later, he found himself descending into a cold stone corridor that seemed to have no end. Eventually they arrived at a large wooden door. The guard knocked, and it opened.

A Dawnir stood looking down at Jeryd, who gazed back in awe.

"An investigator here to see you," the guard announced, then marched away.

Jeryd stared dumbly up at the creature, at the tusks, at the sheer height of him.

"Ah, a rumel!" the Dawnir said, very slowly as if he had just rediscovered speech. "I haven't seen one of you for so long! Please, please, step this way." His voice was thunderous, unexpected.

"Thank you." Jeryd flashed his medallion with its ancient symbol of a triangular crucible, as proof of office. "Investigator Rumex Jeryd, and I take it you're Jurro?"

"For what a name is worth, that is correct," the Dawnir replied.

Jeryd watched the creature with fascination. Twice the size of a human, covered thickly in hair, it was an intimidating sight. "I fear I didn't think you really existed, they were so keen to keep folk away from you."

"Really? How intriguing. You know, I was beginning to think I didn't exist either. They keep me locked up here . . . well not really locked up, but where am I to go? It isn't safe for me to venture into the city so they say. Apparently it is the priests, mainly, who don't want me around. That's why so few people know I'm actually here. They are worried that my presence might offend their little religion. But some of your people leave me little offerings outside my door, and I trip over them when I go to relieve myself. But there is hope yet, for I am to accompany a few soldiers on a trip north. I might enjoy that, because you know, it's not much of a life here."

He indicated the rows of books with his massive arm.

"I don't know, though. Maybe sitting around reading all day is better than seeing what I might do."

Jeryd tried some small talk. He already liked the Dawnir, despite his apparent tendency to perorate. "Must have a lot of knowledge, all these books."

"Yes, but they don't offer answers to the real questions of the world. Our world is so old, the sun so red. Philosophers have speculated things should surely end at some point, and I would agree, if only to confirm the air of melancholy that everyone seems to possess. So, rumel, what is it *you* seek?"

"Your wisdom, Jurro." Jeryd reached under his robes to bring out the scroll, then handed it to the Dawnir, who stood towering over the rumel, as he examined it held between forefinger and thumb.

Jeryd said, "This is confidential information, I hardly need to tell you."

"Why would it be confidential, since you obviously can't read it."

"Yes, true." Jeryd grunted a laugh. "Anyway, it's between us, if you can translate it for me. They say you're an Ancient."

"Ancient in body only, I fear. I have no memory before my days here in the city."

"Does that mean you can't read it?" Jeryd said, feeling disappointed.

"I didn't say that," the creature thundered, possibly frowning under heavyset brows, Jeryd couldn't be sure. "No, I have all my books, and I have studied many ancient languages in the hope of tracing my past. I learn new words all the time. Even yesterday I discovered our word for the Jorsalir has deep origins."

Jurro gazed for some time at the scroll, then brought a candle closer to it. Jeryd flinched, thinking that his only real piece of evidence might be about to go up in flames.

"Yes, I think I can interpret this for you," the Dawnir said eventually. "Would you like some ink and paper to take it down?"

"Please."

The creature searched for several moments under stray piles of books until he found a blank piece of parchment and a quill. "Here you are."

Jeryd sat down at a table, ready to write.

"It reads: 'We have the facilities and the capabilities. We could probably remove five thousand in a few days, then bury the dead at sea. This can be done secretly and with ease. I can confirm there are enough underground passages to facilitate your plans for cleansing. I refer to the old escape tunnels, so the very age of our beloved city suggests she would permit the removal of such a blot on her surface.' Then the rest of the writing seems to be smudged, blurred with damp perhaps."

Jurro ceased reading, looked up at Jeryd. "Have I given you news you didn't wish for, investigator?"

Jeryd inhaled deeply, considering what he had just heard. He rolled up the parchment with his notes and placed it under his robes. "Jurro, you did just fine. Many thanks for your trouble."

Five thousand dead? Jeryd thought. *What the hell's going on? Is this really something planned to happen in the city? And even so, why would the Council want to kill five thousand?*

"Where did you obtain this document?" The creature handed the scroll back to Jeryd.

"Somewhere too high up for my liking," Jeryd said.

"You rumel, tell me, you live longer than humans, yes?"

"Three or four times as long. Why?"

"And that's why there are so few humans in the Inquisition?" The Dawnir fingered a tusk idly.

"The older an investigator, the better, because we can remember cases from a long time back. We're wise to the ways of the city. That's what we tell ourselves, anyway, but the legend has it that this custom was from the original treaty when we jointly founded the city—to keep the two species happy. There's not many of us rumel in the Council, so it's a nice concession to have us overseeing the law."

"I thought as much, but it is nice for it to be confirmed. I'm a sponge for facts."

"Maybe you need to get out a bit more."

"I plan to."

✳

"Tryst." Investigator Jeryd leaned into his subordinate's office—a small, stone room with no windows. A lantern stood on the desk at which the young human sat.

Tryst looked up from the documents he was working on. "Jeryd, please, come in." Tryst stood up, motioned for Jeryd to enter the room.

The rumel stepped in, then he looked behind the door before shutting it firmly. He glanced at the plate of fried locusts to one side. *Always eating, still as slender as a Salix tree, damn him.* "Working on anything special?"

"Just going over financial accounts from one of the smaller Council treasuries. I'm looking out for any movements of monies that could be of interest." Upon seeing Jeryd's expression, he then added, "You look as if you've something on your mind."

Jeryd keenly wanted to discuss what the Dawnir had revealed, but not just yet. Aide Tryst wasn't quite senior enough to be entrusted with something so . . . *profound.* And besides, Jeryd had his reservations about the man's character. "I wonder if you could do me a favor, as I had some new ideas about the murder of those councilors. I think we were right at the beginning—in suspecting the prostitute—

though I haven't got anything solid yet." Jeryd related his latest thoughts.

Tryst leaned back in his chair, the lantern light casting a savage shadow across his face. "Sounds worth looking into, but what did you have in mind?"

"I want her shadowed," Jeryd explained. "Maybe you could observe her for a few days."

"Are you too busy yourself then?"

He's shrewd, this one, Jeryd thought, his tail twitching in irritation. "Yes, I am. I'm seeking out a motive, so I want to spend the next few days examining Council activities."

"Okay," Tryst said. "I'll start later today."

❅

All through the afternoon Jeryd scrutinized his notes, tried to work out how everything added up. Perhaps a little self-indulgently he had seated himself in the corner of a favorite bistro, ordered a sweet pastry and a beaker of hot juniper tea. What he was doing was too sensitive to be pursued within the Inquisition chambers.

He was getting really paranoid.

What did it all mean? Why would one of the esteemed Council be planning the death of so many people? Was that why Ghuda and Boll were killed? Did someone find out what they were up to? And, above all, who was the coded message from? At least, he had Tryst watching the prostitute. Hopefully the young human would find out something useful.

The bistro was fairly quiet. Across the stone-flagged room sat an old couple dressed in matching smart brown tunics, like they used to make down Foulta Gata when the cotton boom was in full swing, a classic Villjamur stitch. They were sitting drinking tea, each reading a book, perfectly comfortable in each other's silent presence, and every time the man finished a chapter he would look up and smile at his partner. A few weeks back, Jeryd would have found the pair simply depressing, but now he warmed to such a display of affection.

This was a time of day when the city would pause. The morning throng had had its moment, the bustle had gone, and in the bistros you mostly found only those who chose to drink alone to ruminate.

Even the serving girl looked a little distant, either anxious to go home or taking a moment to relax before it became busy again.

Jeryd contemplated his next move on the Council, how he would spy on them, digging deep in order to find out who was working on what. He would send a message, to each councilor in private, warning how their lives might be at risk unless they opened up. He folded up his notes, threw some coins on the table and turned to leave, eyeing the old couple as the man brought his loved one's hand to his lips.

What a city, Jeryd thought. *What a place to live, despite the extremes of existence here. The epic and the everyday, they're just two aspects of city life.*

All in Villjamur.

CHAPTER 28

✳

Nighttime, and none of the city bridges were visible, let alone the spires they led to. Thick, immovable, a fog had rolled in from the coast, and Aide Tryst walked cautiously along the snowy cobbled streets, one hand shoved deep in his robe pocket, the other clutching half a roll-up of arum weed, his feet tingling with the cold. The snow had been relentless the last few evenings. Where it had been cleared by seawater, you had to pick your route with caution. Each day there were stories of people breaking arms and legs. Despite the threat, children walked along the same streets waiting to meet their snowball destiny.

Lamps offered faint orbs of light at regular intervals, which prevented him from getting completely lost.

And it certainly makes trailing someone fucking difficult, he thought ruefully.

Few people about, though he could hear the keening of a banshee, somewhere in the distance. It sounded as if it originated from somewhere further down in the levels of the city, maybe in one of the many underground passageways or derelict buildings—at least he hoped it was nowhere close by. He swore he heard a sword being drawn from its scabbard, and Tryst cursed that he was having to be out so late. He took a final drag on the arum weed before dropping it into the slush.

*So, Jeryd isn't only content with confining me to the lowest ranks of the In-
quisition, he also sends me out in the freezing fucking cold, so that I can watch
a whore.*

At least he now knew more about his superior's vulnerabilities.
Tryst was intrigued by something that Chancellor Urtica had said in
one of the Ovinist meetings: that no matter how stalwart a man pretended to be, it was usually his heart that let him down—and, more
importantly, let him be brought down. Many a great man was destroyed in some way by the affections of a lover. On hearing this,
Tryst decided Urtica was one of the wisest men that ever lived.

To rattle his boss, Tryst could simply kill Marysa. But that seemed
too brutal and, besides, he didn't really wish something so cata-
strophic on the rumel. A degree of respect was something that remained between the two of them: their relationship was complex and
adversarial, but couldn't be severed entirely. There were no black and
whites here, where the textures of their lives crossed, linking positively
whenever they shared a joke or discussed a certain case they were
working on, and it wasn't a simple matter of hurting him too badly,
but just enough, just a little lesson, a firm mental slap. No, he wanted
to *disturb* Jeryd rather than destroy him, and then still have him solve
the murder of the councilors. That was something dear to Urtica's
heart, and therefore dear to his own.

Tryst stepped into a wide piazza, near where the prostitute lived by
Cartanu Gata and the Gata Sentimental. The sound of laughter from
a doorway, the *clink-clink* of glasses, shoes sliding on stone. Where he
now stood you could hear a symphony of these subtle sounds of the
night, seemingly coming from everywhere. Someone coughed behind
him, but there was no one solid there, only a long shadow darting
across the stone. There was no wind here, the buildings being high
and crammed together, so the smells of incense and fried food
reached him invitingly, with little obstruction. Ahead of him through
the fog was the bold glow of one of the bistros. He remembered the
prostitute saying how she hung around these places a lot. Perhaps she
was there now. As good a place to start looking as any. Tryst walked
toward the light, heard the soft rhythm of lute and drum.

The bistro was filled, mainly with hooded customers who preferred their own company by the looks of them, and Tryst thought

he'd blend in nicely. He took a seat near the edge of the room, far away from the stage at the end of the long stone chamber. Through the heady smoke, serving girls sashayed to and fro between tables, in the dim light of candles and the torchlight that lit up the stage.

Up there, on the stage itself, a cultist was making several golems dance to the music provided by a drummer and a lute player. The cultist, clasping a relic in his hands, commanded the statues, one by one, to make their way to the center of the stage, where they would gyrate fluidly, while the audience gasped and applauded in between flashes of purple light. To finish the set, he then made one of the statues spread out its wings and fly in a circle over the heads of the crowd, before it once again transformed into stone.

A girl came to Tryst's table to take his order of Black Heart rum and shark's liver paste on coarse bread. When she fetched the bottle he asked her to leave it. If he had to spy on a prostitute during an ice age, he might as well stay warm while he was doing so.

A fat woman came on stage next to read some bad poetry about the dying earth, and though she had no decent cadence to her delivery, no one there seemed to care. The lute player came on again after, and remained for some time, preoccupying himself with minor chords and relaxing sevenths.

Tryst kept an eye on all the customers that came and went from the bistro, deciding eventually that indeed most of the clientele were men. The females were largely staff, and Tryst pitied them for the looks they were getting. Some of these men were old enough to be their grandfathers, but their frail hands grabbed whatever flesh they could reach, as if these youthful bodies would be the last thing they would ever hold. Everywhere in this city now it seemed such desperation was manifest.

His thoughts inevitably drifted from Inquisition business to his commitment to the Ovinists, and to Chancellor Urtica in particular. His mentor was an inspiring man: charming, bright, his dedication to Villjamur unquestionable. It was hard not to want to get involved with anything he was linked to. Like so many young men, Tryst was infused with a burning desire to succeed, to *achieve*. Life was stretched out ahead of him, a freshly plowed field waiting only for his potential, and Chancellor Urtica could help him harvest it.

As the lute player paused for a sip of lager, the sound of murmurs and whispers drew Tryst's attention to the door. The prostitute, Tuya, was walking in from the fog, a silky grace to her stride, a look of deep remoteness in her eyes.

Tryst took another sip of rum as he watched her glide between the tables. She was wearing a carmine cloak, not unlike the color distinguishing the city guard, but carefully tailored to cling to her voluptuous curves. A lock of red hair curled down across her stubbornly beautiful face, whose other half—the half with the scar—was covered by a headscarf. She approached a table near the front of the stage, typical of someone wanting all the attention she could get. As she took off her cloak, revealing a green dress that seemed to contradict most of the city's current fashions, more than a little of the conversation in the room fell silent. Her skin shimmered in the dull lighting, and smoke drifted away from her somehow, as if allowing everyone there to get a better look.

She sat alone at that table for around a quarter of an hour, the serving girls bringing her drinks simultaneously from two different admirers. She accepted them with grace, but didn't acknowledge whoever had bought them for her.

Men passed close by, but she barely gave them a glance. After a while, she rolled herself something to smoke, probably arum weed, lit the end of the roll-up in a candle flame, then leaned back and exhaled the smoke. Her eyes remained fixed on the lute player, still singing moodily on top of his morose chords.

It was going to be a dull night for Tryst if all she did was sit and smoke and drink. He'd just have to wait until she left and then follow her home. One way he could get inside would be if he propositioned her as a customer, but then she would recognize him. Although maybe that wasn't a bad thing, as he could use their brief acquaintance to become intimate with her. If she would only let him into her world. Then he could take a closer look at her paintings, and perhaps they might reveal some clues.

Since his training as an Inquisition torturer, Tryst possessed a secret stash of subtle powder, sannindi, that he could use to his advantage. Essentially a truth powder, supposedly it could only be obtained through official Inquisition channels, but it still found its way into the hands of illicit dealers as "love potion." Just a little sprinkle of it into food or drink, and people became remarkably amenable. Jeryd certainly wouldn't approve of him using it, but Tryst didn't care. He reached into an inside pocket, pulled out the paper wrap. The red powder was inside, not enough to make her pass out, but it would alter her mind enough to make her very helpful with his inquiries.

He picked up his glass and the bottle of Black Heart rum, and headed across the smoky room to her table. "Looks like you've got no company either. Mind if I join you?"

She looked up at him then stubbed out her roll-up of arum weed. "Well, well, it's the human Inquisition officer. Your life's obviously as dull as mine in that you find yourself in this low-down joint. And I had you for a worthier sort."

She indicated the chair next to her. "So what brings you here? How's your friend, Jeryd?"

"He's fine." Tryst sat down and began pouring each of them another drink. He offered her some more arum weed, pre-rolled.

She took one, saying, "Thanks. It's a nasty habit. So has he got back with his wife yet?"

"Yes, they're together again." Tryst set the bottle on the table. She seemed genuinely happy at the news. Strange, he contemplated, living through other people's happiness.

"That's nice to see true love lasting, not just strangers shacking up with anyone convenient to hide from the ice." She pulled out another roll-up from her pocket, lit it in the candle flame. "So, are you here to spy on me?"

Tryst chuckled, glancing up at the stage. "If only." He locked eye contact with her, then released it. "No, I'm just killing an evening on my own. You know how it is."

"Another night in Villjamur," she sighed, exhaling smoke. "I suppose being in this city does that to you. So many people everywhere and none of them cares for you. Not one bit."

"A little morose."

"The city, or what I said?"

Tryst liked that. She was certainly entrancing, despite the melancholy, maybe even because of it. "I'm going to get us another bottle."

He motioned for a serving girl to come over. The girl gave that typical waitress nod-and-smile, then turned to leave.

Tryst said, "What do you think of that one? Pretty or not?"

As Tuya studied the girl as she walked away, he covertly reached out and sprinkled some of the sannindi powder into her drink.

She shrugged. "All right, I suppose, but you could do a lot better."

"Well, I'm usually pretty picky, so it must be the Freeze, like you said." He raised his glass. "Here's to shacking up with anyone."

She laughed dryly, joining him in the toast.

*

Half an hour later they were back in Tuya's room. It had taken them some time to climb the intervening levels as the streets were so icy. She was already drowsy, because of the effects of the sannindi. Her place was dark as they entered, so Tryst lit a lantern, and as soon as it came to life, he could see the copious amounts of ornaments and antiques crammed into every available space. With so little else in her life, she had to fill it with something, he guessed.

She was now getting amorous as a side-effect of the drug, but he didn't take advantage. After all, she was now under suspicion of murdering two of the most senior administrators in the city.

One of the doors to the balcony was fractionally open. Because of the noxious smell of paints in the room, he assumed she left it open to let in some fresh air. He walked over to shut out the eternal winter. The landscape had been reduced to a few lights. Everyone was where they should be, in bed, or somewhere warm. Then faintly, he heard some chatter from the streets, two blades clashing, a cough of laughter. Probably a couple of youths testing each other's ability with a sword.

Tuya slumped onto the bed clutching her head in her hands. She glanced repeatedly up at Tryst, then began to loosen her clothing. While she was occupied, he decided to examine the room to see if he could find anything. Uncertain where to start, he moved over to the covered canvases stacked in one corner of the room. *Paint,* after all, was the only clue Jeryd had found.

Besides several large canvases there were a couple on easels and a dozen much smaller items of art on the side. All were concealed beneath heavy cloth, so he uncovered the first to reveal a large image of an animal that he couldn't identify. Whatever it was, it had several limbs beyond necessary. Its shape suggested something primitive; it generated a distinct feeling of unease.

"Would . . . would you like to spend the night?" Tuya asked tremulously.

She had closed her eyes, was lying on her side on the bed, wearing only a corset. Tryst could see the hideous scar on her face clearly now. He ignored her, and scrutinized the paintings further.

"You're a handsome one," she snickered. "I'd like it if you did. Come on. You know you want to. You men are all the same."

"Maybe," Tryst said. "Just a moment."

She sat up suddenly. "What're you doing? Don't look at those." She pushed herself off the bed, stumbled forward into his arms, her bare feet sliding on the tiles. She was surprisingly heavy, as he eased her back on the bed. "Don't look at them," she repeated.

"Why not?" Tryst said soothingly. "I think you're a wonderful artist. I want to see your *real* talents."

"Really? You're not just saying that?" She sounded confused again. He knew the drug would affect her for a little while longer.

"No, I'm not just saying it," he said. "I want to see more."

"But . . ." she trailed off.

He could sense her frustration now as she battled with the effects of the sannindi powder. She wanted to order him away from the paintings—the need so clear in her eyes—but she also seemed to desire to please him, to offer him anything she could.

Either way, he didn't care.

"I want to look at your paintings," he insisted.

She began to take off her corset.

"No," he commanded, and grasped her hands softly at the wrist. She looked genuinely confused, then gave him a smile tinged with venom.

It said she hated him, without saying anything at all.

"You're a beautiful woman, Tuya," he said, to reassure her. The last thing he wanted now was to create a scene. "But I don't think we should, because you don't really want to."

He pushed her away slightly so that she fell on the bed. She sighed and closed her eyes and just lay there, with her corset still intact.

Tryst walked back to the canvases, this time unveiling another.

What magic is this?

He lurched back in shock. A blue shape appeared to be emerging from the canvas, pumping up and down as if it were someone's breathing chest. No form to speak of. Tryst stared at it for some time. He wanted to question Tuya about it, but thought better of that.

With caution, he revealed another, this time a sketch of the city as seen from her window. Nothing remarkable there. With his eyes fixed on the pulsating blue form, he pulled back the cloth on a fourth painting.

He took several steps away in disgust, holding his hand to his mouth.

Tuya still lay on the bed, staring up at the ceiling. His face creased in horror, Tryst examined the image before him: a hacked-open carcass that seemed altogether too real. A heart—or something resembling one—beat inside it, and streaks of red paint, possibly even blood, had dried while dripping down the canvas. Whatever was in place of a face stared back at him with one unblinking eye. He looked around the room and picked up an empty candlestick and prodded the thing. It squelched away from where he applied gentle pressure.

What the hell is this? Tryst wondered. *Is it alive?*

"What you . . . doing now?" Tuya said suddenly behind him. She was grasping a knife, pointing it at him threateningly. "Get away from them!" she hissed.

The drug was obviously wearing off, fast.

Tryst stood with hands raised, palming the air gently. Trying to disguise his panic, he said, "Hey, I'm only looking at what you paint . . . It's truly . . . remarkable."

"Just get over by the bed." She sliced the air as if to reinforce her words. She looked vaguely ridiculous waving a blade around while wearing only a corset.

He did as she ordered. There was a knife concealed in his boot, but he did not want to use it yet. Manipulating her mind would be a much more powerful weapon, if he could get inside her. It was what torturers were trained to do, seeking to work a little beneath the surface.

"I don't mean any harm, Tuya," he said, noting the slight drowsiness still in her eyes.

She looked at him uncertainly, and he could perceive that she didn't quite know what to do next. She held the knife too close to her, so she wouldn't strike him with it yet.

From her behavior, these monstrous paintings suggested something deeply personal.

"Tell me about your art," he said. He glanced to and from her creations, noticed they were still throbbing dully. She turned toward them, and he acted quickly. With the same candlestick, he leaned forward and struck her across her head, and Tuya stumbled, but remained upright, so he hit her twice more, with sharp and clinical blows.

She fell with a groan to the floor.

That was not what he had wanted, but she had forced it hadn't she, so it had to be done. He placed the candlestick down, then began to rummage through her bedside drawer. He picked out a couple of belts, then tightly bound her hands and feet. There'd be no more of this delicate, tiptoeing around the issue. There was some serious shit going on here, and he was going to find out what the hell she was up to.

He left the room silently, taking one last glimpse at the horrors on the canvases.

❋

An hour later, he was in possession of more sannindi from his contact on Sigr Gata, enough this time for a prolonged session with Tuya.

Those paintings caused him distress and he wanted answers.

When he got back, there she was, sprawled face down on the floor wearing her corset, just as he'd left her. Tryst slung his damp outer cloak on a chair, lifted her back up against the bed, then ran his palm across her scalp to feel the bruises. They weren't too bad, and she groaned in his arms like a lover seeking comfort—ironic, and he knew it. Tilting her head back further, he tipped a larger dose of sannindi down her throat.

While he waited for her to wake up, he stood in front of the paintings, shaking. He couldn't get used to the horror of these depictions, despite his years spent in the Inquisition torture chambers. This was a different horror, however, some artificial life force pulsating impossibly before him. With one finger extended, he poked it several times.

His immediate thought was that this must be some cultist evil, manipulating the arts of the Dawnir. Why did she have such monstrosities in her room? How did she sleep at night with these things hidden only by a cloth? Was it her who had painted something that could come alive? Or did she purchase them from a cultist?

There was coughing behind him, obviously some of the powder having caught in her throat. He stepped toward her. "How're you feeling?" he asked.

She looked up at him through the hair covering her face. "I feel terrible," she croaked, then ran a hand across the top of her head, delicately tapping the lump that had formed there.

"Good," Tryst said. "Now I want you to tell me the truth."

She brushed a thick tress of hair back behind her ear.

"First of all, your name?"

"Tuya Daluud."

"Your age?"

"I . . . honestly, I don't know," she replied.

"Okay, Tuya Daluud. I'd like you to explain those paintings to me. Tell me, why do they appear to be *alive*?"

"They *are* alive."

"Ask a stupid question . . ." Tryst murmured. "Well then, how've you done it?" He knelt down before her face-to-face, in an almost threatening manner—their pose a corruption of a lover's kiss.

"Many years ago I formed a relationship with a cultist. To keep things short, he provided me with special materials. A couple of relics. He showed me some techniques that would breathe extra life into my art."

"Why would a cultist care about that?" he sneered.

She made full eye contact. "Because he was in love with me."

"Ah, yes," Tryst said. "He paid for your body, and you called it love—is that right?"

"It wasn't like that at all. He only paid me the first time . . ."

"I'm sure it wasn't really the first," he said, hoping his sarcasm would provoke her.

"Why are you being like this to me? I've done nothing to hurt you."

"True," he said, and slowly untied her. "Now, let's have a little tour of your gallery, shall we?"

She explained it all, each painting, from conception to creation.

Behind the ones that Tryst saw first lay even greater horrors, and he would never forget them. What he had at first found disgusting he later deemed cruel, since her creations did genuinely appear to be alive, but not in any way he was familiar with. For an hour he was shown the intricacies of her paintings, the body shapes that appeared to step out of them. Most of her creations were now set free, somewhere across the Archipelago, on journeys of their own. One image intrigued him particularly: a clay sculpture of a reclining dog. It moved its head around when she neared it, as if it fed off her presence. The creature was totally black, except for eyes possessing a fragile emotion. How could anything so unreal have a life? It broke all known laws, all religious teachings, every philosophy he'd known.

"I've one more question," Tryst said, as the clock tower rang out the thirteen chimes of midnight. "Why do you make these things?"

She turned to a lantern resting on a chest of drawers, stared at it as if it was a beacon of hope. "I think, deep down, it's because I can. You don't know how rewarding it feels to have your creations come to life. No one does, so I can't begin to explain. That way your art takes on a life of its own. I remember when I was much younger, people criticizing my paintings for being lifeless. Now I can make anything come out of these canvases, and they behave according to my wishes—even if they die shortly after. And I do it because . . . well, because I'm lonely. This is a big city, but I feel like a stranger in it. My family died years ago. I've spent all my life here, so where else would I go? There's nothing for me in one of the far-off villages of some backwater island, and I wouldn't fancy my chances out there in the Freeze anyway. No, I'm trapped here, a permanent stranger. Perhaps it makes my job easier. When men have finished with me, they go back home to their wives, their families, and I know they wouldn't want me to walk up to them in the street and say hello. So every time I make love to a stranger, it makes me a little more distant, a little more solitary. A little more scarred."

Tryst brushed her sadness to one side. "It's possible, then, for you to create a living creature simply to *murder* someone?"

She was silent for some time before answering, frozen in posture, so he could not tell what she was thinking. "Yes, of course. And I suppose you'd want to know why I did it."

Tryst waited for her to go on.

She continued, "Ghuda talked a lot over the pillow. It's like a confessional, and you'd be surprised to know just how many secrets are whispered to a woman like me. He may have been a little drunk, of course, but he started ranting about the refugees, and how they should be eliminated, that they disturbed the central plans of the Council. He claimed they were parasitic scum who deserved to die before they could leach the Treasury dry. So much disease among them, too, threatened the survival of the city, so he and Councilor Boll were working on certain plans to bring about their *removal,* and there were others involved, too. It wasn't difficult to work out what he meant and I couldn't let him continue, Tryst. I just couldn't let them destroy the lives of so many."

Tryst was concerned that she might know Urtica's secrets, of his own involvement in them. "There were other ways to act, you know. You should have informed the Inquisition."

"You think I'm stupid? You think you lot would have been able to do anything? Solely on the word of a prostitute?"

That means Urtica is safe. Tryst felt a surge of relief. "It doesn't mean you can just kill whoever you want, contrary to the ancient laws of this city."

"You're going to arrest me, I presume?" she said, her gaze focused on the floor tiles.

He considered this point for a moment, but he had another idea. This woman might have some definite use for him. And afterward, he would turn her in, of course. Meanwhile, he had a way in which he could make Jeryd suffer, nothing too serious, just a little mental fun—a little revenge for blocking his promotion. And then he could feel justice had been done, an eye for an eye.

Tryst regarded her canvases once again. "You say you can paint anything, and then make it come to life?"

"I can try," she said nervously, "What d'you have in mind? Are you not going to arrest me then?"

"I'll tell you what," Tryst said. "You seem like a sensible sort of woman, so I'll let you keep your freedom if you can do me a favor."

"What . . . what sort of favor?"

"I don't want sex, Tuya, it's your art I'm concerned with."

"My art?"

"I want you to paint a woman for me. Can you make her stay alive for just a very short period of time?"

"I've not created a human for what seems like . . . forever."

"Not a human, more a rumel. If you can't, I will have you placed in the city jail pending execution."

"What do you want her for?"

"Firstly, you must control her so that she does only what I say— just for the short time she's alive. And I want you to make her exactly how I describe."

"I don't have a choice, do I?"

"Not really, no. And you will not say a word of this to anyone, not if you wish to go on living."

"So, what do you want this woman to look like?"

Tryst proceeded to describe Jeryd's wife.

CHAPTER 29

※

SHE COULD TURN STONE INTO LAVA, SEAWATER INTO ICE SCULPTURES, could make plants grow rapidly to the height of a building. She could create devices to flood the land with fire, and just as quickly quench it.

But she could not find Dartun Súr, Godhi of the Order of the Equinox.

Papus sat in the darkness and silence of her stone-built chambers, her fingers steepled, brooding over the situation while staring at the floor.

She hadn't disclosed her full concerns to the red-eyed commander regarding what Dartun had been up to. He was clearly the one responsible for raising the dead. The real questions were how many of these walking dead were there, and what were the consequences?

Papus had known about Dartun for most of her life, because ever since she joined the Order of the Dawnir, rumors had persisted about his lifestyle, his abuse of Dawnir technology. She herself was the most skilled of all at using relics—or that was what she honestly believed, up until Verain's visit. For years she had climbed through the ranks, watched others around her misuse the technology and die in accidents—her own great love, with whom she had hoped to abscond, included. It was all about maintaining image, being a cultist, and her whole family had belonged from time immemorial to the same, ancient order, the oldest of the cultist sects, a line stretching back generations. Most of her remaining kin were now in retirement on Ysla, well isolated from the rest of the Empire. But she was still here in Villjamur, still driven and still working and still competing.

Still Papus loved her work. What made her feel alive was the thrill that she might discover something completely unknown on any day, that she might then understand the universe better than anyone, that she might occasionally assist the advance of civilization in some small way.

And all the time, in the background, Dartun was quietly making a mockery of her.

People whispered about the Equinox. They gave cultists a bad reputation. There were questions regarding their ethics. But, knowing how Dartun liked to perpetuate his own myth, she had ignored the tittle-tattle up to a point.

Now he had gone too far.

He'd tampered with the fabric of life, and it was now a public affair. If he was indeed raising the dead, he had to be stopped soon. If what the girl, Verain, had claimed was true, then he was messing with basic universal configurations. There were codes of behavior as old as the city, among the cultists, insisting that they should consult each other on controversial matters.

If Dartun's order wouldn't respond to her demands that he divulge any activities to do with raising the dead, then it would be tantamount to a declaration of war.

There hadn't been strife between cultists for thousands of years, ever since the original disagreements that had spliced them into their separate orders.

Things were suddenly looking complicated.

She sighed. This was not like in her youth, all those years ago on Ysla. The cultists' isle had been unlike any other island in the Archipelago in geological, botanical, or entomological terms. Its climate was warmer, for a start. But then it had been augmented so much by the various cultists inhabiting it using their relics that it no longer much resembled the island the original Dawnir had created. Lush green meadows, ridges of igneous rocks, crescents of beautiful white beaches, deciduous trees budding and shedding in rhythm with the artificial seasons. And those open blue skies always visible from the hilltops. All the cultist orders were entitled to have use of land there. Their different divisions possessed lodges scattered around, or gathered in village complexes, where their members were able to interpret relics in comparative solitude.

It now seemed a world away.

Her mind drifted back to Dartun, and then she made her decision. His tampering with the forces of life and death was simply wrong, and his reckless opening of doors to new worlds posed a risk to all these islands lying under the light of the red sun. Clearly, it was her responsibility to bring him to justice.

✳

Through the dark alleyways, where the city's snow-scrapers hadn't yet ventured with their shovels, she marched with the letter she had resolutely composed. No lanterns around these parts of the city, but it was a clear evening, and the twin moons illuminated the treacherous snow clearly. Glowing paths stretched in front of her. Although not particularly late, there was no one else visible, few footprints. There were obviously better places to be than out in the cold. One hand was buried in her pocket, wrapped around her ultimatum. She had to present it in person, alone, but several steps behind her were other members of her order, armed with *Sterkr* relics. She was not quixotic about this business. She wanted some protection, but did not want her arrival to seem intimidating. Not yet.

Papus reached the inconspicuous entrance, knocked several times before a hatch slid back aside and a frosty welcome was muttered.

"I want to see Dartun Súr, as a matter of urgency," she demanded.

"Not gonna happen without an invitation," came the response.

"If you don't let me see him urgently, it will mean a massive rift between our orders," she said, and slipped the missive through the bars.

"Hang on," the voice murmured, then whoever was behind the door was no longer there. Papus waited in the cold, reflecting that Dartun was probably on some far-off island as Verain had suggested.

Eventually, the door opened, and one of the Equinox stood facing her.

"He's not here," he said, her letter visible in his hands.

"Where is he then?"

In the poor light of the doorway she barely perceived his shrug.

"I want some bloody answers. Maybe you can help me instead."

"Listen, lady, I don't know what you're after. I told you, I'll give him your message when he returns."

"You're not following," Papus snapped, discreetly dropping a relic from her sleeve into her hand. "I'm not going anywhere until someone senior from your order talks to me."

"I just told you . . ." he began menacingly.

Papus thrust the relic toward him, a bolt of purple light crackling around his body, an electrifying net.

His mouth opened wide, displaying a scream, but no sound came out. After a moment he collapsed onto the floor in soundless agony.

The letter of warning drifted down beside him as she leaned over his body and pulled the door behind him. Then she slid the ultimatum underneath it, as bolts of energy continued to skim around the rival cultist. By now, members of her own order exited the deep night and hooked ropes around the fallen man, and dragged him back down the snow-filled alley, all the time sparks of purple light radiating about his writhing form.

"An eye for an eye," she said with satisfaction as, at the narrow opening of the alleyway, she crouched to deposit another device that fired a single sheet of purple light across the ground. The light disappeared to leave the snow untouched, deleting all marks of their presence there.

Snow continued to fall leisurely as if it had all the time in the world.

CHAPTER 30

✳

"Where's the big freak?" Apium said, before yawning and stretching with the grace of a tramp, astride his black horse.

"I take it you mean Jurro?" Brynd said, after considering for a moment that he himself was the freak, or maybe Kym—men who loved other men, and who'd be killed if discovered. He could never shake off the paranoia.

A unit of troops was assembling between the inner two gates of Villjamur. Brynd had ordered for twenty of the Night Guard, which included some new promotions from the best of the Dragoons, recruited after a little necessary training. There had been a night of induction, as cultists from the Order of the Dawnir used their skills to enhance the new recruits' physical capabilities, their sight, their hearing, their resilience. Brynd had forgotten just what ministrations the Night Guard had to endure in their first evening joining the elite.

Brynd had ordered up a hundred men and women of the Second Dragoons, and a hundred of the First, all of them mounted on horseback and battle-ready within half an hour. Also he was waiting for a Dawnir cultist to join them.

The horses shifted on the muddied ground. The temperature having plummeted even further recently, Brynd wore several layers of clothing, with a fur cloak draped across his shoulders. He guided his horse in front of the assembled Night Guard. Like himself, they were uncertain as to what sort of combat they were expecting. No reliable news had materialized, no firsthand reports from trustworthy sources. All the information they possessed so far was recycled rumors of grotesque beasts tearing down towns and villages, mercilessly slaughtering everything in sight. As his troops chatted idly to relieve themselves of anxiety, the sound of hooves on the cobbled streets beyond informed him that support was now arriving.

The Dragoons were arrayed in full battle splendor, rousing an inevitable sense of military pride in Brynd. They came off the cobbles onto the snow-covered mud. Beneath their furs, metal glistened in the morning light: body armor and chain mail, nothing ornamental but simply designed for fighting with efficiency. Spears protruded over shields, swords hung at sides. Within moments they had lined up, awaiting Brynd's commands. And through the gates rode a lone cultist, clothed elegantly in black. The magician rode forward with casual arrogance, bringing his horse up alongside Brynd's.

"Sele of Jamur," Brynd greeted this new arrival, noticing the cultist was female. She had a weathered face and sunken blue eyes as if she was prey to some addiction. *Have they given me a magic junkie?* he wondered.

The cultist returned the greeting. "So, when do we leave?" Her voice was weirdly elegant.

"As soon as our friend the Dawnir arrives," Brynd confirmed. "Have you brought much of your technology?" Her horse was loaded with considerable baggage.

"Enough," she replied, eyeing the gathered soldiers. "Why aren't we sailing from the city docks?"

"Because ice sheets have already formed on Jokull's northern shores, to some extent, and navigating those waters will be difficult. It will be much quicker to sail from the east side of the island. I didn't catch your name by the way?"

"My name is Blavat, commander."

"Well then, Blavat, it seems we are now ready to leave." He nodded toward the gate. The Dawnir hovered there nearly having to crouch under it.

Brynd began to walk his horse forward to greet the creature.

"Commander Brynd Lathraea!" Jurro shouted across the intervening distance. Four crows sprung suddenly from the walls, and burst in a ragged flight away from the city as the Dawnir's plangent voice echoed around the confined space between the gates. "Sele of Jamur! I have brought some clothing and some books to read on the way, but did I need anything else?"

"Sele of Jamur, Jurro. No, you'll do fine as you are."

The giant approached, casting a great shadow over Brynd. All the assembled troops stared in amazement at the creature's size, its curious goatlike head, its tusks. By now a throng of citizens had also gathered, staring and pointing. You could hear the squeals of children as they set eyes on this curious piece of history. Few people there would've had the intelligence to recognize this apparition as the sole survivor of the Ancient race.

"Are you all set, Jurro?" Brynd inquired.

The creature paused to contemplate the question in a slow exaggerated manner. "Yes, I am. I'm looking forward to our little adventure."

"You realize the danger of our mission?" Brynd warned. "This isn't a holiday. You're not obliged to—"

The Dawnir raised one massive, hairy hand to silence the commander, leaving Brynd vaguely insulted, though he knew Jurro meant no harm. "I have longed for years to leave this city, having almost been a prisoner at the Empire's invitation for far too long. They kept me sweet with endless studies, but there is no use reading about the world from a book, when one can see it with one's own eyes." He prodded a chunky digit under his own eye, as if Brynd didn't know what an eye was.

"Looks like we're all set then." Brynd pulled his horse back, and trotted alongside the ranks of the soldiers. They presented a solid display of the military force that had kept the Empire intact for generations.

Orders were given for the gates to open, and the Imperial troops rode out of Villjamur. Faintly, Brynd could hear the cheers of the populace left behind, as their troops set off to engage in some far-off battle. It seemed one of those patriotic reactions that had echoed through the ages. Or perhaps the people were cheering because for the first time in ages there was a tradition to cheer about.

As soon as the outer gate was opened, the refugees crowded around the emerging battalions. Overflowing feces from the latrines and smoke from pit fires combined to provide an intense odor, while behind them their tents stretched across the tundra like a city of cloth. Dogs ran in purposeless circles, ducking under hung-up washing that had frozen solid and didn't even move in the wind. The muddied road to the east stretched right alongside this hellish encampment. Grubby men wrapped in innumerable layers of rags pawed at the horsemen pleadingly, while the sight of a mother carrying her dead child in a sling was almost too much to bear. Brynd suspected that his guilt at ignoring them would come back to haunt his dreams. Everywhere there was hopelessness.

✳

"These refugees . . ." Chancellor Urtica stood at the window, focusing his gaze through the spires toward those camped outside the gates of Villjamur. "They annoy me somewhat."

Tryst stepped out of the shadows. "You wish them to be eliminated now, sir?"

Urtica peered back at him, still gripping the windowsill. "Timing is everything, my dear fellow. Indeed timing is everything. Of course, I wish them gone, disposed of, because they're a blight on the Empire. Remember this city is a city of legends. Long have poets written about the nights of Villjamur. We can't have their like here, no."

"And your plan?" Tryst asked. "Is this why you asked me here?"

"One of the reasons, certainly," Urtica said. "But I also wondered how you were getting along with our little friend, the rumel investigator."

"Not bad," Tryst said. "He's keeping very quiet about the murders. Makes me think he knows something. He doesn't usually keep everything quite *this* silent, though."

Urtica said, "You suspect he'll find the murderer?"

"I'm certain of it," Tryst said, hoping he could mask the fact that he himself had caught her already. Once he had finished with Tuya, he'd make sure she was arrested and executed, but meanwhile he had his own schemes to pursue. Yes, timing *was* everything. In the meantime he didn't want to consider his actions a betrayal of Urtica's trust.

"I have received numerous requests from the Inquisition hierarchy about permitting Investigator Jeryd into the Council chambers for extensive questioning sessions. I am however wary of allowing such a move."

"Certainly not, chancellor. I have taken moves already to ensure that Jeryd is sufficiently distracted."

"Good." Urtica scrutinized Tryst till the Inquisition aide felt nervous. "Tell me, as his assistant, what do you yourself know about these murders?"

"Very little," Tryst lied, "because there isn't much to go on. It seems each councilor was hunted down with a purpose. By some savage creature, in each case."

"Creature, you say." Urtica's expression revealed surprise. "Hmm, these are indeed strange times. I have had reports of the dead rising up to walk among the living . . . but that is strictly between you and I."

"Of course, chancellor. Of course."

"Our military operations must not be declared openly, though news will filter out eventually."

"Who do we fight?" Tryst asked.

"The Varltungs. I'm slightly concerned not to have heard any further intelligence yet. The routine garuda flights have stopped. Not only that, but we've thousands of stinking refugees outside our fucking gates, living in their own sodding filth and disease. It's only a matter of time before their diseases reach into the city itself."

"You have schemes in mind, sir?"

"Indeed I do, Tryst. Indeed I do. Another reason why I wanted you here was to pick your brains."

Urtica walked to the door, opened it to check if anyone was around. He then locked it, drew Tryst into the furthest corner of the room. "We swear to the Ovinists now," he said, and Tryst understood what he meant.

Urtica placed an arm around Tryst's shoulders. "Say our new Empress were to sign various decrees to . . . *eliminate* these refugees. Say she set things in motion secretly, and they were suddenly . . . *revealed* to the Council and the Inquisition. What would be the official outcome as denoted by the laws of the Empire?"

"Well . . ." Tryst began pondering the question, while he tried hard to recall his studies of the ancient and complicated laws of the

Jamur Empire. "It would be considered an act of conspiracy of genocide against her own people—against the free people of the Empire.
At the very least she would be stripped of her title, and probably executed. But this all depends—wouldn't it be tantamount to a coup?
How do we get the military on our side?"

"The military do not serve Rika directly. They never served Johynn
either—they take orders from the Council, so as to prevent a dicta-
torship. That's why he never trusted any soldier apart from Commander Lathraea for most of the time. Don't worry—I have pacts in
place with certain senior officers."

Tryst felt proud at this sign of proximity to his Ovinist leader, infatuated by their closeness. The man had thought of everything. He
was an inspiration.

"Now then, what I'm about to tell you will be extremely confidential. I will reward you with immense power after this is done, for I
myself will ascend the ranks. At the very least you shall step from
grade Minoris to Majoris . . ."

Power.

The dialogue had moved on, but the word still hung in the air like
a noxious odor. Power was what he should have achieved in the Inquisition, and it was power that Jeryd had denied him simply because
of his race. Power was what he wanted so badly, to prove himself worthy.

Tryst said, "I will honor your confidence, Magus Urtica."

"Good. Now, I fear this next discussion will require us to be somewhere even more private. Shall we?"

✳

On one of the bridges overlooking the frosted spires, and well above
this city suffocating under snow, Urtica discussed his concepts. It was
to be a quick maneuver, a simple, brilliant plan. They would forge a
decree of execution for the thousands of refugees, and have Rika's signature on it. He would say that it was signed in the presence of not
only Urtica but also Tryst as a casual member of the Inquisition. He
would make it appear as if Rika was issuing an order for the Inquisition torturers to go about removing the refugees and killing them. He
could say that the Lady Eir would be there too, and forge her signa-

ture as well. Kill two birds, as it were. Other Ovinists could join in on the fun and pretend to have been "witnesses," and those members in the Council could say that they had been asked to consult her on logistical matters about removing corpses from the city on a large scale.

Forgery: such a blissful art.

Ancient laws would then spring into motion—that no ruler can harm those under the starred banner of the Empire—and Rika and Eir would be arrested. Then executed. Chancellor Urtica, as now hero of the moment, would himself be Emperor—the first of a new lineage. The Jamur Empire would be finished. The Urtican Empire would begin. All the while, no one would really notice if, given the right amount of stealth, *Rika's plans* for removing the refugees went ahead . . .

Tryst felt satisfied as he looked upon his city. Felt proud to be involved with the genius that was Magus Urtica. Despite the Freeze, Tryst had suddenly regained a sanguine outlook on things.

CHAPTER 31

❄

"WHAT D'YOU MEAN, WAR?" DARTUN SAID, WHILE CHEWING A HONEY-oat biscuit. He was in conversation with a flickering image beaming from a brass device beside him onto the snow in the shadow of a dead tree. The image was blurred, but recognizable was the voice of one of his order back in Villjamur.

"Papus has taken Guntar as a hostage," the voice continued, while light quivered on the snow. "She demands your presence."

Dartun laughed before taking a last bite of the biscuit. He dusted the crumbs off his fuligin cloak still considering their position. The air was still, and the temperature had dropped rapidly the further north they had sailed, but at least a relic had kept the worst of the weather away during this journey. Dartun had acquired a pack of dogs and a sailing vessel from some corrupt traders on the south coast of Y'iren—having ripped through empty space to get there—as far as he could manage with the help of his precious relics.

Last night he had dreamed of death, or so he supposed. In his sleep the sun had faded from red to something darker and dimmer, and then to nothing, till all around a city, Villjamur perhaps, the streets were blackened. Rows upon rows of torches burned to provide light, and frozen hands reached out all around to touch him. It was then he had woken and, not for the first time, he felt deeply connected to the world, and sensed that it, like him, was dying.

The dogs began howling further up the shore.

With Verain and his two most trusted cultists, Todi and Tuung, Dartun had traveled to the northeast of the Boreal Archipelago, sailing through the thick ice sheets as far as they could go. A dangerous way to travel, filled with breathless moments. Todi was young, blond, and eager, offering a keenness that meant he was trustworthy. Tuung, however, was older and a balding little man with enough experience to have become cynical, with the need to think twice about matters; he constantly wore the expression of an angry tortoise. Both being of the same stocky build, there was something about their natures that made Dartun consider they could be father and son.

Sled was now the only way to travel since he had no relics enabling transportation. He had abandoned the last one just to get from Villjamur to Y'iren, thus saving himself the chore of traveling as far as the others must do with the undead. That meant Dartun couldn't simply rip through space to cross the islands any more, and dryly he contemplated the fact that he was becoming just like a lay person.

"This is serious," the image on the snow declared, slipping in and out of focus, the voice strangely ambient. "She's accused you of tampering with ancient laws regarding the use of Dawnir technology to do wrong. Started quoting a whole load of shit about regulations— it's very angry stuff, and could spiral out of control back here if we're not careful."

"She's not really much of a threat," Dartun muttered. "I suspect this is more about jealousy than anything else."

"Sir," the image protested, "they'll torture Guntar—kill him even. They now know how you've been raising corpses. She wants to unite all the other sects against us. If that happens, they may have us all killed. So what should we do?"

It was a situation he had anticipated, that Papus would be so self-righteous, as if she herself was the moral centerpiece of the Archipelago. He wondered vaguely how she had come to know of his animation of corpses. Those whose transformation was incomplete he had simply released, perhaps a careless decision, but he did not possess the heart to kill them, they were so very *nearly* life. But the problem with the undead was that they were so unreliable in their different states of decay. And even these failures were side effects of his greater aim, to breed perfect undead men and women.

A private militia. His protection.

"Sit tight, and see what happens," Dartun sighed. "Let Papus make her moves if she wishes. It will bring her little benefit."

"One final thing, Godhi," the image communicated through static. "That Randur Estevu, he says he's finally got the money together. I assume this was some private business of yours."

"Yes, yes . . ." Preoccupied with his own thoughts, Dartun had very nearly forgotten the young man who wanted him to find a way to let his mother live.

"Well, he wants . . . know when he can pay . . ." The image flickered, and the voice became distorted before returning to clarity again.

"Did you just say he wants to know when he can pay me?"

"Yes," the image replied.

"Right. Okay, first you'll need someone who can gain access to my private chambers." Dartun then recited information about assembling certain relics so that even from here he could have the Dawnir technology manipulated in the manner he wished. And it wasn't difficult, ironically, the grand concept of extending life, it was just that only he knew the correct procedure and had kept it to himself for as long as he could remember. None of his fellow cultists would realize what they were creating from following his instructions. Although the methods were clearly not permanent—as he knew all too well now—it might at least give this wretched woman a little extra life.

Dartun said, "If he comes tell him the process will be ready in ten days or so. And I take it there's no issue with the others from the sect in bringing the undead out to me?"

"No, all is as you scheduled."

"Very good." Dartun now manipulated the device so that the projected image faded to nothing, and the air around him was filled with an absolute stillness. But Dartun couldn't work out why he felt a sudden nervousness; he assumed it might be because he was so near the final stages of what he fervently hoped to achieve. There was always that creeping suspicion that nothing would be at the end of his journey, merely a simple reaffirmation that he could not live forever no matter how he tried to engineer it.

✳

Tineag'l: the mining island lying north of Y'iren, and here the massive mineral belt had long been a supplier of much of the Empire's metal ores, an old industry of long-suffering workers and slaves. Snow had fallen evenly across the tundra, its serenity undisturbed except when auks darted out of the thick larix forest, their ragged shapes bursting starkly across the horizon. Much of the island's northern shores had once been heavily populated with dozens of mining communities stretching far beyond the Ring of Iron, as the largest of the Empire's industrial regions was known. Towns and villages were composed of sprawling wooden structures rather than the grand stonework of Vill-jamur. Men covered in black dirt would drag their feet toward the mines while women in dowdy clothing would try to scrape a living providing stores and taverns and brothels. Tribal slaves were treated well, the Council would say of this place, better than if they were merely given poor wages. It was a poor argument to own another person, in Dartun's view, but seemed symptomatic of how things worked in the Jamur Empire.

It was difficult to avoid the detritus from decades of excavations, and the roads interlinking such places were little more than well-trodden paths. There was a continuing problem with wolves scavenging in the scraps of food and Dartun was amazed that people would choose to live here, but he supposed that the mines at least provided a livelihood of sorts.

Their group had passed around the outskirts of several such settlements, but there was now no one here to be seen. It wasn't what Dartun expected. Was this due to the Freeze? Was it now so cold here that the inhabitants had been forced to evacuate? It was unlikely, he thought. The richer or more desperate residents would have sought shelter in the Sanctuary City, definitely, but there were bound to be a few hardened types—rumel even, with their more resilient skins—that could survive a harsher environment. There were still deer around, so the farming communities should at least still survive being here. But where the people were was a mystery.

"Dartun." Verain trudged toward him through the thick snow, her arms elegantly extended to each side as she navigated cautiously.

Her eyes shone with excitement. "We've found two hunters from the Aes tribe just up the way." She gestured toward the shoreline. "I think they can give news of why this island is deserted, although so far we can't quite understand one another."

Dartun took her gloved hands in his. "Thank you for telling me." He reached for the communication relic, held it beneath his cloak.

She smiled. She may have begun to feel a faint pity for his eccentricities.

Slipping now and then, Verain led him down a bank of snow, and he was forced to clutch thick clumps of ulex for stability. He could see Todi and Tuung still in conversation with the two tribesmen. The natives were dressed in furs. They both carried bows and hunting knives. Their faces were broad and tanned from a life in the sun and snow.

"Greetings, warriors," Dartun addressed them in Sula, the common language of the Aes. "The weather has turned for the worse, has it not?"

"You speak our language, magician," the taller man said. They had to be brothers. Dartun could barely tell them apart, but for the high cheekbones of the shorter man. "That is surprising."

"I've used my long life sensibly," Dartun replied. "So, what news is there on this island?"

The tall tribesman regarded the other, while the shorter one nodded imperceptibly, indicating it was him who was the thinker of the two. An icy wind whipped by them suddenly, and both warriors tilted their heads slightly as if to listen for the sounds of the wild.

They're dressed to hunt—or be hunted . . . Which?

"Creatures now stalk this island, magician. They are not natural to any animal group we know of."

Dartun wondered for a moment if any of his undead could have escaped and strayed this far north, without being directed by his sect. But surely that was impossible. "Creatures?" he queried.

"That is why we've traveled here. Because our people have sent us to keep watch over things, according to the directions of shell readings."

"Watch over what exactly? Is this why there's no one around?"

The tribesman nodded. "No one is around because of the creatures. They have snatched the people out of the cities and villages."

"What creatures?" Dartun demanded, growing impatient with the limited vocabulary of Sula.

"I am not sure if they have a name," the hunter responded. "They are like creatures of the sea, yet they walk on the land. They are like nothing I can precisely describe."

Bipedal? "They walk upright?" Dartun marched two fingers across the palm of his other hand. "On two legs? But they come from the sea?"

"Yes, they walk like you and I do, but they have a shell like a lobster—or a crab perhaps I should say. A dark red shell the color of the dying sun. This makes it difficult for our arrows because they cannot pierce the shell. We have tried to hunt some down, or rather other hunters of our people tried. Our folk were killed very quickly."

Dartun was amazed at these accounts. "Are any of them still around?"

"It is possible." Both men shrugged. "They're too difficult to catch. They have killed so many."

"How many?" Dartun was eager for more as he'd never read of such a creature in any of the Archipelago's bestiaries. He felt both excitement and a threat, and this sort of thing appealed to his essential nature.

"Nearly everyone on the island," the short man said casually, his voice as calm as if he was describing the weather.

"*Everyone?*" Dartun whispered. "But there must be hundreds of thousands on Tineag'l. Surely they can't all have been killed?"

The tall tribesman grunted a laugh. "Tell me, how many people have you seen since you arrived here?"

Dartun saw the truth of what he said, and the concept sickened him, yet there was still some base, primitive reaction that excited him. Such was his constant thirst for knowledge and understanding. A new, unknown race was a sensational piece of information. "Please, could you tell me more about these creatures?"

"We have told you all there is. We are sorry, magician." The two of them then headed back to their horses with that same annoying calmness. One added casually, "There have been great problems for us with the coming ice."

Ice. That word again—changing the fabric of the world, changing people's lives, their homes, their thoughts, bringing an unsettling texture of uncertainty about whether things would ever be the same again.

Ice. That was the reason he was now able to head for the Realm Gates since sheets of it had formed artificial land where previously maps had indicated only water. Could that bridge have allowed a new race to enter the Archipelago? Could these creatures have exited through the same gates that he was hoping to enter?

Dartun regarded his fellow cultists, who had soon lost interest in a conversation where they could understand little or nothing. The three of them were shuffling around idly in the snow, kicking up small mounds with their boots.

Todi noticed him watching them. "What's up, Godhi? What did they say?"

Dartun rubbed his forehead as if to stir himself to some new state of alertness. "To be precise, they said that there's some pretty major shit going on."

Verain approached, took Dartun's arm. "Should we be worried?"

Dartun explained what he had learned so far, while the other three simply stared at him as if he was demented.

Dartun summarized. "There has been genocide. The island has been cleansed."

Their moods darkened considerably.

"Come," Dartun announced, heading toward the dog pack. "A little research is perhaps in order."

✳

Dogs dragged the four cultists skidding along by sled into the nearest township that hadn't suffered too much from incursions of snow. Settlements located on particularly exposed slopes had been, without their human population, covered completely. Villages had become corpses. Dartun had halted the dogs more than once, thinking that they should have reached a town clearly marked on his maps. He laughed morosely when he realized it was under snow.

Eventually they came to a settlement sheltered under a titanic outcrop of sedimentary rock. Dartun believed the place was called Bronjek, but it now bore little resemblance to the bustling town he had once heard of. The main street was little more than a muddy track, trodden by a thousand pairs of feet and rutted wheels and dog sleds, between wood and metal shacks that appeared to lean against one another for support. Thick shutters obscured most of the windows, but a few of these were open—despite the freezing cold—and that was the first indication something wasn't as it should be.

The sign on a tavern said "Open," but there was no one to enjoy its hospitality, no hospitality to enjoy, this once-busy street now a ghost of its former self.

There were dark smears across walls, and the odor of urine, something internal now exposed. Blended with the mud, it caused the town to smell like a macabre farmyard. A careful look would discern arcs of blood splattering wooden and metal panels of shacks. Whatever had caused this had visited the place quite recently. The sheer silence and absence of life in the latticework of streets engendered a sinister sensation. There seemed a thousand possible hiding places for those who had butchered this entire community.

Dartun dumped his heavier furs back on the sled in case he had to move quickly, then resumed the investigation. Soon he thought he could hear something. "Stay together," he urged to the others, and they huddled together like children, clutching various relics that could kill a man in an instant.

A muffled, animal whimper.

A sharp inhalation of breath originated from somewhere behind a nearby building.

Dartun strode across the slippery ground, reaching in his pocket for one of his relics, though he realized suddenly it wasn't necessary.

What remained of a young girl lay naked on the ground, her entrails emerging from a horizontal slit in her stomach, while a famished dog was loitering nearby with blood on its maw. Dartun waved his arms to scare the creature off, till it finally trotted away through a gap between the shacks, stealing a cautious glance backward every few moments until it disappeared.

Dartun crouched next to the girl's body; he saw several bones of her ribcage were exposed and the flesh of her scalp peeled back to reveal a tiny piece of her skull glimmering white. With gloved hands he prodded her arms in turn, and they flopped aside, half severed from her torso. Something had actually tried to remove her bones, but apparently had given up. There was no way of telling what had been used to slice her open.

Was it some creature's claws that did this? But why was she left here and yet no others?

The whisper of feet approached through the snow behind, and then Verain was in tears, Todi and Tuung peering over her shoulder. "Is that . . ." she sobbed. "What . . . ?"

"Stay back, Verain," Dartun commanded. "All of you, go and keep watch." He gestured them away.

He studied the body once again. Although he had often raised the dead, there was nothing Dartun could possibly do to help this girl. She had been torn apart too cruelly to restore to living form.

What would do such a thing, and why would they try to pull her bones out? Was it intended as some warning? No, they would've left her in a more prominent position. This one has been discarded, as if she was merely waste.

Although the issue intrigued him scientifically, he was emotionally disgusted by this discovery. If a new race had arrived on the islands of the Empire, what interest could they have in killing Tineag'l's population in such a barbaric fashion? Although, from another perspective many of the tribes in these regions had thought the same about the Empire stealing their lands.

Dartun assembled the others to follow him on a thorough tour around the town's haphazard streets hoping to make some sense of these disturbing scenes. They examined the smashed buildings, doors hanging off hinges, tools strewn outside doorways, fragments of splintered wood littering patches of red snow, broken swords lying abandoned in the alleys. This had clearly been a terrifying struggle.

As he studied the tracks in the snow, he began to build a picture of what must have happened. From the north, they'd come, these creatures, and had smashed their way along every house systematically, driving residents into the open where some were slaughtered. Bloodstains were not frequent enough for complete eradication on the spot, which meant the town's population had been driven away, herded like animals. There were heavy tracks leading back to the north.

More corpses were discovered, people who had met death in their homes: two more young children, a baby with its head removed, five elderly men, six old women, their bodies dismembered at the backs of buildings. One old man's body was lying in his yard clutching a piece of Jorsalir artwork in his frozen hands: a depiction of Bohr and Astrid embracing, and Dartun could not help reflecting on how useless that holy trinket would have been in the victim's horrifying final moments. What faith he must have possessed to think it might protect him from the terror.

The last discovery was the most disturbing: an elderly woman stripped naked, three savage slices running down her torso. She lay in a metal bathtub filled with bloodied water. The stench was overpowering. Todi was sick so he had to leave the room. Again it appeared that some of the bones had been removed from her body, particularly her pelvis and tibia. Her right arm had been totally severed, lying in several pieces that were tossed aside across the room, while her left hand still clung to the rim of the bath, fixed there with ice.

Dartun opened the shutters to allow in some fresher air. The view was of rolling hills in the distance, over which several flocks of birds arced in peaceful flight patterns toward the south, escaping the cold. The air was still as the sun broke through the clouds.

"What d'you make of all this . . . madness?" Tuung asked, stepping alongside Dartun at the window. There wasn't a great deal to look at from there, but both men had seen too much inside.

Dartun sighed. "Dark times, my friend. Dark times."

"What's caused all this? Why is it happening?"

"I'm beginning to see some shape in these horrors. I suspect that the human population on this island was preyed upon by an alien race of intruders those hunters saw. And they've all been rounded up and herded out of this town. Where to and why? Who the hell can say why?"

"It's all so senseless." Tuung slapped the windowsill in fury. This was the first time Dartun had seen someone as dogged as Tuung seem so totally frustrated.

Events such as these altered people.

Dartun said, "I suppose that it's not senseless to them. You're seeing things from a human-centric perspective. I suspect they don't think in the same way that you and I would think."

"I don't follow you. Are you getting all philosophical again?"

"Listen. Why would they leave the bodies of just the old and the very young?" Dartun said, gesturing at the old woman's remains.

Tuung shrugged. "I guess they're the weakest, therefore the easiest to kill? I don't know."

"Exactly so," Dartun replied. "They're the *weakest*. The handful of bodies we've seen so far have been either young children or the old.

Those are the frailest forms of human or rumel. Every corpse has had its bones partially or completely removed. It's as if they opened them up to examine the bones, and then just discarded the corpses. As if they were not considered good enough."

"So they're, what, after our bones or something?"

Dartun snorted a humorless laugh. "That's a strong possibility. They've definitely taken people captive. And appear to be deliberately hunting mankind. Maybe even rumel, too, as we haven't seen any of them around either."

"Bloody sick if you ask me," Tuung muttered.

"That's life," Dartun said, "once you look at it from a viewpoint other than our own. They're just doing what this Empire has done for thousands of years to other cultures, and to other species. Pillaging their worlds for the sake of adding *value* to our own." He added: "And we call ourselves an enlightened civilization."

"It's all right for you," Tuung grumbled, running a hand over his head as if to highlight the signs of aging.

The comment, casual though it was, struck Dartun hard as his gaze lingered on the woman's remains. Death was such a strange phenomenon because everyone went through life hiding from it, fearing it, yet it was the only inevitable outcome. But there was nothing inevitable about the way this woman had died, butchered in her moment of relaxation while lying in a warm bath on a cold day.

Life was never long enough, was it? He understood that better than most.

"Come on," Dartun said at last, and began to lead them away from the disturbing scene. "We now find the Realm Gates, we investigate my final theories, and only when we have done so successfully will we return."

Dartun paused on the muddied doorstep, his breath clouding in front of his face. In that intense air he felt you could breathe the terror pervading that desolate town. You could feel it seeping deep in your bones, into your blood.

✳

They rode away from the dead town toward their agreed meeting point with other members of the Order of the Equinox. Arriving early, they had to wait there for two days in the freezing cold. Red sunlight forced its way through the fat clouds that obscured these vast northern skies. Everything around them seemed more capacious—or rather as humans they felt smaller compared with the empty environment. Life out here was much harsher than in the city. Nature dominated. Ridges of hillsides sloped steeply, snow slanted perpetually across your vision. It was humbling. Snow-buried tundra grasses stretched for leagues in every direction, punctuated occasionally by thickets of larix or betula. Sometimes a wolf would stray past in the first or last moments of the day, imposing its long shadow over the snow, while overhead the cry of birds—terns, gulls, falcons, and nearer the coast, gannets—would add an eerie chorus that only heightened the pervasive loneliness.

Dartun, however, was grateful for this isolation.

✳

They had almost begun to lose track of the days when Verain spotted three longships approaching up Tineag'l's western coast, almost veiled in the spray of the surf as it surged on the rough seas. That morning had brought a stronger wind, and with it the weather had taken a more severe turn.

"Dartun, they're here," she announced, rousing him as he reclined against a tree trunk, his boots sprawled out in front of him.

"You sure it's not the Empire's forces?" he demanded, glancing to the tents in which Todi and Tuung were still sleeping, then over to the pack of dogs who were huddled for shelter beside a windbreak.

"They carry no Imperial banners. And look there." She pointed as a bright flash of purple light streaked up into the cloud base, like reverse lightning.

"It's them all right," Dartun agreed. He paused briefly to embrace her and kiss her on both cheeks. Almost wincing, her reaction indicated she wasn't that comfortable with his closeness. She was like this from time to time—why then did she stick with him? Could she not leave him because of fear?

Dartun proceeded toward the tent, pulling back the flap to kick Todi and Tuung awake. "They're here. Get ready."

The two men groaned. "Not another freezing bloody day," Tuung complained.

"Indeed." Dartun reached into one of his bags, drew out a brass tube, stepped outside, and set it in the snow for stability. He took off his gloves and made some subtle adjustments to the dials, then lunged for safety toward Verain as a thick bolt of purple light burst upward with an explosive roar.

Dartun turned his attention to the ships once again. The vessels lurched lackadaisically, like old marine beasts, and were steered shoreward to the source of the signal.

✳

The four cultists and their equipment were pulled down by the sled to the shore with the sleet now driving straight into their faces. They arrived at a rock-littered beach. Dartun dismounted, and stepped over to inspect the boats towering above him in the shallows. Originally hijacked by political dissidents, these three imposing boats had once been based in a military port further south. Military runework was carved into the hulls. On board, several members of the Order of the Equinox were standing ready, looking down at their leader.

"Sele of Jamur!" Dartun shouted above the smash of the waves. "You couldn't have arrived a moment too soon. Where are the rest?"

The answer to that question came soon enough. Within the bell, five more vessels of equal dimensions had arrived, lining up alongside each other in a haphazard fashion. They had voyaged in small groups, not wanting to draw attention, and had gathered further down the coast to make the last lap to this neglected corner of a fading world. Gangplanks were thrown down, and soon around fifty Equinox cultists began disembarking.

And the undead were unloaded.

Two hundred, male and female, human and rumel, in varying states of decay came shambling through the water to reach the rockshore. Their arms swinging by their sides, they seemed unaffected by the harshness of the weather, the gray tint of exposed flesh showing through what little clothing they possessed.

They marched in neat rows, this militia, to stand in several lines against the upper shore, their rags fluttering like crippled banners in the breeze. Unprepossessing as they looked, Dartun knew he needed this protection. Papus might come after him even here, and he did not know what lay waiting for him the other side of the gates.

Packs of dogs were fetched from the ships, ripping at the cold air in excitement. Following them came yet more of the undead, this time carrying equipment, parts of sleds to be assembled, weaponry and relics and minor armor. Dartun was pleased at such efficiency. This counted for nearly all of the Order of the Equinox, leaving only a handful of cultists back in Villjamur. He felt much safer now, the mere presence of his kin lifting his morale.

Throughout the morning he briefed every cultist in turn on what had been discovered on the island.

Brutal killings.

Alien species.

The grotesque filleting of the victims.

Theories were discussed, methods and solutions bandied about, but one thing was certain: they had to move quickly so as to be prepared for any attack. Dartun stressed the importance of marching across the ice sheets to find their new enemy's location. He was convinced it would be at the Realm Gates, which represented a new level of knowledge entirely.

Later, dog teams began dragging the cultists—a bizarre train of magicians—along the coastline, the army of the undead jogging along to the rear, all heading now for the northern shores. There they would venture out across the ice.

To the possibility of new worlds.

CHAPTER 32

❄

THE GARUDA FLIGHT LIEUTENANT COLLAPSED ON THE TILED FLOOR OF one of the highest-level rooms in Balmacara, a misshapen heap of ruffled feathers and shattered armor. Blood speckled his white facial plumage, and his arms quivered as he tried to regain an upright position. Today, Chancellor Urtica couldn't be bothered with such drama.

"What's your news, flight lieutenant?" Urtica resumed his meal of oysters and mussels as he regarded the sprawling form of the bird-soldier dispassionately.

The garuda crawled a little nearer to the fire, leaned up against the wall of the hearth so that the flame cast quick-moving shadows across his sharp features. Urtica looked up again.

Forgive me, chancellor, the soldier began in hand-talk. *It has been a long flight from the war zone.*

"Get on with it." Urtica motioned with his fork for the soldier to continue.

Chancellor, I fear I bring bad news. The garuda's gaze darted about with fear.

"Well I assume our occupation of Varltung has not been easy then?"

The garuda made a strange sound. *Our forces never found the opportunity to advance by longship as planned. It appears that our invasion force was defeated by the ice. The army therefore had to progress by foot, but the ice was too weak to support them, sir, it collapsed under their weight. Many of them died during the night in the freezing waters. After that, local tribesmen came light-footed from across the island of Varltung, but our commanders would not accept their aid.*

Although inwardly fuming at this devastating news, Chancellor Urtica managed to maintain an air of calm. "Tell me of these losses."

We have only a few hundred men left from an initial force of four thousand.

"Only a few hundred," Urtica mumbled, finally rising from his chair. This was an embarrassment beyond belief. He approached the hearth and reaching for a metal poker, began to slash at the fire, sending sparks showering upward. As the overseer of military assignments, this was an extreme and personal humiliation. Men could easily be replaced, couldn't they, but such a failure would haunt his reputation eternally.

"Well, we must take that island no matter what," the chancellor said. "I will *not* have the Jamur Empire suffer defeat. I will not allow it. Whatever it takes, it must be ours, d'you hear?"

He wafted the poker around the garuda's head as he spoke, but he wondered why he bothered to lecture a dumb, valueless soldier. He wondered then of what message the Council would have to issue to the people. He could see what to put on the news pamphlets: a Varltung massacre of our brave fighters in the ice, a vicious terrorist atrocity, savage barbarism on our democratic collection of nations . . . Such sentiments, he realized, would even provide an excuse for an all-out campaign to control more resources during the Freeze.

"Get some rest, flight lieutenant," Urtica ordered, resuming an illusion of calm. "Soon I'll be expecting you and your fellows to fly out from the city with instructions for reorganizing every soldier we can spare. Soon, everyone available will be marching eastward for a concerted attack on those Varltung bastard tribes. There'll be no prisoners taken—I want every adult male on that island killed, every boy decapitated. Towns to be burned to the ground. So go rest now. Tomorrow is going to be a busy day for you."

Yes, chancellor. The bird-soldier pushed himself fully upright, then staggered out of the room.

As soon as he had gone Urtica hurled the poker across the chamber. Two servants came in to investigate, but Urtica dismissed them with insults.

This military loss was almost as embarrassing as losing Imperial territory. What would people think of him—and of the Empire he now piloted?

Just at that moment, in the midst of his paranoia, Councilor Delboitta entered the room. In her skinny old hands was a document that might at least relieve his stress temporarily. He studied her gaunt features, those prominent cheekbones, highlighted by the firelight. A few strands of gray hair tinged her otherwise black hair.

"Chancellor Urtica." She spoke in a crisp, precise way, a woman who made you listen carefully to every syllable. She had heaved the door shut behind her, leaving the two of them in total privacy. "Magus Urtica—may I call you so here?"

"Yes, but only quietly," Urtica said. "Even the walls have ears— this is a government building after all . . ."

She was a handsome woman of nearly fifty years whose husband, also an Ovinist, had died three years ago.

"What d'you have for me, then?" He guided her to the table. "Some oysters?"

"Thank you, but I've just eaten." She unrolled the parchment well away from the food, then held it in place with a couple of wine glasses. They both leaned in close, little telltale suggestions in their breathing. So he hoped.

She indicated first the ancient runework inscribed on the document, and the correct stamps to indicate the authenticity of it. It was an order, ultimately, that would confirm the ascension of Urtica to Emperor. It made Rika out to be a mass murderer. This would then be delivered to the starving refugees in the form of largesse. They would hopefully die in large numbers, and cease to be a damn burden. All traces of Imperial failures: gone.

"Perfect," Urtica breathed, allowing his gaze to drift down the ancient letter-craft, the runes and seals so true to the Villjamur standard legal documents that it seemed impossible to know it was forged.

"When will you get their names on this?" Councilor Delboitta looked up at him wide-eyed, as if she worshipped him and would do anything for him—or at least he liked to believe that.

Urtica wanted as few people knowing he would forge the signature himself, but she was Ovinist. She was on his side. "I'll add their signatures on this before the sun sets tomorrow. I've been spending some time studying their handwriting, so it shouldn't take too long. Then I'll present it to the Council." Urtica's pride swelled at his own ingenuity.

"And you're sure the Council will accept such a claim?" Delboitta's eyes positively glistened as she gazed intently into his face.

He knew of the secret numbers of Ovinists in influential positions. There were enough politicians who were promised positions of power, enough men and women seduced by rewards to commit to his schemes; guards were under his influence, Inquisition officers freely accepted his coin, and where cash hadn't done the trick, he'd lined up plenty of Caveside gangs to intimidate anyone who might get in his way and give them something to think about. Everything was in place.

After taking supreme office he would initiate his schemes, an inchoation for more aggressive politics. Control over the means of production would be given to only the most profitable landowners. Slavery would be extended for greater productivity. Those at the very top would be rewarded handsomely. The Empire's wealth would flourish.

"I have made more than enough preparations . . ." He trailed off remembering his military defeat. He would divulge that in time, and ascertain a way to blame it on the Empress's strategies.

"And then we'll arrest them, the Empress and her sister," he said. "Perhaps best at the Snow Ball, so that every gossiping bitch and bastard inside this building will immediately start spreading the news. I want her deposed quickly and . . . well, I see myself as a likely elected candidate to replace her, don't you think?"

Delboitta grinned her agreement with impeccable teeth. She then reached up, caressing his cheek, followed her hands with her lips. "Does this mean," she whispered, moving her palm to his groin, "that you'll let me please you, *Emperor* Urtica?"

For a moment he couldn't work out which was the bigger turn on: her suggestion, or his future title.

CHAPTER 33

✳

"Who are you, really?" Eir whispered, her hands on Randur's hips.

They were rehearsing a slow dance that evening, the *Yunduk,* and the only communication so far between them had been Randur whispering softly in her ear to correct her posture. No music this evening to accompany them, but they now understood the rhythms by heart, a liquid grace in every step. They were practicing in one of the many unused corners of Balmacara, a disused chamber long forgotten by most of the inquisitive courtiers.

The more reticent he was, the more she wanted to know, the more she needed to understand him. After years spent in isolation among Imperial tutors and the urgent whispers of guardsmen, this islander had burst into her existence and already shown her more of life than she had ever known. Even his most casual comments suggested an exotic origin, his very presence spoke of some *other* place, a region perhaps physical or possibly mental, it didn't matter, just that it was somewhere not bound by stone and ice like her childhood environment.

And she had seen beneath the veneer of his arrogance.

"I thought we'd been through this stuff already."

Her fingers tightened, gripping his waist. "We have, and yet we haven't. I want to know who you actually are, Randur Estevu."

"You'd only be disappointed," he suggested dismissively.

"I'm not so sure I could be. I find your efforts on behalf of your mother are very honorable."

"I'd rather not talk about that."

"Tell me," Eir changed the subject, "instead of just sleeping around, have you ever *actually* been in love?"

He stared down at her, and by his hesitation she knew that he was surprised.

She continued, "What I mean is, in love with anyone other than yourself."

He laughed, drew their bodies even closer so that they were touching at the waist for the next dance sequence. Their steps flowed smoothly, beginning to be expressive of new depths, and wherever his feet went she was there with him, in unison, in perfect time.

"No," he replied. "Being in love hasn't really been my *style*. I never really cared much for the girls on Folke anyway. To begin with, they were all a little unclean for my liking."

"You've very high standards for someone coming from such a poor region."

"Wasn't always like that," he grunted, and she felt a sudden guilt that she had labeled him in such a way.

After a moment's thought she said, "I thought as much. Your manners are far too good, for one thing. You eat well. And I've noticed how you always let a lady step in front of you when proceeding down corridors."

"That's not always for their benefit," he smirked.

"Randur, come on, be serious."

"Sorry." He grinned. "We were once a very wealthy family, before the Empire really took a grip on our island. The one thing I've learned is that opportunity is linked to wealth in Jamur territories. Whoever owns the most resources has the most power and influence and opportunity, and that's just not how life should be. You—you can do anything you could think of in these halls. But back then we once had servants and all that, then we lost our land—my mother never really told me how, but we lost it anyway. Everything was gone; but she brought me up well. She brought me up rather strictly, perhaps. My father, you see, died before I ever got to know him, and I had a couple of sisters but we were never that close. So everything was up to my mother." After a pause, he added, "I owe her a lot."

"From all you've told me, you shouldn't blame yourself for what happened with her. You're a good man, Randur Estevu."

He shook his head, self-consciously, as if only just beginning to comprehend himself. "Not really. I'm a liar, a thief, a womanizer, and I get in too many fights—a good deal because of the way I dress. I try not to hurt anyone unnecessarily in the process, though."

"But it's what you are attempting to do, that carries real honor. This is an age with no great battles to speak of, no heroes for future stories. I think it's intensely honorable that a son should want to give his mother the chance to live awhile longer."

He said, "It's not as easy as that."

"Talk, Randur," she urged, dancing a thin line between mockery and seriousness. What would it take for her to get this man to really open up?

"Have you ever come to feel so indebted to someone that, on reflection, everything you've ever done merely seems to have let them down?"

She said, "Is this your way of freeing yourself from that guilt then? If you can employ a cultist to add years to her life, then you feel you have redeemed yourself?"

"Think you know so much about me?" he bristled.

"I find you fascinating, that's all," she said, wanting to add, *in ways you'll never quite know, at this rate.*

"Well, if I'm that much of an open book, you certainly don't need to try to get me to talk further." He then steered her into another sequence of moves, where the woman did the leading. She wasn't quite managing it properly, forcing herself into awkward body-shapes, so he had to keep repeating those same steps until she could do them without thinking.

Eir suddenly felt the need to be more honest about how she herself felt. "Randur, I find you're quite different from other men about Balmacara. You never try to impress me, and you don't compliment me for every little thing I do. Quite the opposite, in fact, because you're downright rude to me at times, and so flippant, and . . . Well, whatever in Astrid's name you're doing, it makes me more interested in you."

"Makes sense, I suppose, what with my dashing good looks."

"You know, I've also worked out that you only joke because you're uncomfortable with being honest."

"Crap, my lady," he muttered.

"Followed by rudeness when you're obviously wrong about something."

Silence for a while, their feet moving with precision across the stone floor.

"One thing more," Eir finally said. "Given your certain, shall we say, moral indiscipline . . ."

"Yes?"

"Why haven't you tried it on with me?"

"Because I value my life for one thing. I don't fancy being castrated and my manhood hurled over the city walls. Also, your position, you've got official channels, as it were, in which you must operate."

"So, would you otherwise? I mean to say, if I wasn't the Empress's sister?"

"Well, you've got a great little behind, Lady Eir, a cute smile and more than a handful of the right things in exactly all the right places. Sure, why not."

Something about his directness, the obvious fact that he didn't care what he was saying, was *so* refreshing. And she liked that. She wanted to possess the ability to whisper dirty and loving things to him in return. "Officially, you have my permission to make a move."

"Fair enough." He shrugged. "That would be the easy thing to do, wouldn't it? But I'm not that predictable."

She stepped back. "Randur Estevu . . . you infuriate me at times!"

"Hey, relax. I was only joking."

After she had calmed, they resumed the dance steps and kicks and flourishes. He placed his body against hers, the palms of his hands resting on her shoulder blades. "I know you like me, Eir. This isn't cultist science we're talking about, just a guy and a girl, and it's all a bit inevitable. You're a handsome woman, I'm a pretty man. Anyway, the day you offered to pay my debts, that was a decent indication of your feelings."

"Well, why haven't you reacted?"

He leaned in close to her ear, the space between the two of them becoming charged. "Because, Stewardess, we must think only of the *dance* and for success there are certain *tensions* that must be maintained. You do want to be seen as the best at the Snow Ball, don't you?"

She was so stunned by his serious response she did not know how to reply. Instead she blurted her response. "So even if I offered myself naked, you still wouldn't want to . . ." She wanted to use his words, but couldn't. "Take me?"

"I couldn't because I respect you too much for that."

"Oh. Right." She could not resist taking advantage of this closeness, because, to hell with the dance, to hell with etiquette of the court, she wanted him *right there and then.* His cocksure brashness had reduced her confidence, and now she wanted to impose upon him her Imperial stamp.

She slid her hands further up his lissom body, gripped him, angled her head, kissing his neck, and as she tasted his skin he gave a sigh. His heart pulsed against her breasts. His arms had fallen uselessly to his sides, but soon he took hold of her head, drew her lips closer to his own. A slight groan, more rapid breathing.

She moved away slightly to regard him, and all he did was stare at her in confusion, struggling to read her. Surely this inveterate romancer would know better how to react at a moment like this?

He tried vaguely to say something, but she pressed a finger to his lips. It took all the strength of will she had to turn away, to move across to a wall tapestry. She pulled it aside to reveal a window through which a wind blew from across the city. She waited for him to come to her, determined she would not turn back to face him, the spires and bridges meaningless and empty under her gaze.

But he didn't come near, and she was driven to ask, "Has the great Randur Estevu finally been silenced?"

She heard his footsteps approach, felt his words brush against the back of her neck: "I don't know what to do now."

"You're no amateur, from what I've seen."

"Those women . . . they didn't matter. It's just that I'm not sure what I feel right now. I mean, ever since you offered to help me . . . well, I'm just not sure what it is that's going on in my head. I don't want you to think you've bought my attention."

"Perhaps you have genuine feelings after all?" she said, expecting some witty response from him which was calculated to anger her.

Instead he said, "I know I'll end up hurting you and I don't want to do that. Like I said, I feel I'm in your debt."

"There are ways of clearing such debts."

"Wouldn't that simply make me a man-whore?"

She shrugged. "Not if you *wanted* to do it anyway." She felt a little desperate and out of control.

"I thought ladies in high positions had responsibilities about how they acted."

"After all this is over, the dance, I mean," she said, "when you travel back to Folke, won't it be dangerous?"

"Probably," he said. "Time is fairly urgent, because she hasn't got too much of it left." His tone changed, became brighter. "Anyway, if you want to, we can slip down Caveside tonight and practice before the ball. There's a street dance organized, so Denlin said, and I think we should go, because it'll get you used to dancing in public. You've enough time to slip into something a little scruffier—if you have anything scruffy, that is. It'll be cold and dirty."

"I'm sure I can find something suitable for the occasion," she said. "You certainly take me to the loveliest of places."

❋

With some urgency they moved through the narrow streets, their footsteps light on the cobbles. They had tricked soldiers in Balmacara into thinking Eir was retiring early, wasn't feeling well. Eir herself felt a warm thrill of anticipation at the venture. Occasionally, she gripped Randur's hand when descending steep stairwells. The sky was a dull smear of blue-gray, the air filled with snowflakes that fell so hypnotically slowly they seemed stationary. Icicles glinted on the bridges as if they were decorated with daggers. People seldom ventured outside in the evenings these days, but you could see their faces peering from between curtains, gloomy silhouettes staring from their warm prisons.

Eir had chosen to wear a tight-fitting brown garment, and purposely made her dark hair a disheveled mess so that she wouldn't appear wealthy. It felt liberating, to strip herself of normality and forced manners.

They walked the vacant, snow-slushed streets leading to the caves, the real Villjamur. Being packed together so close, she liked to think that each house would share some heat with its neighbors. And at least here there was shelter, while other zones of the Empire would be struggling with the encroaching onslaught of ice, struggling to find adequate food. It was no wonder that despite such urban hardships she had witnessed, the refugees had accrued outside the city gates. The poverty in her own city had been revealed to her, and as they continued along the streets she passed more homeless people: young girls her own age asleep in decaying archways, rumel families staring lifelessly into contained fire-pits. Her wealthy existence had been so disconnected from it all. She had not known until Randur pointed this out, and just the one visit down here had opened her eyes. She never knew the city possessed such darkness. If she had known how the world really worked, would she have done more about it?

Through labyrinthine passageways, into a well-lit stone square, overlooked by cramped terraced housing, where women leaned out of narrow windows to men who called back up to them from below. A sense of ritual. Someone began beating a drum and a few of the gaudily dressed women sidled into the center of the scene, while old men sat together on benches in the corner, smoking pipes and talking loudly, their faces displaying a happiness she had not witnessed since the temperature began falling.

"Randy, you made it!" She recognized the voice as Denlin's. "And you've brought your girly. Ain't that swell."

"Denlin, you old bastard." Randur turned instantly back to Eir as if to apologize for his language, then back to address him. The old man slapped Randur on the shoulder and gave a low bow toward Eir.

"Not here, Denlin," she hissed. "Here I'm just like any other woman."

"Sure you are." He smiled.

"No, really. Tonight I just want to dance."

"That'll be the lad speaking, I reckon." Denlin turned to study Randur.

"It's not like that," Randur protested. "She's her own woman, this one. Takes more than a fool like me to have an effect."

She liked the reference to her being a woman. For some reason it seemed important.

"If you say so," Denlin said. "Anyhow, looks as if they're ready-ing . . ." He indicated the couples poised to take to the music.

Eir watched with wonder as the local women guided the men, so naturally led them. Rhythms became precise, fast, heavy till footsteps became quickly moving across the square. The dancers kept calling out to each other, drawing attention to the next flamboyant move. They kicked in the half-light and the scene filled Eir with a primitive excitement.

"You ready?" Randur whispered, and held out his hand to her.

"I'm not sure," she faltered. "They're so good. I don't want to em-barrass you."

Denlin interrupted, "Whale cocks, lady. Get out there and enjoy yourself. This is about fun, not being all prim and proper."

So they joined in the *Formanta,* more about leg movements than anything else. She didn't like this one too much, hadn't practiced it to the extent of the others, and at first she felt awkward, to be dancing here in front of all these strangers. But with increasing confidence they weaved a complex pattern through the other dancers. There was exhilaration and tension and poignancy. Their contact soon began to transcend the postures. They held each other intimately, for an age it seemed, in that forgotten corner of Villjamur.

With these humble people she felt totally at ease for the first time in her life. This was an unlearning of her childhood, stripping away her pretentiousness, her airs and graces.

At the end of the first few dances, Randur poured the two of them some cheap wine, while she watched the revelers around her. People talked in shadows, laughter spilling across the cobbles. Children ran to meet the adults who had just performed, staring at them with a re-newed sense of awe. No doubt at all about this, these people had more fun than any she had ever witnessed in the fore-city.

As the evening crept on, a wide variety of dances were performed. They both became inebriated and their rehearsed postures collapsed regularly. She found it hilarious. Inside her mind there was a letting go of something she didn't realize she was unconsciously clinging on to.

✳

Hours later, people began to leave. The silence of the drums left her feeling vaguely disappointed. Torches burned down low. Denlin had left earlier with an old woman, their arms linked, and Eir felt this was heartwarming somehow, and perhaps this was just how you felt about other couples when you were falling in love yourself.

Eir and Randur danced quietly across the courtyard. She was drunk, perhaps, but she desired him, right then, in whatever way it could be offered. She wasn't aware of the rules of such a situation, and was tentatively exploring the limits of her own self. A line had been crossed and she realized that she could not simply return to being who she was before she met him. There was no going back. It surprised her pleasantly to understand that she could now only push forward.

"What are you thinking?" she asked. "I need to know."

"Nothing much."

She liked the way that there were just the two of them here now. It brought a surreal texture to the scene, as if the sun had finally died leaving only the pair of them on earth. Utterly alone.

"It must be something. I can tell by the way you're looking at me."

"You wouldn't like to know," he said.

"No, I *would*." She was willing the words into his mouth.

Randur absentmindedly placed his hands on her waist.

Finally he said, "I was thinking how . . . how much I'd like to take your clothes off."

"Here?" she said, considering her heart might stop beating. His language was so *direct*.

Eir looked around to make sure their conversation wasn't being overheard, and by that gesture she let him know his suggestion was all right. Randur bent down to kiss her neck.

"How do . . . how do I know that you're not just treating me like any other conquest?" She could barely voice the words, so tightly was she holding on.

"If I said anything, would it matter anyway? You'd always suspect me of not being serious, wouldn't you?"

Eir didn't know what to say so she just moved toward him and kissed him with a startling gentleness. His hands shifted up around her back, slid down to her thighs as she shuddered in anticipation.

She led him by the hand to the corner of the square, then down a small alley that she had barely noticed earlier.

Randur said, "You sure you want this?"

"Yes." She laughed at his sudden uncertainty.

"You've never, uhm, done this before, I take it?"

"If I said anything, would it matter?" she replied, and he seemed to like that.

"Wouldn't you at least prefer to be somewhere more comfortable?"

"I've spent my whole life being somewhere comfortable," she said, then pulled his shirt off him, dropped it to one side.

Randur spun her around so that he stood behind her, a perverse version of one of their dances. Gently, he then guided her through maneuvers that seemed so natural simply because he made it all so uncomplicated, his stubble brushing down her shoulder, his hand gliding across her stomach, then lower. She groaned with relief as it finally worked its way between her legs.

All sense of time disappeared entirely as she became lost in the rhythms of the most primeval movements yet . . . until afterward, with Randur's back against a wall and Eir in front of him with her head buried in his neck, surrounded by the darkness, and, aside from the thumping of her heart, she could hear nothing.

CHAPTER 34

✳

Investigator Jeryd regarded the morning sky.

He could almost enjoy it, way up here at the higher levels of the city, away from those Gamall Gata kids and their little missiles of snow. Here, he didn't have to look over his shoulder at every heartbeat, questioning where they'd be, or if he was in their sights.

The rumel was getting some fresh air while he talked to Tryst about developments. Jeryd wanted to clear his head, hoped for some inspiration regarding the murders of the two councilors. Time was passing, and there were too many things to think about. There had been further tensions developing between the city's people and the refugees. The mood of the situation had been heavily influenced by Council pamphlets that suggested the citizens of Villjamur ought to stay away from those seeking asylum due to disease or potential criminal activity. Jeryd knew fear was being utilized—there were now more soldiers on the streets, more citizens were being stopped and searched at random to hunt down illegal immigrants. In response to the fear, over the past few evenings, several long-range arrows had been released from the city's bridges toward the refugee encampment. Just about anyone could have fired them—it was claimed—but names and addresses began to fill the fringe pamphlets such as *Commonweal* before soldiers could confiscate them and cover up the incident.

Jeryd had to deal with so much.

People shambled by them churning up slush with their boots, while men were heaping the snow on the sides of the streets. Much of it was then taken on carts and dumped in the sea, but as soon as they had cleared one area, it began filling with a fresh layer of snow. This was the sort of scene that might provide a bittersweet nostalgia in his old age.

Jeryd found a kind of stubborn pride in the people, in their dogged defiance of the Freeze. Life went on, they didn't moan. Small open fires were now permitted at intervals along the streets to keep the traders warm, the constant trails of smoke drifting above Villjamur. Traders couldn't restock their supplies of furs quick enough, and fights broke out regularly among customers over various new skins freshly imported. There was an awkward moment between a group of rumel and some men he knew to be Caveside gangsters, which reminded him of scenes from the rumel riots fifty years back.

He turned to Tryst. "Found out anything more from Tuya then?"

Tryst shook his head. "She's very elusive. I'm hoping to get somewhere sooner or later. I've found a convenient balcony nearby where I can hang about and spy on her. But she doesn't entertain that many customers."

"I suspect she's made enough money over the years already," Jeryd murmured, gazing into the snow once again. "Only got herself to look after, and I think she feels trapped by the concept of money."

Tryst sniffed, shuffled back and forth indecisively, his gaze fixed on the ground. Suddenly he asked, "How's Marysa these days?"

"Grand, since she's moved back in with me." Jeryd gave him a sideways glance. "Why d'you ask?"

"No reason really. Just that I thought I spotted her, at the Cross and Sickle the other night."

"You what?" Jeryd was genuinely surprised. It was not her sort of venue.

"She seemed to be in a meeting with some gentleman, that's all. I didn't actually speak to them, just saw them over in the corner."

Now what the hell's that about? Jeryd turned away abruptly. "Come on, I'm freezing my tail off."

They headed back into the Inquisition chambers, where Jeryd

began lighting a fire. He remained silent while it built up to a fierce glow. Tryst pulled up a chair to sit alongside him.

Eventually, Jeryd spoke up. "Cross and Sickle, you say? When was this?"

"Two days ago," Tryst replied. "It was fairly early in the night—I'd say about the eighth or ninth bell. Is everything all right, Jeryd? You look a bit worried."

Jeryd said, "Yes . . . Yes, well, it's just that she told me she was out with a friend, that's all."

Tryst leaned back, stretching his legs before the flames. "Oh, well then. Nothing to it."

"What did he look like?" Jeryd said.

"Tall, dark rumel, but no one I knew of. A swarthy chap, with a decent set of robes on him. They seemed like good friends, anyway. There was a lot of laughing, you know, like people who go a long way back. Old friends."

Jeryd said, "Doesn't sound like any of her old friends that I know of. Anyway, she told me she would be meeting a woman."

"I wouldn't worry too much. Probably a chance encounter. You know what people are like."

"Right . . ." Jeryd said. What Tryst just said had made things worse.

Tryst stood up. "Now I'd better get back to watching Tuya."

The rumel watched Tryst leave the room and was left alone with the crackling fire. He became increasingly lost in his thoughts, his suspicions.

✳

That evening he arrived home early to the smell of warm bread. It should've filled him with anticipation, but he possessed little appetite.

He took off his cloak, shook the snow from his boots, and placed them by a fire in the kitchen, where Marysa was busy baking. She was humming one of those popular tunes from ten years back, the sort they would be singing in all the bars, and that poignant memory seemed to unbuckle time in his mind.

"You're home early," she observed as she kissed him on the cheek.

Is she surprised? Was she expecting someone else?

"Yes, I couldn't seem to get any work done today, so decided I needed time off to think."

She returned to kneading dough. "I'll be finished quite shortly. I just want to make a few more rolls. It makes a change from all my other work."

"Great," he said halfheartedly, then left the room only to berate himself. Why was he feeling so negative toward her? He didn't know anything for certain, yet he was already being short with her. What would he be like if something really was going on? He took a step back to watch her, but far enough away so that she couldn't see him in the shadow of the doorway. And he watched her, as if for the first time, because it seemed important now, to think of these little things.

Slender for her age, she had kept her figure well, and was certainly attractive. Other men would be interested in her. Jeryd's mother had always said that if anyone, male or female, wanted a good night's sleep, then they should choose a plain-looking partner, but he rarely shared opinions with his mother on matters like that.

Maybe Tryst was mistaken, maybe it wasn't Marysa that he had seen.

Jeryd couldn't help but feel a deep pain when he thought about her with another man. It made him feel weak, vulnerable, angry. Had it been months earlier, when she was no longer living with him, it wouldn't have been so difficult. But it was the fact that she had come back to him, and he loved her with an intensity greater than he could remember.

He deliberately clunked against the door frame, and Marysa glanced his way before returning her concentration to the rolls. "Everything okay, Jeryd?"

He stepped back into the kitchen. "I never asked about your evening with Layna."

"We had a nice time, thanks. I hadn't seen her for far too long."

"Where did you end up?"

"We stayed at her house, because she didn't fancy venturing out into the snow."

"Tryst thought he saw you at some tavern."

He thought he noticed a small change in her posture, some tension there perhaps, or a little uncertainty.

She said, "On the way to her place, you mean?"

"I'm sure he said you were in a tavern, but he could've been mistaken."

"Oh, it couldn't have been me. I was at Layna's all the time. We stayed at home and talked. She's got some new guy on the go who treats her so well, as his equal, and he sounded lovely."

Jeryd wasn't reassured by this. Maybe it was his naturally cynical nature after having worked for so long in the Inquisition.

✳

Late afternoon sunlight broke through the clouds highlighting some bizarre texture in the sky. The city's spires and bridges sparkled. Tryst had opened the balcony door to help rid Tuya's room of the acrid stench of her painting materials. The chill in the air was enough to sharpen his senses again. He rested his chin on steepled fingers as he regarded the sculpted Marysa before him. Tuya was crouching on her knees as she made some barely noticeable alterations to this creation.

Tryst had drugged the woman earlier, keeping the dosage safe but regular, so that he could manipulate her more easily. He felt pleased with himself, in fact was getting a kick out of his recent elaborate manipulations. He had planted in Jeryd's mind a seed of doubt about his wife's fidelity, and soon he would show Jeryd a display of his wife in action.

"There," Tuya murmured, then pushed herself upright, a sheer blue gown clinging to her curves. Tryst considered that a baser man than himself would take advantage at this moment, but he possessed good morals.

"She looks . . . utterly real," Tryst admitted.

Indeed, the clay female woman was an exact replica of Jeryd's wife, though he had never seen the latter naked. By her stillness, she looked like a statue, however, and Tryst wasn't quite certain what would happen next.

The previous evening, Tryst had led Tuya to observe Marysa in person as she walked through the frozen streets. The advantage of working so close with Jeryd was that he could learn most of his wife's idiosyncrasies. Tryst had even thrown a purse, spilling coins at Marysa's feet, so that Tuya would be able to get the closest possible examination.

Tryst fully intended to be present when Jeryd encountered this. That would be too much of a treat to miss.

Within the bell, Tuya had gone on to perform some strange rituals with a collection of relics. Tryst observed her as best he could, asking occasional questions, but she was vague in her answers. There was obviously a history to this woman that was never going to be discussed.

Dawnir magic was beyond him, beyond any normal person. To him there seemed no way of understanding it. He just sprawled on Tuya's bed, waiting for the animation to begin. The statue of the female rumel began to glow, then faded. Glowed and faded. He tried to say something but Tuya waved him to silence, the woman now deep in concentration as she walked around the statue, touching it in places, a hint of eroticism to her gestures. The fake rumel began to twitch slightly. Its arms jutted forward as if to embrace someone, then relaxed. The sculpture slowly performed arm and leg and head movements, as if learning these for the first time, getting used to its own body. Discovering motility.

Then suddenly it began to move with the flowing grace of the real Marysa. Somehow Tuya had managed to capture the very essence of Jeryd's wife in her art. The woman was *more* than a mystery. Tryst slid off the bed, the hair on his arms standing on end. Here in front of him was the power of the Ancient race, operating specially for his benefit. It took half an hour to dress the figure in the style favored by Jeryd's wife. That didn't have to be perfect, because Marysa's tastes in clothes were varied.

As they applied makeup, the sculpted Marysa sat at the dresser, silently staring at herself in the mirror.

Tuya finally collapsed on her bed with exhaustion, saying to Tryst petulantly, "Is that all you need me for? Why are you still here anyway?"

Time to drug her further, but he didn't have enough supplies on him. He picked up an ancient tribal decoration, comprised of long strips of colored beads hanging from a sphere. He swept it in an arc and struck her across the head. She slid to the floor with a grunt, a small trickle of blood oozing onto the tiles.

The fake Marysa glanced across at him with a look of surprise on her face, then instantly she had become motionless, as a statue once again.

"It's okay," Tryst said. "She's a criminal." Why was he talking to this thing? It certainly didn't feel right. Did this creation have emotions? It still stared at him unnervingly.

He threw the artifact on the bed. "Don't go anywhere," he muttered, then walked out into the cold night.

Clouds had obscured the stars, but that meant it wouldn't be as cold as it had been recently. Out in the street, he glanced up at Tuya's balconied window, the lantern still alight inside, and he wondered again at the powers that the Ancients had once possessed before they disappeared from history.

CHAPTER 35

H E KNEW THAT YOU GOT GOOD DAYS AND YOU GOT BAD DAYS. IT WAS THE life of an Inquisition officer. It wasn't the sort of career that just any-one could do, because you saw some harsh things on the streets of Villjamur.

Dawn on a Priests' Day, a hundred and forty years back: the bod-ies of three children found naked and butchered in the good side of the city. Their internal organs littering the cobbles, fresh blood sparkling in the light. It was his first solo case and according to the Council they had to make sure none of the nearby wealthy residents saw it. *That's the thing about this city: you've always got to keep the rich ones happy.* They eventually traced the deaths back to a Jorsalir priest, and had to keep that quiet too—the rules were that the Inquisition had to keep the Jorsalir happy. Jeryd caught the bastard, made sure justice was served, but it wouldn't be talked about in any of the taverns.

Given all the horrors he'd witnessed, he expected that he would be able to cope more easily with the crap life threw at him. Hell, he'd even put up with those little buggers on his street, allowing their snowballs to crash into him, into his house.

But Jeryd was a broken man.

Tryst had suggested they go for a quick drink after work and Jeryd thought why not? He could do with putting a few opinions about the world across a table.

Snow was frozen solid along the streets before it could be scraped away, and he had to cling to windowsills along the terraced housing to make sure he didn't fall over. He noticed however that Tryst was taking him toward Cartanu Gata, where Councilor Ghuda was murdered.

So, there they were, finally, the two Inquisition officers, enjoying a drink. They made it to a nighttime tearoom called Vilhallan, named after the original city, and, judging by the decor, Jeryd assumed it had been around for just as long.

"Nothing's original," Tryst confessed. "Everything's a carefully contrived copy: the furniture design, the bars, the colored lanterns."

He was right. It was a dreary looking place.

Jeryd said to him, "Not really my scene," as they took their seats at a small wooden table in a secluded corner.

It wasn't much to speak of otherwise. Little candles clustered on tables threw light upward onto the faces of the customers. It made everyone look sinister, as if they were here for any reason other than pleasure. There was a tribal drummer in the room beyond and someone playing an instrument he'd never heard before. Jeryd got the feeling he had arrived on some far-off island of the Empire.

"So, you come here often?" Jeryd said, and laughed.

Tryst merely smiled and gestured to the serving girl, who was dressed in some mysterious black outfit with over-elaborate collars and cuffs. Jeryd could never keep up with fashions. He could never keep up with Villjamur. Sometimes he thought the world was now something he'd never understand anymore.

"What'll you have, gentlemen?" she asked.

"I'll just have black tea," Tryst said. "And if you've got any pastries, I'd love to take a look."

"Of course," she smiled. "And you, sir?"

"Tea with milk, thanks. No pastries for me. I'm watching my weight."

"You've been up to that Council Atrium quite a bit recently . . ." Tryst offered, obviously curious.

He'd been to the Atrium four times already to interview a selection of councilors but he'd been coming up against a brick wall. No one would tell him anything. After that initial lead of something involving the refugees, there was nothing to go on and Jeryd was beginning to feel depressed. And it seemed Tryst couldn't find out much about Tuya, either, despite tracking her for so long. Tomorrow Jeryd thought that he might go and interview her again himself. But suddenly tonight, Jeryd began to trust his aide a little more. The man made the effort to spend time in his company, and he had been loyal in his work in recent months. Maybe they could put the whole promotion business behind them, and carry on like they used to. Maybe Jeryd was being too harsh on him, too paranoid.

"I suspect something," Jeryd said, "that's not related to the murder of the councilors."

"Go on," he replied.

He paused as the girl brought the teas, and the pastry menu for Tryst. He took only a moment to point to a couple of the choices, then she walked away.

"You know the Ovinists?" Jeryd asked.

Tryst held his gaze for a moment. "Yes, I do . . . well, I know *of* them, anyway. Why?"

"They're a weird little cult with some strange plans it seems. They're banned, of course, being an alternative religion."

"Except on Priests' Day," Tryst reminded him.

"Yes, except then. Anyway, I found some documents while searching their offices, and I think that Boll and Ghuda could have both been practicing members."

"What was it you found?" Tryst looked suddenly interested.

"I found a message to one of the councilors from someone in that organization." Jeryd leaned forward, keeping his voice down. "It hinted at a massacre. Thousands of refugees would be slaughtered. It's a plan that seems to have been cooking for some time."

Tryst was frowning. "That sounds . . . just too crazy. No one would allow it."

"Don't be too sure. Remember we live in unusual times. These murders in the Council. All sorts of strange rumors from abroad, too."

At that moment, the waitress returned with Tryst's selection, and he commenced eating.

Jeryd sipped his tea, and went on. "What I'm saying is that anything can happen, and Villjamur's got a checkered and violent history. A massacre of its own people wouldn't be at all out of place."

Tryst remained a bit quiet for Jeryd's liking. Just then Tryst stopped eating. His eyes suddenly widened as he gazed over Jeryd's shoulder.

Jeryd turned, and there she was, his wife, Marysa, sitting at a table with another rumel. They were holding hands—he could see it in the dim candlelight and her face was full of joy and interest. Her companion was some smooth bastard with white hair slicked to one side. Jeryd didn't want to believe it.

He made as if to stand up, but Tryst grabbed his sleeve, shook his head. "Jeryd, I know what you're thinking, but you don't know anything yet, and also think of your reputation among the Inquisition—"

"To hell with my reputation," he growled, but his resolve weakened. Jeryd took several deep breaths, and sat back down to watch the *couple* more closely.

It was her all right, Marysa, laughing eagerly at his jokes and flashing him glances once reserved for Jeryd. The way he touched her hands, the way she flirted with him in return. He pressed his lips against her fingers as she held them to his mouth. The look of anticipation in his eyes, the promise of something Jeryd assumed was only for himself.

Jeryd glanced at Tryst, who shook his head firmly, though he had been watching them, too. "Drink some tea."

"You think a fucking cup of tea's going to make me feel better?" People nearby looked their way.

"No," he said quietly, "remember, Jeryd, you're a gentleman and a fine investigator of long standing. You're not going to blow all that in a fit of jealous rage in a public place."

Tryst made a quick hand movement across Jeryd's drink.

After a few minutes where he could feel a strange rage take charge of his body, Jeryd stormed out of the tearoom and left Tryst alone there. Into the Villjamur night, skidding on the ice sheet so that he fell flat on his face. His tears fell onto the ice.

Jeryd made it home, eventually, with more bruises than he ever sustained in the course of Inquisition duties. He changed his robes of office for something more casual, started a fire, brought down a bottle of some old vodka, the sort that burns the throat. He wanted some control over things, over his life, and the drink felt like it could help.

He slumped in a chair by the fire, drinking and totally miserable. Outside, somewhere in the distance was the keening of a banshee. Another death, but that would be the job of some other poor bastard to investigate. Jeryd could not help wishing that Marysa's new man was the one the banshee was screaming about.

He sat waiting in the darkness for her to come home.

✳

She came in much later, a fluster of scarves and robes.

Marysa was acting as if nothing unusual had happened. The way she looked at him—all warm and loving—disgusted him. He was so unusually angry he felt as if some drug had taken hold of him.

She leaned forward to kiss him on the cheek, the ghost of another man on her lips. He was amazed that someone who was blatantly cheating on him could act so innocently.

"It doesn't get any warmer, does it?" she murmured. "So, how was your evening, dear?"

"Fine," Jeryd replied tersely, working out how best to approach the subject of her betrayal. He wanted to say so many things. To tell her everything he had witnessed. As she was hanging up her outer garments, he hurled the heavy mug from which he'd been drinking straight at the back of her head. As it exploded in a ceramic shower, he felt like some animal thing had taken possession of him. Like chemicals that weren't meant to be inside of him had affected his thoughts.

"We both saw you!" Jeryd yelled out to her unconscious form, half in tears, fighting to maintain charge of his throbbing mind.

No response from her.

In all his decades in Villjamur, and during all his years in the Inquisition up to that point, Jeryd had never struck a woman. Men who did disgusted him, and now Jeryd disgusted himself. It was as if something had claimed his body, making him act with impulses he would have normally kept under firm control.

He felt drugged.

He knew all too well that there was a fine line between sanity and madness.

✳

Later, Jeryd was aware of a knock at the door. "Sir, it's me, Tryst. I was worried about you. Is everything all right?"

At last a friend, someone who can help. Jeryd rubbed his eyes because he'd been crying for so long and now felt numb as he was recalling what he'd done, as if he was starting to have no memory of the event. Jeryd let him enter amid a blast of cold air, and then tried to explain what had happened. He stared at the unconscious form of Marysa, who was breathing so faintly that he wanted to weep again.

Jeryd was glad that Tryst was there. Right then, he needed someone who could think clearly, because he damn well couldn't.

"You hit her?" he gasped.

Poor guy, he shouldn't have to see me like this. Jeryd remained in a stunned silence, sheer disbelief at what he'd done.

After leaning down to examine her in the shadows of the sparsely lit room, Tryst suggested they move her to the bedroom. Luckily there was no sign of wounding, and he was greatly relieved that rumels rarely bruised.

Every now and then he collapsed into sobs, whereupon Tryst tried to comfort him with a gentle hand on his shoulder. They carried her up the narrow staircase, to the marital bed which by now had changed all meaning for him. Her tail slopped limply, but her face was the illusion of peace. He covered her up carefully, then Tryst led him downstairs again.

"Aren't you going to reproach me?" Jeryd said finally.

"No, of course not," Tryst said emphatically, and Jeryd felt an instant surge of relief.

"You're a good man, Tryst. A good friend." Jeryd wanted to shake his hand in gratitude, but felt too ashamed for that. What he'd done was *unforgivable*. If Tryst told someone and Jeryd lost his career, it was nothing more than he deserved.

Tryst calmed him down. His tone was assured, and that's what he needed right then, the sound of someone in control, any sort of control in this madness. Jeryd stood up and went over to look through the window at the snow gathering on the ledge again.

He began to sob helplessly at what a monster he'd become.

"Try and forget it," Tryst urged. "You need to concentrate on your work now. Concentrate on those Council murders." Then he paused. "Maybe she'll forgive you, in time."

If she left him after this and never talked to him again, Jeryd wouldn't blame her. For some reason, the thought of her being with someone else wasn't the main issue anymore. He didn't know what was. Maybe he just didn't care about anything anymore.

"Let's go for a walk, help clear your head," Tryst suggested.

Before they left the house, Jeryd wrote a note to Marysa, then tore it up. What the hell could words do between them now? Anything he might say would be deeply inappropriate and he imagined her reaction upon reading it in the morning.

As they walked the dark streets, it was the sheer coldness of the city that gradually brought him to his senses. Even when he slipped on the ice and mildly twisted his ankle, Jeryd didn't care. He felt he deserved the pain, as if the elements and Villjamur itself were slapping him down with a vague, ironic sort of justice.

CHAPTER 36

❋

THEY CAME TWO HOURS BEFORE THE DAWN, DRESSED BLACKER THAN THE shadows of the street itself, two dozen cultists from the Order of the Dawnir, and they gathered in numbers outside the simple wooden door. Papus placed a metal box containing a *brenna*-based relic at the base of it, altered the settings subtly, retreated.

A few heartbeats later, the door exploded, shards of wood clattering on the cobbles and the neighboring buildings, an abrupt hailstorm of splinters. In the following silence, her cultists entered the city headquarters of the Order of the Equinox. Shouts and screams were soon heard from inside. Knives were drawn. Quick battles fought in the gloom. Only the gargle of blood exiting a throat indicated a death rattle.

They used several *aldartals* to freeze the men and women of the Equinox in time—poised in moments of confusion and terror for several minutes—before binding them with ropes. Any that weren't thus immobilized were killed. Dartun's own relics seemed to inhibit the effectiveness of many of her own devices, so much of what went on happened in real time. The bitterness of ancient rivalry had now reached a violent climax. Papus expected answers. Her previous threat—the hostage she had taken—had not produced a response from Dartun. She would search this building until she knew what secrets were hidden here, and what truths she didn't yet know about Villjamur, about the lands of the red sun . . .

About Dartun himself.

In many of the rooms there was only candlelight at best. Still, it was enough for her order to go about their search. She had planned this in detail. Thirty-four of the Equinox were captured, tied up, dragged out into the alleyway. She figured there would be at least another forty members hiding here, now fully aware of the break-in. She whispered strategy, signaled by hand the parts of the building to be investigated. Some of the corridors had been blocked by simple energy shields, relics being activated within the stonework. Simple enough to remove—they were meant for common burglars rather than to deter cultists. Progress through the complex of secret corridors and hidden rooms was efficient.

Shards of the Equinox technology were shot at her cultists, ripples of purple light cutting through the air. The darkness allowed her to see them easily, but she soon lost the ability to see clearly in the dark because of the constant flares of light. Papus tripped more than once, her palms stinging as they slapped against the cold stone floor. She could hear gasps and shudders of breath and coughs of blood and muffled cries. She could only hope they represented the defeat of the Equinox. Then these private battles ceased.

A signal was sent along the line of her order, back to the front of the building. Torches were ignited. There might be plenty of new technology here, an abundance of unfamiliar relics, that she could steal information from.

She began to search thoroughly, although not sure exactly what she was looking for. Every stone-built room was well kept, no cobwebs in any of the corners. Wherever she stepped she found herself surrounded by intricately decorated artifacts, all alien to her eye. They had to be Archipelagan in origin, but suggested far more ancient technologies than she was aware of, perhaps not even of this world. Bizarrely inert instruments, unknown carvings, rune-work she didn't understand, scrolls written in Dartun's own code, and every new discovery made her feel less sure of herself, a cultist who was diminishing in quality.

A strange smell came from one side of the complex of chambers. This arterial architecture, so typical of this ancient city, meant it was difficult to locate at first. Such was the design of Dartun's home, each room prompted a sudden self-awareness so you felt as if you were exploring some aspect of your own mind and not just another room.

When she found the source of the smell, she wished she hadn't.

She called more of her followers to her side, standing in a large room with a curving, tiled ceiling, as if it was a cellar. The temperature seemed as cold as the snow outside. More lanterns were brought into the room, and as each extra light arrived, there was an audible gasp.

The room was fifty paces long, around twenty wide, and at the far end against the wall were the partially decayed remains of human beings, all shackled by an iron ring around the throat. Laid out on tables in two rows before these dead were crude shapes covered in cloth.

Papus stepped forward and, one by one, revealed what lay beneath.

"By Bohr . . ." someone whispered.

Mounds of flesh were heaped in metal containers, glistening under the torch in her hand. Bones jutted out from some of them, as did an array of metallic instruments that she assumed to be some kind of relic. Her vision drifted across each container in awe.

"Shit, it's moving!" she gasped, and gestured with her torch at one particular lump of flesh. As more light was brought to the table it was clear for all to see that the flesh-heap was rising and falling like some half-asleep beast. Vaguely hypnotic, utterly disgusting, the mound suddenly rolled over to reveal human organs underneath. Everyone groaned in revulsion. What she took for a mouth opened and closed cautiously, with a crepitant noise as if always taking its dying breath. Blood skimmed in intervals just under the surface of some strange, flaring epidermis.

Behind her, a man vomited.

What the hell was Dartun doing? This atrocity had to be immoral, in any age, in any society.

"What d'you think it is, Gydja?" one of the younger girls of her sect inquired. Her dark, slender features displayed a helpless fear and confusion.

"It's obviously some life-form, although nothing I'm as yet aware of. I'd be interested to see if the banshees recognized this thing as a living organism or not."

Comments were passed back and forth, theories offered then dismissed. There was nothing to be certain of except that Dartun had been working on a horrific project. He was utterly insane.

"I want at least two of you here at all times monitoring this," she instructed, staring at the nearest mound of mottled flesh. "We'll examine these relics that Dartun's been using. I want to know everything that's gone on here, everything that bastard has planned."

She headed back through the corridors, deep in thought. At times, feeling faint, she closed her eyes, paused to lean against a wall, just one thought in her mind disturbing her.

The difference between life and death isn't all that great.

If Dartun had the power to reassemble life, that put the whole of the Empire at risk. For the greater good, no cultist should monopolize that knowledge.

He had to be stopped immediately.

✳

The next evening, from the depths of her order's headquarters, Papus directed that the remaining members of the Order of the Equinox be tortured. Having been stripped of any hidden relics, they were left shackled in holding cells beneath Balmacara. After, she had managed to persuade the men and women of Villjamur's Council to allow the city's most skilled torturers to apply their talents. The Inquisition was only too happy to oblige, eager for the knowledge that would be shared.

Their methods would be brutal in this case, but were merited to try to discern whatever evil Dartun was devising.

Of the forty-three prisoners, seven men were tortured in front of the women. They were stripped naked, and bound spread-eagled across a stone plinth, awaiting the Pear of Anguish to be inserted. An ancient tool, this was a metal pear-shaped device inserted into the anus, and, with the touch of a tiny lever, it unfolded like the most cruel of petals in bloom.

Papus watched this, utterly unmoved. The men were crying and screaming, and they froze then jerked as the metal pears were inserted.

Perhaps it was because the members of the Order of the Equinox had become accustomed to a comfortable lifestyle that the confessions came quickly and efficiently.

One by one, they told her all, the confessions spilling forth in their eagerness to oblige. It was the degree of Dartun's knowledge that shocked Papus initially. How a cultist could know so much about the occult world was unheard of, even by her own advanced standards. The information revealed about him was alarming: he was immortal, had lived for hundreds of years, had uncovered the key to longevity. She now had to discover this for herself by searching his headquarters more thoroughly.

At one point she asked, "Does he have anything to do with the so-called draugr sighted on this island?"

Yes, he created them. Yes, he could raise the dead. To breed an army, they explained, enough of a safety net to deter those who might stop him. Also, to protect himself from whatever lay in the other realms beyond.

That brought them back to the subject of the Realm Gates.

She marched back and forth in agitation in front of the remaining prisoners, the facts underlying everything were coming to a head: the things Verain had warned her of were true. She felt extremely naive in her ignorance.

✳

"This is indeed a serious business," Chancellor Urtica whispered to Papus later, as they stood in a corridor of Balmacara. "You tell me all these things about dead creatures walking, and then you warn that he will allow such dangers to spill over into our Empire. I'm not quite sure I completely follow what you mean, but I understand there is a risk. Therefore, do what you feel necessary to stop him."

Papus nodded, but kept silent. They paused while a patrol of city guards marched past them. She glanced awkwardly at Urtica, who now leaned against the wall opposite while the guards said the Sele of Jamur. Shortly after, a stream of servants walked by with food dishes for some of the councilors.

"Fucksake." Papus then drew a gold-colored *aldartal* from her cloak. Urtica looked on surprised as she then triggered the dial on the device.

Servants paused in midstride still holding their trays, guards froze in midstep. Even the flames on lanterns were stilled. A time-delay relic, and she and Urtica were now in their own separate time system. She said, "We've not got long."

He looked around at the people in suspension, then raised an eyebrow. "Impressive."

"If you want Dartun caught," Papus said, "I'll need military transport—longships, sleds, that sort of thing."

"Yes, yes, of course. Whatever you want, just ask."

"We'll be leaving the city immediately."

"Right, wait here a moment," he said, entering one of the clerk's rooms nearby. He returned with a document bearing his personal seal. "This should be all you need."

"Thank you, chancellor, I'll not stop until I find him." As she took the document and slid it into a deep pocket, the stilled figures in the corridor came to life, blurred at first like in some kind of smeared painting, and then they continued performing their errands and routines in real time.

CHAPTER 37

✳

It was the flutter of wings that woke her, a faint sound at the periphery of her senses.

Tuya pressed herself up, pain shooting along her arms, muscles spasming unnaturally. Why did everything suddenly ache so much? She brushed her hair from her eyes, squinted into the light that fell upon her face through the partly open window. Through blurred vision she could make out a blue shape hovering up by the ceiling. A freezing breeze exploded into the room, spiraling leaves and snow over her in arcane patterns.

"Who's there?" she asked, her voice alarmingly weak. She was a strong woman and wasn't used to feeling so helpless.

There was no reply. Street noises drifted up to her window from outside, chants of traders busy in the irens. It was obviously well into the day, but she felt so disconnected from time.

As a blur of blue shot down toward her bed, she instantly recognized one of the images she had painted several weeks ago. The bat-like creature stared at her, the size of a child, and as far as could be judged from its furry features, she saw pity in its glossy, dark eyes. She had no idea it had survived this long, seldom giving much thought to what became of her many creations. She was touched it had returned to her side.

At that moment, as a sudden revelation, her current predicament rushed to the front of her awareness.

Tryst had not only beaten but also drugged her too, the bastard.

Escape was the priority. Tuya stood up, then immediately collapsed. The muscles in her legs would barely function, and it was as if she needed to relearn basic movement. The creature waddled down from the bed, holding its arms and wings out wide. After it helped her up, she sat down weakly on the bed.

"Why have you come to help me? How did you know I needed help?"

It seemed unable to speak. Could it even understand her?

After she composed herself, she limped around her room to pack some belongings. She got changed with a frail caution. When she had taken what she needed, she tried the door to discover it was locked. She couldn't find her keys anywhere, and struggling with the door proved futile.

Again her strange blue creation came to her side and she backed away as it contemplated the solid wooden door. It extended its wings, and with a down-thrust it rose into the air, hovered then circled, flooring ornaments and antiques, before hurling itself at the door.

Wood and metal shattered simultaneously into minute blue sparks.

The door and the creature were no longer there. Tuya gaped in disbelief at this strange self-sacrifice by one of her creations. Sadness overwhelmed her. This was, ironically, the most love any creature had ever shown her.

But this was not the time for pathos. A bag of her belongings in one hand, she stepped out to commence her escape.

She needed to clean herself up, to get her head into some sort of order.

Who could she turn to?

CHAPTER 38

✳

Longships banked toward the east, cautiously navigating the complex and treacherous sheets of ice northwest of Villiren. Brynd looked out across the water, checking to see where the wind blew strongest past the jagged outline of the coast, the ice, the limestone cliffs. As soon as they were through the darker waters, the ship's sails snagged tight as skin, and the vessel suddenly lurched under gathering momentum. But the crew of the ship had also anticipated this, adjusting her sail accordingly. There had obviously been ice breakers out earlier along the length of this coast.

Then it presented itself, Villiren, one of the largest cities in the Boreal Archipelago, one of the most lawless places in the Empire. The city's harbor was perched between two wide cliff faces crawling with birds and pterodettes. A few renegade garudas were about, shadow communities of them living deep in the cave systems.

Villiren was the commercial hub of the Empire, strategically located between several mining islands like Tineag'l, where ore was auctioned and taxed and distributed. Traders of Villiren had made a fortune providing for the Imperial armies. The people of Villiren had been "rewarded" with democracy, even though they voted for someone who served the Council directly—not Brynd's idea of what democracy was. The city had expanded rapidly in recent years under the new portreeve, and this was often at the expense of labor rights. Many of the poor had been cleared from their homes in the face of Imperial progress, and were left with no choice but to work in mining communities further north.

An immense citadel loomed over the harbor. Turrets dominated every angle of the walls, and aside from the immense archways made from bone and the Ancient Quarter, the structures tended to be flat and featureless, a drab and endless latticework of streets, not at all like the grandeur of Villjamur.

As their longship navigated through the ice-plates, Brynd noted an alarming number of small vessels close to the harbor walls.

Apium joined him up on deck. "Well, here I am, back at this shit-hole. Still, maybe a fat purse will compensate me for the lonely nights ahead.

"Anyway look at that—"

Brynd interrupted his reminiscences, gesturing toward the hundreds of boats packed into the harbor, many left untied as if their owners didn't care about them any longer.

Apium came and put his gut on the side. "What d'you suppose has caused that?"

"Either escaping the Freeze," Brynd frowned, "or something to do with the killings on Tineag'l."

✳

It could've been merely smoke from the fire with some spices sprinkled on it for extra aroma, but Brynd just knew that wasn't likely. This was the chamber of Fat Lutto, portreeve of Villiren, after all. The haze was intense, making him feel drowsy. Brynd couldn't put a name to the drug he smelled, but it was close enough to arum weed. Probably some new variety that Lutto had nurtured for a little extra kick.

Bizarre sounds came from the middle of the chamber, which was decorated richly with purple cushions and silk hangings.

Brynd approached the source of the commotion, shouting, "Lutto, is that you?"

"What? Who? Who goes there?" A mound of flesh pushed itself up from the tangle of bodies, grasped for a sword lying by the cushions. "I'll have you, getting in here like that! I am well connected with gangs!"

"Portreeve Lutto, it's Commander Lathraea."

A perspiring brown face leered through the smoke, a wedge of a mustache dominating it. Two bright blue eyes fixed themselves upon Brynd, before widening in recognition. "Commander Brynd! What a pleasure! Just give me a second." He abruptly dismissed the three naked rumel girls, a brown-, a black- and a gray-skin. They threw on their robes, and scampered out of a door to one side. The gust of air let in began to clear some of the smoke.

"That's better." Fat Lutto waddled toward Brynd with all the grace of an old lady wading through shallow water with her skirts hitched up. He now wore a silver silk robe that billowed around him like a tent. "And how's my favorite soldier these days? You bless Lutto with your presence with no warning. How kind. Or perhaps he comes to save Villiren in her time of need!"

"Rumel girls?" Brynd asked.

"Indeed!" Fat Lutto smiled, clasping his hands together. "Tough skins you see and there's little chance of little Luttos coming forth." He stroked his mustache thoughtfully. "Has my favorite warrior come to help us in these troubled times?"

"Everyone seems to be talking about troubled times," Brynd observed. "Yes, we're here to investigate the incidents on Tineag'l. And at your request, I believe."

"At last! This humble city can't put up with all these exiles for much longer. No, sir."

"Exiles?" Brynd said. "Why didn't you mention that in the message you sent to Villjamur?"

"Um . . . I hadn't enough details." He held his arms out wide in despair. "There were too few details then, but now I'm burdened with too many!"

Brynd said, "I hope you haven't been neglecting your duties?"

"Would Lutto consider such a thing at the Empire's expense? I am, after all, her most loyal servant."

It was almost as if Fat Lutto was trying to *convince* himself that he was honorable. "What more can you tell me of the situation?"

Fat Lutto gestured for Brynd to sit on some cushions, then began to describe at length what had happened over the past few months.

At the start they had come in ones and twos, the refugees, in small and optimistic groups. Some came for the opportunities Villiren presented with the Freeze clamping down on their livelihoods in the wilds. But then people started to arrive in volume, families crammed on hazardous vessels, not a few of them drowning in the ice-cold waters.

Their stories were all the same.

The Claws, or the Shells. That was what the invading race had been labeled by locals. Either way, the news was the same: entire families, then hamlets, then towns, and more, wiped out in the course of just a night. Large numbers of people had gone missing. Some were killed, with their skins ripped off. It seemed only the young and old were spared capture, but ended up dead. The invaders were hideous to observe: walking crustaceans that showed no regard for life. And no one knew where they had come from.

Brynd listened to these stories in silence, vaguely aware of the irony that many tribesmen had once spread similar tales of the invading Imperial forces through the ages.

But this was a crisis far worse than he could have imagined. This threatened not just the Empire, but all human and rumel life indiscriminately.

"All you're telling me," Brynd said finally, "this is absolute truth. None of it's your usual exaggerations?"

"Exaggerations?" Fat Lutto affected to look mortified.

"Well, there's the time you spread gossip that some of the Kyálku had sailed across from Varltung to merge with the Froutan and provoke a rebellion on the Empire's shores—all so that you could charge protection money throughout Villiren and Y'iren? Remember that?"

"Such accusations! Lutto is hurt!"

"So why didn't you send any further messages?"

"To be honest, no messengers dared leave the city." Lutto placed a fat hand on Brynd's shoulder. "You may think it isn't often I show anxiety, but I have never seen such a crisis. We've already accepted a few hundred into our city, but more are waiting on Tineag'l, trying to make their way across the ice sheets. More will die.

"And within months the ice sheets will be too much to disperse. A path will be formed directly between Tineag'l and Y'iren. Leading right to this city. What then?"

Brynd said, "I'm surprised you haven't made a run for it already."

"You joke, of course, Commander Brynd! But, there is safety in these walls. This is a fortress city, after all, with many skilled fighters."

"I want you to tell me every possible thing you can about the position of these refugees on Tineag'l, which of their settlements have been attacked and where they intend to sail from. Can you manage that?"

Fat Lutto nodded, his chins wobbling. "To save our city, I'll do anything."

✳

Brynd ensured that his military were properly housed for the night at one of the empty garrisons at the northern periphery of the city, overlooking the crowded harbor. They were to be kept off the city streets, as Brynd knew only too well what kind of trouble they might get into.

The Dawnir, Jurro, was provided with a chamber all to himself, seeming happy enough to spend his evening alone with his books. The last thing Brynd wanted was a panicking city assuming a savior of sorts had come to the rescue.

Hopefully the operation would be straightforward enough, though Brynd wasn't certain as to the enemy's capabilities. The next morning he ordered that all the empty boats abandoned in the harbor should be reclaimed, tied together, and then be towed by several Jamur longships to the southern shores of Tineag'l in preparation for evacuation.

As he lay awake that night on a makeshift bed in the garrison dormitory, even through the thick walls and above the snoring alongside him he could hear the faint sounds of laughter and debauchery from the city beyond. It made him wonder how life could go on in this way with a crisis looming that could soon be tearing the population's lives apart. How much did they know of this threat?

✳

Unable to sleep, he finally pushed his sheets aside, dressed himself in his uniform, went outside to stand on the long balcony overlooking the harbor. It was ice cold, and what clouds that had followed them during the day now moved southwest. Stars were reflected in the water, the harbor stretching down in a sweeping arc from left to right and, from where he stood, he could see the lights of colored lanterns burning all around the city. Stray dogs and massive trilobites shuffled between upturned crates on the stone docks below while people walked home in twos and threes through grubby alleyways behind flat-topped buildings.

Brynd wanted to think about almost anything just to take his mind off tomorrow's operation. He thought of Kym; one particular night the two of them fucked on a balcony, the risk of getting caught seeming a thrill at the time—merely a warming feeling now.

Such absentminded retrospection delayed his observation of two figures standing in the umbra further along the balcony. It was Apium, and the cultist Blavat.

As he approached them, Apium inquired, "You couldn't sleep either?"

"No," Brynd replied. "When there's a big day ahead, I never can sleep easy."

"Been far too long since we've had a proper big day," Apium grumbled. "If it wasn't for that business at Dalúk Point I would've totally forgotten how to fight by now."

"Unlike you to be so glum," Brynd observed.

The stocky soldier merely shrugged.

The cultist turned to face him, her aged skin somehow timeless in the starlight. "You want me to light a fire to get you warm?"

"Please," Brynd said, gratefully.

She reached into her pocket, twisted something. A purple light started from nothing, and she set it down on the edge of the balcony until it soon transformed into a welcome glow.

"Handy, that," Apium commented in admiration.

The three of them stared out northward, toward Tineag'l. Brynd couldn't imagine what state the refugees would now be in. It could take days to reach them, and you had to factor in how far the ice sheets had descended, and how much distance they would have to travel on horseback.

"I won't necessarily be able to get you out of any difficult situation," Blavat said dully, now gazing into the fire. "Don't start thinking we cultists are the stuff of epic poems. We're ordinary people, just like you."

"So who did you piss off back home?" Apium inquired. "Since you're the lucky sod who's forced to come out all this way north with the army, instead of keeping your arse safe and warm in Villjamur."

"There's a certain amount of loyalty owed to the order, but Papus is a bit too fond of being in authority. She doesn't like her position challenged and apparently I became a bit too popular with the rest of my order. Times are uncertain, and she wanted to make it very clear who is in charge, especially right now."

"Especially now?" Brynd queried, surprised at the intensity of her tone.

"Yes, it's all to do with Dartun Súr of the Order of the Equinox. Papus hates him, even holds him responsible for the draugr. I don't know if it's just a personal vendetta, or whether she truly holds the moral high ground. Don't be surprised, if when we get back to Villjamur, you find all cultists are at war with each other. And I was hoping to spend my time quietly on Ysla during the Freeze."

"So this Ysla place," Apium said, "what's it really like?"

"It is an incredible place, you've no idea how much so. There are problems, just like any place, but there is a governing board of cultists from every order who make sure everything runs smoothly. It will be significantly warmer there than elsewhere in the Archipelago, so I doubt the ice will cause too much of a problem."

Brynd interrupted, "I believe you can control the weather there, so why can't you do that for the rest of the Empire?"

"A couple of members of the Order of Natura can alter cloud patterns in order to keep the sunlight on us—also drive snowstorms away—but not for long periods of time. It's a difficult science, and though there is a heritage from the times in our history when the sun shone brighter, we only comprehend a fraction of it all."

For a moment no one said anything, merely studied the city before them. The stars had become increasingly obscured, a bank of clouds rolling in from the north, which made Brynd wonder how long it would be till it started to snow. It didn't surprise him, therefore, when it began, gently at first, and then grew into something more acute.

"Tomorrow's military operation," Blavat said. "How confident are you?"

"Honestly? I don't know," Brynd admitted. "We face an utterly unknown enemy. We have no surveillance information to hand. As far as getting the refugees back to safety, it depends what state they're in. We can only do our best."

"Where do you see my powers fitting in?" Blavat inquired.

"Any medical relics you can apply to the refugees, and, of course, enhancement of our weapons."

"You'll need explosives?" she suggested.

"Yes, indeed," Brynd said. "If you could prime some for us to deploy across the ice sheets, that might be useful in cutting us off—from whatever those refugees have coming after them."

After that the three of them watched the falling snow in companionable silence. Street fires and lantern lights glared defiantly for another bell, but one by one they fell into shadow. Voices in the streets beyond quietened and soon there was only the sound of the wind probing the city's countless alleyways.

CHAPTER 39

✻

THERE WAS SOMETHING ABOUT ELBOWS THAT TOLD YOU A LOT ABOUT A woman, Randur contemplated. You could tell her age easily by the quality of skin there, and no amount of makeup or exercise could cover it up. Eir's elbow-skin was young and firm, he noted, and he considered, for the first time in his life, how he might enjoy watching her age . . .

Blimey, what's happening to me?

These aimless mornings brought Randur much enjoyment, in running his hands in exploration over unknown zones of her body. The inward curve behind the knee, for example: there was joy to be found there. Randur considered her collarbone particularly delightful. And, of course, her elbows.

Randur was in bed with the Stewardess of Villjamur, and they had *made love.* He was acutely conscious of a change in his attitude, an inner paradigm shift—he was a different man now.

One of her legs was sprawled on top of his as they lay there sharing body warmth, perspiring from their recent exertions. Contented. Shafts of daylight infiltrated from behind the tapestries that hung across the window, a cool draft penetrating. Eir turned over so that he lay behind her. He wrapped one arm around her waist and her fingers grasped his lazily. He kissed her neck hungrily.

Randur wanted to savor this intimacy for as long as possible.

They were in love the way only young people can be: full of passion, unaware of anyone other than themselves.

Why did he suddenly feel like this now, for the first time in his life? Randur had read about it in books, never quite believed it; but it had found him too. The days spent together seemed to stretch out forever, and their late-night intimacies made them feel they had been lovers for years. Time itself began to seem a little pointless.

Randur was aware that people in Balmacara were beginning to whisper, asking questions. There were already political maneuvers, he suspected, being concocted in the shadows of the richer taverns, men looking at boys looking at men, and somewhere between them a knife would be placed on the table, his name would be mentioned, some young thing's dreams of riches would blossom.

For them, an unknown outsider such as Randur wasn't meant to be for Eir. It broke the rules, it diluted the concentrated power at the top of the Empire. Secretly her fate had been discussed and decided. Possibly by senior members of the Council. In his newfound bliss, he didn't give a shit what such people thought. Had this cynical island boy finally been hooked? He'd told her everything about himself, his disreputable past.

That was the one honest move he'd ever made.

He had thought once the Snow Ball was over he could simply leave, taking with him whatever cultist trickery he'd bought to extend his mother's life longer. He sighed. That was no longer so easy.

He slid his other arm from under Eir's neck.

"You going somewhere?" she whispered, still facing the wall.

He moved her short dark hair away from her ear, with no specific purpose, just tenderness. He kissed her arm. "I have to go and pay the cultist today. I'd almost forgotten."

"Of course. I'll get you the money." She looked up, smiling softly.

*

Randur felt awkward as he thanked her for the four hundred Jamúns, though she insisted impatiently that money meant little to her. A month ago he would have called her a spoiled brat for being so reckless with it. Funny, he thought, how love can affect your outlook so quickly.

Tomorrow, she reminded him excitedly, was the Snow Ball. To spend a wonderful evening with a man she chose to love. Even someone as cynical as Randur was surprised to find he, too, was looking forward to it. He made a note to examine the latest fashions in the city, then to push it on a bit more, as it was his secret mission to enhance the unadventurous trends of Villjamur.

Down the steps of Balmacara he strode, a sack of Jamúns under his cloak, then out across the raised platform offering views of a fog-caked city. He couldn't see half as many spires as yesterday, but at least it wasn't snowing. A garuda sailed overhead, disappearing into the white, but there weren't as many people out and about these days.

For a quarter of an hour he sought out the street of the cultists, searching his memory for the way there amidst the deceptively surreal routes of the alleyways. Eventually he arrived at what seemed the right location, and frowned to see no door any longer, only a cloaked figure standing guard.

"Morning," Randur said, trying to skim past her.

"Get out," the woman spat.

"I need to see Dartun," Randur protested. "I've something for him. We had a deal."

"He's not here," the woman replied sourly.

"Anyone from the Order of the Equinox?"

She stared at him angrily. "Why d'you want to know?"

After he explained, he was taken inside to be questioned further.

✳

Randur was ushered into one of those dreary underground chambers that Villjamur possessed no shortage of—with minimal light and no warmth. He was instructed to wait on an uncomfortable stool in the corner. Randur was beginning to panic, having all these months assumed that all he need do was hand over the money to the cultist, and his mother would be miraculously saved.

There were sounds: the clattering of a metal door opening, the shuffle of footsteps, heavy breathing nearby. Then someone grabbed his shoulder, pushed him back against the wall.

Another female voice snarled, "Why are you here to see Dartun?"

Randur squinted through the darkness, the fingers tightening on his shoulder. "I was just coming to make him a payment as agreed. And I find out he's not here, and there's some weird shit going on. Now will you let go of my shoulder, and tell me what has happened to him?"

"He won't be coming back to Villjamur."

"But . . . what of the rest of his group of cultists?" Randur was getting desperate. Dartun should have been here.

"They've either gone with him or been arrested. The Order of the Equinox is now outlawed throughout the territories of the Empire."

"Shit," Randur gasped in alarm, then further explained his situation.

"I remember you now," the voice said. "You're the boy I pointed in his direction as a favor, for saving my life. But I can't help you anymore."

"You must. You have to. That's the whole fucking reason I'm even in this city."

"I'm sorry. But you're free to go."

"Can't any other cultists help me? I've got money—I'll show you." Randur stood up but found, after a lengthy silence, that he was now totally alone. Torch light entered the chamber and he was escorted out.

✳

His world had imploded. Lying on Eir's bed later, he felt he wanted to vomit, but instead he cried like a ten-year-old as he told her everything. She sat next to him waiting for him to finish—he knew that, and he felt ashamed, to expose his emotions like this. But, despite her age, she possessed an unexpected motherly quality. He liked that. After that he got up and left, walked for two hours across the city bridges, then returned, damp and cold.

Then he resumed crying.

Eir held his hand. "It's understandable you're upset, Rand, so don't be so harsh on yourself."

She got up and lit lanterns and soothing incense and waited for him to compose himself. He realized he was comfortable being vulnerable in front of her. Soon he began to feel better, until somehow his failings as a son didn't seem to matter quite as much.

CHAPTER 40

✳

THERE WERE TIMES IN HIS LONG LIFE WHERE JERYD HAD BEEN AFRAID. Cornered in an alley with a sword against his throat. Going undercover with gangs in his youth. Chasing suspects along icy bridges and precarious rooftops. Dealing with crime, you'd expect that.

But as he now awaited Marysa to wake from her slumber, he was *truly* frightened.

She had slept right through for two nights as if under some spell. His life was balanced, waiting for these moments for her to wake up. He'd already forgiven her for her misdemeanor. Didn't matter that she'd found something, momentarily, with someone else. That wouldn't be the first thing he would think about when she finally opened her eyes. His tactic was to pretend it had not happened. He loved her so much, it caused him an entirely new level of pain inside.

As the milky light of day began to filter through from the window, he looked around at the clutter of junk filling the bedroom. It was all hers, of course. Jeryd was one of those who didn't care to accumulate anything much. As soon as he'd finished with it, it was gone. His rooms had been bare, before she was around. She'd filled the void systematically, buying steadily over the years, nearly all of it antiques. Maybe much of it was junk, but it was *her* junk.

He had got comfortably used to her filling his otherwise empty life with objects of uncertain purpose, and he'd often wander around the house, simply to uncover items he'd have no recognition of. It seemed to suggest something deeper about their relationship.

As he rested a hand affectionately on her arm, she finally stirred, her fingers gripping the white bedsheets gently. He sprang to life, a silent prayer to Bohr on the tips of his lips.

She lifted herself up, and stared at him vacantly.

"Good morning," he said. "You've slept through two nights without waking. I hope someone didn't try any love potions on you. There's a lot of it about these days."

"Two nights?" she said, her eyes focusing on him intently, a million thoughts clearly darting through her mind. "I had such a weird dream . . . I dreamed I came home and you were really angry. It's strange how real it all seemed. The mind can do scary things . . ."

With those few words he knew he was safe. All he had to do now was behave as normal.

※

Jeryd knew he had to leave the house before too long. Minor cases were mounting up in his office, and he still had to solve the councilor murders. Today not even that tiny snowball army, the Gamall Gata kids, annoyed him. *Jerrryd.*

As he walked the ice-slicked streets of Villjamur he felt in a particularly strange mood. His eyes felt heavy, barely took in the constant streams of people passing him. The keening of a banshee echoed somewhere unnaturally far away. His mind was left abandoned on a melancholy plane neither here nor there.

In the melting sun, an icicle detached from one of the high ledges and shattered on the cobbles near his feet. Not even that could interrupt his torpor.

Reaching the headquarters of the Inquisition, he opened the door of his office to find Tuya Daluud standing there with her back to him.

She turned her head, her thick hair flowing in an alluring arc. You couldn't really see her scar in the dim light. She was wearing a thick black coat and smelled of a decent perfume. She stared at him in discomforting silence, and her eyes looked red and sore as if she had been weeping.

"Can I help?" Jeryd said at last, indicating the visitor's chair in front of his desk.

She shook her head, but he didn't know whether that was in response to the question or to his gesture.

"You look as if you need help," Jeryd suggested.

"I . . . I have some information," she said eventually, and sat down. "It's serious. I feel I need to . . . confess. But I don't know how you'll react and I'm scared that he'll come to get me." The gaze she fixed on him then was deeply penetrating. "I'm so frightened. I've no one else to turn to. You must be the only person in this city who I can trust—you seem like such a genuine man."

Jeryd laid his dark-skinned hand on hers, and she felt peculiarly tender. "You can trust me." He walked to the door, locked it, then started a fire to get the room warm again. He pulled his chair around the desk so he was next to her, wanting her to know he was on her side. "Tell me what's wrong. You said someone was after you?"

She sobbed fearfully. "I escaped him, at least for now."

"Who?" Jeryd tried to meet her eyes, but she kept looking away from him, to the floor, to the desk, to the walls.

"Your 'aide,' Tryst."

Jeryd leaned back with a shocked frown. "Go on."

She began to tell him everything that had transpired over recent weeks: how Tryst approached her, the drugs he used to subdue her, the beatings once the drugs wore off, her uncanny ability to bring to life creatures through her art, how Tryst had abused that secret by demanding a clone of Jeryd's wife so as to play a cruel trick on the investigator. And in the stunned silence you could hear the crack of wood splitting on the fire as it burned. "He hated you to an extent. I think he just wanted to teach you a lesson for something. It was obvious you didn't know what he was up to, and since you seemed to be his enemy, I thought you could help."

His enemy? Jeryd thought morosely.

And then, reluctantly, she confessed to the murders of the two councilors, thus revealing the key piece of information that Jeryd had suspected, but had no proof of—the diabolical plan devised by members of the Council itself to eliminate thousands of the refugees.

About a million thoughts raced through Jeryd's mind. His world had suddenly become so much more confusing, so much more dangerous. He realized that Marysa hadn't actually cheated on him. It was this "clone" that he had witnessed. Despite the surge of relief, in that moment the guilt of his subsequent actions became unbearable.

"Investigator?" Tuya prompted.

He faced her. "Forgive me, Miss Daluud. You've given me such a huge quantity of information that not only affects myself but this entire city, this Empire. But you say Tryst may be coming after you."

"Yes . . . he humiliated me and beat me." Then she collapsed into sobbing, burying her head in her palms. It didn't seem natural for a woman previously radiating such confidence, such strength.

Jeryd clasped her hands in his own. "Tell me everything again—absolutely everything you remember."

The specific details regarding the actual slaughter of the refugees were limited, and Tuya could give only one other name at the center of the conspiracy. Chancellor Urtica, it seemed, was setting the pace on this matter, although the actual means of achieving this remained uncertain. Jeryd realized he would have to alert others within the Inquisition—but only a select few he could trust. If this went to the top of the city's ruling hierarchy, who else might be involved? Could he risk informing his superiors? Or should he handle this on his own? Either way, what would be the consequences? Regarding Tuya herself, should he arrest her or let her free? Tryst would soon find her again, and Jeryd now saw his subordinate in a chilling new light. He realized that he would have to hide her away somewhere safe, for now. For her own good. *But she has committed murder.* Yet it seemed she had killed the councilors to prevent the slaughter of thousands of innocents. Sometimes this city was so sinister, so complicated, he wished he could leave it completely.

He made up his mind. "Don't worry about anything. For the moment, you'll be safe. I'll take care of that but I'll need your help."

❊

Jeryd had decided to allow Tuya to stay at his house in the Kaiho district.

Marysa was there still, thank Bohr, though Jeryd felt a pang of guilt every time she looked his way. She accepted Tuya's arrival without question, so he felt free to return to work.

After spending much of the afternoon thinking about recent developments, Jeryd saw the figure of Tryst walking off through the winding stone corridors of the Inquisition headquarters, heading out into the street.

He followed him hastily into the chill, his cloak wrapped tightly around him.

"Tryst," Jeryd called out across the fresh snow, his voice echoing in the still of the early evening.

The young man stopped to look back and, on recognizing Jeryd, approached. "Investigator, you need me?"

Jeryd looked him up and down, rage fluctuating inside him. He felt a strange respect for the levels this treacherous bastard would stoop to in order to achieve his ends. "Walk with me awhile, I've something important to discuss."

Through the alleyways of the old city, and down toward the caves. They passed two quiet irens packing up for the day, the street traders looking glum at the lack of business in such miserable weather. A few fires were still lit where women sold fried spiced pastries, the smoke trapped ghostlike in the frozen air. Eventually they came to a neighborhood where Jeryd felt able to continue the conversation. Graffiti covered the walls, tags and obscenities and protests of love. Moss gathered where it could in damp corners.

"The councilor murders," Jeryd began, "has that prostitute come up with anything yet?"

"Afraid not, sir." Tryst's calm expression showed no sign of any deception.

"Where's Miss Daluud now precisely?" Jeryd inquired.

A flash of anxiety in his eyes?

"I can't be sure," Tryst replied. "Not at the moment. You wish to speak to her? I think if I have a little more time I could get some answers for you. I'm keen to succeed."

"Are you, now," Jeryd muttered.

"Sir?" Tryst tilted his head, his expression still all innocence. "I'm not sure I follow."

Jeryd looked around, at the run-down stone dwellings with their rotting wooden doors and windows. No one else was nearby. The sun had set almost completely, casting a dreary ambience over the scene.

He said, "I'll be arresting her myself tomorrow, so I fear she'll not be able to help you anymore." Jeryd saw the panic in Tryst's eyes, the collapse of a plan, and continued. "You know, that clone of my wife you both created, even though you already knew that she was a murderer. Withholding information from the Inquisition. That was particularly low, but there are quite a few black marks mounting up against you. Using banned substances to influence suspects. But it isn't that which I'm really pissed off about."

Tryst remained silent, instinctively backing away, nothing but cold stone behind him.

"No." Jeryd looked this way and that. "What I'm really annoyed about is the fact that you dragged my wife into your little schemes."

Tryst finally spoke up, "You were the one who struck her—"

Jeryd thumped Tryst in the stomach, doubling him up against the wall. The rumel then brought his knee up sharply into Tryst's exposed face. Blood flecked the wall as Tryst collapsed into the snow holding his nose.

"Did you drug me too, that night?"

No response till Jeryd kicked his subordinate in the back. The human arched like a bridge, then moaned.

"Yes, but . . ."

Jeryd pulled a blade from his sleeve, stared at the man lying before him. He could slit his throat here and now, and no one would notice. He could move the body to Caveside, where this sort of thing happened daily. But then his rage subsided into something much calmer, much colder. If he did not kill him, Tryst would have to be arrested— but then he might reveal how Jeryd had struck his wife unconscious.

Tryst looked up pathetically, clutching his gut with one hand, his nose with the other. It was in moments like this that Jeryd realized lives could be altered forever.

"I'm . . . sorry, Jeryd," Tryst gasped. "I was angry. I resented you."

Jeryd looked down at him. "There were," he snarled, "other ways to let me know."

"I wanted to make you suffer, so you would know how I felt . . . I deserved that promotion."

Both men remained silent for a while as a banshee screamed somewhere in Caveside. Jeryd again looked down at Tryst and could see the fear in the young man's eyes, as if that sound was a premonition.

Tryst said, "What're you going to do with me?"

What could Jeryd do? He wasn't a murderer. But nor did he want Marysa to find out the truth.

"Here's what I think," he said. "I could knife you here and now, blame it on the usual suspects. There are plenty to choose from. But I won't do that because I, at least, have morals." He put the knife away. "But I don't want Marysa finding out any of this either. If she does, you'll either be a wanted man, or a dead man." He leaned forward to look straight into Tryst's bloodied face. "*That,* I swear by."

"Please, I beg you, just let this go, Jeryd. We can put this behind us."

The rumel grunted a dry laugh.

Tryst continued, "What about Tuya? We know she's the killer. We can get her locked up and we'll be rewarded for solving the murders."

Except there's more to this, isn't there, something to do with a few thousand refugees being cynically exterminated by their own rulers. And exactly how much do you know about that?

Jeryd sighed. "All right, don't come anywhere near the Inquisition chambers for the next couple of days. When you do come back, you'll not be working with me. If you reveal any of this mess, your dismembered body will be found in some alleyway. Are we clear on that?"

Tryst nodded eagerly, dabbing his bleeding nose with his fingers.

Jeryd turned away, headed off down the snow-plagued street.

❄

Jeryd stood looking over the city walls to the refugee settlement, the hundreds of campfires looking hopeless and suffocated by the encroaching night. Streams of smoke wafted from between tents. The barking dogs echoed endlessly across the tundra. There were said to be nearly ten thousand refugees huddled down there, in that expanse between the city walls and the beach. The very spirit of the hell they lived in seemed to rise above like a depressive cloud.

He wondered for a moment if the stories he'd heard were true: that the refugees had taken to eating their dogs and cats, and in some taverns a rumor broke out that they had taken to cannibalism, consuming those already dead from disease or starvation. Jeryd knew the Council were the ones manufacturing such talk, being the only ones allowed to distribute the news pamphlets. The gates of Villjamur now separated those who struggled to get on with death from those who struggled to get on with life. The only thing they had in common was struggle.

Jeryd was going to leave Villjamur as soon as he could. Of that he was certain. Life was too short to waste it in a city whose government would stoop to slaughtering its own. He had enough money to risk uprooting to another city of the Empire, somewhere much quieter. Perhaps on Southfjords, or maybe he could even strike a deal with the cultists and build a cottage on Ysla with its milder climate. Whichever way, his disgust with this city, and himself, meant he had to get out of here. With Marysa, of course. Because he loved her, and that was all that mattered. You went through life working so hard and acquiring all the things that you were meant to. Now some way down that journey, perhaps even too late, Jeryd realized he should have gone in some other direction.

He regarded the clustered refugees once again. How exactly did Urtica intend to kill them all? More importantly, could Jeryd stop it from happening?

Footsteps approached along the top of the stone wall—the figure of Investigator Fulcrom. The wind picked up, racing across the tundra and blasting directly into his face, and it brought him to some new state of alertness. Despite his thick rumel skin, he shivered, drew his cloak tighter around him.

"Jeryd, you've not looked yourself these past few days, and I'm getting worried about you." It was unusual these days for anyone in Villjamur, let alone another rumel, to show such concern, but he knew he could trust this colleague. So Jeryd began to relate everything that had gone on recently—about Tryst and Tuya, the truth about the councilor murders and how these murders were linked to a conspiracy to eradicate the refugees. Behind it all was the secret cult of the Ovinists.

They were clearly involved.

"Jeryd, that's so awful," Fulcrom said, after a moment's silence. "But who is heading up the Ovinists in the Council?"

"Urtica," Jeryd said bluntly.

"Chancellor Urtica?" Fulcrom said in dismay.

"The prostitute insists he was involved somehow. Amazing what a man will tell a woman across a pillow when their business is done."

"I wouldn't know too much about that," Fulcrom admitted.

Jeryd grunted a laugh. "Anyway, something's going to happen soon, but I don't know when. For all I know it could be already happening."

"I can't believe we've got corruption at so high a level," Fulcrom remarked. "It's disgusting, when you consider these people have been voted in by our citizens."

"The Council has always been about maintaining the illusion that a vote gives the people a say in affairs, when all the time they control communication—like generating fear against these helpless refugees. That a democracy? You tell me. But in such an organization the Ovinists would fit very well. What's worse is that this cult has attracted so many powerful members. They could be operating anywhere—even in the Inquisition."

"D'you really think people higher up in our own organization already know about it? The refugees, I mean."

"It's possible. Thing is, I don't want thousands of innocent men, women, and children dying through the devious machinations of my Empire. Not in my name at least. I don't care what the hell happens, but we've got to do the right thing. We must show ourselves to be good people."

Good people . . .

He liked to think that there were some moral absolutes in the world, that Villjamur's rulers had not been reduced to moral nihilism. That good was to be done and to be pursued, and evil avoided. Some things, to Jeryd, seemed natural, an essential part of existence.

It helped, being an investigator, to believe in law.

"What can we do?" Fulcrom rested his hands on the wall, staring out over the refugee encampment. "If something's going on this high up the ranks . . . We'll find ourselves on our own."

"Probably. But, maybe you know other people we can trust?"

Fulcrom said, "Sure. Some good types in the Inquisition. I've inside contacts with the city guard, too, for that matter."

"Good. I'm now going to organize weaponry of some sort. Meanwhile if you can ask every man in the Inquisition you can trust, to watch out for any unusual movement of men. It would need a sizeable operation to remove so many people from outside the city, so there'll be plenty of visible activity. But we've got the law and morality on our side, so if anyone finds out what we're doing, they'll not be able to stop us easily."

"Unless they kill us first," Fulcrom suggested.

"Yes. Unless they kill us."

"But still, if we don't know how Urtica plans to achieve this massacre, it'll remain difficult to foil his plans. How would one eliminate so many people without others soon knowing about it?"

Jeryd was silent as he reflected on this, and could not think of a plausible answer.

It had been a long time since Jeryd had been required to participate in an armed mission, and never on a scale such as this. The last time he had fired a crossbow was before Johynn was born, against a corrupt network of the city guard who were abusing their position to kidnap young girls in Caveside and sell them as sex slaves to private landowners on the outer islands.

This was not a bunch of renegades but the chancellor they were up against. Obviously Urtica was power-mad and hungry for control, prepared to go to any lengths to achieve his insane objectives. Clearly, in his eyes, removing the nuisance of the refugees was a good thing, reducing the strains on the city's resources that would, ultimately, lead to great political unrest. For Urtica to retain his seat comfortably, the refugees had to go.

Both rumel stared out at the familiar evening scene. Theirs would be no easy task, but it was the right thing to do. Jeryd felt a great sadness at the corruption overtaking his beloved city. All that mattered now was that he would do all he could.

CHAPTER 41

✳

ANOTHER ONE OF THOSE MELANCHOLY NIGHTS OF VILLJAMUR, IN WHICH a pterodette called out across the city's spires so loudly it sounded like a banshee. Up here on the top floor of the Imperial residence, starlight clearly defined the rooftops, meaning the evening would be cold and cloudless. Incense burned somewhere, mere hints of it on the breeze, prompting thoughts of some wild ritual being performed in a forgotten corner of the city.

Tryst loved this city and he could easily see how it invoked such passions in people—in Chancellor Urtica, in himself. Raising a corner of the tapestry preserving the still warmth of the chamber, he stared idly out of a window, waiting for Urtica to arrive. There were occasions, in the chancellor's presence, when Tryst felt so much reverence for him that he wanted to be part of his consciousness and see the world through his master's eyes.

The door opened and Urtica marched into the ornate room, with its glittering trinkets arranged around the immense fireplace.

"Sele of Jamur, chancellor," Tryst greeted him.

"What happened to your face?" Urtica paused as he moved closer. "A fight I suspect? I hope you're not attracting too much unwarranted attention."

"No, not at all. It was just . . . well Investigator Jeryd had some sharp words to say to me."

"What about?"

Tryst met his gaze boldly as they eyed each other across the glow of the flames. Tryst had used Tuya to all advantage, now simply wanted her out of the way. He probably would have killed her if she hadn't escaped him and run to Jeryd. Now the damned rumel knew everything. No matter, Tryst would soon have her hunted down, with a reward on her head. "I strongly believe that a prostitute is responsible for the councilor murders."

"A prostitute?" Urtica wore a look of utter amazement on his face.

"Yes, from what I gather, Ghuda spilled certain secrets across a pillow. Disclosures that linked him with you, sir. She learned about your plans for the removal of refugees. She knows who was involved and decided to take matters into her own hands."

Urtica interrupted, "We can't have her blabbing such rumors in case she brings attention to me. She must be removed promptly." The chancellor paused. "Does Jeryd also know of this?"

"I'm afraid so," Tryst said, feeling guilt now for having put his own interests above those of the chancellor. "You see, I had her under confinement, but he took her off my hands. I merely wanted to protect your honor, sir."

Tryst watched his idol with hope, heart thumping in his chest.

"Very good, young Tryst, you did well."

"Sir, I'd do anything for you," Tryst said eagerly. "Anything."

"Still I need to be able to trust you totally. I've seen that you're a sharp man, but can you be loyal?"

"Of course," he breathed.

The chancellor paced back and forth before the flames. "Good. Then I want you to kill both Investigator Jeryd and this prostitute. They must not have the chance to inform others." He leaned forward, continued with a whisper. "Now, I'm about to initiate my plans with the Empress Rika. She'll be arrested tomorrow at the Snow Ball for maximum publicity, with an order for her execution coming the following day. All the Ovinist councilors are ready to support me. Tomorrow night some Ovinist colleagues in the military will begin guiding in some of the refugees in small numbers to meet their fate, all on the quiet of course. They'll make use of some of the precarious tunnels under the city—and it doesn't matter if they collapse on them, does it? They'll think they're been taken to temporary housing within the city, and we can finally start poisoning them one by one. As they are dying we can move them to tunnels nearer the coast. Then I think we can just dump them out at sea. Tryst, I want you there with me, at the center of things. Can you do that, lad?"

"Indeed, chancellor. Anything for you, and for the Ovinists." Tryst swallowed, bowed his head slightly. "One thing though: what about the banshees?"

"What about them?"

"This many deaths—on a large scale. Surely their screams may attract rather too much attention?"

"Leave that to me," Urtica said grimly, and paced around momentarily. "Now, in getting rid of the rumel, I'd suggest some explosives. Make it look like something other than an assassination. I know a cultist open to persuasion, so you can get armed with the necessary equipment to take out his entire house—in case he may have documented his findings. Set a timer to make certain you're clear, but I can guarantee you a good alibi."

A strange emotion overwhelmed Tryst, and suddenly his stomach felt sick. He really didn't want to kill Jeryd. Certainly he had resented the old rumel, but he only wanted him to suffer. Killing him was going too far. But he had to prove himself to Urtica, the man who would soon be Emperor.

✳

Tryst had been traveling so far under Caveside that he feared he'd never see daylight again. Urtica had given him the address of a cultist who worked alone, and, somewhat dubiously, occasionally helping out people when the coin was right, no questions asked.

The bag of money he carried was slowing him down. Colored lanterns lit the way sporadically, casting light on rats and dogs and grubby children playing games among discarded poultry bones.

Eventually he came to a narrow, solitary street, whose habitations were carved into the cliff. After peering around him, Tryst approached the one he wanted, then knocked on the door three times in quick succession.

It opened to reveal an old woman wrapped in a dark red robe. "What d'you want?" she inquired harshly.

"I was sent by the chancellor," he explained. The lines etching her face creased even further, though her eyes were dazzling in the dreary light.

"Urtica, eh?" she said, with obvious interest.

Tryst revealed the bag of money. "I need some devices made tonight."

She eyed it carefully, then himself. "By all means, come in."

The room beyond the rough wooden door was lit by dozens of thick candles. Tryst had to walk awkwardly around piles of books that littered the floor to reach a central table. There were items in bottles on shelves which he couldn't discern, maybe organs of some hybrid beast, and he swore that one of them was moving.

She indicated a chair and he sat down, placing the bag of money on the table. She turned to face a mirror. She removed her hood, combing her hair with her fingers, pulling long, gray strands to either side of her face. There was something distinctly childlike about her manner.

Eventually, she came over to the table, sat opposite him. Her eyes were blue-tinted, and she regarded him with a soft intensity, as if thinking him someone from her past. "What d'you need?" she asked.

"*Brenna* devices for destroying an entire house. And the person within it."

"Four small ones should be enough."

"You'll need to show me how to use these *Brenna* things. I'm not familiar with handling relics."

She leaned forward, her old eyes sparkling. "Don't worry, lad. I'll help you out."

"Much appreciated." Suddenly he felt a little nervous, as if the quality of the conversation had changed. "I'll need a time delay of a few hours before they explode. Could you work that into the magic?"

She said unexpectedly, "Down here, it's not often I get to see someone so . . . handsome."

Tryst murmured, "Thanks . . . Sorry, I don't know your name."

"Sofen," she said. "Not that it means much down here, where so few people ever use it."

"What order of cultists do you belong to?" Tryst said, keen to change the subject.

"I belong to none. Plenty of cultists prefer to work on their own, lad. Less politics that way and you're not bound to follow any particular creed. How's this sound, lad. You stay and keep me company for a couple of hours, while I get your devices made to your exact requirements."

"Company?" Tryst said, beginning to comprehend her innuendo.

She's sick . . . Surely she's kidding? Or is this some test to prove my loyalty to Urtica?

"Don't look so surprised," Sofen continued. "You see old men getting the services of young women all the time, so it should work just as easily the other way."

"Right." Tryst was beginning to feel desperate. He couldn't hope to get Jeryd and his house destroyed properly if he didn't obtain the relics.

"What's wrong?" Sofen interrupted. "You don't find me attractive?"

"It's not that," Tryst blustered. *Although, let's face it, hag, not even the tide would take you out.* "No, it's just that I'm a man of principle."

"Principle," she said. "Ha! What kind of principle is there in asking me for the means of killing another?"

"It depends," Tryst said, "on why and who you're killing."

She observed him thoroughly. "At least you're honest. I like that. Still, my price remains. You pay me and satisfy me."

Tryst considered his options again, and didn't like what he was being faced with.

"Shall I make it easier for you?" Sofen said.

"How d'you mean?" Tryst said, a little uncertain whether or not this was some form of threat.

"Wait a moment." Sofen walked over to a doorway leading into darkness beyond. After reaching to lift what appeared to be a metal mirror off the shelf, she stepped into the umbrae.

Purple light spat outward, no sound with it, only a thin waft of smoke drifting like incense.

Tryst stood tensely alert, reaching for the short sword he carried under his cloak. A strange, almost floral smell caused him to frown.

"Sofen?" he said, and made a step toward the darkness.

A beautiful woman walked out of it.

Tryst was shocked at this apparition and its obvious similarity to how Sofen must have looked when sixty years younger. Her hair was now luxuriant, a glossy black, her eyes still a dazzling blue. Full lips, prominent cheekbones. She removed her outer robe to reveal an elegant white dress, plain but cut to cling to a slender frame, revealing just enough about the body beneath to win his approval.

The new woman spoke, with a smirk. "You can now pick your jaw up."

"Who are you?" Tryst said.

"The same woman you were disgusted with moments earlier." She grunted a laugh. "Magic: it's all wish fulfillment really. This is an illusion of how I once was, and you've got me in this state for an hour, more or less, so take your time."

The transformation was so remarkable, he was truly lost for words. "I . . . don't know." He hesitated.

She leaned in so close he could smell the clean fragrance of her skin, the freshness of her breath. Breasts were pressed up against his chest. All her wrinkles, all the sadness in her expression were gone.

His hand in hers, she steered him toward the darkness.

CHAPTER 42

✳

Rᴀɴᴅᴜʀ ʜᴀᴅ ᴛᴏ ᴀᴅᴍɪᴛ ʜᴇ ʟᴏᴏᴋᴇᴅ ᴅᴇᴠᴀsᴛᴀᴛɪɴɢʟʏ ʜᴀɴᴅsᴏᴍᴇ.

He regularly cut a very fine dash, but now couldn't help but stare at himself in the gold-framed mirror. With his hair tied back, wearing the latest black breeches, a dark blue shirt and matching jacket, a black cloak to finish it off, he looked ready for anything. It was surely what being here in Villjamur was all about.

Eir had even given him some jewelry: a plain silver chain to go around his neck, two rings for his fingers. She had supported him so much that he felt he owed her his very soul, if only he could give it. Eir's biggest gift to him wasn't monetary, but psychological. Perhaps all he'd ever needed was to actually *love* someone else.

Somehow, the importance of helping his mother to survive had subtly diminished.

"Stop admiring yourself in the mirror." Eir walked into his chamber. "You do that far too much."

Randur turned to gaze at her. "You look pretty damn fine yourself."

As she came nearer, her sinuous movements were highlighted by her dazzling new outfit. The striking and revealing dark-red dress that clung to her body made her look so much older, more sophisticated, bringing her curves to his attention. Her hair was adorned with black ribbons while elaborate mock-tattoos adorned each cheekbone.

She approached him with a new walk that was hers and yet also wasn't, and she said, "Am I to take it, then, that this rare lack of words is a good thing?"

"Yeah," he said, then blurted, "Eir, you look incredible."

"Well you don't look so bad yourself. We ready to set off?"

He said, "Yeah, is your sister ready too?"

"She's already on her way down there."

"Who's to be her partner?"

"She won't have one because as Empress she must remain aloof. No one is deemed suitable, I suppose."

"Kind of sad, that," Randur observed, and he meant it.

✳

They entered the ballroom to find themselves the happy focus of everyone's gaze. All of the Empire's most powerful were already present, dressed in their finery. Light skimmed off gold and silver and mirrors. A thousand candles, a hundred lanterns.

At the far end of the room, a band played fast-moving rhythms, violins leading the tune, harps providing the framework.

People gave the Sele of Jamur to her and Randur, and she was as polite as she could be while Randur maintained his cool aloofness.

Everyone was constantly looking at them and whispering. All the Imperial land- and capital-owners, retired military governors, influential civil servants, members of the Council and their partners. She didn't mind their scrutiny, because tonight she was happier than she'd ever been. With Randur's help, she had learned to dance better than many society ladies. There was, of course, Randur himself, who was the most good-looking man there.

Important people—notably the Council—would most certainly not think Randur suitable, not fitting to be part of the mechanics of the Empire. In her mind, that wasn't an issue, and she didn't care. She'd leave the city if she had to, giving up her rank and privileges.

There she was, Rika, in the center of a throng of councilors. She had soon settled into the role of Empress, calm but serious in expression, but knowing how to laugh in all the right places.

Though she loved her, things weren't the same between the two girls. It wasn't that her sister had become a different person, but she would never again feel that closeness of their childhood. As Empress, Rika had now inherited a different set of priorities.

"Look at this lot," Randur murmured dismissively.

Couples moved around the dance floor, segueing between the delicate shapes they made of their postures. Eir looked up at him questioningly.

"Their dancing is totally crap." He shook his head. "We're so much better than this."

Even she, with her recent training, could see how out of time many of them were, how the women didn't seem to move comfortably, their hips too rigid, spines hunched, while the men were even more awkward, clasping their partners with arms made of stone.

"Shall we show 'em how it's done?" he suggested, then stepped forward with a flourish. He held his hand out to her in invitation.

"Could I possibly even stop you?"

Together they stepped onto the dance floor, and it came to her as naturally as walking. Together, the couple sliced an elegant swathe through the parting crowds. Everyone's eyes were now fixed on her, and for the first time, she basked in the attention. Her own hands resting on Randur's hips and shoulders, he led her through the now-familiar movements, and they suggested passion, they *were* passion, and the way they looked at each other linked the feelings together. Their steps, though so precise, created an illusion of a freedom that other couples couldn't come close to, maybe couldn't even understand.

A quarter of an hour later, Randur guided her to one side of the room. "Let's not waste it all now," he suggested coolly.

Her sister now approached, councilors stepping behind, sipping flutes of wine. Rika wore a regal purple dress, more conservative in style than her own.

"Sister," Rika said, "how did you ever acquire such talent and skill. One might almost think you wore relics in your shoes to help you move so gracefully."

Eir whispered the words "This young man taught me well" to her sister, who began to regard the Folke islander in a new light.

"Well, Randur Estevu, it seems I have you to thank for making my sister the envy of every woman in this room."

"An occupational hazard of my lessons, my lady," Randur offered, and smiled and bowed deeply before stepping aside to let the sisters talk alone.

The Empress leaned closer to her sibling. "You seem rather tender toward each other, the two of you. Are you sure—?"

"Would it be a problem?" Eir interrupted.

"Well, there are a dozen suitable capital owners asking for your hand. It is encouraged to secure progress in our territories . . . We do have duties, I think—"

"Let's not talk about that now," Eir said. "Please."

Rika eyed her carefully.

Eir changed the subject. "You seem to have quite a crowd of councilors following you." She indicated the men behind Rika.

"Yes, I feel I've begun to win them over to my way of thinking."

A thoughtful silence fell between them. Eir could not help thinking again of the refugees and those suffering Caveside. This was Randur's doing, this change of perspective, and how different the world now seemed.

They separated and the evening rolled on toward the dance competition. The band began to build up the anticipation, and then the music stopped abruptly.

A sudden gasp from the crowd.

Whispers fluttered all around her.

A troop of soldiers had marched into the ballroom at its far end. Eir gripped Randur's arm nervously. What could possibly warrant such an intrusion? A dozen of the city guard approached her sister, surrounding her.

From behind these armed men, Chancellor Urtica himself emerged, dressed in his full Council regalia. He strolled toward the front of the ballroom where the band leader stood, fuming indignantly.

The chancellor waved him away, turning to face the crowd of dignitaries.

"Ladies and gentlemen, my apologies for the disruption," Urtica began, projecting his voice to the far corners of the room, "but I bring grave news. I regret that I must take Empress Jamur Rika and her sister into immediate custody."

He then paused, as if he was an actor on stage, for further attention, and was greeted with a hushed confusion, as faces tilted toward Eir. The whole scene became a blur of disconnected images.

Urtica said, "I have a document signed by both the Empress and her sister the Stewardess authorizing a mass execution of the refugees now encamped outside our gate."

Several men advanced demanding explanations for the intrusion. Rows broke out, and the chancellor urged his military heavies forward.

Urtica palmed the air, remaining quite calm. "In an emergency meeting of the Council late last night, it became apparent that substantial evidence was building to prove the incident had been arranged by her—four witnesses in the Council, to name only a few. We could none of us stand by such a slaughter of the Empire's citizens, no matter how dire the current predicament. The Council has decided that the Empress should be removed from office, pending trial—a precautionary measure. We merely wish to escort them to more comfortable surroundings for further questioning on the matter."

Shocked, Eir glanced over at Rika, who was staring calmly at the chancellor, a couple of soldiers gently but firmly holding her arms. If the Empress felt any fear, she was not prepared to show it.

Eir looked up at Randur beside her. "It isn't true . . ."

"I know," he said, bringing her closer to him as several of the soldiers approached them.

"Stay away from her," Randur demanded, holding out his palm to deter them. There was a further disturbance behind as a few of the other guests attempted to help the Empress, but the soldiers restrained them, smacking faces and breaking fingers. They weren't messing around.

"Stand aside," growled one of the men, pulling at the arm with which Randur held her.

"Leave her *the fuck* alone!" Randur threw a punch at one of the men, connecting with his jaw.

"Please, stop!" Eir shrieked in alarm.

Two other soldiers grabbed both of Randur's arms, while a third set to work striking him repeatedly in the stomach, with swift and low and focused punches. When they finally released him, he collapsed to the floor, groaning. Another soldier kicked him across the mouth so that he spat blood across the ballroom floor.

"Please!" Eir cried out. "Let him be, I'm begging you. I'll come, just stop beating him." She couldn't bear to think of what else they might do to him.

As the soldiers dragged her away, blades now drawn, she looked back at her lover sprawled on the floor, his hand held out uselessly.

As if nothing had happened, the chancellor continued his speech, intoxicated by his own rhetoric.

"I have taken it upon myself to save our nation from such a perfidious breach of our sacred laws of hospitality. They will go on trial in the morning, and the public will be made fully aware of their attempted acts of terror. I can assure you, we will bring these two evil women to a suitable justice."

Eir heard these final words as the doors shut behind her.

How could this happen?

Why tonight?

Frightened for her life, the guards that had once protected her now hauled her into the darkness.

CHAPTER 43

THE SOLDIERS HAD LANDED THEIR SHIPS ON THE ICE SOONER THAN BRYND had anticipated. Firm ground was still some way to go, but the ice was so thick here that the horses could be safely unloaded.

The horizon was imperceptible, everything cloaked in all shades of gray and white. At least it wasn't snowing, nor was there any particular wind. A lucky time to be fighting, if you could see anything good in it.

With the fresh recruits in the Night Guard, and the extra forces of the Dragoons, Empire soldiers rode together at a steady pace toward Tineag'l. The two hundred men and women advanced quickly through communities of refugees carrying their worldly belongings to the farthest fringe of their own territory. These people had barely stepped out of their villages, and now were struggling for a new existence, finding new boundaries to their lives. Brynd dispatched twenty of the Second Dragoons to see that these people got safely to the numerous vessels approaching the perimeter of the ice sheets to collect them.

To save causing them unnecessary alarm, Jurro was requested to proceed at some distance from the oncoming refugees. This he did with good grace, though they could doubtless see his hulking figure some distance off.

Brynd took a brief opportunity to interview some of the refugees, hoping to learn more of the unknown enemy. But most were escaping in advance of rumors rather than as a result of firsthand confrontation. Younger boys had the look of confused-excitement on their faces, and discussed the possibility of the new race, of a rogue army, of Varltungs, of beings from other worlds, of gods. In the absence of fact, his men would have to ascertain for themselves what lay ahead.

For hours they rode on across the desolate island. Empty towns and villages were all that remained, framed by these vacant-looking skies. The wind picked up a little, stirring a fine powder that clouded the air immediately around them. They wrapped scarves around their faces, vision now coming through a slit.

All that Brynd might have learned about the geography was deeply covered with snow now. They could have been traveling in an alien world.

"We'll keep riding until we find something," Brynd decided, after being questioned about their current objective. He needed a garuda, but there had been none on standby in Villiren.

Brynd cantered up to the Dawnir who loomed over the men about him. "Is this everything you really wanted, Jurro—the military life, as we know it? Not always the most exciting experience."

"It is for me. You forget I've been staring at the same four walls for so many years. None of the previous Emperors would allow me to leave my confinement."

"Any of this prompt some memories then?" Brynd said. "Nothing surfacing in that big head of yours?"

"Nothing, I fear, so far."

"And what're you hoping to find?"

"Anything will do."

Now wasn't the time to be deciphering Jurro's existential crisis.

Another quarter of an hour, and they were riding north again, and Brynd decided to spread out sections of the First Dragoons east and west, hoping to ascertain if there were any signs of life. They would converge at designated locations at every bell to report on any discoveries.

✷

It wasn't long until bad news came. Brynd had waited for it long enough. First, a private had gone missing beyond the town of Portastam, which lay at the center of the island's eastern plains. His riderless horse trotted to a troop of Dragoon soldiers out on a scout. Three followed the horse's hoof prints to investigate. Only one returned, caked in blood and slumped in his saddle. Finally his unit managed to persuade the shivering man to dismount, revealing that his breastplate had been severed cleanly by something phenomenally sharp.

He did not speak for an hour.

When the words came they were initially incoherent, like the mad incantations of a disturbed beggar on the streets of Villjamur. He juddered. Then he managed to gibber about carnage and slaughter.

Brynd quickly organized his remaining troops and readied them for combat.

Blavat spent a moment enhancing the metal armor of the Night Guard with a *vald,* but she could only strengthen Brynd's saber in such a short space of time. He hoped that the technology of the Ancients would last long enough.

The plan would be to stay as one staggered unit, with the two flanks moving forward, the center slightly behind to form a pincer. The soldiers adjusted their armor and withdrew their weapons while the snow came and went in assiduous gusts.

Brynd shouted some final orders and the Jamur forces rode on.

✳

Cresting a hill, they were presented with a small group of unknown creatures. In the thick of the snow it was impossible to determine what they were, but they were massed there like a regimental unit at the base of the slope, about fifty of them in all, and nothing else as far as the horizon. Brynd had to make a snap decision to either retreat or to charge, because his men were clearly visible now—and Nelum gave a nod to confirm what Brynd himself was thinking, so the call was given, and the Imperial troops, who outnumbered the creatures heavily, rode headlong into combat, hooves pounding against the snow.

Brynd's flank spread out along the side with Apium's waiting briefly then following suit, forming the classic pattern of a pincer attack.

The creatures stood their ground, tilting forward in a uniform movement.

Fifty of them versus over two hundred of the best Jamur soldiers.

Brynd's horse closed the distance to pull ahead of the opposite flank, instinct leading at this pace of combat. He brought down his cultist-enhanced saber flaring purple through the falling snow and cleaved the first creature's skull. It buckled to its knees, but still was taller than any human. The other flanks connected, driving their horses over the enemy. The black armor of their enemy was now distinct against the snow as they lashed out with their claws when the Jamur forces were within range. Brynd could hear his troops howling and grunting all around him as he hacked his way through the enemy. Their shells cracked open and buckled under the ferocious impact of his blows. At first they seemed surprised more than anything, presenting not so tough a challenge, but his soldiers began dropping too. From the corner of his eye he spotted the head of a woman Dragoon getting caught in a giant claw and then her skull exploding as it clamped shut. These weren't the usual tribesmen armed with a few arrows.

Soon horses were collapsing around him in spectacular numbers, slamming their riders to the ground, where they continued to fight desperately. Brynd's flank was now severely diminished. In the end the sheer number of Jamur troops began to prevail, and the last of the horrific creatures were slashed down.

As Brynd dragged his horse out of the bloody scrimmage, a quick head count told him there were only around a hundred Jamur fighters left in all. A hundred of his soldiers had died against just fifty enemy troops.

The survivors, men and women, were pulled from the pulpy mass of the dead and dying, and it wouldn't be long until the snow covered this dark stain on the landscape. Brynd was greatly relieved that most of his twenty Night Guard were still alive. He couldn't spot Apium though, so he rode up to inquire of Nelum.

"There," Nelum pointed over to one side.

Apium lay beside his horse, still alive, but in obvious pain, one foot still caught in the stirrups. Brynd jumped down, unhooked the foot, noting that his friend had pried off his breastplate and was gingerly fingering his chest. From the look of it, a fragment of enemy carapace had penetrated through his ribs.

Snowflakes melted on the febrile exposed skin.

"Blavat!" Brynd looked around for the cultist woman, then waved her toward him.

She dismounted, clutching some relics, placed them to one side. The red-haired man was attempting to speak but produced only staccato puffs, and Blavat then examined the wound while Brynd examined her face.

"What d'you think?" he finally asked her.

"I think I can extract it, but it might have penetrated his lung."

"Just do whatever it takes. What about the enhancements we have? Weren't they meant to help with things like this?"

"It's not that easy, since I have no idea what material the enemy's shells are composed of. It's nothing I've ever seen before, and might not be responsive to my relics."

"Commander!" Nelum drew his attention, gesturing toward one of the creatures they had just vanquished.

He turned to Blavat. "Just see what you can do here." She responded only with a subtle head movement that could have meant anything. He was constantly prepared for his friends dying in combat, but it wasn't something Brynd wanted to face now, and not Apium.

Brynd strode over to Nelum, noticing Lupus standing next to him, bow in hand. Two of the creatures had survived, looking like crustaceans strayed from the sea. In some ways they looked partially human, each with two arms, two legs, but replacing skin were those carapaces which made them so formidable. They appeared charred, melted. So this was it then, these were the terrible creatures causing the genocide on Tineag'l. Right now, sitting in a mire of their dead and dying, they didn't look so impressive. Their bulbous eyes were lidless as they twitched in sharp movements. But what interested Brynd most was their reaction as Jurro stepped alongside them with a book, some kind of bestiary, in his hand. "New creatures, how exciting! Let me see if they are included in here . . . Damn this index."

The two captives raked their heads round with *clicks* to acknowledge the Dawnir's presence, then seemed to motion with their limbs in a manner Brynd didn't understand.

It was perhaps a salute, or perhaps some religious gesture. Seemingly they recognized Jurro, which Brynd pointed out to the Dawnir.

"They know *me*?" Jurro stared dumbly.

"From their reaction to you, they're familiar with either you, or your breed."

Brynd wondered what this might mean to one who spent so long hidden in a dark chamber away from prying eyes. Now, to have another creature actually *recognize* him.

Nelum, ever curious, said, "Say something to them, Jurro. See how they react."

As Jurro bent forward the pair of aliens shied away from his direct gaze.

"What do you think, Nelum?"

"Obviously they know what he is, so I'll bet that wherever they came from, there are more of Jurro's lot."

"Want us to kill them, sir?" Lupus inquired.

Brynd shook his head. "Probably more useful alive."

Thunder sounded on the horizon and he walked away to squint through the snow. In this monochrome landscape, it was difficult to locate the direction of the plangent sound.

Then he spotted, to the north, a thin line of black.

Barely noticeable, on the furthest hill.

The only patch of darkness against the gray landscape and pale sky.

"Nelum," Brynd summoned him and pointed. "More of the same, d'you reckon?"

Nelum regarded the horizon. "It looks that way . . . shit. They'll destroy us, that number of them. We'll have to get back to Villiren. Fast."

"It'll take us hours to reach the ice sheets again."

"Not necessarily so. We took a meandering path here, took plenty of stops."

"Yes, fair point."

Brynd gave the orders for the two surviving creatures to be bound, alive, but requested Blavat to use some relic to knock them unconscious. All she could really manage was to reinforce the chains that confined them. That would have to do for the moment.

He returned to check on Apium, who was now fading from consciousness. Brynd had noticed that the shell had been removed.

"You got it out?" he asked the cultist.

"No, it disintegrated while we tried to extract it. The remaining part's still inside him. I'm sorry."

Apium opened his eyes as if hearing this news. "Commander." The word emerged as barely more than a breath.

"Hang in there. We'll get you strapped on your horse and you'll be all right."

Blavat tugged at Brynd's shoulder, hissed, "But he's going to die. We'll never get him back in time. He'll die."

Brynd stared into her eyes with a feral intensity that made it perfectly clear who was in charge.

"But the serious wounding is internal. It's his lungs and—"

"I don't give a fuck. I'm not leaving him here. Numb his pain."

With that he returned to mount his horse, then rode around the remaining group giving orders for an immediate retreat to Villiren.

✳

Apium coughed blood onto the horse's neck, and when that happened you knew things weren't looking good. The rhythm of the gallop was making him feel even sicker, and he had to keep stopping, holding the others up. Brynd was constantly looking round to check if his friend was all right. Truth be told, it was as if he was thieving every last breath just to stay alive, and Apium hadn't a clue how many more hours he would last.

A piece of shell. Just a piece of fucking shell.

It was funny, in a strange way, now that Apium himself knew he was dying, how it seemed to trivialize these final moments. Another irony was that he didn't feel inclined to tell them about the hole in his boot, or about the frostbite that must be destroying his left foot almost as quickly.

"You want to get up behind me?" Brynd asked at one point.

"No, I'm fine. Leave me behind if you need to."

"Leave you with that lot? You must be joking." Apium followed Brynd's gaze off into the distance.

The black-shells had now gathered behind in enormous numbers, a huge line of them now clearly visible. If fifty had taken so much effort to kill, the thousands in pursuit would surely destroy them. Apium was desperate not to hold up the others.

The effect of Blavat's relics consistently failed, and it felt as if he was inhaling knives.

They didn't train soldiers for this shit.

✳

It went on for hours, this stop-start nightmare chase through the dark. The creatures just kept on coming, and as the Jamur soldiers finally arrived at the ice sheets, the number of enemy had merely increased.

Everyone was beginning to fear that they would never make it to the longships in time, and Apium felt the burden of Brynd's soft glances toward him.

"Blavat," he wheezed, unexpectedly.

Surprised, the cultist woman steered her horse closer to his. "Yes, captain?"

"Those *brenna* devices," he whispered.

"What about them?"

"They're primed for our men to use them, aren't they?"

"They're ready to use, yes. What about it?"

Another deep breath that sliced through his insides.

Apium said, "They work in a chain reaction, yes? I think I might be of some use. In getting you lot away from here."

"I can adjust them so as to work in unison, sure. You really fancy taking that lot on by yourself?"

Nothing in her tone to suggest she cared too much, but then why should she? Only Brynd was keeping him with them. "Yes. Now we're on an ice sheet . . . once I let you all get far enough away, I can detonate the devices so as to cut them off. Once we've put water between you and them, you're safe to get back to Villiren."

"And you?"

"We all know about me. Now, line up those devices." He painfully steered his horse toward Brynd.

Apium told him briefly of his intentions.

"That's insanity. We'll get you back."

"Who's the crazy one, Brynd? Who's the one kidding himself?"

The look in Brynd's eyes said everything that Apium already knew. He didn't want to fail a friend, but it just wasn't practical.

"What do you want me to say?" Brynd grunted.

"You're supposed to commend me on a good plan. At least this way my fat carcass will be worth something." Then, seeing Brynd's expression of dismay, "We're fucking soldiers, Brynd, just pull yourself together."

They shook hands, holding their grip longer than necessary.

"Now . . . fuck off out of here while you still can," he wheezed, forcing a smile.

Apium said brief good-byes to the men, who stared in confusion. Then he accepted the *brenna* devices from Blavat, who quickly instructed him in their subtleties.

Into the darkness, he rode for a quarter of an hour until he was face-to-face with the enemy, with nearly every sharp breath seeming penultimate.

He unwrapped all the *brenna* devices. He dropped one to the ground, hearing it ping on the ice. He turned his horse sideways, dropping the others in as straight a line as he could manage, while the pain became unendurable. He deposited the last *brenna* device in the snow, knowing they were all linked up in whatever way Blavat had configured them.

From the clinking and rustling sounds, the enemy had begun to approach

Sliding from the saddle, Apium gave the last-placed device a gentle twist at its top, barely able to see it in the pitch-black of night.

And with snow whipping against him, all alone in this bleak vista, with his lungs finally collapsing, he wondered vaguely what, if anything, would be waiting for him on the other side.

✳

Behind them, the night sky lit up with an unholy fire.

The ice sheets rocked and lurched and cracked.

The survivors were now close to the longships, where a handful of Jamur sentries stood guard. All of them stood watching this last noble act of Captain Apium Hol.

Nelum realized exactly what had gone on, and silently placed a comforting hand on Brynd's shoulder. A small gesture, but enough.

Tonight they had witnessed real heroism and who would have thought it would be Apium of all people. Chubby old Apium, more interested in carousing than soldiering?

No time for sentimentality. Brynd muttered a bitter prayer for his dead comrade and gave the command to head south.

CHAPTER 44

✳

A FRESH LAYER OF SNOW, NOT THAT THE LANDSCAPE NEEDED IT.

That moment when it had just stopped.

A silence even the air appreciated.

The sun, wherever it was behind all those clouds, was setting—darker and quicker than Dartun had expected. They would make some form of camp here, a cluster of canvas tents pinned to the ice. But what comfort would sleep bring being exposed so far away from solid land?

He looked back at the map, then again regarded the terrain. They had traveled up the western coast without yet engaging with many forms of life. The remoteness appealed to Dartun. Maybe dying didn't seem to matter so much when he was surrounded by an environment so detached from normal existence—it was like you were halfway there anyway. Dogs barked into the wind. His cultist followers remained dutifully on their sleighs. Dozens of the undead stood motionless, waiting for further instructions.

They were now crossing the ice sheets somewhere to the northwest of Tineag'l. Just a year ago and they would have been walking on water. Instinctively, Dartun knew that he wasn't far from one of the Realm Gates.

Verain stepped up alongside, placed her hand on his lower back.

Thick clothing, a fur hood, and beneath it all she looked so distant. "How long, do you think?"

"Not far. Two hours, maybe three."

"Are you getting nervous?" she asked.

"Nervous? Why?"

"I don't know . . . because of what we're discovering. Because we have no idea what to expect on the other side of these gates—if they exist."

"They exist," he said. "They most definitely exist."

"So why don't you *feel* anything, Dartun? You seem to have switched off your emotions."

Verain moved to face him directly, placed her hand on his arm in a tender gesture. "I no longer know what to make of you. You summon the dead to your side. You drag us all on an expedition to find another world. What am I supposed to make of it? You've stopped talking to us—to me. It's as if the Dartun I knew has died, and you're not *him* anymore."

Her words pitter-pattered on, and he tried to ignore them. He *was* dying: that was the whole point, wasn't it? But what did she mean, saying that he was already dead? Had he changed so obviously in the face of his sudden mortality?

✳

Night, and a small fire had been built on the surface of the ice, transforming his cultists into strange purple silhouettes. The dogs had fallen silent, bedding down alongside the sledges so that the only sound here was of the wind, haunting and isolating. Undead men and women shambled in patrols around the periphery of the camp. Dartun explained his situation to Verain, and repeated his statement to the rest of the Order of the Equinox. He had never been clear about his immortality to them, but was now candid.

When Verain looked at him he felt for the first time in months that there was a connection. He had satiated her mind. They headed for their tent. As others chatted outside, in the light of fires that spat against the bleakness of the Tineag'l sky, the pair huddled together under the same blankets, finding a renewed interest in the details of each other's bodies. Only since regaining his mortality did Dartun truly appreciate the texture and fragrance of her skin. Subtleties he had forgotten were rediscovered under his fingertips, his lips.

As his mouth now sought the warmth of her neck, there came a cry from outside. Dartun sat up, peering around the tent as if to locate the source there.

It sounded again.

One of his order in alarm or distress?

Dartun looked back to Verain, who reflected his alert gaze. "Let's see what's going on."

They dressed quickly then headed out into the intense cold where he saw his order gathered in a cluster, on a hillock some way off. He trudged through the snow to see what they were all staring at.

"What's going on?" he demanded.

"Godhi, something on the horizon," someone replied.

Dartun pushed his way to the front and noticed a strange glow where the earth met the sky. Directly north, a faint touch of white light shone like a warning beacon against the surrounding blackness. His heart started to beat quicker: could this be what he was searching for? But why could they see it now and not earlier?

"Fetch my maps," Dartun instructed, still staring in excitement. Within moments, someone was thrusting the documents into his hand.

"Not only there," Tuung observed. "To the east slightly, as well."

Dartun's gaze shifted to his right, where another line on the horizon was glowing. And suddenly he recognized them as a row of torches. There must be hundreds of them, at least an hour's journey away.

"Looks like an army of some type," he decided.

"Jamur?" Tuung suggested.

"Possibly," Dartun replied.

"Do you think they're heading this way?"

"How long have you been here watching?" Dartun inquired.

"Not long. Five minutes at most."

"Let's wait a little longer," Dartun said, then turned to the rest of his followers. "Everyone get ready, round up the undead, put out those fires."

He turned to study the first light. It could have been an atmospheric trick but he could have sworn the white glow there had aggregated into the shape of a doorway.

✳

The scout returned, his light sledge fizzing to a halt. Four dogs panted heavily.

"So what did you see, lad?" Dartun raised his voice above the wind. His cheeks were stinging in the cold, so he brought up his hood.

"I couldn't get very close, but that's no Empire army." Todi shuffled nervously on the ice. "Isn't like any tribe I've ever seen, either. I could swear most of them were wearing some weird kind of armor that covered the entire body."

"Did it look like some kind of shell?"

"Aye, I suppose it could, yes."

"What else did you see?" Dartun urged.

"Rumel, too, but not so many of them, though there's hundreds of the armored things. They've pitched a camp by the looks of it."

"And the other light directly north?" Dartun demanded.

"Shaped like a door, just as you said," Todi replied. "It's big—about four men high."

Dartun had no real idea what a Realm Gate would look like, but this sounded encouraging. However, he tried not to become too excited by the prospect of it. And the army camped closer could well have stepped through it. Dartun was aware that something new had come to this island, and it was far from benevolent.

The coming of the ice really had brought a change upon the Boreal Archipelago.

Todi tossed him back the *deyja,* a small device that caused momentary invisibility.

Dartun was impressed by this youngster. Whilst he might be naive, he was always keen to undertake these risky little missions now and then.

Dartun turned to the others. "Prepare yourselves for an operation of stealth, using every device at our disposal. We head for the gate."

✳

But he couldn't hide the normal sounds made by the sleds and the dogs, nor could anything but darkness hide the undead. Dawn was an hour or so away, the horizon not yet purpling as the Order of the Equinox sped across the flat ice toward the north. Sunrise and sunset were a sudden business this far north. The armed undead ran alongside them, an eerily regular patter to their footsteps, as if they had connected to some distant mind in unison. Dartun didn't actually care what they were connected to, as long as they offered him some protection. Whether they were up to confronting this new race that was invading Tineag'l was another matter, but he had his relics, and he was still the most proficient cultist in the Archipelago. Years of acquiring knowledge wouldn't be wasted.

He crouched, his knees pulled up to his face, riding on a smaller sled along with Verain, Todi and Tuung, the three most trustworthy of his cultists. They traveled at the very front of the group, although the *deyja* was in operation so they couldn't be seen, only their trails in the snow.

It wasn't long before he could discern the peregrine army in more detail. Setting eyes on them for the first time in this crepuscular hour, he thought the assembled creatures shunned light itself, creatures seeking darkness. Not the best omen.

Their sheer numbers were worrying, too. Dartun estimated several thousand judging from the extent of their camp. Rumel mingled with the newer race, their distinctive skin reflecting the glow of torches ranged in neat rows to an almost mathematical precision. Dartun focused his gaze on the gate itself, the object of his travel. Of his desire. That way lay his only hope of finding something to prolong his life once again.

The call of some instrument sounded over to the east.

Torches began to shift, clustering in a manner that suggested a disturbance had been spotted. And Dartun knew full well that he was the focus of this attention. He tapped Tuung on the shoulder, who pulled on the reins to halt the dogs. Dartun pushed himself upright, stepped out of the sled. He picked up a *skjaldborg,* a heavy brass box like a traveler's chest, the same device he had designed for the Jamur forces decades ago. For a moment he headed forward as if to meet the oncoming ranks, even though he had his suspicions that they wouldn't be coming in peace. Dartun placed the *skjaldborg* down with a grunt, arranged it in the snow to face toward the intruders. They were indeed gathering in force now, a mass of black soldiers under the fire of torches. Thousands of them. He opened the relic, took off his gloves, adjusted the tiny dials inside. Closed his eyes, sensing the most minor of movements inside. A difficult task to perform in any weather, let alone out here. As the technology clicked into place, he opened his eyes to see sparks of Dawnir power flicker across its open surface. He stepped back, closed the lid, then glanced up to both sides in turn.

Behind him, his order remained still, an expression of fear on their faces.

"Don't worry." He returned back to join them. "They won't get past that for at least an hour."

"Where did you set the limits?" Tuung said.

"I didn't," Dartun said, and from someone there came a gasp.

Dartun put on his gloves and waited.

The army approached at a rapid pace, flaunting no banners—this was nothing graceful. The rumel rode horses, their heads clear above the level of the armored alien race who traveled just as quickly by foot. They could soon see that this wasn't armor, but a kind of shell. Shell creatures with claws, black and fearsome, but Dartun eyed them with a casual regard, as if watching an experiment.

The thick ice vibrated beneath their feet, responding to the bass thunder of animal and warrior. Some from his order beside him gave a mumble of concern. There must have been over a hundred soldiers now approaching them in two columns, and at thirty paces away, the *skjaldborg* was all that lay between them.

Approaching troops and horses collapsed on impact when hitting the invisible wall cast up by the relic, the others colliding straight into the back of them.

Seeing how it was saving them, this relic didn't seem so much a piece of cultist technology as a makeshift prayer.

There were gasps of agony from behind it as the oncomers still desperately piled into the shield. Horses lurched sideways. Metal armor pinged against the resisting emptiness.

Such power gave Dartun a cheap thrill at times, but he maintained his composure.

The shell-creatures seemed totally unable to comprehend what they faced. Fallen companions looked up from the ground with bulging eyes as the horses trampled them. *At least they're not invincible,* Dartun thought, seeing black blood spit against the flat nothingness and ooze down it as if on glass. To the rumel, at least, it soon became apparent that there was no way through, and some began shouting urgent commands to those at the rear. Their language was none that Dartun recognized.

Eventually the turmoil ceased and the rumel stood observing Dartun calmly, militant voyeurs. He turned to beckon to his entourage. "Come on—don't be shy."

The other cultists joined him. ·

"They look just like the rumels you find in the Archipelago, don't they?" Todi remarked.

"They do indeed," Dartun replied. "Which is interesting, don't you think?"

"How so?" Verain inquired.

"Because those ones have red skins, unlike any of ours. Otherwise they seem anatomically identical. Even those shell creatures aren't all that far removed from what we find in our world. They're bipeds, for one thing. Yet if they stepped out of that Realm Gate," he indicated the glow to the north, "then why would there be any similarities at all?"

"That suggests some evolutionary link to our own world," Todi said. "Or maybe we derive from them in some way."

"Excellent reasoning," Dartun said. His mind was buzzing with theories. "One might go so far as to say our ancestors might have shared origins, then?"

Someone on the other side tried firing an arrow, which struck the shield, stopped in midair, and fell uselessly to the ice. Others scraped the invisible wall with their swords. They weren't going anywhere.

Dartun walked in front of them, his arms folded, scrutinizing them. The armor of the rumel was sophisticated, he noted—intricate designs which had their roots in some of the ancient traditions of the Máthema civilization. They clutched swords, bows, small round shields, which meant interestingly that their technology seemed no more advanced than that of the Boreal Archipelago. Dartun wondered how this race might have evolved totally independently of his own world.

Gasps.

Dartun looked round to see a group of shell-creatures begin advancing upward, digging their claws into the wall generated by the relic. He laughed at this absurd vision, but for a moment he wondered just how high the relic's range would offer sanctuary. He certainly didn't want to take any chances.

One of the creatures finally reached the top of the invisible barrier then fell some distance to the ground, not far from his feet. Within moments, as if perceiving his thoughts, the undead soldiers approached it.

"Make sure they kill it properly." Dartun gestured for the undead to move. They shambled numbly forward, inert, eyes focused at a vague distance. Fifty or so had gathered around their intended victim when another creature dropped from the summit of the unseen wall. As it collapsed on top of the undead, there was not a single sound of protest or alarm.

"Enough now," Dartun decided, turning toward his sled. "We head for the Realm Gate."

✳

Dawn broke with ferocious speed, shadows chased off the ice in the blink of an eye. The sled ride was uncomfortable, the entire company remaining silent. It was as if no one even wanted to mention having just encountered things from another world.

Eventually the sledges came to a halt and everyone stepped off and stood in the same flat landscape they had been traveling through for days.

They watched, still in silence, as Dartun sauntered toward the glow of an immensely high doorway, which seemed to hover just above the ice, fifty paces away. A group of the red-skinned rumel stood by it, armed with swords, but showed no sign yet of having seen either the cultists or the undead. Their armor caught the rays of the new day's sun, and their presence made Verain wonder just how many waited beyond.

She watched Dartun produce an *aldartal,* a narrow brass tube em-

ployed to pause time. As he approached, Todi and Tuung put their
two arms around each other, and—

—suddenly were some way off, now taking a few belongings from
their sled. She looked up to realize that Dartun had just unfrozen her
in time, having the *aldartal* still in his grasp.

"You okay?" Dartun inquired of her.

"Yes," Verain said, pulling her hood up and pushing the loose
strands of her black hair under it. Dartun gave her a loving glance.

"We're finally here. This is it," he said with a smile.

"I'm a little scared."

"It's the unknown, that's all. It's all we're ever scared of. I'll look
after you, I promise."

She looked behind them and saw that everyone else was now motionless. Even the undead stood with precision stillness. Up ahead,
the rumel soldiers, too, were perfectly still. In the snowy haze, the
Realm Gate glowed invitingly.

"I'll just get this lot undone and then we're off," he said cheerfully.
Dartun headed back to free the rest of his order from the bonds of time.

He left the dogs in a state of suspension though, as they wouldn't
be required for the next stage of the journey.

As he marched back to join her, everyone else plodded after him.
It was a surreal sight, these few dozen men and women, all cloaked in
black, tramping across an ice sheet.

They continued toward the red-skinned rumels, Dartun pressing
ahead alone, clearly the most eager. There were twenty rumel in total,
but that showed no indication of their numbers beyond. Were these
ones just as wary about being here in another world as she was to be
stepping into one? A bitter wind forced her head down, but she continued walking in the footsteps of the cultist in front. When she
looked up again she noted how the light from the Realm Gate didn't
cast any shadows. Just how ancient was the technology that had created this thing? It loomed higher and higher, and the nearer she got
to it, the more impossibly tall it seemed.

Above the howl of the wind, Dartun was saying something.
". . . we must now remain cautious, because of our lack of knowledge of what lies beyond. Whatever relics you carry, make sure you
have them at the ready."

His form was now almost just a silhouette against the bright light. She sensed him glance back to her and smile, and couldn't help but be infected by his keenness. The man knew what he was doing. For a moment she forgot about their immediate situation, remembered that they were lovers. Just what exactly did he hope to find here? That was another thing about him, the constant air of mystery. Always playing with secrets.

At that very moment Dartun Súr walked with casual grace into another world.

CHAPTER 45

*

Tuya regarded Marysa as the female rumel stood watching the blurred figure of Jeryd pass the front window on his way to work. Faint flurries of snow slashed past the glass, morning sunlight penetrating in between. As Marysa turned to face her, she realized she was pretty for a rumel. Even without youth on her side, she still possessed a youthful charm. Her dark, almost-black skin gave her an exotic air— you didn't see too many of that color in the city, most being brown or dark gray. Perhaps this added an allure of mystery that Investigator Jeryd could never really solve.

The two women now sat enveloped in thick layers of brown robes that did nothing much for either of them except keep them warm. For a long while there was a tenuous silence brought about from suddenly being brought together. Visitors often possessed the power to inflict self-consciousness on their hosts and she could see a hesitant look in the rumel's eyes, as if she too was uncertain at how to handle the situation.

They were startled by the sound of a snowball striking the window.

"Would you like some tea?" Marysa inquired.

"Thanks," Tuya said, "but you don't have to be polite to me. I can easily understand you not wanting someone like me in your home."

Marysa stood up and walked over to the kitchen area. "Jeryd merely said you were in trouble, and that people were after you."

Tuya wondered if Jeryd had informed Marysa of everything she had been through, of the destruction she may have caused. Not something to bring up, though, as it didn't make for an easy conversation.

"I work as a prostitute," Tuya said bluntly.

Marysa glanced back at her. "Oh."

Another snowball hit the glass.

"It's not as bad as you'd think. I'm selective."

So cozy, with the *clink* of cups, the crackling fire, the water boiling.

"I'm in a little trouble with some people who'll be looking for me. They wanted what I couldn't give them." Tuya laughed inwardly: what exactly could she not give a man? "You know, you're really very lucky to have someone like Jeryd. He seems such a good sort."

"He is." Marysa spun around rather too quickly, her expression warning Tuya to stay away from the husband she loved.

"You know, I've never loved anyone like you must have done," Tuya said. "Never even been in love."

"Really?" Marysa inquired, and there was genuine interest in her tone.

"That's right, never. And I'm in my forties. I've not met any man with whom I could form a connection. I suppose, in my job, it's easier if you don't get too attached to people."

"I can understand that."

Tuya continued, "I've had men who've had their little infatuations with me. Lonely men, in particular, seem to become infatuated so easily."

"Why do you do . . . what you do?" Marysa said, embarrassed but curious.

Tuya thought about this for some time. "I'd like to say for the money. It's easy money, after all. I don't have to do much, just use whatever I've been blessed with. But there's an emptiness now that I just can't explain, like a spiritual scar." She touched the side of her face. "Sometimes you know you've walked so far down a particular path that you've nothing left but your dignity. Dignity to keep on down that very same path, even though it's the wrong one. Because when you stop, when you think . . . that's when it hurts the most. Some sort of dignity is all I've got left."

Tuya resisted the urge to cry but she could tell by the fact that

Marysa was now walking toward her that she was failing in this. Marysa placed a hand gently on Tuya's.

A sound now from the roof.

Tuya looked up. "What's that?"

"It's those damn kids," Marysa said, "throwing snowballs at our house. It usually stops after half an hour, but it doesn't half drive you crazy."

A snowball smashed the windowpane and exploded inside, accompanied by squeals of childish laughter.

✳

Now working in his chambers, Jeryd checked his crossbow. They didn't make them now like they used to. You used to get some slick firing mechanisms that were so straightforward to reload. Insert and *click*. The new one he held in his hand was problematic, because you had to insert the bolt so deep before it locked in place. Sure, it fired much further, so they claimed, but you spent far too much time reloading, in which time a knife could rake across your throat and it was all over. He needed something quick and deadly, promising a swift shot in the dark. The rumel held the weapon this way and that, then shook his head. It would have to do.

His colleague Fulcrom entered the room. "Have you heard these extraordinary rumors about the Empress and her sister? They're planning to execute them on the city wall tomorrow evening."

Jeryd whistled in astonishment. "Whose call?"

"Council decision, it seems. The arch-inquisitor approved the judgment apparently. She was planning to have all the refugees killed, but was arrested at the Snow Ball by the chancellor, who intercepted her plans and put both Rika and Eir on trial late last night. Quite the show apparently. They tried to deny it, but the documents were there for all to see, and many of the councilors confessed that Rika had approached them, consulting on issues like disposing of bodies and the likes. Some claimed that the sisters had issued beatings from guards to silence them, and one guard—someone I'm sure has links to Urtica—admitted this. They said they were glad of the opportunity to get it all out in the open. They praised Urtica for his guile in seeing that the Empire's people were safe. And despite all this stuff on the surface, deep down in the heart of the city, it seems people really *are* being taken in to be killed."

Jeryd took it all in, nodding slowly, not really surprised, but it didn't stop him feeling disgusted over what went on up there, in that black vault of Balmacara. "It couldn't be Lady Rika that organized the underground killings. It just couldn't be."

"No," Fulcrom agreed. "I reckon this is to do with certain councilors . . . and Ovinists. It's something much darker to take advantage of this distraction. It's all been worked out in complex detail, so whoever's in the Ovinists . . . well, they're certainly smart."

Jeryd said, "This is Urtica's work, all right, all of it, and we've not got one damn piece of evidence against him. Our only witness, if you can call her that, is both a prostitute and a murderer, and if we say a single word out of line, we'll be thrown in some cell and forgotten about— that's if we're lucky. Urtica must have a huge network of his damn cult in operation, from laborers to Inquisition personnel to councilors. The trial's got to be a smoke screen, something to focus everyone's attention on while he's engaged in the business of genocide."

Fulcrom added, "Updates are being nailed to the doors of every tavern in the city, and even after midnight I saw a huge crowd around one."

"Did you see what it said?"

"Said something about the dark Empress turning on her own people. If he genuinely has organized all this, then he's the master propagandist. I can't believe the audacity."

Jeryd laughed. "If you've known politicians for as long as I have." He shook his head, remembering the news stories that the Inquisition had to keep under wraps *for the good of the people* so they were told. Cover-ups of the murders of union leaders, the provision of weaponry to various rival tribes to destabilize a region, servants charged with spying. "They were bad enough before these Ovinists got involved, the ubiquitous bastards."

Fulcrom frowned. "Ovinists are everywhere," he said. "Can we even trust each other?"

During the pause, the two rumel eyed each other steadily, knowing the question was totally unnecessary. Jeryd chuckled to himself and muttered, "Fulcrom, if I was an Ovinist, the first thing I'd do would be to make sure I was in a better job than this."

Fulcrom seemed to like that.

Jeryd continued, "So who the hell d'you think will take over the Jamur Empire? Can you imagine that pompous git Urtica being in charge?"

Fulcrom shrugged. "Not our call to make."

"No, indeed." Jeryd took a moment to rid himself of splenetic thoughts. "So, to business. We've got some people to save."

Fulcrom moved nearer to Jeryd. "Soldiers have made some movements around one of the tunnels. It's the one they're letting the first wave of refugees into, and it's one of the older tunnels. I've got it marked on a map."

"Good," Jeryd said. "Any idea how many?" *So this is it. It's really happening.*

Fulcrom shook his head. "No, all I got was the tip-off. As for some help, I've managed to round up a few of the young investigators who still have principles."

"Can they be trusted, though?"

"They know what they're in for and just how secret this must be."

"Fair enough." Jeryd knew he could rely on Fulcrom's selection. "There's just one thing we've to do on the way."

✳

Jeryd knocked hard on the metal door of Mayter Sidhe's house of banshees, as Fulcrom glanced left and right along the snow-covered street. Only a few people were out and about, hunched under so many layers of clothing that you could hardly see their faces.

It took much longer than usual for the door to open. That alerted Jeryd's suspicions, but he knew something was definitely wrong when Mayter Sidhe answered the door herself.

"Investigator," she said, her blue eyes a shade dimmer than previously. She glanced nervously at Fulcrom.

"It's okay, he's with me," Jeryd said.

"You'd better come in," she beckoned.

No fragrance this time, no welcoming fire. The place was as cold as the street outside. A couple of chairs were broken and left in the shadow of the stairway.

"Where are the others?"

She gestured for the two rumel to sit down, but they insisted on standing.

"Why are you here?" she asked.

"We just want a chat," Jeryd said, and told her everything he could about the threat to the refugees, going on to state that he would appreciate it if the banshees would forbear to draw attention to any conspirators' deaths that might occur during his intended raid on the tunnels.

"This explains much," she sighed. Her expression was full of sadness.

"Explains what?" Jeryd said.

"Wait here a moment." She left the room and returned with one of the younger banshees, looking like a smaller replica of herself.

Jeryd was about to say something, but Mayter Sidhe held up her hand to silence him. She turned to the girl. "Show the investigator."

The young woman shook her head, manically, her eyes filled with a fear Jeryd had never seen before.

"Show the investigator," Mayter Sidhe repeated insistently.

After a moment, the girl opened her mouth.

Her tongue was missing. Scar tissue had already begun to blossom. Jeryd grimaced, glancing at Fulcrom who also looked appalled. The girl began to sob, then hurriedly left the room.

"A few nights ago," Mayter Sidhe said calmly, "some masked men broke into our house. They did this to everyone—took the tongues of everyone apart from me. I was the only one not at home. A couple of the girls bled to death on their beds, including my youngest who was only ten."

"Who did this?" Jeryd asked horrified.

"I wasn't here to see. And none of them can now tell me exactly what went on. All my girls are forever silenced."

Jeryd couldn't find the words to express his disgust.

"So you see," she continued, "someone has already asked for much the same favor that you did, just a little more forcefully."

Mayter Sidhe would say nothing further.

Jeryd knew instantly what was going on. Whoever intended to kill the refugees had realized that the banshees would soon raise the alarm over death on such a large scale. Their screams would inevitably draw in someone to investigate.

So the witch women of Villjamur had been made inert, silenced for good.

✳

Jeryd greeted the assembled investigators with a curt nod as they huddled in a damp, mold-covered underground passage. There were a couple of sword tips poking out beneath cloaks, and a ceaseless drip of water somewhere added to the gloom of the melancholy room.

Jeryd had considered it best for everyone to remain anonymous to each other, so he had assigned each of the young rumel a number from one to ten. After briefing them all precisely, he and Fulcrom again consulted some maps. Networks of passageways as old as civilization itself were already committed to memory and the two rumel had discussed the best access routes, the best exits. There was one way out for those refugees who were being brought into the tunnels. Two if you included death.

Jeryd finally checked the crossbow hidden under his cloak, checked the knives tucked in his boots, the small sword that hung at his side.

Now, off to work.

✳

Down here the passages were so narrow in places that you had to walk sideways. Jeryd wondered what kind of people were of this slender girth a thousand years ago. Where there was no light, you relied on touch to get you through until you reached the next shaft of light illuminating the path. The walls were damp and cold, with lichen and mold proliferating wherever light struck the stone. Their companions were the usual rats, which was only to be expected. Still, at least there were no damn spiders—he shuddered to think how he'd react to spiders in such a tight space as this, and in front of so many other men from the Inquisition. Above them, Villjamur was experiencing another day, just like any other, unaware of the thousands of people whose lives were now under threat.

For half an hour they traveled underground until it was too deep to expect any external light. Fulcrom carried a torch ahead of Jeryd to guide the way, while boots shuffled reassuringly behind.

Into Villjamur's heart of darkness.

According to intelligence reports, refugees would be brought here in small numbers and disposed of over a long period of time. The first and unluckiest refugees were going to be, or already were, confined in one of three escape tunnels leading over to the west. As to how the refugees were to be killed, no one yet knew. Perhaps it would be a simple, brutal execution by the sword, but, on this scale, who would have the nerve to do that to the Empire's citizens? There would be so much panic probably, so maybe the methods would be more discreet, more subtle.

Fulcrom paused, held out a warning hand that Jeryd saw only when he had walked into it. Everyone else stopped.

"What's up?" Jeryd whispered.

Fulcrom held a finger to his lips, tilting his head as if to better hear some sound. Jeryd listened too. Faintly, they could hear voices through walls. How far away, he could not decide.

"I'd say they're a level below us," Fulcrom ventured. "We're not far off."

Jeryd replied, "Where will the city guard be?"

"Probably at the entrance to that same level. There are three access routes, and we're following one of them. They, however, will most likely approach from the direction of the Council Atrium, so we're fine here."

"Press on?" Jeryd suggested.

"Hold this a moment." Fulcrom handed Jeryd the torch, then he took off his cloak and let it drop to the floor. Everyone followed suit till their metal weaponry glittered openly in the torchlight.

Jeryd handed back the torch and began loading his crossbow.

✳

The small band of investigators approached the next stairwell leading down. No guards were in evidence, but Jeryd's heart still thumped in expectation. He leaned over to Fulcrom, whispered, "Put the torch out now?"

"Sure. Then give it a few minutes to let our eyes adjust."

They stood there in darkness and listened to the groans and whispers of people massed below them. This pitiful sound at least meant they were still alive. Jeryd felt spurred on by pity and determination. If there was any good left in this world, he would have them saved.

Water dripped all around them and the slightest breeze came from some concealed opening further along.

"Let's go," Fulcrom hissed.

They shuffled forward as one, Jeryd opening one of the pockets containing his crossbow bolts. His nerves vibrated, surprising himself that an old rumel could still feel intensely.

A single torch was fixed to the wall at the far end of the passage. Rat-shadows moved constantly, distracting the eye. Further along sounded voices, footsteps.

Jeryd and Fulcrom both held their crossbows up, ready to discharge. The investigators around them drew their short swords.

A soldier suddenly turned a corner, spotted them, reached for his sword, and just as he was about to open his mouth to raise the alarm, Jeryd loosed his crossbow. The man's head snapped back as the bolt struck him full in the face; he collapsed under the light of his own torch.

Jeryd reloaded, advanced to check upon the guard. The splattered blood on stone told him all. He nodded to Fulcrom, gesturing him forward. At this point, the corridor angled to the right, leading into darkness.

In their silent progress another guard was dispatched before he could react. After compacting his body into a dark corner, they continued on toward the sound of voices.

Around another turning, there were two further guards, and the noise was increasing. Two shots: one soldier dead, the other merely wounded. Immediately the younger investigators rushed forward, swords out ready, while Jeryd and Fulcrom reloaded. The sound of clashing metal. When Jeryd arrived at the corner he saw his colleagues engaged in combat with three more city guards. Jeryd prepared to fire again but it was unnecessary. All three of the soldiers were soon dead, blood pooling around them.

We're close now, Jeryd thought.

Again they hauled the corpses to dark corners. "Good work, lads," Jeryd commended them.

Forward, again with weapons ready, to a well-used corridor. They passed an arm detached from its body, dried blood arcing up the walls in a manner suggesting an execution.

Another soldier was posted outside a closed door, and the look on his face said he didn't want to be there.

Fulcrom's distant shot wasn't clean, so Jeryd was obliged to fire his at closer range, his bolt catching the man in the throat and throwing him back against the stone. Jeryd searched the body for a key to the door till Fulcrom pointed out that it wasn't locked, merely bolted shut from the outside.

Into the room beyond.

Tryst looked up from the table, two guards hovering behind him. "What the—?"

"I might've known you'd be involved, you bastard," Jeryd spat at him.

The younger investigators came swarming past him and the guards backed off, outnumbered. They dropped their swords with a clang and held up their hands. One of the investigators looked back to Jeryd questioningly.

"We can't take any prisoners," he sighed.

Swords were thrust below the breastplate of each soldier, and they fell to the floor in disbelief like drunks at the end of a long night out.

Jeryd stepped toward Tryst, who had now backed against the wall.

"So you're an Ovinist, too," Jeryd said sadly.

Tryst managed an uncomfortable nod.

Jeryd grunted a laugh. So his own subordinate was really working for Urtica. Somehow that didn't surprise him. The depths this man had already gone to were ridiculous.

"How can you be here? You can't. I mean—"

Jeryd thumped him repeatedly in the stomach. "*What* exactly do you mean? Don't think I won't rip out your fucking tongue if you don't."

Tryst eventually stammered something of a response. "I . . . set cultist devices to work on your house. They should have killed you."

Jeryd glared at him. "You mean my home is rigged to do what exactly?"

"To explode . . . I didn't want to. I was forced to."

Jeryd thought immediately of Marysa sitting at home with Tuya.

"Why should I believe you?" Jeryd said. "After all your damn lies."

"Jeryd, I really think you should go back home to see everything is fine. Forget about these refugees—they mean nothing to the likes of us. Just go and we can forget all about this. Come on, Jeryd, I know we've had our ups and downs."

"Ups and downs? You bastard. You've betrayed me. You've betrayed yourself." Jeryd lowered the crossbow, and Tryst relaxed. In one fluid movement, Jeryd swiped the weapon across his assistant's face, knocking his head back hard against the stone. Tryst fell with a gasp, and Jeryd kicked him once in the stomach. "Now tell me what the hell you're doing here. You're obviously involved with killing off the refugees but how?"

His boot across Tryst's throat, the crossbow aimed.

Tryst weakly indicated the table on which stood several bottles of liquid and some measuring instruments.

"Go have a look," Jeryd urged to Fulcrom. Then, to Tryst, "How were you going to do it?"

"Toxin sprays and serums. Kills painlessly within the hour."

"How many have you killed so far?"

"Only about fifty."

Jeryd said, "And how many are left down here?"

"Hundreds, but thousands are to come at a later date. We wanted to get rid of them slowly so as not to cause suspicion. We've only taken the first batch . . ."

"Where are they? Through there?" Jeryd indicated a door at the far end of the same chamber.

Tryst nodded.

For a moment Jeryd considered what value Tryst still presented. Then he thought about his home, about the deadly threat to Marysa.

"Who's behind all this?"

Tryst lay still. Not a flinch or flicker. Instead he stared past Jeryd at the ceiling, a glazed look in his eye as if he was already dead.

The old rumel looked down at Tryst.

He thought of his own wife.

He thought of the deceit.

Jeryd fired a bolt through Tryst's eye.

Reloaded.

He took out his knife and slit the man's throat before fiercely regarding the others. "We can take no prisoners. Remember, no witnesses."

"Right," grunted Fulcrom, turning away.

*

The stench of them came first. The crowd of prisoners had been held here for only a short while, possibly only a day or two, but without food and water. Hundreds of faces, the first wave of people destined to be poisoned, tilted toward the investigators without a sign of either expectation or fear—just resignation. Men and women with children in their arms, slumped against the walls or sprawled on the cold stone floor of the wide tunnel, with just the few rags and blankets they had carried with them for warmth, unaware they'd been brought here to die.

Jeryd walked around them, telling them of their situation. Told them of the threat. Did they understand him, did they believe him? Did they want to leave and enter the ice again?

Among them lay the dead, one or two with the living still clinging to them. Bodies turning blue with poison, bodies shriveling like fruit . . . One of his men was retching violently behind him, and Jeryd could hardly blame the man.

People began clamoring for food and water, but all Jeryd could offer them was their freedom—a concept that seemed to confuse.

"We have to get you out of here," he called out repeatedly. Then, to Fulcrom, "Let's open up the other end of the tunnel, wherever that is."

Jeryd left two of his men by the door they'd come through, and eight of them now progressed through the crowd of refugees to investigate what lay ahead. The air seemed oppressive. Occasionally a woman would scream, and a man would groan.

They finally reached another makeshift door, metal and firmly closed. He knew a sentry would be posted beyond it, so they eased it open a fraction, then kicked it wide. Fulcrom's crossbow bolt caught the single soldier who was already rising from his chair, then they rolled his body into darkness.

The further they progressed, the colder it became, and despite there being no light, Jeryd sensed they were close to the exit. Eventually they were making headway by touch alone along a narrow passageway, yet as long as they were in darkness, nobody could see them.

Then finally it came, freedom.

A burst of light and cold air, followed by the adjoining wastes of a refugee camp—a battered tent-city, dying fires, black silhouettes of trees on the horizon, wind wailing in across the tundra. And if you looked back you could see the outer wall of Villjamur looming, which these unfortunate people had been staring at optimistically for months.

"Go and lead them through," Jeryd ordered to one of his men. "Force them, if necessary, if they seem unwilling to leave shelter."

It took them an hour to get everyone out. The refugees came shambling out into the open, with obvious reluctance. They stared at the snow as if they had never seen it before.

Their joyous liberation was something of an anticlimax.

Jeryd, for his part, felt more depressed and exhausted than he had ever done in his life.

When the last child had trotted free, Jeryd dispersed his anonymous band, their Inquisition medallions being enough to see them safely past the soldiers at the gates.

Fulcrom now faced Jeryd, a look of misery upon both their faces, and they were searching each other to find the right thing to say.

"It doesn't feel as good as it should do."

"No," Jeryd agreed.

"They could die even sooner out here, in this ice," Fulcrom observed.

The younger rumel was right. The Freeze itself would most likely kill them sooner or later. Now they were merely refugees once again outside the gates of Villjamur, and what could they do now?

"Do you want to get back to your house?" Fulcrom suggested.

"I should." Jeryd shuddered. "There's a danger that Tryst might have been telling the truth for once in his miserable life."

"I'll go with you, in case I'm needed."

What a strange feeling it was to have a colleague thinking after his safety.

✳

As the street wound its way upward in a gentle arc, they trudged the cobbles doggedly feeling their thighs ache. Jeryd contemplated how old he was getting.

Fulcrom suddenly pointed out a black trail of smoke wafting across the wind-tossed sky.

Jeryd began to run up the hill, leaving Fulcrom pointing behind him, fearing the worst.

Toward the smoke.

Toward his house.

Passersby in the street stared at him because so few people ever ran these days, what with the constant snow on the streets. Even a dog barked in surprise. Then he fell on the ice, struck his knee on a cobble. Cursing, he pushed himself up and limped on.

✳

Fulcrom arrived a moment later to find the old rumel on his knees in the snow, in front of the debris of his home. Fragments of wood were strewn across the entire street in countless splinters, broken bits of furniture were smoldering, roof tiles and shattered glass lay everywhere, and where Jeryd's house once stood, there was now merely a ragged hole.

Fulcrom walked over and placed his hand on Jeryd's shoulder. The old rumel was gently pawing at some fleshy remains.

Fulcrom cringed. It could once have been a foot.

A young investigator approached, a gray-skinned rumel not long signed up.

Jeryd tilted his head toward him as if he could offer him his life back.

"Were you first on the scene?" Fulcrom inquired.

"Yes, sir. My name's Taldon, and I've been here a quarter of an hour. We've searched the remains and we've found one body so far, but no one could have survived this. The damage is immense."

Jeryd began to shake violently. Fulcrom released his shoulder, gestured for Taldon to go.

"I'm . . . I don't know what to say. I'm so sorry."

The old rumel merely sobbed, clutching at the snow like a child. Fulcrom couldn't believe this. After all Jeryd had done for the city over the years, to receive such recompense. Because of Tryst. Or Urtica?

"If the chancellor wanted you dead, Jeryd," Fulcrom advised, "it's probably not too safe to hang around here long. He might still be out to get you."

"A moment," Jeryd sobbed. "Just give me a moment."

"I'll take you home with me. Then I'll look after it all, okay?"

A scream, a female voice calling. Marysa came running through the snow.

Jeryd looked up as she ran toward him, her hair bouncing.

The two of them hugged each other so tight they might have become one entity, and still Jeryd would not let her go.

At last, through his tears, he asked her, "How did you . . . survive?"

"It was those kids with the snowballs. They smashed a window and I went out to chase them away down the street." She began to cry too, perhaps imagining for the first time what could have happened to her. And Fulcrom loved this irony, that Jeryd's tormentors, the Gamall Gata kids, were responsible for saving his Marysa.

There were about eight of the same kids hovering nearby, though empty-handed now. And Jeryd smiled at them, waved, then he laughed through his tears.

The kids shrugged, a little confused, and a blond one shouted, "Sorry about your window, Jeryd. We didn't do the rest though, we swear."

"I know," Jeryd said, a peaceful smile on his face. He began to chuckle, tears in his eyes. "Don't worry, I know."

Fulcrom wondered about the woman, Tuya, who was presumably dead—no one could have survived an explosion like this. From what Jeryd had told him, she'd led a lonely life, and he felt sorry that there was no one to mourn her, no one to even know she'd been killed. How many faces must she have seen in the night? There were hundreds of thousands of people in Villjamur, and hardly any of them would have meant a thing to her. He felt a pang for her exit from the world, despite having never known who she was.

People moved on, and the Gamall Gata kids trotted off, all apart from the blond and redhead, who stayed for a little while longer, looking on as the snow fell in thick, heavy streaks while Jeryd and Marysa remained in the cold, clutching each other as tightly as they could.

Kneeling in the wreckage of their lives.

Interview with Chancellor Urtica, to be nailed to the door of every tavern and Jorsalir church by order of the Council.

HISTORIAN: Thank you for seeing me, chancellor. Can you just confirm, for posterity's sake, why you've organized for an interview to be issued across Villjamur?

URTICA: Certainly. We're about to organize the executions of the Empress Rika and her sister tomorrow, and we will be starting the Empire afresh. I have been selected as the only candidate to go forward and construct the new era—an era of more open politics, with nothing to hide. What more suitable a manner to do this than with interviews? With pamphlets circulated around bistros, taverns, and whatnot, I can communicate with the people. I am, after all, a man of the people. So it is a new kind of leadership, and it is time the people had honesty from their leaders—not as before with a madman and then a murderess!

HISTORIAN: Well that certainly sounds encouraging. Now, could you tell us a little about the strange circumstances surrounding Rika's exit?

URTICA: I'm very sad to see that a woman would want to do something like killing her own people. It was simply wrong. I found out about it, of course, and I investigated further—it was clear that Rika and Eir had signed a document requesting the refugees be killed. The Inquisition followed it up, of course. The Council decided that this level of deception is unacceptable, so I did what I could to save thousands of lives and my efforts were rewarded by the Council.

HISTORIAN: Will you therefore be letting the refugees in as a peace offering in these dire times?

URTICA: Unfortunately no, the refugees suffer from dreadful diseases

that could harm our people. And it is suggested there are tribal terrorist factions among them who wish to penetrate the city in order
to destabilize our democratic ways. We cannot permit such a risk.
Unfortunately, this might also mean that we must conduct more
searches on the streets of the city—in such treacherous times, we
must join together in purging Villjamur of such evil, tribal radical-
ism.

HISTORIAN: There were rumors of a botched military operation on the
far side of the Empire recently. Could you enlighten your subjects
as to those events?

URTICA: These are searching questions! I shall remain honest with
you: several regiments of our brave soldiers were crossing an ice
sheet when a savage band of Varltung warriors used cultist trickery
to destroy them. Our troops didn't stand a chance. As a result, I will
be declaring open hostilities against all Eastern tribes and, as soon
as is possible, we might initiate a full-scale invasion.

HISTORIAN: Some people have suggested that your missions to the
Varltung islands might be merely to claim more resources. What do
you say about this?

URTICA: It is utter nonsense.

HISTORIAN: Has your ascent to the most senior position of the Empire been challenged in any way?

URTICA: Well, it's important to remember that I was in a hugely senior
position even within the Council. Perhaps second only to the Empress in terms of role. Due to this fact, that I helped to save thousands of lives, and also that several other Council members
supported me for Emperor, the majority vote was with me. We are
not a barbaric people—of course the matter was debated heavily,
and this is a democracy we live in, after all. I was the chosen one.

HISTORIAN: Chancellor Urtica—soon to be Emperor Urtica—thank
you for your time.

URTICA: Thank you.

CHAPTER 46

✻

Randur tramped along the streets of Caveside, collar flipped up, head down, a couple of bags slung over his shoulder. He was a totally focused man. His ribs still ached from the beating he received from the soldiers in Balmacara. The dogs that ran around his feet were skinny to the point of death, with no energy even to bark and he knew that feeling all right, was himself close to it right now.

He approached Denlin's house, then stopped and stood looking at the door. If he was the religious sort he would have said a prayer right now, because things were that bad. He couldn't believe what had happened, how his life had changed so quickly. One moment she was in his arms, amid the dazzling pinnacle of wealth and society, all elegant postures and smiles, the focus of everyone's gaze. And now she was locked away with an order of execution hanging over her.

Randur didn't believe for a minute that she was guilty. She didn't have it in her, and he knew her almost better than anyone. And he couldn't believe her sister capable either. This had the trappings of a setup, but it was outside his control. You couldn't fight directly with people that well connected, with that much influence. His problem now was how to get her out of there. If he succeeded, from that point on he'd be a hunted man, so he had to get himself well clear of Villjamur too.

He banged on Denlin's door, glancing across the decaying structure of the house. There were architectures in this city that were beyond his comprehension, astonishing in either their complexity or simplicity, employing layers and techniques that were alien to more recent craftsmen.

The door creaked open. ". . . fucking knocking at this time? Oh, Randy lad, what can I do you for? You look right pissed off." Denlin, standing in white nightwear, waved him in.

Randur said nothing as he passed through the doorway and dumped his bags on the table. "You alone?"

"No, I have several of the most sexually active women in the city keeping my bed warm," Denlin muttered as he closed the door.

Randur sat down at the table.

"What's wrong then?" Denlin took a seat opposite him, poured himself a cup of water from a jug, gesturing for Randur to help himself. The young man shook his head.

After a moment, Randur opened one bag, pulled out a purse of money, the same purse that Eir had given him as payment for Dartun Súr, and clutched it on his lap, frowning in contemplation of some distant fury. "I need you to gather together some of the toughest men you know. And to get hold of some swords."

Randur explained the dramatic events at the Snow Ball, explained what his plans were.

Denlin observed, "A right bollocksed-up situation."

"You could say that. But can you help? Look, Den, I need your help now in a big way. It's more than likely I'll need you to leave the city with me, and I've no idea when we'll ever get back. *If,* that is, we survive. We'd be going up against the city guard, and up against the Council. It won't be pretty, however . . ." Randur opened up the bag of money then began to count it all out, all in Jamúns. Every next one that he placed on the table, Denlin whistled softly, his eyes growing wide.

Randur said, "I realize that it seems a lot, but this is for you if you help me out. It might go some way to providing a decent life for your nieces during the Freeze. It'll buy them a nice education, decent food. Because you yourself might not have much use for it if you're on the run. As for the rest of this money, well, we're going to need the best weapons, the best fighters—a private army, if you like. Possibly the roughest bunch—ones most likely to have grudges against the Council and their kind."

"Shouldn't be too hard, that," Denlin muttered. Then, "How many men do you need, like?"

"However many it buys. It's real danger money, but I need enough men to overwhelm the city guard."

Denlin said, "And you want me to go with you, after it's all done?"

"Yeah, we'll need some extra protection. You used to be a demon archer in your younger days."

"Aye, I was, lad." Denlin wore that distant look of a man remembering his youth, of those bittersweet regions that only he could explore. "This lot could keep the girls living well for years. A rare chance, given all the misery around. So to rescue this girl of yours, you'd give up any hope of helping your mother?"

There was no way Randur could rationalize his answer. It wasn't simply a question of which one he loved more—there were different kinds of love involved. All he knew was that he must follow his current instincts. Maybe he'd regret it in the future, but he was someone who made this sort of decision on impulse. "It was her money to start with," he mumbled.

Randur held eye contact with the old man, and something passed between their glances. "I really need your help, Den."

"Aye, count me in. I never got to be a proper hero in the damn army, but maybe I can be to my girls instead. So, when d'you need these fellows by?"

"Tomorrow afternoon at the latest. The Council plan to execute Eir and Rika at sunset."

✳

They began to gather inside the Garuda's Head, sixty-six of the roughest types money could buy. The landlord reckoned he had never seen such a profitable evening. Randur had paid for only one round though. Clear heads would be needed. Denlin mingled with the throng, a socialite among these down-and-outs. There were about twenty rumel, brown-skinned or gray-skinned, and thirty-four humans, their faces mostly concealed beneath their hoods. Some of these thugs were even meant to be from the underground anarchist group. There were weapons in abundance. Denlin had even managed to get hold of two garudas who had been sacked from Imperial duty. Fortunately, Denlin knew the hand-language they responded to.

As he murmured instructions to several of the gathering, every now and then the old man would gesture toward Randur. Scarred heads would turn in his direction, and Randur would shuffle nervously under their gaze. He had made a point of not carrying the rest of the cash on him. One payment up front, the rest securely hidden till later. Denlin himself had thought it best this way.

Denlin struggled to climb onto a table, clasping a spoon and a metal tankard. He rapped the one on the other to get everyone's attention. A reluctant silence fell. "Right, you lot, I've gone through the details with all of you individually. Now, Randur here is going to say a few words."

Randur leaped onto the table with his dancer's agility, conscious of how sixty-six people looked four times as many when you were stood up in front of them.

He cleared his throat. "You know the arrangement. I'm betting most of you don't care about that. But there's something else I need to say. We have to save two innocent women from this bastard Council, the same one that uses its powers to keep you lot trapped down in the caves year after year. Here's your chance to put one over on the fuckers, and to make some cash in the process."

A cheer went up around the tavern. They liked that. Randur glanced across at Denlin, gave him a relieved grin.

Randur detailed what was essentially Denlin's strategy. The old man had the better knowledge of the city, of how things worked, of how public executions were conducted. It wasn't a wonderful plan. It wasn't even a particularly well-thought-out plan. But Randur hoped it would suffice. The councilors themselves wouldn't provide much opposition, being politicians, not fighters.

It was street thug against soldier, the rough stuff.

Randur himself would at least offer some fine sword skill, a little flair maybe where it was needed.

In response the hired men thrust their fists in the air, an eerie unison to the gesture.

One by one, the participants slipped out of the tavern till Denlin and Randur stood staring at each other in sudden emptiness, and the evening seemed to take on a new quality entirely.

"Your weapons," Denlin said finally, heading behind the bar and returning with a small bundle of blankets.

"I'm not fighting with cloth," Randur quipped.

Denlin heaved it onto the bar counter with a *clunk*, peeled back the material to reveal a couple of swords, newly crafted, simple and slender, without much ornamentation.

Randur lifted one to test its weight. "Shit, you've excelled yourself, Den. Where did you get these?"

"Finest backstreet smith in the city. They breed 'em tough, down Caveside. Tough metal. Tough men."

Randur lifted the sword this way and that, then strode through a few moves, fetching glances from the landlord. "That's a better weapon than any in Balmacara."

"Of course," Denlin said with a genuine satisfaction.

Randur returned to check the other sword was identical.

"Who's the other sword for?" Denlin inquired.

"It's for Eir," Randur explained. "And now we'd better get going. We've got garudas to catch."

✳

It was difficult to judge when the sun was setting, since too many clouds obscured it. There was no snow, at least, which would make things easier for the garudas.

All available spaces between the two encircling walls were people-thick. Against normal practice the guards had let them in to watch this historic event. Much of the city had gathered, citizens leaning from every convenient window or balcony. Randur himself was standing with Denlin and the two garudas on a rooftop though the wind was so vicious it was likely to transform their bones to ice. In this light the garudas looked more decrepit than previously. One of them was missing feathers in places, and its beak was heavily scarred as if it had been tortured long ago.

The house belonged to a woman of the court he had spent a couple of evenings romancing, and she still succumbed to his charms. It gave the four onlookers a view of everything they needed. They could see all the three walls surrounding the city. On the outermost one, the two young women would be executed, and that was the one Randur had to get to. That wall was fairly narrow, which would work in their favor since only a couple of soldiers could come against him at a time.

"Den, why're there so few guards?"

Denlin sniffed, scrutinized the scene. "You're right, lad. Haven't a clue. Perhaps there's something going on somewhere else. Something not that good, I'd wager."

"You reckon that explosion we heard earlier was anything to do with it?" Randur suggested.

"Who knows, lad. Rumor is that a house collapsed, so I doubt it."

Randur explored his paranoia. "Another thing, have you heard a banshee scream recently? I haven't heard anything for a day at least."

"Perhaps no one's died," Denlin said. "Though I doubt that."

A soldier garuda circled the city, seeming to cast a lingering glance their way, but with this many people about, they probably would not be the only suspicious ones to watch. Not in Villjamur.

Drums from somewhere, a slow beat, deep and low.

This was it then. Randur and Denlin braced themselves, and Denlin signed to the two garudas. He reached into his pocket to pluck out his horn.

They waited anxiously.

Eir and Rika were escorted forward from a doorway, guards in front, guards behind, ten in all. Two at the front held bows ready-drawn. The two women were bound by rope at the wrists, and were clothed in the same brown garments that all prisoners were forced to wear. As they commenced the long slow walk to their fate, people cheered or booed from below. Randur had heard about the poor excuse for a trial, the rushed legal procedures and could only speculate about what had gone on behind the scenes. Randur phased the distractions out of his consciousness, tried to concentrate on *Vitassi*, taking his mind somewhere where his emotions wouldn't get in the way.

Deep breaths.

Denlin suddenly blew the horn.

Down between the walls, a fight started, people pushing and shoving toward a troop of soldiers stationed near the gates. Randur thought he saw one of them get his head sliced off. More cheers followed. A soldier on the top of the wall halted the grim progress of Eir and Rika. The crowds below seemed to drift in liquid form, pushing back and forth. One of the inner gates began to close, then for no clear reason, stopped halfway. The guards on the wall looked to each other for some kind of direction. The two archers were now pointing their bows down at the surging tide of people, awaiting instructions.

Denlin produced a bow of his own from under his cloak, flipped the garment aside to reveal a quiver full of arrows. He took aim and fired. By the time the first archer was struck, Denlin had reloaded. He missed the other archer by a handspan, took aim, fired, narrowly missed again.

"Damn wind," Denlin grumbled. Then he made a sign to the garudas.

As the birds seized hold of the ropes already fixed to the belts of their two passengers, Randur gripped his sword in readiness.

The crowd underneath began to riot while Denlin and Randur were pulled skyward, sailing above the scene below of thousands of citizens crammed between the walls.

A soldier-garuda shot toward them from one side.

Denlin looked up in time and aimed and fired. The arrow struck the bird-man's face full on. The creature spiraled into the crowds below, which parted with a liquid elegance suggesting they now moved as a single entity.

Across the first and second walls, dodging arrows from the archer still standing. More arrows whipping from all sides now, but the garudas flew on regardless, hauling Randur this way and that, and it took determination not to be sick from the erratic flight.

The garudas landed simultaneously on the outer wall, with a skidding clamor of boots on stone. Then they released the men onto a surface that could only be four paces across, with nothing either side to keep them from falling to their deaths. More arrows sang past as the garudas took off and faded into the great cityscape above the rioting crowds.

Now for the hard part, Randur thought, as he turned to face the remaining soldiers.

He noticed how the guards had left Eir and Rika standing alone.

Denlin kept taking aim from behind him but his arrows weren't much use against the men's armor. As arrows pinged off the metal, Randur drew his sword, and stepped forward to meet the first of them.

Their heavy broadswords suggested they would be slow in such a narrow arena, which brought a confident smile to his lips.

The first made a lunge at him, bringing his sword down to clang against empty stone, but Randur had skipped back and now flicked his blade up through the soldier's hand, and as the soldier gaped at his wound in disbelief, Randur kicked behind his knee then pushed him over the rim of the wall. Randur drew his other sword and, one in each hand, stared warily at the two men directly in front of him.

Denlin shot an arrow into one's face and with a gurgle he toppled to his death.

"Cheers, Den!" Randur cried out, and began carving into his opponents' frenzied strokes with ease, one sword quickly across a face then, while the man instinctively pressed his palms to the bleeding wound, Randur kicked him off the side harboring the refugees.

A noticeable cheer of triumph from below.

Denlin shot yet another soldier directly in the face, his helmet snapping back into the face of another. Randur continued to ram his blade into any exposed segments of flesh.

Guards continued freefalling to their death.

Down below, soldiers were massing to try to subdue the rioting, not helped by the fact that certain hired thugs kept hauling them to the ground and dispatching them. Then people emerged from the crowds to kick and pummel their victims, venting long suppressed anger on the symbols of power in the city.

At the far end, further troops were gathering at the door giving access to the top of the wall. The few remaining guards approached him cautiously, thrusting their swords toward him reluctantly. Randur took them two at a time, tuning into his peripheral vision for guidance. Quick, subtle strokes. Deft footwork. An arrow from Denlin. It was soon over.

Randur glanced across the wall. Nothing between them and the women except perhaps fifty paces.

They ran.

"Rand!" Eir cried in relief, her brown robe flapping like a flag in the wind.

Randur arrived first and sliced through the rope securing her wrists while Denlin freed her sister. Randur handed a sword to Eir, who regarded it as if she couldn't recognize its function.

"I taught you how to fight, but not to kill," Randur panted. "I promise you it's not much harder. You up for it?"

"Yes, I am," Eir replied without hesitation, but with a look of terror on her face.

Randur indicated the soldiers now approaching, some way further along the long wall. "Those heavy swords impede their movements, to our advantage."

"Did you organize all this?" Rika gestured to the commotion down below. The crowds had overpowered the military and violence had spread out to the neighboring streets. The whole chaotic scene possessed a surreal texture, spoke of the power of the people, the power of long-term resentment. What had begun with just a few dozen brawlers now absorbed hundreds, the spirit of the city changing before their eyes, generating a confidence that came from citizens rather than their rulers—a true democracy. You would soon hear these screams and shouts on the far side of the Empire.

"Den, mainly them," Randur said, pointing to the soldiers behind. "Not quite the time for a debate though."

Randur then gestured for them to hurry. "There's a boat waiting for us right now in the underground docks. We need to fight our way down to the tunnels running under the city." He reached into his boot for a knife, which he handed to Rika. "You may need this."

"I am not really the kind of woman to consider violence as a solution." Rika handed the knife back.

Be awkward, why don't you. Randur frowned, sliding the blade back in his boot. "Righto, my lady, but you don't mind if we kick a few arses to save your own?"

Denlin interrupted, "City soldiers are nearly here and I'm almost out of arrows."

Randur said, "Rika, you stay behind us. Right, Eir, let's show this lot a little *Vitassi*."

The pair stepped forward with their swords up at the ready. The soldiers stared at Eir with confusion, a young woman of her pampered lineage preparing to meet them in conflict. Randur utilized their momentary hesitation to lunge out and rake his blade across one face.

Before retreating, Eir swiftly repeated his gesture, and Randur noted her remoteness with approval. It was never a simple thing, to wound for the first time.

Two men crumpled to the floor, another came in place. Randur slipped on the wet stone, tumbling into the other man. They rolled awkwardly, pushing each other away from their own weapons. Randur reached for the man's head, smashed his skull and kicked his body sideways off the wall.

He pushed himself up as another two soldiers shuffled forward. Eir faltered and Randur shouted for her to continue, to concentrate.

Side by side they were blocking blows, stepping gracefully out of the direction of strikes, and Eir learned from their opponents' mistakes, waited for them, then wiped the razor-edge of her short sword across their necks or hands, never enough for a direct kill, but they collapsed off the wall to their deaths. Every time they did Randur could see something fade within her.

Denlin warned, "Last arrows," and killed two more.

"Keep an eye out behind us for now, Den. Me and Eir will get rid of this lot easily." Randur noticed how Eir seemed enhanced by his boast of how effectively they worked together, regained her composure and put her mind into a protected place. She began a series of new moves that were far too complex for the guard she now parried with, overwhelming him with pace if not strength, till a swift diagonal stroke saw him paw his throat in panic. Then she kicked his weakened legs from under him and he buckled forward.

One by one, the opposition was decimated.

The four of them finally had a clear path to the doorway. The riot below had moved away from the gates entirely, absorbing new energy in the ancient streets nearby, and already two trails of smoke rose from the lower level of the city.

They moved to the narrow stairs, which spiraled down.

"How come there're no more guards?" Eir panted.

Breathless, Randur replied, "Rioting . . . All the trouble on the streets . . . Weren't prepared for it to get out of hand."

"Smart," she gasped. "And all Denlin's idea?"

"A master plan," Denlin wheezed, and nearly tripped over the bow strapped across his chest.

✳

The two guards standing sentry at the bottom of the stairs were dead before they even realized what was happening, and their departure was marked by a web-trail of blood against the whitewashed stone.

From then on, Denlin directed the small group along a complex of side-alleys, then down into a passage leading under the city toward Caveside, and all the time they could hear the crowds shouting in anger above them, a thousand feet thundering on a trail of devastation.

At one point Eir dropped her sword and staggered against the wall and began to cry. Randur held her in the darkness. "What's wrong?" he asked soothingly.

"I helped kill . . . I've never done anything like that."

"It's all right." He'd been stupid to expect she could just take someone's life like that, without feeling anything. Denlin was just about apparent in this darkness, but the old man seemed patient and understanding. Rika was close but silent.

"You were saving your own life," Randur whispered to her, pulling her closer to him, then helping her to her feet. "You had no choice. I promise you that when we're out of here, you'll be fine. You'll be fine." It wasn't a good time to tell her that she might never get over it, but she would have to block it out or they would be hunted down and slaughtered. She cried into his shoulder for several minutes while Denlin marched back along their route to check if they were being pursued. When Eir had calmed herself and he could feel the tension released from her body, she apologized. "I'm being so ridiculous. Now isn't the time."

"You're just being human." Randur repeated over and over that she would be back to normal as soon as she was out of the city, and that she had to put it out of her mind. All the time praying that sometime soon she might begin to believe the lie herself.

✳

On and on, through passageways and down steps that had become so worn they were rounded treacherously at the edges. Ancient, ancient corridors.

Denlin was relying on memory to guide them. Randur wasn't so sure of the reliability of that, but the old man had surprised him more than once. They trudged for the best part of an hour in near-darkness—and in silence, so they could hear if anyone was approaching.

Eventually: the sound of water.

"Are we close now?" Randur inquired.

Denlin said "Yep" with satisfaction.

Eventually, bits of daylight pooled in patches, as the rock around them changed texture, and the familiar smells of Caveside became intense.

"This is it," Denlin announced in triumph.

Eir said, "Won't they be out looking for us?"

"Probably," Randur replied, "but down here is unlikely. Anyway, with all those opportunities for looting above, I think we'll find Caveside is almost empty."

Rika interrupted, "So we've come so far—how do we proceed?"

Denlin beckoned, "Follow me."

Down further hidden alleyways and along backstreets which few knew of, even in Caveside. In his heightened paranoia, the shadows moved like live things. Cats craned their heads in curiosity, leaping from wall to wall in the darkness. Randur noticed how Denlin constantly looked this way and that, and he wondered if the old man was thinking how he might never see these familiar streets again.

The Garuda's Head was unusually closed, a man slumped in front of it, either asleep or unconscious.

"Wait here," Randur instructed the women. Eir drew her sword just in case.

The two men walked around the back of the bar, then returned with Randur's bags, and a replacement quiver of arrows.

From one bag, Randur dug out some female garments. "Bit more stylish and probably warmer than what you've got on."

"Thank you," Rika said graciously, as she and her sister began pulling on layers of clothing. Randur and Denlin kept a lookout. It was strange to see Caveside so empty.

"Ready," Rika decided at last. "I want to tell you how truly grateful we are."

"Sure," Randur said, thinking that it was only for Eir he was doing this.

"Pleasure," Denlin said. "But not over yet. We need to sail through the caves first, and past more military stationed outside. They should be stretched, what with the riots, like, but there's bound to be a few on watch."

"Sail?" Eir asked.

"Yep," Randur said, "the last of our money bought us some kind of boat. It's no longship like you're used to, but it'll get us the hell out of here."

"Let's go then," Denlin declared.

Randur hauled the other bag over his shoulder.

"What else have you got in there?" Eir said.

"Just my clothes. Why?"

Eir sighed.

❋

The city docks at the far end of Caveside were crammed with fishing vessels of every kind, a line of them packed in tight along the harbor-side, the only safe getaway route left open for them. Randur had slipped out first in stealth and cut down two of the soldiers on patrol, dragging their bodies into the water. One fisherman turned from fixing his net, saw the incident, then waved casually before ignoring them again.

The small group climbed aboard the small boat that was waiting for them—a fishing boat offering little shelter—then pushed off. Soon the wind blustered through the caves, bringing fresher air with it.

Denlin explained, "We'll all need to row until we can get the sails up."

It took an immense effort to push their craft through the water.

"Bit of a step down for an Empress, this," Denlin joked.

"I will do my bit," Rika said. "I am quite capable of being treated as an equal."

An arrow pierced the water right beside them. A soldier was firing from a vantage point just ahead and to the left.

"Get down," Randur urged the two women, and ducked down himself.

The old man brought an arrow to docking point and let fly.

It connected with stone. He repeated the action while the boat edged forward. The soldier didn't dare to return fire while Denlin was aiming at him. "Good thing I brought so many arrows, but I don't want to waste them on this bugger."

Oars split the water, and helped by the current they made progress. Now they were out of view, Denlin picked up his oar to quicken their pace.

No conversation passed between them; they were all preoccupied with a determination to escape.

Ten minutes later and one of the moons became visible, the sounds of rioting became sharper, despite the greater distance. They were outside. Randur opened his bag and pulled out a couple of blankets and offered them to the women. He took time to wrap Eir up snugly, enjoying the moment of intimacy.

"You not going to wrap me up too, eh?" Denlin said. "I'm old. I feel the cold."

"Can we relax yet?" Randur said.

"Once the sail's up." Denlin fiddled with ropes and set up a small mast. He unfurled a sail that snagged tight as the wind caught it, and the boat lurched. The oars were pulled in.

Randur sighed physically, and feeling mentally drained he turned to Eir, who nestled into him, her head resting under his chin. He didn't feel the need to talk right now. All he wanted to do was fall asleep beside her. All that mattered to him now was Eir. And here she was, in his arms, so things were fine.

"Where to now, then?" Denlin said, pulling him back to reality.

Randur glanced across at Rika, whose arm rested on the side of the boat as she sat gazing out to sea. She nodded vigorously, then spoke, almost to herself. "Villiren. That's where Commander Lathraea has gone."

"Brynd?" Eir asked, shuffling upright.

"Yes. My name needs clearing. In fact, both our names do. Chancellor Urtica has corrupted the whole city hierarchy, and now only the commander will believe me—even though the military will serve whoever's at the top. I just know he'll believe me, and do what's right. The last I heard, he was heading for Villiren. We shall find him there, and then he can advise. Ask yourself the question: can we allow Urtica to steal from us the Empire that generations of our family have ruled over? No, I'm still Empress, so it's my duty to resist him, and this is only the start of things. We can't do that from here, as we are clearly going to be outnumbered. So we need to go to Villiren."

Randur didn't think it mattered much who led the Jamur Empire—nothing seemed to change anyway, and the Council made all the decisions. Didn't fancy explaining that to her just yet though. Instead he muttered, "There was me thinking I'd got the girl and that was it."

Denlin said, "And I can kiss good-bye to putting my feet up and growing old disgracefully."

"Denlin, Randur—I owe you great rewards. Please, will you stay with me?"

"I'm going where the lad goes," Denlin replied.

Randur turned to Eir. "I go where this one goes."

Eir shrugged. "Well, I don't fancy being constantly hunted down and then slaughtered. So I guess we're all in this."

Her sister leaned back with a sigh.

Doesn't anyone just want a quiet life? Randur thought.

"Thank you," Eir whispered, words meant for his ears only. Her glistening eyes fought back tears of exhaustion.

Given all the problems of this world, Eir offered him so much comfort, and that was maybe enough, wasn't it, just to find someone to love, and to get through life with that person alongside you, because there were no certainties in this world except maybe uncertainty itself.

As the boat was dragged by the breeze, he could see the orange glow of light in the windows of a handful of houses along the shore, warm and inviting but distant and untouchable, and it was as if they weren't just sailing away from Villjamur but from all the comforts and luxuries they had been used to, from their own lives as they had been lived.

From the world as they knew it.

ABOUT THE AUTHOR

MARK CHARAN NEWTON was born in 1981 and holds a degree in Environmental Science. After working in bookselling, he moved into editorial positions at imprints covering film and media tie-in fiction, and later, original science fiction and fantasy. NIGHTS OF VILLJAMUR is his first novel, but he is just wrapping up the sequel. For more information visit his website markcnewton.com or follow him on Twitter at twitter.com/MarkCN. He currently lives and works in Nottingham, UK.